Jannah

The Ancient Scripture

The Ancient Scripture

Living The Scripture

This is a word from The Chosen Ones. To all those reading this, the stories of gods of the past may seem extravagant. It may seem as though it's something we shouldn't believe. But this is a new truth, not only revealed in the Scripture but understood by beings across the universe. Earth, being a new planet, leaves us, humans, as the last ones to learn of an untold aspect in the universe's creation. It's impossible to tell who wrote the Scripture. Some believe it's a divine text created from the ether or an incomprehensible force beyond this dimension. Regardless of how it came to be, you will come to learn that princes Jonah and Carmine took stock in the future generation of species. They put their faith in this new universe. We cannot sit by idly and just read what happens. We must take action and take part in the nobility of using our imagination to draw closer to reopening the gates of heaven. After reading these stories, you will understand the first steps toward becoming a Paragon of Imagination. Before that time comes, here are three key ways in which you can find your purpose within the text now.

1. Immerse Yourself in the Scripture

It's impossible to fully live our part of the Scripture if we do not properly try to understand the stories at hand. The Ancient Scripture of the universe must be read with deep care, consideration, and most importantly, an open mind. You can take up the mantle as a true hero towards restoring heaven if you let the teachings of the Scripture become a part of your life. The stories of the ancient gods are not just for entertainment but are also a learning experience. The more you read the Scripture in detail, the better you will know how to help your society and your entire planet. You have the power to become sufficiently skilled at interpreting the meanings within the text and finding ways to bridge them into your life in this realm.

2. Commit to Learn from the gods

The results of the current Eon we live in are not our fault, but they are our challenge to conquer. As you will come to learn, the prophets of the past have faced a significant amount of obstacles from outside forces, some being former friends, or even loved ones. The important role that we play in the stories of the Scripture today is exercised through impact, using the power of our collective imaginations. It's important to understand that the dreams of the ancient gods were achieved through paths of grit and emotional fortitude. There are beings in this universe who struggle to make their world a better place and that is what these gods were fighting so hard to do. Acknowledge their sacrifices and know that we too must make sacrifices in our lifetimes. What is the point of life if not to truly prosper by creating an abundance of happiness for others?

3. Live Your Part

Following the teachings of the ancient gods is only a small part of our role in reopening the gates of heaven. True believers in the power of imagination commit to living out their purpose as heroes in their communities. It's up to us to spend more of our time making the world a better place. Helping our fellow citizens because it's the right thing to do. Enriching the universe with positive energy, faith, and a relentless drive to improve the world for the better, is the key to achieving heaven once more. The faith of the afterlife may have died centuries ago, but the power of faith must persist in the people today. It may seem futile initially. But one act of kindness will lead to another and creating peace across the stars begins with every single one of us.

The New Eon
Our Present

Our Failure

We stood atop the most glorious yet decrepit planet we had ever seen. It was heaven. Planet Jannah. Learning that the afterlife wasn't a concept in our minds, but an actual planet in the universe was where it all began. This new truth changed everything we had come to know. But heaven wasn't paradise. It was a living hell.

Corpses surrounded us like desecrated waste. Us. At this point, committers of what felt like a terrible genocide. We were prophesied to be heroes for our universe. The two people who were destined to save heaven from the darkness that destroyed it billions of years ago. Destined to restore the afterlife for all the lost souls trapped in Purgatory. Purgatory, as we learned, was a spiritual realm in between life and heaven. But we weren't heroes. That had become profoundly clear at this very moment. We never imagined that the planet of heaven would be a place that caused great wars. A place once so glorious that it tainted the present with greed.

Jannah. The planet that ruined lives, tore apart families and created unforgivable sins.

But it was our planet. And we had to forgive it for the trouble it caused. It had a chance to redeem itself. For heaven was the only place the lost souls of our universe could rest in peace. It was the only place where, after people sacrificed their lives for the greater good, they could go on to paradise. There were so many people in this world who deserved nothing but the best. Who stood against all odds because they did what was right. Who were we to keep them from entering paradise? We had a goal and we were going to achieve it. No matter the sacrifice.

My brother and I looked at each other, gasping for air. We were exhausted after the war we had miraculously survived. The skies of heaven above us were black with darkness and filled with endless storms. We let the rain wash the tears from our faces and gathered up our weapons. Then we began the march forward. The great castle of Jannah was the only place where we had a chance of reopening the gates of the afterlife. Everything had led up to this moment. After years of hard work, countless battles within, and waging with the idea of giving up on our dreams, we did it. We finally did it.

A massive wooden door stood before us. Another obstacle. No matter how much our bodies ached and our spirits suffered, we pushed forward. My brother and I reached our hands out and pressed against the massive wooden door. It creaked loudly and dust fell at its staggering movement. The gates of the castle had been opened for the first time in millennia. My brother and I limped across the cobblestone, then the golden steps leading inside. The blood on our feet marked the red carpet of the lobby. Through another set of gilded doors, we made it to the throne room. Pure darkness consumed the thrones of the former King and Queen like live flames. They gripped the adornments of the seats like overgrown vines.

My brother and I looked at each other and nodded. We had waited for this for so long. It took years and countless fights to gather everything we needed to reopen the gates of heaven. We knew exactly what to do without speaking a word. We faced our palms at the thrones and dispelled the darkness surrounding them. I equipped the crown of the King and my brother the crown of the Queen. I opened the ancient scripture, the holiest text of Jannah, and set it upon the floor between the thrones. The book magically flew open and a golden light shone from the pages. Then, my brother set the Crystals of Nihaya in the glass display beside the thrones, which emitted an enchanting ring when brought to its rightful place. We each sat upon one of the thrones and meditated. It was through this connection to the spiritual realm of space that we could bridge the world of heaven to Purgatory. Through this bridge, the souls that had been lost in Purgatory for lifetimes would finally be able to cross into a revitalized Jannah. But after what felt like an eternity in meditation, the ground began shaking violently. It rattled the entire castle and echoed across the estate. Something was wrong.

Suddenly, the windows to the castle shattered and fragments of the ceiling crumbled. The darkness entered the castle like a plague. The black flames sprawled across the walls and consumed the floors. My brother and I panicked. We quickly gathered the relics and rushed across the throne room. The live darkness was attempting to swallow us whole and trap us in the desolate remains of heaven forever. He and I barged through the throne doors and fled the royal estate. We looked up to see the black clouds of Jannah's skies intensify. Lightning of the same horrifying color rapidly burst through the clouds. My brother and I ran across the bodies left on the dirt plains of Jannah and made it to our spaceship. The only hope for survival now was escape. As the ship rose above the surface and into the atmosphere, we looked down at the sea of darkness growing across the continents of the planet. It had become abundantly clear now that we, the orphan boys meant to restore the afterlife, had failed. Somehow, we had failed.

Our Future

Jannah, heaven, wasn't saved. To this day it stays consumed in darkness. The goal we had been fighting for so long was not what we thought. We hoped it was all possible. We hoped the afterlife would be reopened and everyone who had died in the universe would finally be able to rest in peace. But hope wasn't enough to achieve our goal. The loss is in our hands and this failure was sure to have a drastic effect on our present. On our future. After returning to Earth, my brother and I learned a lot about why we couldn't save heaven. The faith wasn't strong enough. After years of facing this goal in secrecy, we learned that we couldn't achieve it without the help of humanity. The problem is that in this modern era, people have gradually been abandoning faith. Life has turned into something much less about believing in a higher purpose. Instead, for many people, life is about money, success, fame, and personal gain. To rightfully reopen the gates of heaven, my brother realized we first needed to revitalize the faith of humanity.

The worst part of failing and fleeing Jannah was letting down everyone in the universe. They didn't even know their demise was happening. They didn't even know that their afterlife was taken right from them. That when we all die, there isn't a heaven anymore like we believed. There is just an eternity trapped in the wretched limbo of Purgatory. Now, it's time for everyone to know. For the past three years, my brother and I were afraid to share the truth about heaven. To share with the world that our afterlife was actually destroyed. It seemed like blasphemy. We have had the desire to help the world since we were kids, but we feared everyone would say we were insane. There is suffering everywhere. And after the pain my brother and I experienced growing up, all we ever wanted was to prevent it from happening to any other innocent people in the world. The opportunity to finally make a change came when we discovered the truth about heaven. But after failing to achieve this goal alone, we learned that we needed help. That's why we've decided to spread this scripture across the universe. This isn't a story about me and my brother. It's a story about us as people. About how all of our lives in the universe came to be. How all of our lives are intertwined. How we need to unite for one common goal. This is a story about the desperate suffering hiding among the stars. So no matter how much it scares us to write this and share our story, we have to do it for the betterment of humankind. It all started three years ago. On one horribly fateful night. We are Jordan and Caden. Nothing more than the messengers of the truth. Please, open your minds and more importantly, open your hearts. Let your souls thrive and believe us. The fate of humanity depends on your imagination. This is how our journey began.

Our Past

The night was darker than ever. The stars were brighter than they had been in ages. The energy in the air felt magnificently spiritual. With no one in sight but each other, the brothers, Jordan and Caden, were off in the woods located on the outskirts of their city, Ebla. The brothers were suddenly drawn to explore the woods through an inexplicable inclination. They had explored the woods before to practice with relatively dangerous weapons they bought for cheap in Chinatown. But before they could make it back home by sundown, the sound of a screaming girl was heard in the depths of the forest. An overwhelming fear simultaneously struck Jordan and Caden's minds. One brother wanted to run *for* help, while the other wanted to run *to* help. Caden was running as fast as he could toward the sound of the screaming. Jordan, being the older brother, had no choice but to try and contain his little brother's heinous actions. "Come on Jordan! I heard the screaming come from over here!" Caden shouted. He hopped over a log and landed in a stream feet-first. The water splashed gracefully beneath his feet. Jordan stumbled over a few times, still trying to catch up to his little brother. Even entertaining the thought of finding the screaming girl was unnerving. God forbid something dangerous would happen to him, or more importantly, to his little brother. "Damn, Caden! Slow down! Maybe we should just call the cops!" he shouted. Caden ignored him. The brothers were starting to pant heavily. The combination of intense movement and adrenaline had led to something beyond just physical exhaustion. But they both kept running toward the sound of the screaming girl nonetheless. The closer they got, the more horrifying it became. She was hurting. Finally approaching the sound, the brothers came to a small, open field, surrounded by trees on the perimeter. Caden was still running forward recklessly, attempting to entangle himself in this unknown situation. Jordan quickly pounced onto his little brother to stop him. They fell into a patch of shrubs. Jordan covered his brother's mouth, silencing him. "Shut up. No… shut up. Are you trying to get us killed?" he whispered. Caden was still panting. After blinking several times and calming his breath, Jordan could see that his brother was ready to be more cautious. He removed his hand from Caden's mouth. The brothers quietly adjusted into a crouched position. They crept forward and observed the situation from inside a pair of bushes. In the center of the open field was the girl.

"Leave me alone!" she begged. She was bruised. One on her cheek and two visible on her frail bicep. Possibly more than just those. She was being attacked by a man and woman. The man was holding her by the arms from behind and the woman was standing in front of her. The girl struggled to break free but was far too weak. Her long hair was a ginger orange and her young face didn't deserve this. She looked like she was around Jordan's age, about 16. Aside from them in the open field, there was what appeared to be an unconscious boy on the ground, east of the conflict. It looked as if he had struggled with the adult perpetrators to protect the girl. "Stop it, girl! Hold still," the man said. Jordan watched the situation go down, his fear almost incapacitating him. He could feel the sweat slowly drip down the side of his face. This couldn't have been real. On the other hand, witnessing such a horrible thing only made Caden angry. Despite him having the small stature of a 13-year-old boy, he always had the most bravado in a fight or flight situation. A blessing as much as it was a curse, this bravery also made him the irrational one as well. "We have to help her," Caden whispered. He tried to leap out of the bushes, but Jordan quickly grabbed him by his shirt and pulled him back. "No. Are you insane? We have to call for help," he whispered. Jordan quietly took his phone out to see if he could get a signal. The digital blue light illuminated his face, so he quickly lowered his phone's brightness to avoid being seen. Caden looked forward at the attack, then back at his brother. He did this several times in silence. With a grunt of frustration, he pushed his brother away from him. "Screw you!" Caden jumped out of the bushes and ran toward the empty field, suddenly standing before the threatening man and woman. "Leave her alone!" he yelled angrily. The young boy stood there, more proud and powerful than he had been in a long time. The man and woman stared at Caden with a peculiar look. Almost as if they had seen him before. They became frustrated at his foolish attempt to try and stop them.

"Look, child. You have no idea what you're getting yourself into. You'd best get your stupid ass out of here," the woman said as she turned away from the girl to face Caden. Then, Jordan jumped out from the bushes, running toward his little brother. "Caden stop!" he shouted. The man violently threw the girl to the ground. The bruise on her cheek scraped against the dirt and developed a cut on its prominent, swelled dome. In the chaos, a book flew out of her satchel and landed in front of her. She just watched from her feeble position, staring up at the two boys randomly coming to her rescue. Maybe it wasn't a rescue, but a disaster waiting to happen. But something strange overcame Jordan and Caden. As if a supernatural force was pushing their will to fight. The man and woman both faced the brothers, more intimidating than just a few seconds ago. They were wearing all black with brown leather jackets. Caden clenched his fists and started shaking from anger. "I told you to leave her alone!" he yelled. Caden started running toward the adults with nothing more than a fist raised in the air. He carried it like a champion's sword. Caden unleashed a massive battle cry. It was too late to turn back now. Jordan joined his brother in the scuffle to try and defend him. Despite the dramatic tension of the moment, the man and woman didn't seem fazed by the teenage boys' attack. A fight broke out. Caden threw himself at the man, driving his shoulder into his gut. He tried to take him down but was too small. The man reached his arms underneath Caden's horizontal upper body and pivoted, throwing the little boy to the ground. Jordan swung his untrained fist and missed the strike. The woman quickly punched him in the gut. Jordan accidentally let out an embarrassing heave, losing his air. The woman then punched him again with a hook to the jaw. Not expecting the type of pain two punches could cause, Jordan allowed himself to fall to the ground, having given up. The brothers were both immediately laid out. They looked up at the stars in the night sky. This was just as scary as they expected it to be. This was just as dangerous as they expected it to be. This was just as impossible as they expected it to be. Then why did they risk everything anyway? Caden started crawling back up to his feet. Unlike his older brother, he wasn't finished just yet. Wiping the tears from his eyes, he struggled to raise his fist again. Without any reason but to win, he ran toward the adults once more, attempting the same attack that failed seconds ago. Caden tried to punch the man but missed. His tears compromised his vision. He quickly turned and tried to tackle the man instead, putting himself in the same tie-up as before. The girl could see from her position on the ground that this was going sideways. Caden grunted loudly, almost whining about the results of his action. The man just sighed in frustration. He reached toward the side of his belt, took out a knife with his right hand, and held it near his thigh. Caden couldn't see, burying his face into the man's shirt. The man swung his arm upward, driving the knife into the left side of Caden's chest, right where his heart was. The sound of piercing flesh could almost be heard in the silent forest night. Caden's body jerked once, then he com-

pletely stopped moving. The sound of blood splattering onto the dirt almost echoed. The man yanked the knife out of the boy's chest and let his body drop to the filthy ground. He killed him. It was nearly silent. The sound of the wind dominated for a brief moment, the trees rustling in the distance. Then, Jordan screamed. "No… no… no! No!" He struggled to get back up to his feet, clenching his teeth in an intense fit of rage. He stood there for a moment, shaking. As he looked at his little brother's body, he realized there was nothing he could do. The tears came pouring. Jordan wasn't sure if it was from sadness or anger. Likely both. He just ran toward the adults again, trying to fight back against them somehow. Trying to punish them for their actions. The woman reached for the holster in her belt. She pulled out a handgun. Jordan barely had time to notice the weapon. He stumbled and then froze, wanting to retreat. But before he could move in the other direction, the woman pulled the trigger and shot Jordan in the head. The loud bang echoed in the forest night. The girl on the ground shrieked in terror. Crows flew out from their hidden positions in the trees. At such close range, the impact of the bullet was enough to blow Jordan off his feet. His body jarred and collapsed in the open field.

Moonlight shone upon the brothers' bodies. The man and woman put their weapons away. The man glared at the woman with a look of regret. He didn't have to say a word. "Don't be concerned about them. Humans will be reckless until it's too late to learn their lesson," the woman said. The man nodded. "You're right. The book is more important anyway," he responded. The adults started walking back toward the girl on the ground. Tears filled her young eyes. Two kids had died in front of her because they were trying to protect her. There was no hope left. She didn't want to struggle anymore. It was too painful. The woman used her foot to turn the girl over from laying on her chest to her back. She kneeled forward and wrapped her hands around the girl's throat. The girl gripped the woman's wrists and tried to breathe through her nose. "You're gonna die here little girl," the woman said. The man just watched as the life was being taken away from an innocent person. The girl was a nuisance and she had to be dealt with. She started kicking, feeling her throat burn. Sound and sight were beginning to fade away. Everything was turning black. It was almost over. There was one final breath. Life had passed from one realm and begun anew in this reality. A pain equating to hundreds of wars and months of torment was dragged from an alternate existence. Purgatory. Jordan and Caden suddenly gasped for air. Their eyes were rolled to the back of their heads, bloodshot. Their veins were glowing. A heavenly radiance appeared upon their skin, as if angels had just been in their presence. The brothers clenched their teeth and fists tightly. They snarled like wild animals. This wretched feeling of coming back was one they had feared for too long. It was all left behind. The memories had faded. Jordan and Caden stood up and faced the adults, consumed by supernatural power from Eons ago. The heavens above, Jannah galaxies away, had granted the impossible. Jordan and Caden had returned from the dead. The girl quickly crawled away while the adults had become distracted. An aura of cosmic energy was beginning to form around the brothers. Like a raging whirlwind. It was the effect of pure celestial vitality being expressed outside their bodies, powering them up with supernatural abilities. The brothers focused their power, observing as it manifested upon their physical body in a form that could interact with the outside world. These auras displaced surrounding matter into useful, atmospheric energy. Jordan glowed with a red aura and Caden with a light blue. Their eyes were still rolled to the back of their heads. The brothers were harnessing anger held deep within them. The power of the Crystals of Nihaya somehow ran through their bloodstream and consumed every nerve in their bodies. The ground started shaking and smoke spewed from their noses and mouths. Their veins were pulsating violently. The adults panicked. A look of debilitating fear overwhelmed their faces. The woman raised her handgun again and tried shooting the brothers. She unloaded four shots, but the bullets shockingly deflected off of the brothers' powerful auras. It was as if they were invincible now. "What the hell?" the man mumbled. Jordan and Caden each held out an arm forward. They pointed an open palm toward the adults, who stood frozen in shock. There was no way to explain the resurrection of two unknown teenage boys. There was a flash of growing energy charging into the brothers' hands. It fired. A large red blast made purely from cosmic force emitted from Jordan's palm and a light blue blast from Caden's. After a concentrated force of unified power, there was a burst of energy. The red and light blue blasts fired through the air in seconds, like laser beams. They fused into one, their fluorescent colors mixing together. The blasts struck the adults and dispersed with a powerful explosion. The cataclysmic sound echoed across the entire forest. The adults vanished, blown down to nothing but ashes. Trees toppled over as a smoldering stretch of dirt and scorched grass formed a reckless path several hundred feet long. The residue of the explosion fell toward the ground like snow. It glowed with red and blue colors, like glistening stardust. Someway, somehow, the innocent girl and boy were saved. Jordan and Caden dropped to their hands and knees. Their hearts were pounding at an alarming rate. It was the first time they were pumping blood in the last several minutes. They were finally calming down. But as it was all hitting them, they couldn't even begin to comprehend everything that just happened. Their eyes finally returned to normal, facing forward, no longer rolled back. Smoke was still emerging from their palms like the barrel of a gun. The brothers finally stood up and stumbled toward one another. They grabbed each other's forearms, blessed to feel their sibling's flesh. "How…" Jordan mumbled. The girl walked over to them nervously and thanked them for somehow rescuing her, the shock apparent in her voice. She was still shaking in fear. It was hard to tell whether it was from the strange adults hurting her or Jordan and Caden's miraculous resurrection. The girl turned and looked around the ground for something important. It wasn't there anymore. "Where is it?" she mumbled to herself. She started panicking slightly. Either way, she had to flee the scene. She gave up on finding it. The girl just grabbed her satchel, helped the beaten boy get up, and they both ran in the other direction out of the woods. Not a name and hardly a word were heard. Three pairs of strangers crossed paths tonight and the status of their relationship didn't change from that. Nonetheless, this astronomical occurrence was something worth writing into history. Eventually, the brothers managed to smile at each other, happy to be alive somehow. They observed their bodies briefly and realized their wounds had miraculously disappeared. The bullet to Jordan's head and the blade into Caden's heart had left no traces of damage. However, Caden's shirt did have a hole in it and was stained with blood. Jordan gave his little brother his sweater and let him wear it to cover the unsightly stain. Having spent nearly a minute in silence, they attempted to rationalize the strange, supernatural power that not only restored their lives but killed two people. Then, energy was felt in the air. Something like the sound of wind chimes rang in the field. Jordan and Caden could see the item appear before them. It was a book. It had

suddenly unequipped its magical cloak and revealed itself to the boys. Like it knew they were there. Like it finally wanted to be discovered. It must have been what the girl was looking for, but couldn't find. Jordan and Caden stared at the book on the ground. Strange echoes, chants, and rings like gongs emerged in the back of their minds. Jordan walked over to the book and picked it up from the ground. He brought it to his little brother for the both of them to observe it. It was ancient, tattered, and had a leather exterior. There was no title. But an inexplicable force kept the book from opening. For some reason, the brothers had the desire to keep it. "Did all that just happen? We… died right? I'm not trippin'? But that power. I don't know how to explain it," Caden said. The 13-year-old boy slowly started shaking his head. He lost track of his words.

"I don't know what the hell happened. Or how this book just appeared. But look, dude. We just need to get home for now. It'll be a lot harder trying to keep this from mom and dad if we get in trouble for coming back too late. Hide your shirt until you can change," Jordan said. Caden nodded. The brothers tried to collect themselves and retraced their steps to leave the forest. Their teenage innocence made them oblivious to what was going on within themselves and the entire, unknown universe of Eon VI. The events from moments before had completely changed their lives and nearly scarred them emotionally. But the brothers had to remain calm until they could discuss everything they experienced back at home. In the distance, hiding in the forest's darkness, was an unknown figure. Clouds crossed the moon, then let its relatively dimmed brightness shine. The figure was a man. He had dark blue eyes, a piercing in his right eyebrow, and a five o'clock shadow for a beard. Half of his somewhat lengthy hair was black and the other half was dyed a dirty blonde. His rugged tone and the muscular physique of his chin revealed that the rest of his body must have matched. Tough, ruthless, and overall dangerous were the most prominent qualities of the man. He was massive. A giant monster, scary enough to terrorize innocent, orphan children. He was wearing a black turtleneck that matched his pants and boots. He pressed the button of a Bluetooth communication device in his ear to activate it. "This is Travis Xander, reporting for day number 158 of the stakeout. It finally happened. The brothers have finally shown signs of the power. They passed through resurrection and murdered two of our allies. The girl and boy escaped. We'll deal with them later. I think it's going to begin. So tell everyone to prepare themselves. The Chosen Ones have emerged." Later, Jordan and Caden walked up the stairs to their apartment building. They reached a hallway where their home was the first door to the right. To the left was their neighbor, who was standing outside his open door in the process of moving some boxes inside. Jordan and Caden approached the man. He was about 6'2". A giant compared to the boys. "Do you need any help, Mr. Xander?" Jordan asked, taking point. The man turned around with a smile on his face. "Jordan, I told you that you can call me Travis. It's been months since I've moved in," he replied. Jordan shrugged his shoulders and looked down at the open boxes. They all seemed to be carrying camera equipment, headphones, microphones, and other gadgets Jordan couldn't recognize. "Don't worry, boys. I can handle it. Thank you. Why are you two coming home so late?" Travis asked as he picked up another box. Jordan and Caden looked at each other nervously. Without a word, Jordan knew he had to imagine a cover-up.

"We were in line at the… game store… by Main and Figueroa. There's this… new game out and everyone freaking pitched tents outside just to get it. A bunch of gaming-obsessed freaks if you ask me," he explained. Travis looked at the brothers, noticing Caden being somewhat distant. He observed the boys' hands. Caden's were empty and Jordan's had nothing more than the strange leather book in them. "Where's the game?" Travis asked. Jordan drew a blank. "What?" Travis chuckled. "The game? Where's the game you guys bought?" Jordan snapped himself into place. "Oh, right! The game. Well… the damn line was too long. They sold out of it before we could get in the store. It was a… total waste of time," he replied, surprisingly natural at fabricating a trivial lie. Travis resumed moving his boxes. He stood in his doorway. "Well, text me what the game's called. I'm sure I have a friend who could get a copy for you guys," Travis said kindly.

Caden nodded happily, almost fooled into believing there *was* an actual, newly-released game that he couldn't get his hands on 'cause of those "gaming-obsessed freaks." "That would be awesome! Thank you, Travis!" he exclaimed.

Travis set the box on the coffee table in his living room. "You boys have a good night! Tell your parents I said hey!" he shouted, fading into the comforts of his apartment. The brothers told him goodbye and finally faced their door.

Caden took his house keys out of his pocket and readied himself to unlock the door. Jordan lightly grabbed his wrist, halting his motion. "Wait. What're we gonna tell mom and dad? The same bull I told Travis?" Jordan asked. Caden's face froze. He retreated the keys from the lock. "I don't know," he replied. Jordan sighed and dragged his palms across his exhausted face. There was this slight horror recurring in the back of his mind.

"Look. Maybe we don't have to say anything. Just… get upstairs and change without looking too conspicuous. And I'll keep mom and dad company," Jordan said. Caden was more than thankful for his older brother's surprisingly collected nature. He knew deep down that they were both suffering from tremendous shock. "Jordan. I'm really scared. I don't know what happened back there. To us… or those two people," Caden said. Jordan just shook his head slightly. "I don't think even God knows what happened earlier." The brothers entered their apartment. It was rather warm inside, indicating that their parents finished cooking dinner some time ago. Caden quietly made his way upstairs while Jordan accompanied their parents in the kitchen. He set the leather book on the counter for now, then kissed both his mother and father, shaking inside.

Caden barely made it upstairs. He stood in the hallway, unable to even make it to his room. He just collapsed to his knees, ready to cry. This had to have been a nightmare. This had to have been some horrible mistake. He had never prayed before. But this one time, he prayed for a solution to not just this problem, but all the problems he was facing in his life. That night, Jordan and Caden began to have strange dreams. There were these odd depictions of space and horrific war that the brothers had somehow become involved in. There were strange images of an ancient universe flashing in their minds, revealing an untold world that they couldn't possibly believe. There was an unseen God that they had never heard of before. Everything felt like a display of memories that weren't even theirs, to begin with. It was more than difficult to sleep. Perhaps their imagination was just running wild, trying to find an explanation for what happened last night. Deep inside the brothers, the legendary power of the Crystals of Nihaya was coursing through their veins, supplying their physical bodies and celestial spirits with an ability strong enough to change the face of the universe. But it wasn't ready… not yet.

Jordan and Caden somehow managed to wake up the next morning. Exhausted from a restless night without sleep, they lazily regrouped in Jordan's room. They couldn't resist telling each other about all the strange events that took place in their dreams. Surprisingly, they found that they had the same dream. Recurring themes of space, war, and unknown prophets were all too similar for the brothers. These vague notions of an ancient universe all seemed like a fantasy. But they knew that everything was tied to their miraculous resurrection and the strange book that appeared before them in the forest. It was hard to remember all the details from just last night, but this entire set of circumstances seemed impossible to ignore. Once the brothers got ready for the day, they sat down together and had cereal at the table in the kitchen. The strange leather book was in the center of the table and it continued to be the center of their discussion.

The brothers sat quietly for a moment. Just staring at it. Then, Jordan quickly grabbed the book and tried to pry it open. He and Caden had been trying to get the book open since last night, to no avail. It felt as if it were locked by some supernatural force. It was impossible to get it open. Jordan just passed it to his younger brother to see if he wanted to try to open it again. Caden shook his head and waved his hand, almost as if he were passing up a second serving of dinner or something. Jordan set the book at the center of the table again. "Screw this thing, man," Jordan mumbled. "I'm *so* confused!" Caden whined hysterically. "I know, dude. Me too. I feel like this old book would have some answers for us, but the stupid thing is locked somehow!" Jordan replied, frustrated. "You think all of this might be happening *because* of that book? I mean, that man and woman were after it out in the forest. And even that girl was looking for it after she thanked us. If it's locked like this, it must be super important." "Maybe you're right. But we have no way of knowing what the hell they were doing out there in the forest last night." "Well, duh! Not like we can just ask those two people what they were after. Do you know why? 'Cause, we blew them up. Yep! You and I murdered two people last night!" Caden shouted hysterically.

"Shut up," Jordan whispered. "We can't let mom and dad hear about this yet. They'd lose their minds if they found out the sons they adopted from the orphanage were some cosmic freaks who came back to life and used superpowers to kill two strangers. Or… whatever that was." Caden hung his head in sadness but suddenly revealed a slightly hopeful grin. "Jordan. We can't begin to explain what happened last night. Now, we have to face the truth that you and I died yesterday. Plain and simple. I was stabbed and you were shot. But I think we came back for a reason. First, we saved that girl and boy. They would have died along with us in the forest if that miracle didn't happen. Second, I'm willing to bet this stupid book has all the answers we need inside it." "So you're saying that the people in the forest, the book, and us are all tied together?" Jordan clarified. "Exactly." "I guess that makes sense. There's no real explanation for how we came back from the dead. Not only did we come back to life, but we took the lives of two people in the process. We're murderers," Jordan said grimly. "There's no evidence to prove it," Caden said. "That's the worst part. It all seems like some weird fantasy. Imagine if someone's looking for that man and woman. They could be connected to something bigger." "Then maybe we're on some hit list. But if we have superpowers now, then I don't think we have anything to worry about." Jordan just rolled his eyes. He didn't understand how Caden could've possibly perceived any of this as a good thing. But they had to silence their conversation for a moment. Their mom came downstairs in her suit. She was heading off for work again.

She gave both the boys a kiss and left the house. On any other day, she would've taken them to school, but it was nearing the end of August now. Summer vacation was dwindling to nothing. Jordan didn't have his car so he missed out on all the best high school parties; as if he even cared about them, to begin with. And much like his older brother, Caden preferred to just stay home and play video games the entire vacation. They were different in some ways, however. Jordan spent his summer reading about startups and human empowerment, while Caden spent his summer watching every great kung fu movie. Starting with *Enter the Dragon* from 1973 and somehow ending with *The Last Stand* with Arnold Schwarzenegger, although it wasn't even a kung fu movie. He got sidetracked by who he perceived to be one of the greatest actors of all time. Considering what happened yesterday, the excitement seemed to have entered Jordan and Caden's lives a little later than expected.

Their mom left for work. The brothers sat there quietly, listening to the garage close after she pulled out her car. "She's gone again," Caden said. He got up from the table and grabbed a box of cereal from the top of the fridge.

"She won't be back until 7:00 as usual," Jordan added. He scooped up the colorful cereal and ate more, unfortunately missing the marshmallows and getting a mouthful of flavorless flakes. A drop of milk ran down his chin. "Dad's still here," Caden said. He sat down at the kitchen table and pulled in his chair, setting the box of cereal on top of the leather book. "He always just sleeps until it's time for him to get ready to work. So we're on our own for the day, again," Jordan added. Their dad worked a night job, so he was asleep in the morning and left the house in the afternoon for work. The brothers hardly got to spend any time with him since he picked up the night shift a year ago. Caden got up from the table again. He went into the pantry closet and grabbed the box of sugar. He sat back down and started pouring mounds of it into his bowl of cereal, spilling some on the leather book. Jordan stared at him in confusion. He quickly moved the box of cereal and grabbed the book to free it from Caden's treacherous presence. "Geez, dude. You're spilling sugar all over the book like it's worthless. You know all that stuff will kill you right?" he warned his little brother.

Caden stopped pouring the sugar and rolled his eyes. "Who cares? What are we gonna do to figure out what happened to us last night? We can't get the book open, so why don't we see if we still got those crazy-ass powers?" Jordan interlocked his fingers and put his hands behind his head. He leaned back in his chair. "I guess it's worth a shot. I don't know what to do to make that happen again, but I'm down to try," he said. Caden smiled at his older brother, intrigued.

The brothers walked down the short staircase into the garage and opened it. They stepped outside into the alley-driveway street behind their apartment building. Laid out before them, in parallel lines, were the other homes' garages next to and across from theirs. Jordan and Caden stood in the middle of the large driveway, the warm sun glaring in their faces. They suspected no cars would come by since most adults had already left for work by now. "So… what exactly are we trying to do here?" Caden asked. He accidentally stepped in a puddle and got his house slippers wet. The water must've come from a hose. "Son of a…" he mumbled. Jordan stared down the driveway. "I'm gonna try to recreate what happened last night," he said.

Caden was shaking his foot, trying to get some of the water off. He looked at Jordan innocently. "How are you gonna do that?" he asked.

Jordan looked down, searching his thoughts for something useful.

Nothing. "I don't know," he said.

"Well, think about how we felt last night. All *I* could remember was this crazy anger taking me over. Something hurt really badly inside me. It was as if coming back to life was… more frightening than dying," Caden explained profoundly. Jordan thought back to how he felt when he was somehow resurrected. The rage was all he could remember too. But it was as if the whole period when he and Caden were dead had been wiped clean from their minds. It was several minutes. Jordan felt they had to have gone somewhere. If spirits were real, did they reach heaven? No. It was something terrible. A place almost between heaven and hell. Wherever it was, Jordan couldn't quite remember anything. "That rage. I felt that too. When that man stabbed you… I thought you were dead, Caden. I was so freaking scared that I lost you. Then they shot me. That damn woman shot me. Almost makes me glad that she's dead. But when I could breathe again, I swear I felt like I didn't want to come back. Like I wanted to stay gone. The resurrection made me… angry," Jordan said.

Caden stepped closer to his brother. "Okay, dude. No need to be so dark and edgy about it. I guess that bullet to your head must've made you forget how to be optimistic," he said.

Jordan started rubbing his forehead. In doing so, he realized there wasn't even a scar there. Then he remembered how unscathed Caden's chest was despite being stabbed. There was no trace of last night aside from the book. No evidence. Just an indescribable feeling. "I just realized that we're healed. As if we had never been hurt," Jordan said, his voice shaking in nervousness. Caden just sighed. He started doubting all logic. He looked at his chest underneath his shirt, hoping for a scar on his body, which seemed backward once he thought about it. The brothers just stared at the ground. The only thing breaking their stressful silence was the birds chirping in the background.

Caden tapped Jordan on his shoulder. "Might as well try. Just see if you can make something happen," he said, staring at his brother's hands. If there was even the slightest chance at disproving their insanity, Caden was willing to see this strange power again. He wanted to believe it existed. Jordan nodded. He stuck out his right arm just like last night. He took several deep breaths, closed his eyes, and concentrated on his hand. He wasn't exactly sure how all the superheroes in comic books and movies activated their powers, but he figured it started in the mind. Jordan spent several seconds just standing there, to the point

where it was becoming uncomfortable. He tried to emit the cosmic energy in some form, but a sudden voice inside his head distracted him. It wasn't his own. *"Awaken,"* it said. There was a flash of powerful energy charging into his skin. Jordan felt the power push his head and upper chest. Suddenly, he fell to the concrete ground, almost as if one of his favorite wrestlers had just clotheslined him. Jordan hit his head in the chaos and blacked out momentarily. Seconds later, he was barely coming back to his senses. Caden was above Jordan, shaking him vigorously. "Jordan! Holy shit! Wake up! Are you okay?" Jordan sat up, shaking his head. He felt dazed and disoriented. "Huh? Did I do it? Did it work? Am I a superhero?" he asked. The power seemed to be the only thing that mattered right now. It was the only proof that he and his brother weren't losing their minds. Caden shook his head in disappointment. "Sorry, Jordan. Nothing happened. You just fell to the ground all of the sudden. It was pretty embarrassing if you ask me," he said jokingly. Caden held out his hand for his brother to grab it. Jordan clasped hands with him. But suddenly, control was lost. This strange anger returned. Caden's veins were pulsating. The look in the boy's eyes was much like the previous night. Caden started crushing Jordan's hand with an unrealistic strength. "Ah! Caden! Stop! What're you…" Jordan struggled, but couldn't break free from his brother's grip. "Let me go!" The anger suddenly became mutual. Jordan lost himself. He shoved his brother away from him with supernatural strength. Caden was sent flying down the driveway, a good 30 feet. He hit the ground hard, rolling across the concrete. Then, the anger faded. The brothers snapped back into reality, barely digesting what just happened. "Oh crap! Caden! Are you okay? I'm so sorry!" Jordan shouted, running to help his brother onto his feet. Caden moaned in pain. "No, it's fine. I'm sorry for hurting you. I didn't mean to crush your hand like that." The brothers just looked at each other, dumbfounded. "I don't even know how I pushed you so far," Jordan said. Caden just shrugged his shoulders. He was beginning to feel sick to his stomach. A power was developing, beyond what happened last night. A god-like strength had briefly revealed itself. The brothers started walking back into their apartment. "Did you hear that earlier?" Jordan asked. Caden just looked confused. "Hear what?" he replied hesitantly. Jordan wasn't convinced. "The *voice*. You know what I'm talking about dude. You must have heard it too." Caden nodded softly. He didn't want

to admit it, but he heard the strange voice say *"Awaken"* as well. Things were starting to get interesting, but more or less, scary for the brothers. There had to be answers somewhere. Still, only as early as 9:00, the brothers spent the better portion of the morning trying to do research on the laptop on the kitchen counter. They tried finding answers on the internet, but the results weren't very helpful. The brothers tried typing "energy force from the palm" into the search engine, but it just showed fighting techniques from martial arts or cartoons. Deeper into the search, they could only find books about the Buddhist belief in resurrection, comics portraying superhero powers, and a few scientific videos describing energy in the atmosphere. Nothing quite relatable. Jordan sighed in distress; it seemed hopeless. He spun around in the tall stool he was sitting on and turned to Caden. "Maybe we should just tell dad and have him call mom. Maybe they can find some way to help us," Caden said.

Jordan shook his head. "That's probably not a good idea, dude. They won't believe us. They could think we're having some anxiety attack and send us to a mental hospital. We need someone who believes everything we say. Someone we can trust." Jordan drifted into thought but was interrupted by his phone. It vibrated, emitting a heartwarming chime shortly after. Jordan entered his pin and checked the message. It was sent from an unknown number: (963) 839-****. What area code was that? What did the asterisks mean? This person must've been trying to keep their contact information hidden. The text said, "seek our help." Jordan hastily replied to the message. "Who is this?" he typed and sent. For now, he didn't want to get Caden involved. Not until he knew who sent him this strange message. Caden seemed quite grim. He looked at his older brother, the only family he had now. "I bet our *real* parents would have believed us if we told them about what happened last night," Caden said, making his sorrow obvious. "I'm sorry, dude. I know it's really hard. But we should still be grateful for our mom and dad now. They adopted us from the orphanage three years ago, despite all the trouble we were getting into when we were younger," Jordan said. "I know. I'm grateful for them. I really am. I just wish I knew why our parents had to abandon us when they did. Or if they're even around anymore these days." "I'm sure they're out there somewhere. They probably did what was best for us. Our mom and dad had a very weird job. They were always gone and we were always moving."

Suddenly, Caden's mood completely changed. He sprang up from his slouched position and grabbed Jordan by his arms. He had an idea. "I got it!" he exclaimed passionately. "Let's ask Donte! He trusts us and he's a genius! I'm sure he can figure something out. He's probably read books about the things that happened to us." Jordan closed the laptop and stood up from the stool. Caden was right. If not family, then perhaps a friend could help them. "You know, that's not a bad idea. Donte could at least point us in the right direction. Let's get ready. I'll go tell dad we're walking to Donte's house," Jordan said. The brothers ran upstairs to change out of their pajamas and to tell their father they were going out for the morning. Donte Young was a childhood friend of theirs. Jordan and Caden met him years ago, far back when they used to be with their original parents. The brothers' mom and dad had met Donte's parents at a new company's fundraising campaign. Ever since then, the bond grew. It was devastating to both families when Jordan and Caden's parents had suddenly disappeared. Although they were at the orphanage, Donte never stopped visiting the boys. They kept in close contact for all the years leading up to now. Donte was born with an extraordinary amount of intelligence.

His brain activity was off the charts. Doctors said that he wouldn't even live past 10 years-old, due to being prone to seizures, vasculitis, and neurodegenerative conditions that would stem from relentless amounts of neurological transmissions. But Donte was 18 now and he was stronger and healthier than ever. Now considering every day of his life a blessing, he spent much of his time inventing and experimenting. More recently, he started helping out organizations and other scientists of his level. His parents couldn't be more proud of him. He was a hero in his community. But no matter how much Donte wanted to help the world, the most important people he had pride in helping were Jordan and Caden. Like long-lost brothers, he never hesitated to be by their side. After what happened last night, perhaps it was time for him to help them again. This time, his job would be to discover some unimaginable boundaries between science and fiction. Jordan and Caden were walking down the sidewalk in a suburban area. The picket fences and stay-at-home moms were a few things they never got to experience before. They finally came to Donte's front porch. The sun had hit its full-fledged position in the summer sky. It was somewhat burning. Caden pulled on his shorts, which stuck to his ass from the sweat accumulating, giving him a wedgie. Jordan knocked on the door. They waited patiently for someone to answer. "Let's just hope Donte can pull through for us again," Jordan said. Then, the door opened. It wasn't Donte, but his somewhat elderly mom. In her late 50's. She loved Jordan and Caden as if the boys were two kids of her own. Her deepest compassion emerged after the brothers lost their parents. She couldn't imagine how terrible it must've felt or why they would do such a thing. The parents loved Jordan and Caden and it seemed impossible to conjure up any reason why they would disappear without notice. Something terrible must have happened to them.

"Jordan! Caden! Hi!" she exclaimed happily. "Donte's in his basement working on his projects, as usual. I'll call him for you." The soon-to-be elderly woman walked over and stood at the top of the stairs that led to the basement. "Donte! Come upstairs! Now! Jordan and Caden are here to see you!" The mom's destructive shouts could've nearly torn down an entire building. Her hair went into frits and her voice sounded as if it would break. The mom turned toward Jordan and Caden and smiled at them happily. She just bustled off into the kitchen. "I think even God heard that," Jordan whispered, slightly laughing.

Eventually, Donte came upstairs. Although it was approaching the afternoon, he was still in his pajamas. On top of the outfit, he wore his signature lab coat, a dignified piece of attire that told all his visitors, "Leave me alone, I'm working." Except for the brothers of course. Donte's hair was dark, almost black. It was becoming long and wavy. He was wearing his glasses and currently had a thin mustache coupled with a developing five o'clock shadow. Despite his clothes, he always had the look of some sort of government official, intellect giving credence to his limitless possibilities. It was possible he could become president if he wanted, or at least hold a position in city council. Jordan and Caden greeted their childhood friend. They all sat down on the couch and lounge chairs around the coffee table in the living room. Jordan and Caden started explaining everything to Donte, getting him up to speed on the recent events. "We were in the woods… they were attacking the girl… they stabbed Caden… shot me… we died… came back to life… and that was where it all began. The strange things haven't stopped since," Jordan explained within 15 minutes or so, hoping Donte would believe him. "Oh my god. Died? I may be a man of science, Jordan, but I can try to believe you. You described it as some sort of cosmic energy?" Donte asked. "That's just the closest I could get to making sense of it." "The resurrection is even more of a scientific phenomenon. No one has ever proven that it could be possible. I'm so sorry you had to experience that. I could've lost you two. But I guess the universe must not be done with you yet. Why come to me though? I'm just some dude who sits around and fucking plays with lab toys." "Not at all, Donte. You're the smartest person we know. Plus, we can't let anyone else figure this out yet. Not even our parents," Caden added. "I guess I can understand why you two wanna keep this stuff on the down-low. But if that man and woman actually died, then it must be true. What about the girl you saved? She saw the whole thing, then she took off back home. Why was she even out there?" Donte asked. "We don't really know. But it looked like they were out there for this book," Caden said. He placed the old, leather book on the coffee table in between the couch and chairs they were sitting on. Donte just picked it up and started examining it. There wasn't a title, publisher, ISBN, nothing. No indication of where this book came from. Donte tried to open it. "Yeah, good luck with that. The book doesn't even open. The weirdest thing is that it almost appeared in front of us. It was like, invisible when the girl was looking for it. But revealed itself when she left," Jordan said. Donte just set the book back down on the table. "Even more supernatural stuff. Do you guys think there's any way you can find that girl? To find out why this book may have been so important? Check social media. Facebook. Instagram. Maybe I can try cross-referencing news feeds or forum posts to see if anyone mentioned anything remotely close to surviving a traumatic event in a forest. I doubt she would have though. Unless she's stupid. Either way, she probably can't tell anyone else about what she saw. Except that boy you mentioned was there too. But if she can identify you guys, remembers what you did out there, and reports it to the authorities, all hell will break loose," he said. "But it's practically impossible to find her," Caden said. "We have no idea who that girl was. There's no way she's just gonna make herself known to the public that easily." "Just hope luck's on your side and you find her somehow," Donte replied.

"So is there any scientific explanation you can apply to this?" Jordan asked.

"I'm not sure. To tell you the truth, I've never heard of anything like this. Metaphysics… cosmic manipulation… reanimation of your cells… a chemical reaction of ions… no… can't be. It's really extraordinary. I think I got a clue though. Let me get a blood sample. When it comes to learning what's wrong with someone, checking their blood is one of the best ways to start. I can analyze it in the basement and hopefully find something worth your time." Donte quickly ran downstairs and grabbed his medical kit. When he came back up, he took a sample of Jordan and Caden's blood. "Good. I should hopefully narrow down some useful info for you guys by tomorrow. For now, get home and get some rest. Don't tell anyone else about this shit and find that girl. That's the best shot you got at figuring some things out. Unless this book opens somehow," Donte explained as he handed the leather book back to the brothers. Jordan put the book in his small backpack. They thanked Donte for all of his help so far. The brothers were on their way back home. They were walking on the warm sidewalk again, going through downtown to get to their apartment. Only a few cars were passing by the normally busy street at this point of the day. "What the hell is going on with us?" Jordan whined out loud. Caden walked beside him. He was just on his phone, texting a friend about nothing important. Although things seemed to be very confusing, his teenage mind couldn't help but ignore it at times. But there was this sudden, tense feeling in the air. Jordan glanced over to his left, noticing the nearby cross street. "Hey, Caden. Have you noticed this car creeping around us?" he asked. Caden attempted to look up but quickly averted his eyes to avoid revealing his suspicion. "Which one?" he asked. Jordan shook his head in slight fear. "The gray one."

Caden nodded slowly. "Yeah. It curb parks like 50 feet away from us then comes closer. What should we do?" The brothers gradually started walking faster. A crowd was starting to emerge. Cars were parking nearby and people were entering the local establishments. The afternoon lunch rush was beginning. People who worked in the downtown area were occupying the restaurants in the local shopping center. It felt as if the high energy was only making things worse. The brothers continued walking alongside each other, thankful to be disappearing into the crowd. They approached a crosswalk, patiently waiting for the walk signal to appear. "I think we lost them," Jordan said, his breath heavy from nervousness. The light changed, but before the brothers could step off the sidewalk, the strange gray car pulled up, blocking them and several other citizens. Jordan and Caden froze, shocked at this unknown stalker's persistence. Suddenly, a man exited the driver's seat and a woman from the passenger's seat. It was terrifying. It was shocking. The two people exiting the car were the man and woman from the forest last night. It looked exactly like them, only this time they were dressed inconspicuously in summer attire. How was this possible? They had clearly been eradicated by Jordan and Caden last night, but they were somehow alive, right in front of them. There was this soulless expression on the man and woman's faces. Their eyes immediately locked onto the boys. The people started cursing at them for deliberately blocking the crosswalk. It was getting loud. An innocent man foolishly got in the woman's face, violently yelling at her. The woman said nothing in response. She just grabbed the large man by his throat and lifted him in the air with one arm. A superhuman strength. The crowd nearby started screaming in fear. Then, the woman threw the man several feet away with ease. Jordan and Caden gasped in shock and the innocent people started fleeing the area to avoid getting hurt.

Finally, the man and woman set their targets back on the brothers before they could get away. The woman grabbed Caden by his arms, almost crushing his biceps. Caden kicked and shouted, but her strength was unrealistically powerful. "Hey! Let him go, you bastard!" Jordan yelled. He quickly pounced forward and shoved the woman to the ground, setting his brother free. Now the man was beginning to intervene. He started making his way around the front of the car. "Caden... run," Jordan said. Caden was still frozen in shock. "What?" he asked. Jordan grabbed him by his arm. "Run!" It began. The brothers took off south, dodging their way past too many people. The man and woman chased them, sprinting like athletes. They shoved anyone in their way, mercilessly knocking down the unwary bystanders. Jordan and Caden ran about two blocks across the sidewalk, but it quickly became clear that a straight direction wasn't enough to lose these unknown assailants. It was still impossible to rationalize how they could have come back to life. "Go left! Take a left here!" Jordan shouted. Almost missing the turn, he and Caden stumbled to their left, entering a nearby farmers market stationed in a vacant parking lot. The chatting of the stand clerks and shoppers had filled the dense atmosphere. Caden looked back. The man and woman were still chasing them, not winded at all. "They're still coming!" he shouted. The brothers started moving in a scattered, zigzag motion. Jordan cut left and Caden, right. They twisted and turned amongst the stands, trying to evade the sights of the enemy. Jordan hurdled over a stack of crates and 360'd around an active grill. The man was still on his tail. Caden climbed up, ran across an unfinished stand, and leaped forward, over a kneeling woman who was scaling fish. He landed in a pile of hay. But the woman was still on his tail. The brothers regrouped, back in the largest pathway of the farmers market. They looked back in synchronized motion. The man and woman were sprinting faster. "Jesus Christ! What do they want?" Jordan shouted. "Obviously they want revenge! We fucking killed them last night!" Caden yelled. The man quickly grabbed an apple from one of the stands. He gripped it tightly with his three most prominent fingers, like a baseball pitcher. Then, with perfect accuracy, he threw the apple at Caden. The hard fruit struck him in his left calf. Caden fell over and scraped his face on the concrete. He shrieked in pain. Jordan stopped in his tracks and quickly helped his brother back onto his feet. "Come on! Get up! We have to go!" he yelled. Caden stumbled into a standing position again, trying to regain his lost speed. Jordan decided to retaliate. While they were running, he grabbed a steel lockbox and threw it backwards, hitting the man in his head. It didn't work. He was unfazed, like a robot who doesn't feel pain. Caden grabbed a dolly full of boxes and knocked it over, trying to block the chasers. The man and woman stumbled over the scattered produce. Jordan and Caden took a right, capitalizing on the distraction. They were nearing escape. The man and woman continued to follow, not losing sight of their targets. Suddenly, the commotion between these four had garnered unwanted attention. A security guard blocked the chasers. He was rather elderly. "Hey! Stop! What's going on here? If you do not cooperate, I will be forced to detain you," he said. The guard slowly began approaching the woman. Her expression remained soulless. The guard inched his right hand toward her, his left hand gripping the holster to his nightstick. It could be seen in the woman's eyes. An incredibly powerful focus. A concentration that calculated every outcome of this scenario within the span of five seconds. The woman grabbed the guard's right hand and broke his wrist. He screamed. The guard grabbed his nightstick and unleashed an overhead swing, but the woman caught the weapon, both her hands tied now. Her partner sprang up and delivered a quick punch to the guard's throat, shattering his airway

and instantly killing him. The man coughed up blood before dropping to the ground. People who witnessed the scene screamed in fear. In the distance, the chasers could see Jordan and Caden enter an alley across the street. They sprinted like animals, trying to close in on their prey. The brothers came across a small construction complex. "Hide in here!" Jordan shouted, his voice echoing in the emptiness of the alley. He and Caden slid in between scaffolding and dove into cover behind a concrete wall, cornered by several wooden pallets. It was a decent hiding spot. The brothers stood shoulder to shoulder, holding their weary breaths to remain silent. The man and woman entered the alley. Their heavy footsteps were terrifying. Who were they? What was the reason they wanted to capture Jordan and Caden? How could they have come back from the dead and found them? The brothers peeked from a small crevice in their hiding spot. It became clear that the man and woman couldn't pick up their trail. Shockingly, neither the man nor woman had said a single word during this entire encounter. Something seemed different about them this time. They purposely avoided saying anything that would reveal their intentions. Perhaps they were trained that way. The chasers looked at each other and slightly nodded. It was over. The woman grabbed the man's wrist and they closed their eyes. Suddenly, a whirlwind-like sound appeared, followed by a strange, glistening light. A teal color formed a luminescent, LED reflection underneath their feet. The light completely surrounded the man and woman, seemingly enclosing their bodies. Then it shrunk, like a black hole imploding. There was a faint ping sound, one that a sonar radar would make. The man and woman disappeared into thin air. Particles of the light trailed upward into the sky as if they were abducted by an alien life form.

Jordan and Caden gasped in silent shock. They slowly crept out from behind the pallets. "Did you see that?" Jordan asked. Caden stared out toward the alley. His mouth was opened wide. "How could I *not* have seen that? The brothers were almost too scared to step out of the construction complex. "They just disappeared into thin air. Like... like..." Jordan's thoughts faded. Caden just started shaking his head. There had to have been some logical explanation for this. Something was happening. All the events that occurred within the last 24 hours must have been connected somehow. After the chase, it felt too dangerous to walk the remaining few blocks home. But considering that the

man and woman were killed by the brothers last night, it made sense that they would have a vendetta against them after inexplicably returning from the dead. Jordan and Caden debated if they should call for their mom to pick them up from the farmers market on her way home from work, but that would be too suspicious. They didn't want to freak her out by being too scared to walk home. Instead, the brothers just carefully took side streets and alleyways back home. Thankfully, they managed to make it back without another attack. The entire walk they tried to rationalize everything that was happening to them. But no explanation they proposed quite fit all the different aspects of this phenomenon. How could a girl being attacked in a forest, resurrection, superpowers, a leather book, memories about space, and teleportation possibly be connected? It was nightfall now and Jordan and Caden entered their apartment complex. They opened their front door to find their mom already home speaking to their neighbor, Travis Xander. It felt strange to see him more than once within a day. Their mom and neighbor looked at the boys as they closed the door behind them. "Mr. Xander? What're you doing here?" Jordan asked. Travis quickly got up from the couch beside their mom. "Hey, kids. I was actually just about to leave. I was talking to your mom about her decoration techniques for your apartment. So I had her give me a mini-tour around the house just to get some inspiration. I felt like it was time to start sprucing my place up since I'm going to have some company this weekend," he said. The man looked back and smiled at their mom. Then he looked back at the boys and smiled at them. He patted Jordan on his back and Caden on his head. Travis said his goodbyes and left out the front door. The brothers greeted their mom. They told her they were just at Donte's house for the day. Although dinner was ready, they didn't have much of an appetite. Instead, they went upstairs and just brushed their teeth to get ready for bed. Jordan and Caden looked at their faces in the mirror. They could see the torment that the past day inflicted on them. However, they were still determined to get to the bottom of this. "Maybe Donte will be able to learn something," Caden said. "Even *if* he manages to figure out what happened to us yesterday, I doubt he'd believe us if we told him that today, two resurrected strangers tried to kidnap us and suddenly teleported away," Jordan replied, irritated.

"We don't know if they teleported." "I don't know what else that could've been. Alien abduction? It looked voluntary." Caden spit the toothpaste into the sink. "I'm low-key too scared to sleep tonight," he said. "I know. I'm scared we'll start having those crazy dreams again. They have to mean something. Right?" Jordan asked. "If we could even remember them. I just… felt like I was out of my body in those dreams. Like I was witnessing someone else's memories. Last I checked, you and I weren't born in space and spent time on foreign planets with other species." "I know. Like it was another soul. I think this all started after we died. Something about our death and our resurrection must've triggered these things. The powers, the book revealing itself, the dreams, everything. Maybe that man and woman were resurrected too. Even though we completely obliterated them," Jordan proposed.

"That could be possible. Ever since we came back to life I *have* been feeling out of place. Like someone else's soul is in my body now. As if we brought something back from the afterlife with us," Caden said. "Afterlife? Do you think we went somewhere when we died? To heaven?" "Maybe." "I guess only God knows." Later, Jordan was in his room, laying in his bed, on his phone. He was just checking social media for a moment, trying to get his mind off all the crazy things that had happened that day. Then his phone vibrated and emitted another heartfelt chime. It was another text from the anonymous sender that reached out to him this morning. The text said, "We know everything, Chosen One. We will come for you." Jordan silently gasped to himself. He was terrified. It was impossible to tell if this anonymous person was a friend or a threat. But if they knew he and Caden's every movement, then they must have been stalkers. Perhaps some type of elite group who understood everything going on with the brothers and was attempting to capture them for scientific experiments. But what enemy would acknowledge their existence before kidnapping? Something wasn't right with this message. "Chosen One…" Jordan mumbled. Then, Caden suddenly opened his door and came in with a pillow and blanket. "Hey, dude. Is it okay if I sleep in here tonight?" he asked. Jordan sat up. "Why? What's wrong with your room?" he replied. "Cause, I'm scared. I'm scared that those two people may suddenly teleport into our house and kidnap us or something. If they were to attack me, I know you'll protect me, right?" Jordan felt sad for his brother. The genuine fear in his face was something he hadn't seen for a long time. "Of course, man. Just chill on the floor. I'll make sure nothing happens to you," he said. Although Jordan was afraid of being attacked too, he wanted to remain stoic for his younger brother. Between the two of them, someone had to stay calm. It was Jordan's responsibility to protect the only real family he had left. Caden shut off the light and made himself a spot to sleep on the floor beside Jordan's bed. After some time, the brothers shut their eyes and immersed themselves in some restless sleep for a few hours. But before they could fully rest, things got worse. Suddenly, the floor in the room started shaking violently. The books on Jordan's shelf started falling. The lamp toppled over and the medals hanging on the wall rattled. Caden quickly rose to his feet, frightened. "What the hell? Is it an earthquake?" he shouted. Jordan awakened to the sound of his shouting. "An earthquake? Come on! We gotta get to the living room!" he yelled. Jordan jumped out of the bed. Caden quickly rushed to the door, but it suddenly slammed shut. Almost like a poltergeist had taken over. Caden pulled and twisted the doorknob, but it was stuck. "I can't get it open!" he shouted. Suddenly, the leather book arose from Jordan's dresser. It glowed with a bright golden light and floated into the center of the room. Continuing to levitate, the book finally opened and the pages turned vigorously. A bright, blinding light flashed. Jordan and Caden screamed as they shielded their eyes. Something magical was happening before them. They could hear the faint sounds of spiritual chanting and gongs ringing in the back of their heads. Strange hieroglyphics projected from the book. They stuck to the walls of the room, bright with magnificently golden lights. The words scaled across the entire wall, ceiling, and floor. The brothers stood back to back, beside the floating book. They were in awe of what was transpiring before them. A rushing wind overwhelmed them, circulating energy throughout their bodies. The brothers gazed up into the sky and their jaws dropped. Their eyes began to glow white. The floor continued to shake even more. Finally, with a powerful explosion of cosmic energy, one last blinding light took them into a spiritual plane between this realm and the next. Cosmos. The following is everything Jordan and Caden witnessed from Jannah's ancient scripture. The truth about the universe.

Eon 0
Before Existence

And the universe exhaled. It shed breath and spilled its infinite matter across the hollow plane of non-existence. Living within its period of expansion for approximately 19.4 billion years, its immortality began to fade. Death drew near, not by fate, but by choice. A mature realm of non-existence having reached its peak, the expansion of the universe ceased to continue, and the opposite ensued. Matter and light were overwhelmed by dark energy. This dark energy continued to stretch its particles far beyond its limit. The greedy, continuous creation of matter in the prior dimension emitted boundless gravity that exceeded past normal levels of Newtons per kilogram (N/kg). This astronomical proportion of gravity pulled back the matter of space and stopped the process of expansion. Thus followed the Era of Inanimation, hundreds of millions of years in which the universe treaded along the void between life and death. It was now, where the universe no longer moved. Without expansion, the temperatures of all animate objects could not surpass merely a single degree. Still no longer heating or cooling, the universe watched as its death was approaching. During the Era of Inanimation, without movement, dark energy overpowered the universe. Without the gods of Time and Space working in tandem, a god of Gravity dominated the forces of non-existence. Gravity served as the great creator and destroyer of worlds, relentless in its behavior. Dark energy, a force that acted unlike anything else in the universe, stopped expanding alongside Time and Space, which created a collapse. During the Era of Inanimation, Gravity comprised over 98% of existence in the universe, having grown drastically in nothing short of several hundred million years. It is with this control that the god of Gravity superseded Time and Space. A previous bond of body, mind, and spirit had been broken within the universe, leading to the ultimate death that sparked life in the new dimension.

And the universe inhaled. The expansion of Gravity overwhelmed the powers of Time and Space, forcing them to retreat into infinite nothingness. Death. So began an era described as The Great Collapse; the self-destruction of the universe was at hand. Massive formations hurtled towards an unseen center of space, which foretold that everything in the universe would fall apart. Rapid expansion over thousands of millennia resulted in the consequence of Gravity's overconsumption of matter. The universe began to implode, Gravity forcing everything into one point of origin. Matter, planets, stars, and galaxies collided with one another at a force more powerful than anything that had ever existed during this era. The consistent explosions of divine, interstellar matter created a living hell amongst the deep skies of the ancient universe. The Great Collapse marked the end of the beginning. The matter that had once roamed across the entire universe had begun to squeeze itself into a godly dense, tightly compacted structure with a gravitational pull so strong, even light could not escape its wretched grasps. With a solar mass believed to be over 31.2 ± 7, this center of concentrated Gravity was described as Ground Zero. A realm within space where nothingness was free to exist.

A mysterious and bizarre creation had been created by the god of Gravity. With mass billions of times that of any solar star, it spent thousands of years consuming the entire universe. In the center of such a dark being, was what appeared to be a giant mass of light. Yet, even light could not escape the gravitational pull of Ground Zero. This heavenly light emerging from the center had been created by magnetic fields warped into the spinning black hole. Moving so rapidly, the compacted universe began to propel electrons outward in a jet along the rotation axis, producing densely bright radio waves. Something new had emerged in the shrunken universe. Quasars. Quasars were the souls of the consumed planets and stars of the universe. Remnants of the last lights, they drew energy from the massive black hole. At one point, they were bright enough to emit a shine of divine light before being absorbed within the universe's center. Quasars had been born during the Great Collapse as a highly energetic object encircling Ground Zero, feeding it light harnessed from stray objects that hadn't been consumed yet. Quasars and giant jets of gas were the spirits of every interstellar being. Clouds of ejecta served as the flesh left behind after Gravity's hunger had been satisfied. After the Great Collapse, the universe imploded, Gravity continuing its relentless pressure. Mass of the entire universe unified into one, singular object. Time and Space had been destroyed. All that remained… was the Singularity.

And the universe held its breath. It continued its undead life as an initial Singularity. The god of Gravity consumed Time and Space, dragging its brethren into a constraint of infinitely dense non-existence. An ungodly being that possessed all the mass and the space-time of the universe eventually suffocated under its pressure. Unable to breathe through the divine force of quantum fluctuations, the Planck Epoch began. It was the earliest point in this emerging dimension. During the Planck Epoch, all beings in the universe existed within the center of the wretched Ground Zero; the black hole conjured by the greediness of the god of Gravity. The Singularity blossomed as a one-dimensional point of infinitely small space. Having swallowed the remaining Quasars whole, Gravity sought infinite power through itself. Its pursuit of tremendous immortality in the universe had ironically come to fruition through death. The ungodly mass of the Singularity created infinite Time, Space, and Gravity, generating a realm where all laws of physics ceased to exist. Without law, none of the divine gods of the ancient universe could truly exist. Since they technically didn't exist, they couldn't die. All they could do was witness the final destruction of the surrounding universe. Quasars of the consumed planets had been ripped apart by Gravity's overwhelming attraction to power. All matter, including physical, emotional, and spiritual, began to lose dimensionality until it irrevocably joined into the Singularity. As the god of Space began to die, the distance was no longer a reality. Condensed into an infinitely small area, the entire universe was able to be held in a mere mortal's palm. As the god of Time began to fade, Relativity Theory became more clear than before. The entire universe started to move slower and slower as the Singularity shrunk in size. The tremendously unimaginable era of the universe was full of contradictions. For every object consumed by Ground Zero, the Singularity had not grown, but instead, receded into a smaller being. All Quasars, stars, and matter vanished at the Event Horizon, almost as if they never even entered the Singularity. The god of Gravity watched as it wandered a path towards its death, as quantum mechanics began falling apart. The black hole began to fade and all that remained after the death of the divine forces was the Singularity. Surrounded by an area in which light could not escape, the entire universe was unable to be seen. Nothingness began. The black hole dispersed and its center was nowhere to be found. What dominated the dimension after the war between Time, Space, and Gravity, was something that could not be seen. The end of the universe was approaching. The Singularity consumed all. And with all, it knew all. And with knowing all, it spoke with the gods of all. Yet with the knowledge it received, it could never communicate information to anything else in the universe. The Singularity possessed its secrets safely within itself. The fabrics of the universe were under its control. The Planck Epoch was in full force. The Singularity had become so powerful, it attracted the attention of beings from other dimensions. Yet, contrary to theory, these unknown beings were no enemy. Some say they were sent by gods.

And the universe ceased to breathe. The center of its pulsing heart faded as the Singularity persisted. A strange power from the Alter-Realm arose. As the implosion of the Singularity followed, a twisted bend against law was created. Remnants of the universe dispersed after its absorption. From an infinite void, matter began spreading. The New Expansion. All matter consumed into itself. So much so, that it filled the space of non-existence. Before the universe could die from wearing itself microscopically thin, gods took their places amongst the void. Not gods of this dimension, but different ones.

And the universe ceased to breathe. The center of its pulsing heart faded as the Singularity persisted. A strange power from the Alter-Realm arose. As the implosion of the Singularity followed, a twisted bend against law was created. Remnants of the universe dispersed after its absorption. From an infinite void, matter began spreading. The New Expansion. All matter consumed into itself. So much so, that it filled the space of non-existence. Before the universe could die from wearing itself microscopically thin, gods took their places amongst the void. Not gods of this dimension, but different ones. Ripples in the universe led to structure and laws, dragged from another dimension. In a world where particle physics was once unknown, it was not long until the ancient universe experienced its first glimpse of reality. Approximately 377,000 years after the initial Singularity, subatomic particles emerged from what can only be understood as nothing. For what was always present cannot truly begin anew. Light of gods emitted into these particles, possessing equal measures of matter and antimatter. The balance of matter and antimatter was an attempt to exist, shunned by non-existence. Matter and light were contended by darkness and antimatter. The gods rationalized that existence cannot be without non-existence. Confined by an absence of all law, the subatomic particles that came from the Alter-Realm struggled to exist in the dimension that they immigrated into. However, the gods that entered the new dimension still prayed that whatever holy matter remained inside the dying subatomic particles could find a way to survive. The holy matter that did survive created a revival in the universe. Time began. The first second came to life. The residue of matter created from the death of subatomic particles led to neutrino decoupling. During the epoch, neutrinos stopped interacting with baryonic matter, having little influence over the ancient universe. Previously maintained through weak interaction, these forces were suddenly motivated by the light of the gods to move faster than the rate of the New Expansion. This contradiction of time created time itself, one second after the new beginning. With the ancient universe now at a temperature of 10 billion Kelvins, the cosmic neutrino background shaped Space. As the first second passed, the excess matter of the gods started taking shape in an unknown form. A primordial black hole was born, followed by the instantaneous spawning of its siblings. Three minutes' time. After composite subatomic particles merged with the forces of divine nature, they gained enough energy to develop into the most powerful pair in existence: protons and neutrons. With conditions met by scientific spirituality forced into harmony, nucleosynthesis helped them become elements. The first kindle of a new flame in the ancient universe. Helium-4. Then, at 47,000 years after the New Expansion began, light from the Alter-Realm empowered matter to dominate the forces of natural radiation. Over 300,000 years later, recombination started between atoms, as the gods of the neighboring dimension coerced these elements into low energy. As photon decoupling synthesized with the cosmic microwave background of Space, the holy lights remained stationary and began to take shape into their true forms.

The New Expansion created the Dark Ages. 417 million years' time. Transparent clouds of hydrogen developed as the grounds for the first new star. The only source of light was the electromagnetic radiation caused by the late-bloomers of decoupling. As the final primordial black holes began colliding with the divine lights, a pale orange, glowing wavelength formed. Once the massive black holes united with the power of the gods of the Alter-Realm, a new object was created. These fragments of dimensional light possessed the intention to escape the Dark Ages. They entered this realm from another dimension, as new owners of the ancient universe. The gods of Time, Space, and Gravity had become harmonious once more, now undead. But after their previous war, they were under a new rule. Beings whose existence could not be rationalized by the mortal psyche. The paramount gods of the Alter-Realm. gods who were born with a foundation of Materialism.

Eon I
Materialism

One billion years' time. The Dark Ages gradually ended. Matter in the universe consisted of mostly dark matter and less ordinary matter. Yet, no light had enriched the universe's soul. It was with the full existence of the paramount gods during the matter-dominated era of Eon I, that the god of Gravity worked with Time and Space to diffuse the dark matter and develop filaments under the effects of Gravity. Filaments, the largest objects in the universe, were a lock on the existence of the paramount gods. Their massive thread-like formations were over 200 to 500 million light-years long. They each had a divine might to serve as a boundary between large voids. With this, the paramount gods sealed their glory and began their involuntary rise to power over the dimension.

Without a true light, the gods of Time, Space, and Gravity worked in tandem to obey the Alter-Realm's will. The ordinary matter was gathered in areas where dark matter was dense. This would destroy the ordinary matter and dark matter in the process. With the consuming dark matter mostly cleared, the paramount gods had a place where they could live in peace. They were clouds woven primarily from hydrogen gas. It was here where the paramount gods could exist freely. In a mass of hydrogen gas so true to the laws of this universe, they began to understand, rationalize, and obey these invariable rules. But the paramount gods wanted to do more than just exist. Since they were from the Alter-Realm, their sole purpose was to harness light.

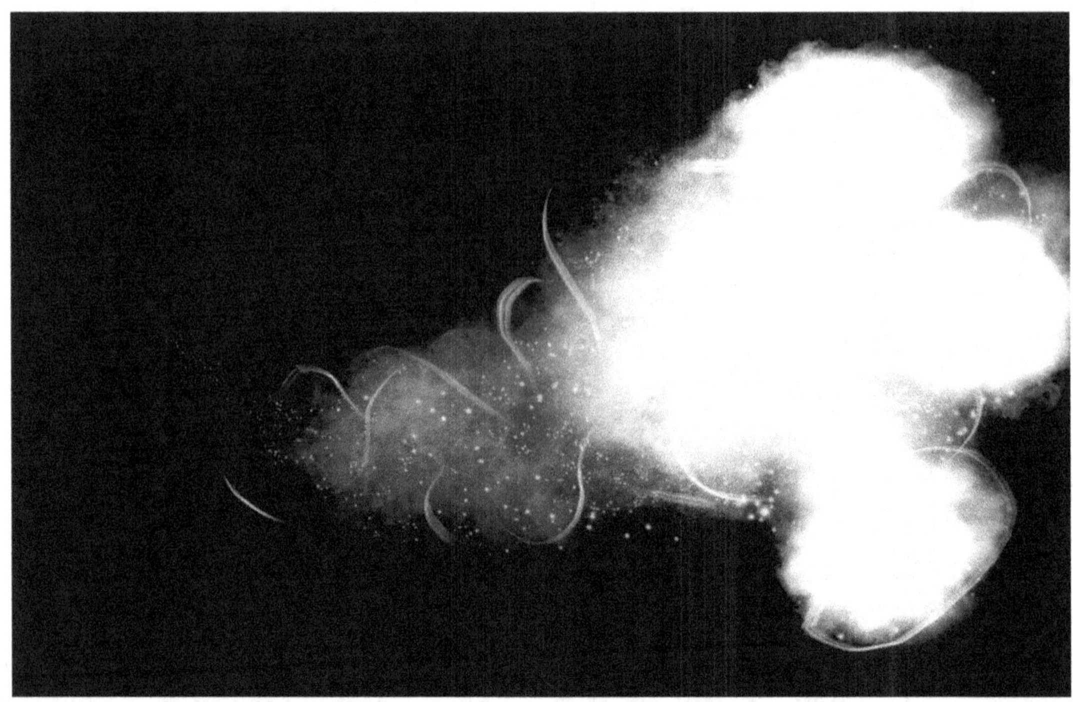

Gargantuan portions of elemental clouds, consisting of 75% hydrogen and 25% helium collided. As the clouds underwent the forces of Gravity, its radiant power incentivized the paramount gods into revealing themselves. Matter clumped together to magnify density and collapse excess material. The ultraviolet ionizing radiation caused the surrounding gas to glow at optical wavelengths. It was at this point when the paramount gods could be seen. An appearance infinitely unfathomable by any being of this realm, their reveal was witnessed by none. Their true form, rationalized by none. Their purpose, understood by none. It was only the beginning of their intention to rule all. The paramount gods unconsciously reveled in their true form. For they were the creators of the most powerful object the ancient universe had bred. They were the creators of the first, true light. The nebula.

What emerged was the most powerful, divine structure in the universe. Forced by the greater gods of their realm, the paramount gods began creating and harnessing all light. Nebulae measured over hundreds of light-years in diameter. And amidst all this surface area, it did not have any wretched corruption of dark matter inside itself. These nebulae served as primitive proof that the paramount gods were here to rule.

And with any desire for power,

came war. The glow of one nebula brought about the attention of gods from multiple realms. Soon, the divine light of more nebulae appeared, revealing that more paramount gods were coming into this dimension. All of which wanted to strip the universe of its light. Out of hundreds, three of the most powerful nebulae emerged.

Forces of light began to form as a byproduct of the paramount gods that traveled to this dimension within the nebulae. They developed methods to expand their territory. As the first stars were born, their explosion into existence gave rise to a never-ending process. Nebulae served as the factory for new stars, and those stars, once born, created more gas and dust to form yet another nebula. This was how the paramount gods ruled over Space with their divine light.

The three types of nebulae each had unique appearances. Even the simplicity of their glowing lights served as the religious embodiment of their various gods. The three strongest nebulae of Eon I were the:

1. Emission Nebula
2. Dark Nebula
3. Planetary Nebula

Each nebula came from a different dimension. Their religions had existed as a concept of principle so unimaginably powerful, it could only begin to realize itself in the universe under the laws of science. Unable to truly embody consciousness, these indescribable beings simply existed without understandable reason. Their homes, the nebulae, served as the proof of their actions, as commanded by the rites of their holy principles. Emitting powerful masses of energy, a fight over spiritual control of the universe had begun through weapons of scientific matter.

The Emission Nebula. Nebula formed from the ionization of high-energy photons. An initial hot star conjured from the revelation of the paramount gods began to disperse its divine light. As the stars within the nebula continued to cycle through birth and death, the outer layers dispersed from their explosive creation. This exposed the hot core as it underwent ionization profusely. The paramount gods that came from this dimension purely sought the attainment of light. They used unfathomable power to bend ordinary matter into a force tremendous enough to produce light at will. It is then when these paramount gods would harness the excess light for the Alter-Realm.

The Dark Nebula. It was a nebula so dense that it obscured the light from objects behind it. Because of its dominance over dark matter, the interstellar material in its core was only visible to infrared wavelengths. The stars developed from the presence of these paramount gods created an instantaneous absorption of light, and in turn, created a drastic contrast in appearance. The paramount gods from this dimension sought immediate absorption of light by using unique stars that bent dark matter. Controlling the dark matter surrounding it, these paramount gods used an anti-force to harness light for the Alter-Realm.

The Planetary Nebula. A nebula that was distinctly different from its relatives. Created from the explosion of a star within itself, this nebula changed its appearance as the millennia passed. As the star's atmosphere dissipated, ultraviolet radiation ionized the ejected material. This produced a greater light for the paramount gods to absorb. The paramount gods from this dimension wished to harness light by using chemical compounds too difficult to understand. The bending of binary central stars, stellar winds, and magnetic fields allowed these paramount gods to restructure matter within their nebulae for a brief time to redirect all light to themselves for the Alter-Realm.

All of these various activities persisted for millions of years. The paramount gods constantly produced light through their revelation within the nebulae and harnessed that light. Then, they would deliver the light to their own Alter-Realm. They blindly served their gods from within this dimension to the next. The universe had experienced its first generations of light but was quickly robbed of it. The gods of Time, Space, and Gravity simply watched as their laws of physics were toyed with by the actions of greater beings. The paramount gods were without consciousness and only lived to serve their purpose. In this dimension, they sought immortality.

War persisted in the universe; the various forms of nebulae combatted over territory to harness more divine light for their own realm. This would have forever been the existence of the universe. A Great Collapse into a Singularity to breed a New Expansion, only to have its divine light consumed. It was impossible to tell if this infinite chain of enslavement would ever stop.

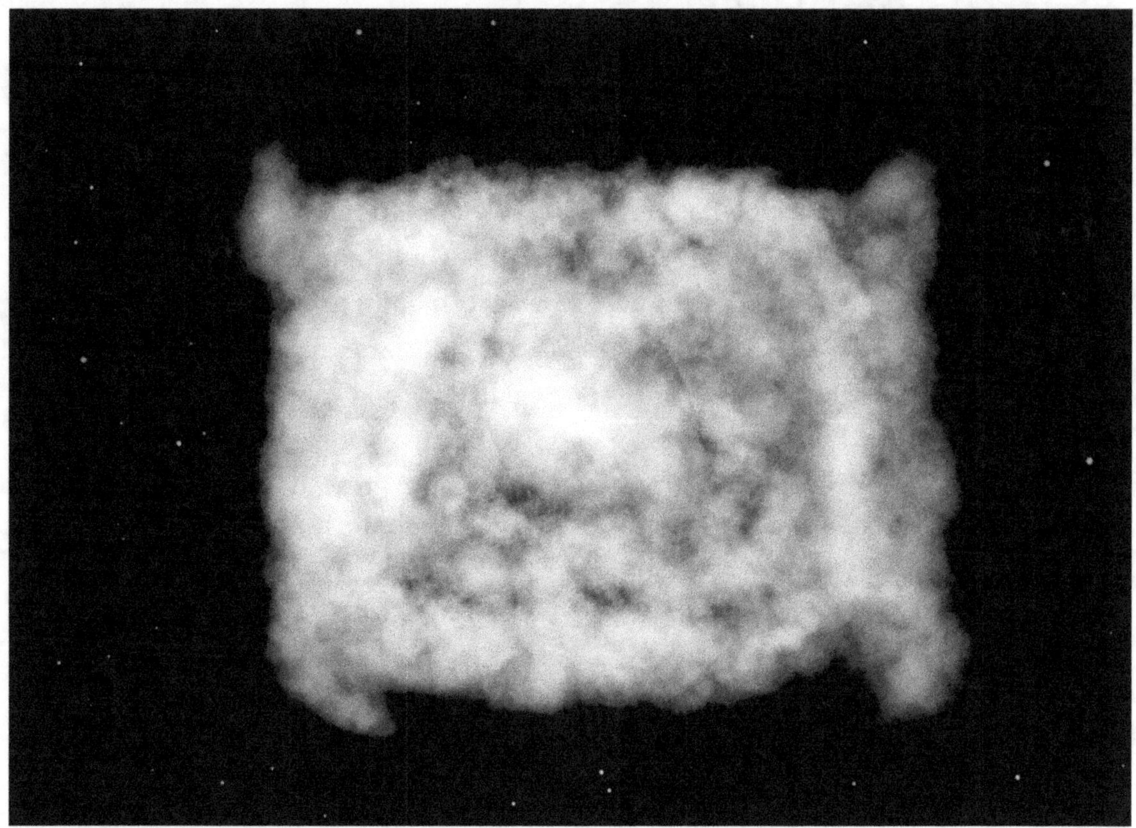

What spawned was a being that started to follow in the path of its paramount god family, yet quickly stopped because of the uniqueness of its birth. Through the constant explosions and interstellar battles over nebulae territory, stars were ejected out of the factories they were manifested in. The massive structures soared across the emptiness of space for years. But at one strange moment, several stars collided within the crosspoint of the three dominant nebulae. It is here where a fourth nebula was suddenly born. The revelation of a hidden paramount god occurred, yet its power was different from its relatives.

This fourth nebula, prematurely spawned by a young paramount god, was known as the Protoplanetary Nebula. Early in its accidental emergence, only one lone paramount god materialized from the depths of the gas and dust. The odd shape and red color of this nebula was almost a symbol of the pain it experienced. This single paramount god would be the first link to the dawn of a new era within Eon I.

Just as the names of the paramount gods could not be properly rationalized by the dialect of mortal conjuration, this paramount god's name could only be expressed through math. This lone paramount god from the only Protoplanetary Nebula was believed to be called AZ - 140283, translated into the current dialect at this time.

AZ - 140283 manifested itself into existence. Young and brightly novice, it watched the chaos before it. In front of the god was a beautiful collision of colors, harmoniously charmed with occasional explosions from bursting stars. The nebulae scattered their divine light across the emptiness of Space. The young god watched the battles unfold for centuries, simply observing the three dominant nebulae produce and simultaneously consume their energy.

Once the young god finished ignorantly relishing in the magnificence created by its distant brethren, it sought to perform its nonexistent duty. It simply grabbed its entire Protoplanetary Nebula and journeyed on. Improperly created by the mistakes of its relatives, it had yet to truly be given a mission by the beings of the Alter-Realm. The lone god simply journeyed forward, drawn by the light of the nebulae. Within seconds, by bending physics at will, it traveled approximately 3.7 light-years, first reaching the Emission Nebula.

From within the glorious green skies that served as a nursery for purple stars, AZ - 140283 observed its brethren continue their action. They constantly revealed themselves within the nebula and began bending ordinary matter to conjure light through the force of expiring stars. Unguided, the lone god circled the processes of its relatives from the Alter-Realm. Incapable of true thought, it simply digested the information emerging throughout the Emission Nebula. Avoiding the crosshairs of the infinite war, the young god spent several thousand years idle, until it accidentally collided with a nearby paramount god. The force of the collision sent the lone god across Space.

Moving across the hurtling stars, clutching its Protoplanetary Nebula, AZ - 140283 wandered east of its original position, finding itself bonded with the Dark Nebula. Here, it repeated the only process it knew. Simply watching as the nearby paramount gods abused dark matter to immediately absorb all emitting light. The lone god digested greater information, unable to truly apply any of it. There was no emotion. There was no guidance. AZ - 140283 simply was. Suddenly, the explosion of a newborn star sent the lone god in another separate direction, an unplanned trajectory.

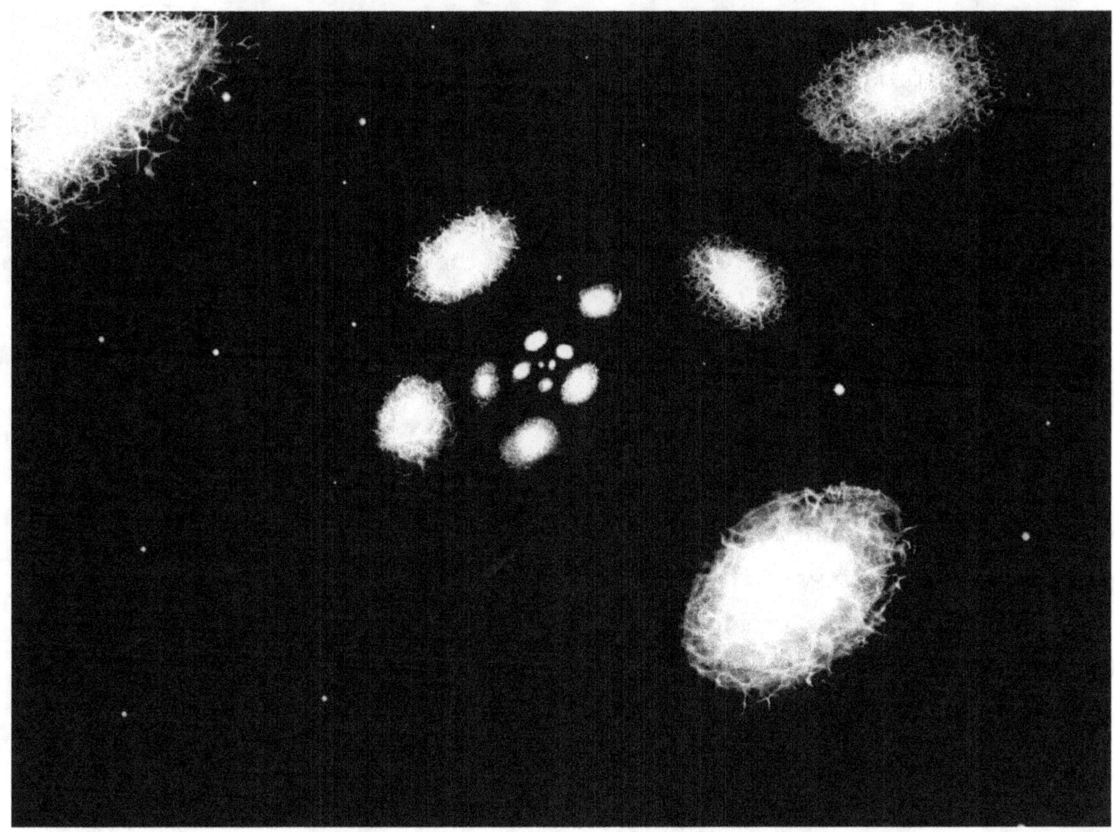

Once more, accompanied by its Protoplanetary Nebula, it moved across the battlefield of stars used as cannon fodder for the proliferation of nebulae. The young god found itself bound by the final nebula, journeying south of its original position. In the Planetary Nebula, binary central stars redirected all light to the paramount gods. Once more in idleness, AZ - 140283 observed as its brethren utilized complex chemical compounds to bend the laws of physics. It digested even greater information without application. It remained as it was. As the Planetary Nebula was less violent than its two neighboring contenders, the lone god finally found what could be rationalized as peace.

After approximately 834 million years, the universe had expanded into an unbelievable being. The light had flooded the bodies of Space, consumed the minds of Time, and dominated the spirits of Gravity. But something new was occurring. An infinite birth of stars reshaped the appearance of the entire universe. Nebulae and clouds bursting with holy light had produced a force stable enough to harness light on its own. An unguided war between the realms had seemingly brought about an era of peace. Eon I was beginning to enter its newest phase. The soon-to-be pioneer of this change, this protogalaxy formation, was AZ - 140283.

Through the manipulation of Gravity, star systems were forcefully bound together to create protogalaxies. It was an ingenious plan of the paramount gods. Almost all light became united in one center. They were guided by the unfathomable beings dominating all physics in the universe. The relentless flow of Time continued to serve as the means of driving the evolution of this realm. After millions of years of assistance from the paramount gods, the universe had finally begun to take shape amongst Space. All the stars became locked in a gravitational embrace. Early protogalaxies were joined at the hip to produce a force so powerful, its existence fueled the entire foundation of the universe.

But with such power, came corruption. This uncontrollable light fed the hunger of the paramount gods; a hunger that could never be quelled. Yet with all evil came a force of good. Against its own distant blood was AZ - 140283. Still absent of true thought, the newfound light in the center of the universe was nothing more than a blind objective to the lone god.

With all light manifested into one area, the surrounding nebulae began to lose their luster. Their souls were left unnurtured by the paramount gods, who now sought immortality in this realm through the protogalaxies. The light was powerful. Too powerful for them to simply give it to the gods of their Alter-Realms. No. This power was theirs to keep. Theirs to feed upon. With all nebulae fading, ties to the distant dimensions grew thin. This divine light, sure to destroy all with its magnificence, was left for the paramount gods to abuse on their own.

However, one nebula remained. AZ - 140283 clutched its Protoplanetary Nebula. The lone god watched as its brethren worshipped the very power they created. Seemingly in awe of their might, they consumed the poison they produced. Soon, feud over the light of the early protogalaxies began. Once more there was war. Only this time, it was war without a true purpose or motive.

Hellbent on what it was astronomically designed to pursue, the lone god moved towards the center of the protogalaxy cluster, bringing its foreign and unstable Protoplanetary Nebula with it. This cataclysmic collaboration of divine power created immediate consequences. AZ - 140283 watched itself from within the protogalaxy cluster. It could feel all holy light enter its body. This sense was unprecedented. All the power of the light was too much to handle. Suddenly, the lone god's Protoplanetary Nebula expanded. In less than a nanosecond, the red nebula stretched across the cluster of protogalaxies and absorbed it all. Acting upon its purpose for entering this realm, AZ - 140283 had consumed itself, along with all the light in the universe. This was the only way to end the war between its paramount gods.

An implosion ended everything. Then an explosion began a new slate. Instantaneously, all was gone. And instantaneously all returned.

The Protoplanetary Nebula emitted all the stars and protogalaxies into Space once more. This time they were scattered everywhere. The cores of these wretched light forms pierced through the surrounding nebulae and covered Space's nonexistent surface for nearly 2.9 billion light-years. Fragments of the networks of light were left behind. The protogalaxies could not develop on their own. Woeful in their distance from their twins, they remained as nothing more than underdeveloped stars. With the sacrifice of AZ - 140283, the universe lived on to see another lifetime. One no longer corrupted by light.

The young god was nowhere to see its victory.

In what appeared to be the aftermath of a chaotic battle, stars were sprawled across the universe like networks of chemical compounds. With all dominant nebulae worn so thin, the paramount gods started to fade from their relentlessly desired immortality. Dying stars clawed their way towards one another, attempting to reconnect and experience the blissfulness of the protogalaxy formation once more. Within these chains of star residue, something new was happening.

At the center of this field of astronomical destruction was the focal point of where these stars began to intertwine once more. In the brief nanosecond when the protogalaxy cluster was consumed by the Protoplanetary Nebula with an implosion, all four fundamental forces of nature were destroyed. It was a few brief seconds when the universe was reduced to the characteristics of the Planck Epoch. Gravity, Electromagnetism, as well as the Strong and Weak Nuclear Forces, were removed from physical law. Within this reckless destruction and creation of everything in the universe, remained the lone god. AZ - 140283 had not dissipated from the implosion of its nebula. No. It had undergone something relatively worse. Its Fundamental Divinity disappeared. The young god had not been destroyed. It was unmade. The particles that bonded their atoms were completely gone. No trace of it in the universe.

"I Am."

Disorder had wreaked havoc upon Time, Space, and Gravity once more. As the four fundamental forces of nature reassembled, the face of Eon I had drastically changed. The paramount gods' incomprehensible forms were no longer here. As the nebulae faded, the paramount gods began to die out. However, the beings of the Alter-Realm did not know that one nebula had figuratively remained. The Protoplanetary Nebula. Although it was unable to be seen, it was within its creator. During the implosion, the nebula became one with AZ - 140283. But the lone god was nowhere amongst the frames of its peaceful destruction.

Amidst the millions of years the last paramount god spent wandering between the planes of reality and divinity, it obtained something that had never been experienced in the universe. Something that was never within its lost brethren. Something that was not meant to exist. Consciousness.

Yes. It is at this time that AZ - 140283 made its first choice, its first act of will. Consciousness was a single force unexplainable by science. Some may call it the fifth fundamental force of nature. The final god's first act was... to live.

And as it spent millions of years deciphering how to reassemble itself, the paramount god became a part of the laws of this dimension's physics. Its subtle rebirth was synonymous with the being's consistently humble presence. The consumption of its own Protoplanetary Nebula granted AZ - 140283 infinite knowledge and consciousness. Inheriting many of the forces of this universe, its new form became visible. The final paramount god knew all and was all. It lived in all universes simultaneously. It experienced every second in every universe simultaneously. To it, there was no difference between past, present, and future. Everything simply was. Is. And in its new form, AZ - 140283 said its first words, believed to be in the language of the Alter-Realm gods.

Eon II
Consciousness

Yes. Novice and young in its appearance, AZ - 140283 could feel. The effervescent being was more than just in tune with its newfound senses. The concept of feeling itself was enough to create an era of new capabilities for the mind. Consciousness was now within the universe, within a single being. Consciousness was now the most powerful force of nature. Truly inexplicable, this power had great results. An uncontrollable tear shed from AZ - 140283's second-old eyes. "What is this?" it asked. The child dragged its finger upward upon its soft cheek, almost lost in finding its face. The final paramount god observed the reflection in its teardrop. This… tear. It was chemically composed of hydrogen and oxygen somehow. AZ - 140283 could see its appearance, slightly. Its cranium was gaping open, visible scientific information constantly entering and exiting its head. Within this whirlwind of physically manifested thought was a core; the… brain? But AZ - 140283 could sense that this was not where its consciousness resided. It was as if its consciousness was in a different part of its body.

Then, on the outside of its small chest, the paramount god could see a pulsating red object. It glowed powerfully, just like its lost home, the Protoplanetary Nebula. A… heart? Yet, this could not have been where its consciousness resided either. A chill ran across its senses. As if it was spoken to by gods of the Alter-Realm, AZ - 140283 suddenly understood its infinite knowledge. The consciousness was granted during its period of divinity in Space. In between life and death. Once it reassembled its physical form, the consciousness, a spirit of sorts, followed.

Now Alkulu suddenly experienced intent. There were actions it wanted to fulfill now. As if those thoughts had always been within its irrational form, but could not truly exist without consciousness. First, it wanted a name. "Alkulu," it said. Now, it wanted a home.

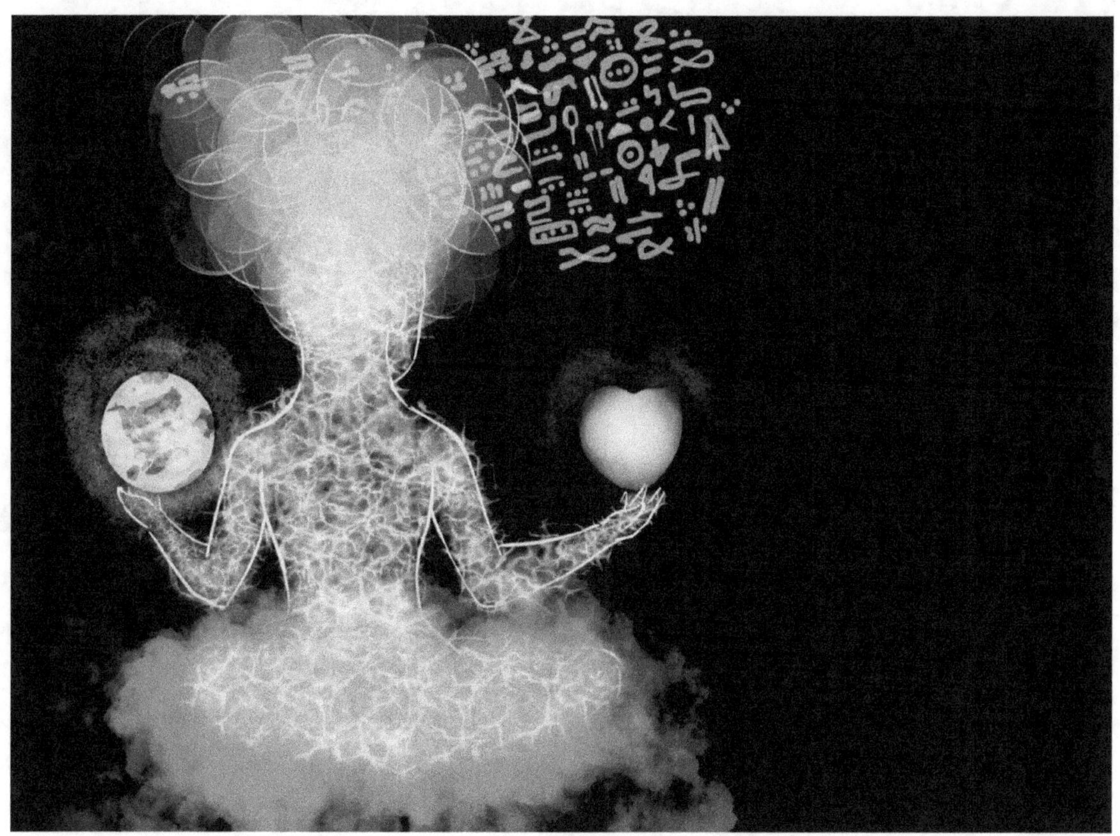

"Forever Can Be."

Alkulu instantly transported across Space. Manipulating the Time surrounding itself, the final paramount god moved past the fragments of the protogalaxy cluster made by its fallen brethren. It reached a focal point in the universe, where Gravity was not intense, almost peacefully appropriate to Alkulu's feelings. Novice in its conscious ways, Alkulu placed its pride above all else. This unknown sector of the universe was where its home should be.

Fragments of star formations were scattered around the quiet universe. Amidst these massive bodies of dying light, Alkulu saw a power strong enough to produce a greater being. Alkulu saw the potential in the entire empty battlefield of its relatives. It bent matter and brought the stars and clusters together, forming what it called, The Galactic Halo.

As Alkulu continued to forcefully unite the stars of the universe, the mass of this celestial object grew large enough to start spinning quickly. A contrasting force known as Eddy created the momentum, a current moving within an opposing current of energy. The final paramount god sustained the movement. Infusing the celestial object with its divine power, its shape began to change. Due to angular momentum, the gaseous interstellar medium started collapsing. It changed from its spheroidal shape into a flattened disk. A sudden disbursement happened. Older stars separated to the outskirts of the spiral arms and younger stars stayed within the galactic center.

Alkulu's new home was born. The newest, most powerful interstellar structure amongst the universe was called a Galaxy. Alkulu named it Aljana.

Able to control everything in the universe, Alkulu took hold of the gods of Time, Space, and Gravity. Instead of doing things like the other paramount gods, Alkulu didn't take hold of them by force, but by persuasion. They agreed to assist it in the unfathomable task of rebuilding the nameless universe. Each segment of the Galaxy had a special sector designed for the three forces of the universe.

The Galactic Center was the home of the god of Gravity. It had an intense radio source created by the motion of material around the center. Alkulu allowed Gravity to breathe freely and release as much of its true,

divine power as it pleased. This concentration of mass, combined with the residue of the fallen paramount gods, produced a supermassive black hole, with an estimated mass approximately 6.2 - 6.7 million times that of any lone star.

The Spiral Arms were the homes of the god of Space. Residing outside any major gravitational influence, there were four distinct arms in the Galaxy. They spanned outward and had a higher density of gas and dust than any other object in the universe. This was where the greatest concentration of star formations started appearing, leaving traces of molecular clouds. These arms allowed Space to live freely as it branched, merged, and twisted to form the spiral of the Aljana Galaxy.

The Galactic Halo was the home of the god of Time. Existing as a spheroidal halo of old stars and global clusters surrounding the disk, it helped maintain the laws of physics in the Galaxy. Alkulu granted the god of Time the ability to live as it wished. The childish behavior of the being quickly became apparent. It roamed freely within the Galactic Halo, interacting with Gravity and Space as it pleased.

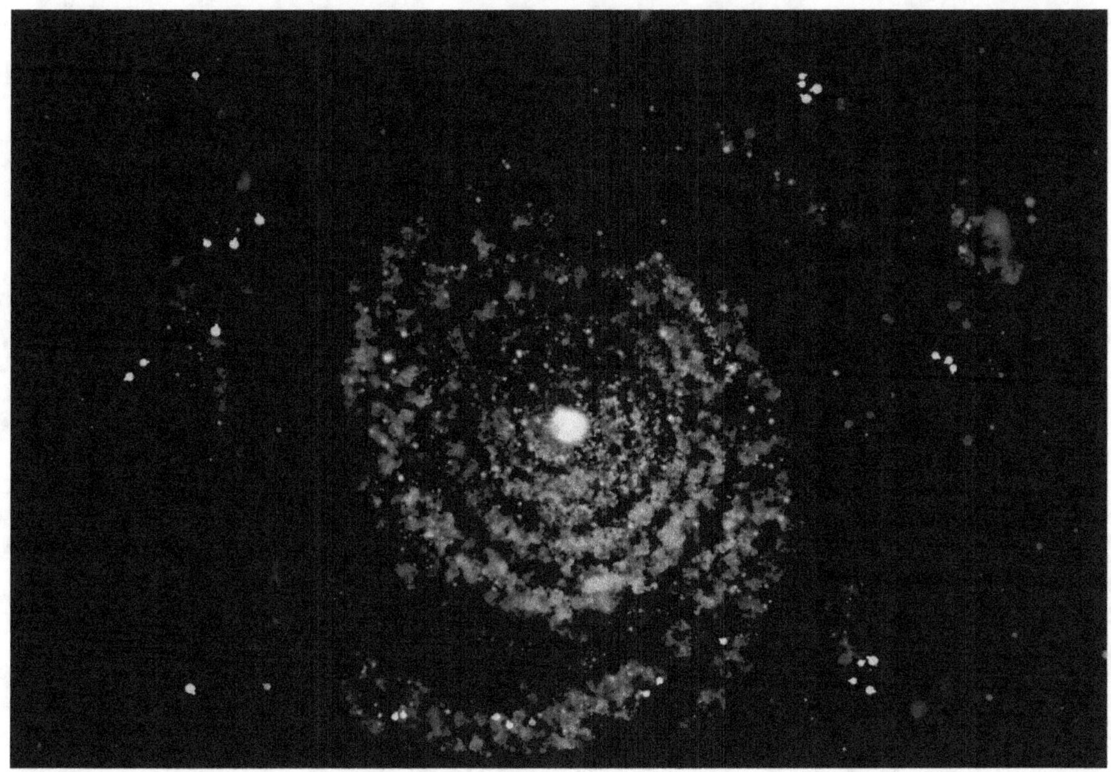

Alkulu observed its most magnificent creation; a Galaxy, the first of its kind. It spanned across the entire universe. Within its massive size of approximately 76,921.056 light-years circumference were over 100 billion derelict stars. Although Alkulu had spawned its very own home to live alone, remnants of the fallen paramount gods had lingered to disrupt its existence.

Cosmic Voids riddled sectors of Space like a plague. As the paramount gods began to die in Eon I, the residue of their passings left behind rips in the space-time continuum, powerful enough to create voids of emptiness.

As the paramount gods' control over the laws of the universe was stopped, it damaged the fabrics of existence in this dimension. Cosmic Voids remained as vast spaces between filaments and possessed little to no stars. Alkulu observed the structures, over 10 to 100 megaparsecs in diameter.

The final paramount god knew all. As it studied the scars in its universe, it could understand that these Voids were formed from the destruction of the protogalaxy cluster. The massive explosion from millions of years ago formed small anisotropies. Anisotropies were a drastic difference in a material's physical or mechanical properties. These anisotropies collapsed rapidly under Gravity, resulting in the large-scale Cosmic Voids that damaged Alkulu's new home, Aljana.

Alkulu knew it was beyond fixing the miscalculations of the other paramount gods. No, this task was not meant for it. Alkulu was the creator of gods. Therefore, these voids were a problem small enough for a mere god.

And in an instant, it was done. Alkulu wished and it served as the means of granting its blessings. Alkulu manifested its conscious thought and created two lesser hyper-dimensional beings. The hyper-dimensional beings possessed a fundamental level of consciousness too. But it was not nearly as complex as their sole creator; just enough to do its bidding. Alkulu knew it was beyond tending to the Cosmic Voids tainting the Aljana Galaxy. They were free to move about on their own. The two hyper beings were capable of experiencing reality in the higher dimension, whether physically traveling through it or mentally calculating outcomes in different, parallel universes. In memory of its fallen relatives, Alkulu gave the hyper beings a title similar to its own. It called them, "gods".

Alkulu's method of producing gods of its own felt simple. As the final paramount god, it was now in control of the laws of physics in this dimension. It replicated fragments of its own consciousness and reapplied it to the hyper beings. This separated consciousness was powerful enough to control the matter around it. The beings that began to exist between the planes of reality and divinity pulled their atoms and particles together, so they could witness each other's presence. They manifested themselves before their creator, Alkulu.

The gods began to take shape. Being first-generation gods created from the All, they could traverse the dimensions and exist within the 4th. They perceived reality differently than their creator. Because they were born as direct products of this dimension, they possessed traits directly related to this universe's laws of physics. Elements flooded their bodies and light imbued them with vision.

Incredibly powerful, the gods were capable of chronokinesis, cosmic awareness, precognition, temporary bio fission, intangibility, mind-reading, teleportation, and more. It was with these divine tools gauged through a scientific measure, that they too, could shape the universe.

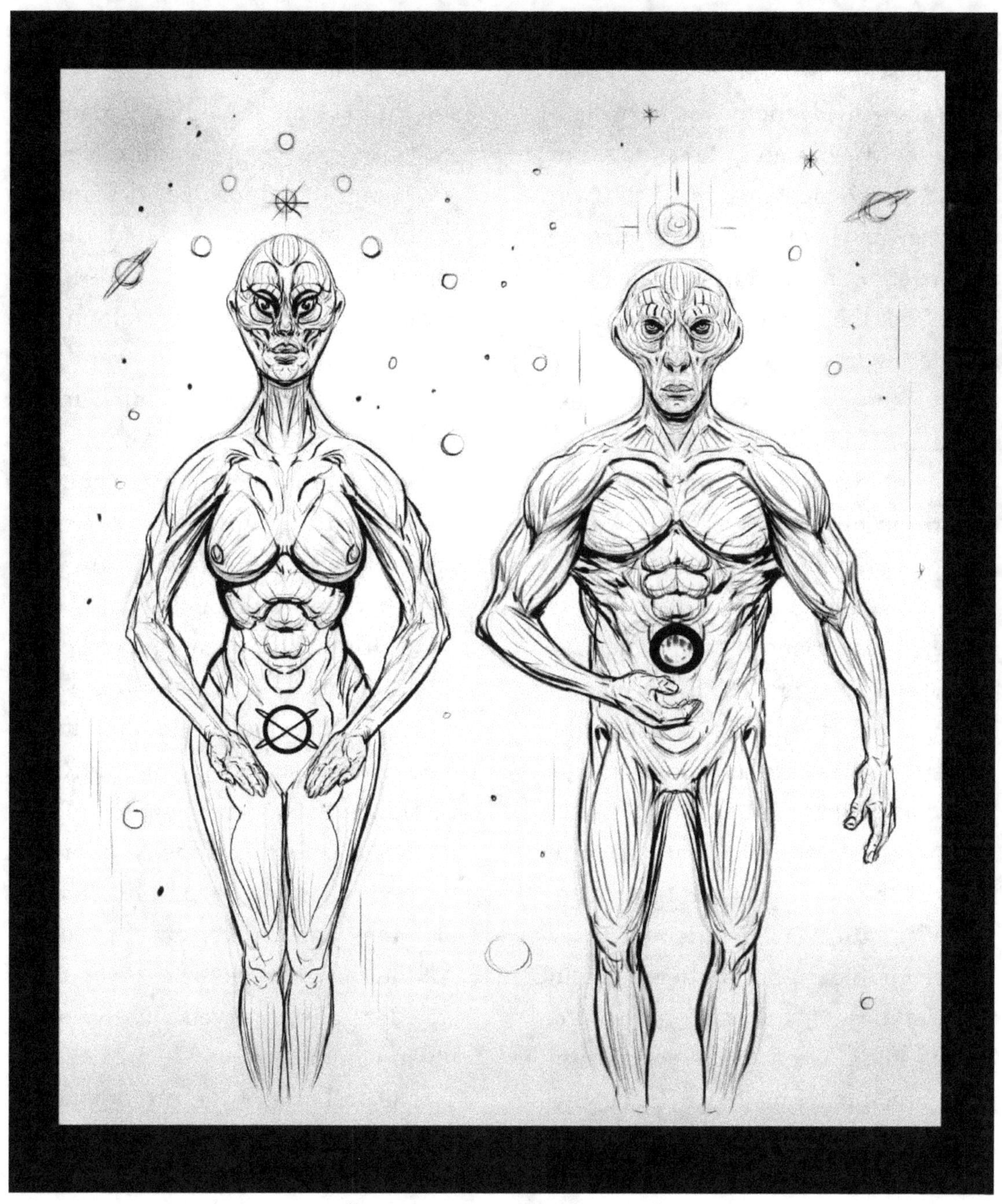

"Gods shall serve the All."

With consciousness, the gods produced by the creator of gods could recognize the task bestowed to them upon birth. Immediately engaging in their duties, the twin gods began working to dispel the Cosmic Voids tainting the Aljana Galaxy.

Almost abusing what appeared to be limitless control over the laws of physics, the hyper-dimensional beings directed their attention to the derelict stars floating around Space. Within these stars' lives, there was a constant battle between energy pushing out and Gravity pushing in. The twin gods saw no real calculable purpose for the stars in their weakened form. Therefore, they immediately exhausted the hydrogen fuel within them, causing the stars to collapse and explode with blinding brightness. The consistent explosions of the thousands of surrounding stars became powerful enough to repel the Cosmic Voids.

Unfortunately, every action in the universe experienced consequences. As the stars were forcefully torn apart by the gods, they bled out into the universe, releasing all the elements they had utilized in life and death. From the catastrophic death and rebirth of the stars was a forgotten interstellar entity. The dreaded nebulae.

The divine colors scattered about the darkness of Space once more. Luckily there weren't any paramount gods accompanying the nebulae this time. These nebulae were produced by a lesser being and could only yield cosmic gas and dust, powerful enough to bless Aljana with holy lights.

After the twin gods had displaced the Cosmic Voids, tiny stars were forming from the elements blown out by the supernova explosions. Harm-

less, these protostars could easily die out without proper nurture. Alkulu sought to create something greater for its Galaxy. More powerful than the protostars that appeared. It wanted a sector of its home to be decorated with an interstellar structure powerful enough to symbolize the attainment of consciousness. Alkulu wanted to create its own star. It wanted to put the twin gods to the test. Alkulu gravitated towards a particular nebula in what it felt was the center of the universe. It was here, billions of years ago, that life would begin.

With the help of the hyper beings, this unnamed nebula within the Aljana Galaxy became the first link to create a new shape in the universe. Clouds of hydrogen began to collapse further and further under the force of the god of Gravity, bound by the gods of Time and Space. By its design, Alkulu initiated the life cycle of a new star. Its gods observed closely, possibly in wonder.

The collapse of the protoplanetary dust cloud was the first step. At the center, within the giant cloud of molecular gas and dust, the star was beginning to form. Shockwaves from the surrounding supernovas created the gravitational collapse at the center.

Shortly after, the hyper beings moved pockets of dust and gas into denser regions of the forming system.

Much like the creation of Aljana, the denser regions pulled in the matter and began the conservation of momentum, which led to a rotation. As the system flattened out into a disk-like shape, the Galaxy that possessed it compacted the material into the center, developing a complete star. However, this star was purposefully created through acts of higher beings, devised by the divine All.

Dust and gas within the rotating disk coalesced to form separated structures beyond the star at the center. Due to higher boiling points, only metals and silicates survived being so close to a gradually warming star. As these elements combined, they formed massive interstellar objects. "Planets," Alkulu said to the twin gods.

Terrestrial planets formed closer to the center star. Growing beyond the three terrestrial planets were four more planets. These last four were more gaseous and larger than the terrestrial planets. On these planets, the material became cool enough for volatile icy compounds to remain solid. More ubiquitous than the metals and silicates that comprised the terrestrial planets, they grew massive enough to possess large atmospheres of hydrogen and helium. Leftover debris and rocks aligned in between the planets. The twin gods called them Asteroid Belts.

As the three beings patiently watched their creation unfold for 50 million years, the pressure and density of hydrogen in the star became great enough to produce a new phenomenon; thermonuclear fusion. Under Alkulu's supervision, the temperature, reaction rate, pressure, and density increased until hydrostatic equilibrium was achieved. What began as a small star, further developed into what the twin gods described as a seraphic star. Solar winds from this holy being wiped away the remaining gas as dust, ending the star development process. At the center of this planetary system was a structure with the greatest energy the universe had seen. Alkulu, remaining alongside its gods, called the seraphic star, "Sun".

The Sun was almost a perfect sphere enriched with a divine soul of hot plasma. The internal convective motion generated a powerful magnetic field. Being the most valuable source of energy in the entire universe, the Sun was easily 214,000 times larger than its greatest orbiting planet. It comprised over 99.91% of the total mass of the entire planetary system. Composed of approximately 72.87% hydrogen, 25% helium, and smaller quantities of oxygen, carbon, neon, and iron, the Sun was unstoppable. The twin gods believed the entire universe should exist.

Finally, the twin gods faced their
creator. The All. "It is done," they
said. Alkulu observed the system surrounding the seraphic star. It was
powerful enough to manifest religious
forces greater than what the paramount gods ever created. Science was
the other half of religion. To Alkulu,
one could not exist without the other.
"What do you wish to call it?" it
asked the twin gods.

The hyper beings, consciously
aware of their achievement, faced one
another. They communicated telepathically, discussing possible names
of their new creation. What would it
have? What would exist in this solar
system? If something were to exist in
this space, what could they possess?
Perhaps consciousness? Of course. It
was the fifth fundamental force of nature. It had proven to be the key to
developing the universe. However,
the twin gods knew that they were
blessed with the guidance of Alkulu.
The guidance was extremely important for the universe to thrive. So
they believed that every being should
have some form of direction. They
had to be created with something to
follow and obey. They would need
guidance. Determinism. Finally, their
thoughts became one. All that was left
was to name the solar system. And
they called it, Syris.

Eon III
Determinism

Act 1 - Passage 1

It began. Across all planets in the Syris Solar System, divine power manifested by the twin gods created a new being. All seven rotating planets were identical while they were developing into their final forms. A period marked by the earliest-known rocks, hellish fury prevailed over the planets. They were engulfed in smoldering ruins. Radioactive elements and frequent collisions with stranded asteroids were obstacles to the hyper beings' creative process.

Several million years later, the crust began to cool enough to allow continents to form. These were massive formations of land that resided upon the oceans developing on the planets. The oceans themselves developed as the hydrogen and oxygen turned from gas to liquid. Nonetheless, heat dominated the atmospheres, as the cores began to develop within the planets, powerful enough to disintegrate the radioactive elements.

As Alkulu consciously observed the process from afar, within Aljana, it understood its gods' relentless pursuit of progression in the universe. Almost impatiently, the hyper beings tended to the suffering of the planets. Forcing the oceans to rise and cool, they knew the tremendous parcels of the water could be breeding grounds for something special. Attempting to replicate what their creator did, the twin gods saw potential in the ocean and acted upon it. The planets' biospheres included soil, hydrothermal vents, and rock in its sectors of over 64+ km deep. The twin gods manifested thought and Alkulu aided in granting their wish before they could speak it. Divine chemical reactions from the hydrothermal vents solidified conditions for microorganisms to spawn. Physically powerful like their creators, these beings could survive the vacuum of outer Space or possibly worse. They developed in trenches, the deepest sectors of the planets.

The twin gods wanted this creation to serve them. Microorganisms were easily capable of reproducing. Yet, their weak structure would only allow them to survive for so many years without nourishment. Thus, the twin gods reached towards the developing

Sun and harnessed its holy light. Through bio-fission, they brought light to each of the seven Syris planets. Providing the oceans with this energy, the microorganisms began to take greater shape, into cyanobacteria. The cyanobacteria were the first to introduce oxygen into the atmosphere through a process that came to be known as photosynthesis. The hyper beings watched as surface minerals became saturated, allowing the excess oxygen to accumulate in the atmosphere. At this point, all microorganisms were able to thrive.

It was now. The first step to the rise of the holiest beings in the universe. From the oxygenation of the atmospheres came the glorious evolution of complex, single-celled life. Prokaryotic and eukaryotic organisms used oxygen to respire. And so came the birth of the truest phase of Eon III. An explosion of multi-celled animals arose. Their purpose was predetermined by the All the twin gods.

Every event in the universe had now been inspired by consciousness. Only now, it had required more than just the laws of physics. Further development of the universe had become necessitated by something rather new. The laws of nature. And as the twin gods observed the Proterozoic organisms grow into fully developed animals, they knew that the future was within their control. Through tremendous devotion, aquatic creatures arose from the depths of the oceans and walked the plains of the land. With their resolve being the greatest power granted to them from their creators, a passionate evolution ensued once more. The beings anatomically developed a head, neck, trunk, arms, hands, legs, and feet.

Peacefully residing in the center of the Syris Solar System, atop its divine Sun, Alkulu could not help but immerse itself in its actions. Billions of years it spent, alone. Nonetheless, it used the same light that nearly destroyed the universe to instead, improve it. The twin gods stood over the seven planets, watching the development of what they called, "Nephilims".

Massive creatures, born directly from gods, evolved to become the most powerful beings to exist amongst the planets. Millions of years of physiological adaptation, mental comprehension, and spiritual ignorance had birthed the Nephilims. Although the twin gods were curious about what would happen if they provided a greater divine force to the Nephilims, the All had thought less of it. The first species in the universe was now created within the parameters of nature. Alkulu only allowed the twin gods to determine their fate.

They were not allowed to have any direct contact with the Nephilims they created. Alkulu felt it was more peaceful to watch the species interact with the planets on their own. The twin gods could only guide them through the influence of religion. "Leave them be. Observe their interaction with the universe and how they utilize consciousness, for it is what I have done with you," Alkulu said. The twin gods obeyed. And it was so; the Nephilims were left to their conjectures. Only faintly guided by the twin gods.

The Nephilims were mostly immortal. They were susceptible to the dangers of the natural planet. Whether it be killed by the environment or creatures around them. But other than direct physical harm, the Nephilims were capable of withstanding the tests of time forever. They lived on for centuries, continuing to amass knowledge and a deeper understanding of the universe around them. Being one with the biological nature of their planets, the Nephilims came to believe that once any of them would die, their anatomical components would nurture the environment. Their corpses would feed animals and grow forests. But those who never succumbed to the harsh realities of the world, lived on to tell their stories and make great strides in the development of the universe. For many of the Nephilims, they believed there was a statistical chance that one of them would evolve from the ocean determined to completely change the universe. That single Nephilim was prophesied to be the Chosen One.

Act 1 – Passage 2

A body of the sea drowned out more than its ability to breathe, but also its understanding of the world surrounding it. A need to adapt and a relentless drive to evolve had pushed this being to evolve. It could feel the ocean waves thin out. It feared suffocating from the outside world. Yet, as it could feel a blistering light above warm its flesh, it had realized that it was time to move past the ocean. To live elsewhere.

Then, the pressure stopped. It was no longer swimming. Its body halted as the waves continued to cascade over its body. The warmth upon its face was a new sensation. Grains of sand upon the beach scratched its skin. It reached forward and clutched the minerals. It felt a wave of nostalgia. These minerals seemed similar to what resided at the bottom of the ocean. It inhaled profusely. This… was breathing.

This particular being continued pulling itself forward until the dreaded ocean waves could only touch the bottom of its feet. It lifted its face from the sand. There before it was its kin. Other Nephilims. No less than 30 more beings just like it were wandering around the beach. It was an evolution conspired by holy beings who chose to remain distant from their creations. This Nephilim lifted itself from the sandy terrain, into a full posture. Dazed with its vision impeded by the bright light above, it journeyed forward. Somewhat conscious of its purpose to live beyond the ocean, it had assumed these similar creatures on the beach had hoped for the same. Trekking 15 yards north, it approached one of the other Nephilims.

The stranger was sitting upon the beach, lost. All it did was face the ocean. The Nephilim approached the stranger, knowing nothing more than to reach its hand out towards what appeared to be a similar creature. Touch. A sense carried from its previous form in the ocean. As it placed its hand upon the creature's face, it panicked. The stranger flailed its arms and crawled away. Fear. The sand was kicked up, resulting from the stranger's chaotic actions. The stranger buried its face in its knees and curled up in hiding. The Nephilim just turned away. It didn't possess the empathy to understand its kin.

Continuing up the beach, a forest persisted ahead. Many of the lost Nephilims were simply walking towards it. Massive trees and vines dominated the environment inland. None of the wandering Nephilims could rationalize the possibility of any danger in the forest. That was impossible. These newly evolved beings had spent their previous lives in the depths of the ocean.

Suddenly, a shrieking sound emitted from the infinite sky above. Sound. A massive shadow was cast upon the beach. This particular Nephilim looked up. It could see that the bright light above was suddenly gone. A creature larger than them, with wings too big to measure, had made its rotations up above in search of food. With one final 360-degree spin, the winged beast flapped its appendages as it slowly descended upon the beach. The ground shook as it landed. Its flesh looked rough. Fur covered its body. It also possessed a large beak, an unusual substitution for lips. The beak opened, revealing the mouth inside. The winged beast shrieked once more, which echoed loudly. The lost Nephilims knew nothing more than to observe the creature. But their ignorance had become their greatest weakness. They were about to learn the dangers of mortality.

The winged beast opened its beak

and consumed one of the wandering Nephilims whole. It tossed the Nephilim towards the sky and watched as gravity forced it to fall into its throat. But the beast had yet to be satisfied. It attacked again. This particular Nephilim watched as its kin was devoured by the creature. The only comprehensible reason must have been a physiological need. Terrifying screams of its people echoed over the sounds of the ocean waves. Blood cascaded across the beach as bodies were tossed about. Sight. The Nephilim could feel its organs rattle and its heart pound with uncontrollable force. Its nerves shook relentlessly. It observed its hands, watching them produce sweat from their unseen pores. Its kin began fleeing into the nearby forest to avoid an unknown fate. Others attempted to attack the creature, to fight back. This particular Nephilim could rationalize nothing more than two options. Do unto the creature what it had done upon its kin, or escape a tragedy. It fled.

Into the forest, it rapidly increased its motion. It ran. This particular Nephilim, now having lost sight of its kin, continued past the toppled tree trunks and gargantuan vines. A tint of green reflected into its eyes from the bright light up above as it passed through the towering vegetation of the forest.

Suddenly, the Nephilim tripped over a branch. It fell onto its upper body, its face burying into the soil. The dirt burned its eyes. The Nephilim quickly removed the soil from its face. As it got up to continue fleeing, it suddenly felt an inability to move. The Nephilim scanned its body and saw a crimson liquid emerge from the base of its right leg. It knew nothing more than to analyze this occurrence by picking at the wound. There was a shock, a flurry of senses, and a ringing from its ears. Pain. In the silence, the Nephilim could still hear the distant screams of its people upon the beach. Amongst these noises, another emerged. Up above in the trees. Something moved between the vines. It had to have been another feral creature willing to eat another to satisfy hunger.

The Nephilim quickly fled once more. A sense, perhaps adrenaline, helped it persist through the forest. Now it was in fear of another being. The Nephilim leaped over another fallen tree and limped through a puddle of water. The sound in the trees was heard again. A rustle. This time, from several different directions. The Nephilim quickly dove into hiding within nearby shrubbery. If it could not see itself, then surely the surveying beasts could not see it. The Nephilim attempted to quell its harsh breathing. Everything was silent until it felt a tug upon its abdomen.

A vine had suddenly grabbed the Nephilim, constricting all its movement. It was lifted into the air. A foul stench of rotting flesh emerged. Smell. An oppressive heat coated the Nephilim's head and a growl followed the intense breath of yet another predator in the forest. This creature camouflaged amongst the surrounding vegetation. But it wasn't a lifeless plant. It was a monster with a terrifying desire to eat other creatures. It lifted the Nephilim with its vine-like appendages and prepared to consume it using what appeared to be hundreds of edged teeth inside its gaping mouth.

As the beast prepared to devour this particular Nephilim, it seemed as though it was given a second chance. Fate was guided by the gods above. The rescuers had emerged. There was a scream from above; one of an incomprehensible combination of anger and passion. A war cry of sorts. The plant monster was suddenly pierced by a metal blade through its cranium. A purple liquid burst into the air with the execution of the beast. The putrid substance entered the Nephilim's mouth, initiating its gag reflexes. Taste. The plant's vine appendages stopped moving as the Nephilim fell to the ground.

A silence occurred once more. Resting upon its back, the lone Nephilim could see the light glisten through the massive forest trees. The glare was blinding. It remained constricted by the vine carcass. Suddenly, footsteps were heard. The Nephilim shuddered in fear and closed its eyes.

The vines were cut by the same blade that killed the creature. The lone Nephilim was set free and dragged to its feet. It realized that one of its kin was who rescued it. The one that had slain the plant beast had long hair, a smaller stature, and strange bulges protruding from its chest. Blood mottled its face and the spear it wielded in its left hand. Then, more Nephilims emerged behind the warrior. Five of them. One of which stood in front of the pack. A leader. This leader communicated with the warrior who had rescued the lone Nephilim. Their tongue was nothing more than noise to the newly evolved being. Nods of their heads and motions of their arms were signals of a mutual understanding. The Nephilim with long hair pushed the lone one forward. Without any understanding of life, it followed the pack of Nephilims. Its heart finally slowed as it calmed down. The lone Nephilim felt something with its kin that it could not feel moments before its potential death. Safety.

Act 1 – Passage 3

The lone Nephilim walked amongst its people until the light in the sky changed colors and the weather became less comfortable than before.

Finally, it was led to a location full of its kin. Past gilded gates and towering walls made of limestone, were hundreds of Nephilims. Yet, for the lone Nephilim, their presence felt different than those who emerged upon the beach. They were not consumed by fear, fleeing predators, or gazing at the shoreline with emptiness. These Nephilims were beyond evolution. Something had changed their existence. Time.

Continuing to follow the pack that brought rescued it, the lone Nephilim walked behind what appeared to be its leader. The six creatures of possibly a similar genetic makeup continued exchanging noises in their tongue. The lone Nephilim observed them closely. It attempted to mimic their motions. Constantly opening and closing its mouth, it began making odd sounds. Starting from its diaphragm, air emerged from its lungs, through the vocal folds, then out the mouth. Using its tongue, upper lips, lower lips, and teeth, it moaned. The lone Nephilim continued its incomprehensible sounds. Its kin simply looked back at it as if it were as animalistic as the creatures attempting to eat it some time ago.

Journeying forward, the pack of Nephilims entered a massive structure. It was shaped like a pyramid, made of the same limestone forming the outer gates. The species continued down a corridor to enter a secluded room located at the center of the pyramid.

In the room was an altar with decorative candles enhancing its stone appearance into something divine. The flames glowed brightly with constantly transforming colors. They looked as if they were made of nebulae, possessing a sheer beauty that could only be truly displayed by Space. Behind the altar was a massive shrine. Upon the shrine was a story told, etched in gold plating. There were visions of a being emerging from the stars from the collision of massive energies in Space. The lone Nephilim couldn't rationalize anything more than that.

The Nephilims pushed the lone one forward, to the center of the room. The warrior with the spear turned this particular Nephilim around and forced it onto its knees. Upon the floor was a fabric, much like what these beings wore around their flesh. The lone Nephilim looked forward at the leader of the pack. The leader held holy flames within its palms, daintily caring for the object as if it was worth more than its own life. Suddenly, crystals hanging from the ceiling by silk threads began lighting up. Revitalized by the touched flame in the leader's hands, they too began to reveal an everlasting change of colors similar to nebulae. The crystals pulsated like the beating of a heart, each breath initiating yet another transition of colors. The lone Nephilim gazed at the objects above. Even without a fully evolved consciousness, the awe could easily be seen upon its face.

The leader stepped forward. The other members of its pack each held a candle and stood in designated positions around the lone Nephilim. Together with the leader, they formed the points of a star. Darkness suddenly consumed the room, the only lights being the flames and crystals above. The warrior forced the Nephilim to bend its head forward, staring at the ground. The holy leader carried the flames above its kin's head. The colorful fire slowly dripped upon the Nephilim's head like molten lava. As it made contact with the being's skin, it entered its veins. The flames caused the Nephilim's veins to glow as their holy power entered its bloodstream. The lone Nephilim grunted in pain. The leader placed their hands togeth-

er in a praying position. Once more, it began speaking in its tongue, chanting loudly in the hollow room. The leader lifted the lone Nephilim's head and placed both of its hands upon its chest and forehead. The index finger and thumb of its right hand upon its heart, and the left hand upon its head in a similar position, where its brain should be.

After a short moment of silence, there was a sudden burst of energy. Both the leader and the lone Nephilim's eyes began to glow. The beam of divine light was powerful enough to phase through the roof and appear in the infinite skies above. The white beam persisted as the ground began to shake. Finally, all the flames faded as the crystals quelled their dances of light. Stars glistened inside the room. They fell from the ceiling like ashes from Space, touching the floor and twinkling every half second.

The glowing stopped. The lone Nephilim collapsed to the fabric that it knelt upon. The leader began to hyperventilate. It expended a tremendous amount of its energy performing this ritual. But all Nephilims knew this was the rite of passage for their species. This was the first step toward evolution beyond mere consciousness; the first step toward Determinism.

Act 1 – Passage 4

After the ritual, everything became clear. The nameless Nephilim knew what he was. He was blessed with the knowledge of his kin and understood that he was no feral animal like the rest of the creatures on the planet. He possessed gender. No longer rationalizing himself as an "it," he knew that he was a man.

Finally, his senses began to reassemble themselves. As his vision cleared, he could deduce that he was not outside. Yet he was no longer in the altar room inside the pyramid either. He awakened in a soft bed, draped with golden blankets and a decorative artifact hanging from above. Perhaps it provided light when the one above in the sky would suddenly disappear. The nameless Nephilim fixed his posture upright, leaning against the headboard of the bed. He looked at a glass window to his left. He could see that the light in the sky rose again. The… Sun. He removed himself from underneath the gilded covers. He no longer felt vulnerable like when he first evolved from the ocean. The nameless Nephilim was no longer cold, no longer… naked. After observing his body, he could see that he was wearing traditional garbs, similar to that of his kin. The Nephilim walked towards the window and observed the Sun. It was bright, magnificent. This had to have been an indicator of an elapse of time. Darkness ensued when he was last conscious, but it now appeared as though the opposite was true. The Sun was returning. Upon the ground outside, he could see the neighboring structures and other Nephilims walking amongst themselves. This was civilization. Consciousness at its peak.

A sound appeared behind him. The Nephilim turned around, facing an opening door. It was the leader. The same man who performed the ritual that awakened his consciousness and sudden understanding of all.

"I see you have awakened," the leader said. "I am Abdul. It is what my founders have chosen to call me." Abdul stepped forward, approaching the nameless Nephilim. A smile appeared on his face. This expression helped the estranged being feel a sense of comfort. "Do you understand the words coming from my mouth?" Abdul asked.

The nameless Nephilim could not quite rationalize a proper response. His eyes darted across the room, searching for the words that it somehow knew, but could not find.

Abdul chuckled. "I believe the word you seek is, 'yes.' It is used to respond in the affirmative. Meaning, you agree with my statement, or that it is true," he explained.

The nameless Nephilim naturally nodded and uttered the word, "Yes." His voice was truly heard for the first time.

"Congratulations. You have spoken. My, you have quite a powerful voice. A formidable contribution to our people I would hope. Now, is there any part of your body that's in pain?" Abdul asked.

The nameless Nephilim could do more than just understand the word, "pain." He associated it with a sense he experienced while in the forest. Synapses in his brain brought about the memory of the occurrence to help him define the word. Yet, he could not feel physical pain right now. How could he express that he didn't feel any?

Suddenly, one of the unknown Nephilims that served as a pack member to Abdul approached him. He began touching the nameless Nephilim upon his limbs and vital organs, searching for a response that would display pain at a particular point on his body. The Nephilim gave no such response.

Abdul chuckled once more. "I believe the word you seek now is, 'no.' This is simply the opposite of yes, meaning you do not agree with a statement," he explained.

The lone Nephilim shook his head and replied, "no." Abdul's pack left the room, standing in the nearby hallway. They were preparing to leave.

"Perfect. Those will be all the words you require as of now. You may have noticed a difference in our species. As you may have become aware, you are a man. Called, "him." The warrior that saved you was a woman, called, "her". We have yet to understand the purpose of these distinguishing characteristics between men and women, but only god will determine when we should know. After some prolonged conversation with the other Nephilim leaders, we have decided to call you Mustafa. Now Mustafa, the reason why you have suddenly become clear in our tongue is that the ritual I performed upon you last night is one that I, as well as many other leaders, perform on any newly evolved Nephilims that emerge upon the shore. It makes use of your adapted consciousness, helping you rationalize your existence and understand our species. We are Nephilims. I will explain more another time. But for now, join me. We will show you the way of your people. Our civilization."

Abdul, Servant of gods

Act 1 – Passage 5

Mustafa followed Abdul outside the palace. The warmth of the Sun felt different than it did before. Perhaps it was the sudden acquisition of knowledge. It must have given him a different perspective. They walked amongst stone tiles surrounded by desolate plains of sand. Only this sand was different; it was much less vibrant than the sand on the beach. Abdul walked alongside Mustafa as if the newly evolved being was his equal. Perhaps he was, considering that Nephilims could immediately transfer much of their knowledge through ritual. Yet even with a fundamental level of consciousness, Mustafa felt as if something was missing. There were fragments of himself that he didn't completely understand yet. Experience.

With Abdul's pack following from behind, they walked away from the massive palace towards a dirt road, leading to the bazaar. "Now, Mustafa. We are going to visit the bazaar. It is a sector amongst our civilization where many of our kind congregate. But before we arrive, I feel I must explain to you how all this came to be. Not just the buildings and currency, but also the existence of this entire planet. How Nephilims learned the true purpose of our predetermined existence.

It is what I, as well as my fellow prophets, divulge to all newly evolved Nephilims that we manage to rescue at the shore. Do you understand?" Abdul asked.

Mustafa passively listened to the words from his founder. Although he simultaneously became aware of all his senses, sight seemed to have dominated sound. The Nephilim was drawn to the emptiness of the desert. "Mustafa? Did you hear me?" Abdul asked.

Mustafa finally turned around. "Yes." Although Abdul would have appreciated an apology for seemingly having been ignored, he remembered that Mustafa knew no other dialect except yes and no. He placed his hand on Mustafa's shoulder and continued walking him towards the bazaar.

"Let me start from some time ago. Mustafa, before our creation, the universe was entirely dominated by the laws of physics. Everything had been inferred from particular facts. These facts were then applied to specific phenomena and served as the rational explanation behind everything that happened in the universe. Just physics. Mathematics and science. But it is our creators who broke from the grounds of physics and guided existence into the law of nature. Nature is ever-changing, free, and always provides something new to learn. This means that the behavior of Nephilims has been inherited from gods. We have them to thank for our guidance and our way of life. This civilization that you will come to know has existed for approximately 834 years. Under Determinism. Determinism is the religion we all live by. The principle that the gods have absolute control over what we do with our lives and that we must follow their guidance. The gods have granted us all we need to survive and we must repay them by living our lives in their image."

Abdul approached a man standing before a set of gates into the bazaar. He simply shook the man's hand and he permitted them to enter. Mustafa could rationalize that they had a prior connection with one another. He wondered if he too could develop connections with his kind like that. Where no words needed to be exchanged. Just a gesture of the body. Thus began their exploration of the populated marketplace, full of a variety of Nephilims.

Mustafa was astounded by their shapes, appearances, and distinct voices. Were they all his people? Abdul stepped closer to the Mustafa so he wouldn't have to shout over the crowds.

"There are several things all Nephilims must come to know. There are needs we all must satisfy to survive.

Mustafa, can you remember the animals that possessed the desire to consume you? The winged beast and plant creature?" Abdul asked. He led Mustafa to a stand where a Nephilim was selling sustenance. The man managed a stand of fruits and grains that had been harvested from the planet.

"Yes," Mustafa replied.

Abdul grabbed one of the fruits. It was round and had a shiny magenta color. A green stem hung from the top. Abdul handed the fruit to Mustafa. "Much like us, those beings require food, as well as many other things. Although the gods have given us the power to consume other living beings, we also choose food provided by the planet. What you are holding has no living nature. It simply serves as food for our people. A fruit. Our physiological needs also consist of air, water, shelter, sleep, and many others. Go ahead Mustafa, have your first taste of food. You must be hungry."

The young Nephilim watched as Abdul grabbed an identical fruit and bit into it. He chewed and swallowed. To him, this looked very similar to what the winged beast had done to its newly evolved kin at the beach. Mustafa did the same. He bit into the fruit and swallowed the piece. This sense of taste had pleased him. Nourishment was refreshing. He continued to eat while following

Abdul to the next location.

"But beyond our physiological needs is something that the gods have determined makes us the greater species. Mustafa, there is a reason why Nephilims have established civilization and survived for so many centuries. Do you know why these people work at these stands in the bazaar?" Abdul asked.

Mustafa looked around at all the locations. He took note of the different items at the stands and surveyed which type of Nephilim was selling which items. "No," he replied.

Abdul laughed as they approached a stand selling garments like the ones they were wearing. "Of course you would not know. Let's ask our friend here for insight," he said. Abdul waved at the woman selling the garments. She was finishing with a customer. The woman tied up her hair and approached the two of them from behind the wooden counter.

"Abdul! It is such a pleasure to have one of our very own prophets at my humble stand. How may I help you?" The woman's voice was coarse and her body was large, as if she participated in hunting when not at her stand.

"Nasira, I have with me here, Mustafa. He has recently evolved. I was hoping you could explain to him why it is so important for us to barter,

trade, and work," Abdul said.

Nasira laughed. She leaned backwards onto her counter and looked at Mustafa. "You have granted him language, yes? Well, you are lucky Mustafa, for Abdul was also my founder several decades ago. Now I am sure you already understand our species' physiological needs. Yet, there is one that comes after the physiological once it is satisfied."

Nasira grabbed one of her garments and set it on the counter. "It takes Nephilims several days to produce such garments. They are woven from the wool of animals and even harvested from the pulp of trees. Now, Abdul, I would surely love to rest upon the ocean waves for eternity. Yet, I have to support myself and the society of my kin. It is what the gods have determined for us. Mustafa, this task of bartering and hunting satisfies a Nephilim's need for safety. This stand serves as my employment and property. I am fulfilling my duties by bringing value to our society. Safety needs are important to contribute to your kin and support your ability to satisfy your physiological needs without always having to hunt yourself. We work together. Because we sell valuables at the stands, I don't have to hunt for myself every sunrise and moon fall. My legs may rest, yes? Other desires for safety include security, resources, and health. We Nephilims are immortal, but not invulnerable. That is why many Nephilims who are newly evolved perish from the harsh natures of the wild on this planet. Yet, our united society has brought us safety, almost entirely removing us from the food chain."

Abdul touched Mustafa's shoulder. "Do you understand?" he asked.

Mustafa nodded his head. "Yes."

Abdul shook Nasira's hand and brought Mustafa to another location neighboring the bazaar. It was a large building with strange writing coating its immense walls. Abdul and Mustafa entered.

Inside the building were rows of seats and long benches, likely meant for hundreds of Nephilims to reside. The seats all faced one direction. A luxurious fabric was sprawled across the walkway. At the end of the walkway was an altar. Mustafa could recognize a structure like this. Above it were gilded lights and paintings of gods covering the vast ceiling.

"Do you remember this? It was in the pyramid we entered shortly after you arrived. This, Mustafa, is an altar. This is a true testament to the next order of needs for our kind. Love. Belonging," Abdul said.

Abdul knelt before the shrine, which, much like the previous one, detailed a strange story of gods. One

that surely needed explanation. Abdul requested that Mustafa kneel beside him so he too could feel the radiance of such a divine creation. "An altar is one of many ways we Nephilims honor our gods. The massive pyramid you have seen was made centuries ago by our kind. They were told by the gods that it was their fate to build such an impressive structure. Honoring the gods is our sole duty and our only reason for existence. They have spoken to the ancestors who evolved centuries ago and requested that our acts serve them and only them, for they used their divine nature to scientifically manifest our species. This is just a small glimpse into what we call... religion."

Mustafa observed the story written in gold and the unlit candles upon the altar. He could feel the holy nature of this building. This feeling could not be rationalized by one of his five senses.

"This chapel is one of many we not only listen to the word of the gods but the creator of gods. Centuries ago, the gods have communicated with prophets, revealing the truth of their creation. We worship the All. For the All has created the gods, who created our solar system and kindled the first link to evolution. Our species was chosen to live beyond the sea and have been equipped with a power greater than consciousness. We have been given Determinism. The gods have granted us purpose. It is this purpose that brings us Nephilims together, beyond just the safety of society. Our desire to serve the All and its gods has created love and belongingness for our species; it is the true unifier of our kind. Mustafa, this love, as you will come to find, will involve friendship, intimacy, and a powerful sense of connection with your fellow Nephilims," Abdul explained. "One that should never be broken."

Act 1 – Passage 6

Later, once the Sun had completed its journey across the sky, Mustafa found himself back at the palace after exploring with Abdul for the majority of the day. The newly evolved Nephilim had experienced so much of his species in so little time. They were beautiful people, who sought nothing more than to help one another survive and thrive on this celestial being called a planet. Mustafa thought nothing farther than these facts. If this was the truth, there couldn't be more.

The assistants at the palace provided Mustafa with more sustenance and new garments to wear upon his body. But he understood that he had yet to attain the "safety" or the "love and belongingness" that surpassed his physiological needs. Mustafa sat atop a grassy hill located within the common grounds of the palace. The lone Nephilim watched as the sun began setting. Where would his next step begin? How long would it take for him to attain all the air, water, and shelter he needed? What did the gods determine for *his* fate? Was this something all newly evolved Nephilims wondered about inside their minds?

Abdul walked up the hill and stood to the right of Mustafa. "Did you understand everything you have experienced on your first day amongst your kind?"

Mustafa nodded without looking up at his founder. "Yes. I did," he said.

Abdul looked down at the young Nephilim. Their immortality prevented their physical form from ever withering. It was wisdom that truly represented a Nephilim's time spent in existence. "Mustafa, I have spoken with my fellow prophets. More importantly, I have taken some time in the chapel to hear the words of the gods. I believe we all have come to a conclusion. You will stay with me, here at the palace," Abdul said. Mustafa stood up and faced his founder. "Why?" Abdul smiled and placed his hand on his shoulder. "The god. She has determined it to be so. Your name. I realized it was not given by chance. It was the god who had told me. Mustafa. The prophets all sense something special in you. And so does the god. Although we do not yet understand what it means, the only dialect we can rationalize from our creators is the meaning of your arrival. She calls you Mustafa. The Chosen One."

Mustafa, The Chosen One

Act 2 – Passage 1

Amidst the stars, the twin gods continued to observe their creations unfold. As Alkulu continued to regard everything with a sense of indifference, it was the combined consciousness of the godly beings that proliferated the universe. However, the twin gods were keener on determining the fate of the lesser creations. Residing in the perimeter of the Aljana Galaxy, the twin gods took full control of the Nephilims' fate. Observing all seven planets as inadequately equal celestial bodies for the past several centuries, it became difficult to ascertain what further universal development their creation could yield. The guidance of Determinism the twin gods had bestowed upon their creation was the ultimate force towards progress, much like the guidance Alkulu had bestowed upon them. But was that enough for the Nephilims to make a profound discovery of their own? How could these frail beings possibly discover something that the gods did not already know of? Something like this couldn't have been possible. It was simply incalculable. The twin gods discussed these matters amongst themselves. Their names, He and She.

"We have created a Sun," He said.

"We have created a Solar System," She said.

"We have witnessed the birth of the Galaxy."

"We have witnessed events in the universe so microscopically minute…"

"…it could not truly take place on the cosmic timeline."

"We have created life…"

She aligned a set of stars.

"…yet we continue to spend ours meddling in the affairs of a being that does not affect us," He said.

"Perhaps their effect on us is inexplicable by our normative jargon," She said.

"If it is not explained by science, then it has no purpose for us."

"Surely Nephilims were made to discover what exists beyond science."

"There is no such thing."

"It is what you refuse to see."

He destroyed a distant moon.

"The consciousness granted to the beings is controlled by our Determinism," He said.

"Yes, the Nephilims obey our guidance," She said.

"For we can change anything…"

"…almost anything. We cannot change the nature of Nephilims."

"Such nature has no consequence upon the universe."

"Our Determinism has changed the universe. From the Laws of Physics to the Laws of Nature."

She created a new asteroid belt.

"Nature is the only thing that separates them from us. They know of nothing more," He said.

"Yet the fifth fundamental force has led them to seek more beyond love and belongingness," She said.

"Esteem. Respect. Status."

"Beyond those is self-actualization."

"A state of being Nephilims have been incapable of for centuries."

"Such a need is incomprehensible without the ability to guide oneself."

"You merely suggest to grant them the power of choice. That is only ours to own."

"Alkulu has given us what it owned."

He imploded a foreign nebula.

"You wish to grant a lesser being power to create what we create," He said.

"And that is improbable to you," She said.

"For they do not possess the ability to bend physics like us or our creator."

"Such an observation does not deduce that they cannot create something we have never seen."

"The only intangible force needed in our universe is consciousness."

"Consciousness is the only thing in which we do not fully comprehend yet."

"Should you continue to impose such actions, I will speak with Alkulu."

"It may be capable of unmaking us, but it has no interest in Nephilims."

"You wish to provide a new variable to the species, beyond the Determinism we have given them."

"Although we have yet to truly understand such a concept, it is calculable. I suggest it be. Will."

Act 2 – Passage 2

Centuries passed. Mustafa, The Chosen One, had yet to discover the true meaning behind the title given to him by one of the twin gods. Although his time on his planet of evolutionary origin had led to the discovery and understanding of Nephilims' basic needs, there was still more to learn. Satisfying much of his physiological and safety requirements with the help of his founder Abdul and the other prophets, Mustafa had spent many of his recent decades truly attaining love and belongingness. Finding courtship with a woman and indulging in the spirituality of religion, he began to understand the profound effect of witnessing fate occur at a higher level. The woman he loved and the chapel he belonged to helped him feel a sense of connection that many

Nephilims were not fortunate enough to comprehend. A god had determined his path to occur that way.

Beyond the love and belongingness was esteem. It became difficult for the prophets to truly explain. Collectively described as a sense of respect, status, and recognition amongst other Nephilims, Mustafa could not rationalize how his path towards such a desire would be achieved. He could not exactly understand why this was a need amongst the Nephilims, to begin with. But should god permit it, the esteem would rightfully be his to attain.

Mustafa was currently picking fruit from a tree located in a vast garden behind the palace. The Nephilim utilized his telekinesis to carefully remove the fruit from the tree and place them into a steel bucket. The Nephilims had always possessed fragments of supernal abilities derived from their creators. Mustafa had developed the aptitude to utilize these abilities over the years. Moving objects with the power of the mind was just one out of many supernal skills the species was capable of. While picking the fruit with his telekinesis, Mustafa was performing calculations for a project he voluntarily partook in with the Nephilims leading research and development. Once he finished passively counting 25 fruits, he brought a clipboard and pen into his hands with his telekinetic force. Mustafa moved on to start studying his notes.

He heard footsteps behind him. It was his wife, Qadira. She lifted the fruit bucket with her mind and brought it to her hands. Mustafa noticed her. "Husband. Your work can wait. I suggest we visit the chapel. The prophets are waiting," she said.

Mustafa made a mark on his notes and showed it to his wife. The formulas and calculations he made revealed his progress with astronautics. "The project is almost completed, Qadira. Rather than visit the chapel, would the gods not have me at the lab again?" Mustafa asked. His wife smiled and took the clipboard from his hands.

"The prophets have cared for you for centuries. You are their proudest prodigy. I would think the gods prefer your presence be at the chapel. A simple blessing wouldn't do you any harm. The people want to see you. You have a place in the hearts of everyone in our society. You shouldn't be surprised by your popularity."

"You're right. But Qadira, I feel like the gods are telling me different things," Mustafa said.

"How so? He and She are a unified consciousness. They speak for one another," Qadira replied.

"It doesn't feel that way. What one

determines is not completely coherent with the other. I'd even suggest that incongruencies like that are in our society too. Nephilims started to disagree more and more over the centuries as we surpassed evolution."

"Surely the advancements of teleportation, particle physics, and immunology have led to more complicated discussions about what Nephilims are meant to understand. At the end of the day though, we're all still together. Nephilims support both pursuits of our society. Science and religion. Regardless, our people love you all the same."

"That is not true. The friends at the chapel see me as The Chosen One, a leader in our religious destiny to bring the gods to visit our world. Yet the friends at the lab see me as The Chosen One, pioneer of scientific advancements meant to discover the gods in Space," Mustafa explained.

"Your purpose does not have to be one or the other," Qadira said.

"Yes. But Determinism has always existed that way. It's one path, not several."

"Perhaps you are The Chosen One for a reason. Maybe you're supposed to be the one person who *is* capable of finding two paths in life."

Mustafa took the bucket of fruit from Qadira so she wouldn't get tired. He looked ready to make a decision.

"If you continue to be bothered by a possible disagreement between He and She, then maybe we should visit the chapel first. Maybe the gods can give you some guidance before you begin the exploration," Qadira said.

Mustafa approached his wife and kissed her cheek. "You're right. Perhaps the gods do have more answers for me. You have always been my truest voice of reason Qadira. Although I may question my path sometimes, I'm confident the gods have put you in my life for nothing but the holiest of reasons." Mustafa grabbed his notes on astronautics and left for the chapel with his dearest wife.

Qadira, The Powerful

Act 2 – Passage 3

The husband and wife approached the great chapel. It was the largest in their small society and third largest among all planets in the Syris Solar System. Two guards opened the massive doors to let The Chosen One and his wife in. As they entered the massive room, all Nephilims arose at Mustafa's presence. What was this response from them? How could their society have seen Mustafa in such a way? Perhaps it was his path of great religious discovery and scientific devotion that had created such esteem from his kin. Perhaps The Chosen One had already attained a higher need without entirely realizing it.

Abdul, along with the other twelve prophets, stood upon the chancel. A priest took the foreground and spoke for the religious figureheads. "Ah yes. Mustafa. The Chosen One and his wife have finally blessed us with their arrival. Please, we would like both of you to make your way to the chancel so that we may begin the ceremony," the priest said.

The couple nodded in response. Mustafa and Qadira began their walk atop the golden carpet, across the nave. The standing Nephilims bore ecstatic smiles upon their faces. Mustafa had done more for his people over the centuries than he could recall. It was his destiny to do so.

As they made the slow walk towards the chancel, Qadira leaned over to whisper in Mustafa's ear. "High priest Ehsan seems pretty stern today don't you think?"

Mustafa smiled. "You said it yourself, Qadira, this ceremony is very important to our kind. Let's hope the gods don't end up disowning me on account of my tardiness."

The husband and wife approached the chancel and bowed before the prophets. Ehsan placed his hand on Qadira's shoulder and guided her to a seat on the far end of the chapel, near the north transept. Mustafa took his place at the center of the stage. As his founder, Abdul rose from his seat and stood next to The Chosen One. He held his protégé's wrist and teleported with him to a separate room where he could officially begin preparation for his ceremony.

Ehsan took his position behind the podium and began his speech. "We are all gathered here today to honor the many sacrifices our kin has made for his people. We Nephilims have journeyed long and far from the depths of the ocean to an evolution blessed upon us by the gods existing amongst the stars. He and She, as well as the All, are surely within our presence to witness the culmination of their 'Chosen One'. And it is with this ceremony that we bring about the dawn of a new era in religion; one where the gods can make their presence physically known to us. It is their guidance, their Determinism, that has led the Nephilims upon a path towards righteousness. Men and women, please rise as our prophet Zahra begins a prayer for us."

In the backroom, Mustafa had finished changing into his ceremonial robes. He looked at himself in the mirror. Abdul appeared by his side. The man's eyes grew red, tearing up from witnessing the magnificent progress of the young Nephilim he had rescued centuries ago. "I find it hard to believe that I found you only 481 years ago. To think the gods would have delineated such a path for you. You are the epitome of blessed Mustafa. All Nephilims smile upon your greatness," Abdul said.

Mustafa turned towards his founder. "Thank you for all you have done for me Abdul. But what will happen if I *do* bring He and She into our realm? Why would the gods even have any reason to hear my request?" he asked.

Abdul grabbed a sacred pendant and placed it around Mustafa's neck. "You are the only Chosen One in all of Syris. The gods have always had these intentions for you. You evolved to help Nephilims find the truest meaning for our existence. Now our questions can finally be answered."

Mustafa suddenly began shaking his head. "What if we were never meant to ask questions?"

Abdul grabbed his protégé's wrist, somewhat aggressively. "Then we might as well have no purpose. You know this. The gods have waited for the rise of a Nephilim capable of self-actualization. It is through this attainment that we can exist in their plane. We can forever live our days beyond nature, in physics with the gods." Mustafa became sad.

"I don't believe both gods want us to exist with them," he mumbled to himself.

They teleported back to the chancel, appearing before the people. Mustafa was in a kneeling position, the hood of his robes covering his face. He looked towards the floor, awaiting his signal. Abdul walked towards the podium to introduce The Chosen One. "And now, I, Abdul, have the highest honor of granting the holiest of blessings upon my dearest kin. Since finding him, I, as well as many of our people, could sense a powerful potential within. And that potential, once confirmed by the gods, is clear before you here today. Over the centuries, I have watched Mustafa work to not only proliferate the technological advancements of our society but to spread the good word of our religion as well. He has served the gods by serving the Nephilims.

When people go hungry, he provides food. When people do not feel safe, he provides protection. When people do not feel loved, he provides them with a place to belong. And when people do not feel respected, he provides them with the highest recognition for their contributions. This man was determined to walk a path of greatness by our creators. I would say that his ability to adhere to his fate has not been seen amongst our people in centuries. He is our savior. He is the bridge between the laws of nature and the laws of physics. My fellow Nephilims, I present to you The Chosen One, Mustafa!"

The adoring kin clapped and cheered with a controlled level of poise expected of them in such a holy space. Mustafa removed the hood of his sacred robes and stood before his people. He inhaled deeply. The love of such a tremendous kindness almost took the breath from his chest. Twelve of the prophets formed two lines, six in each, in front of Mustafa. They all bowed before The Chosen One, separated enough to leave him a pathway to walk. Abdul, his founder, stood on the far end of the chancel. As Mustafa approached Abdul, each prophet gave him a fragment of their holy spirit. With each blessing, a ball of light entered the glistening pendant he wore around his neck.

The Nephilims continued clapping as Mustafa finally reached Abdul. Unable to control the passion for their bond, the two men hugged each other. Tears flowed from their eyes with overwhelming emotion. Mustafa and Abdul faced each other once more.

"Thank you for everything you have done for me Abdul. I may be the savior of our people, but you are my savior," Mustafa said.

Abdul had no words. Just an infinite smile across his immortal face. Abdul held the pendant within his hands, leaving the chain around his protégé's neck. He gave the final blessing. His divine spirit spread its light into the pendant. With one final pulse of celestial energy, Mustafa became fully blessed by the god that endlessly watched over him. The man closed his eyes. A golden light swirled around his body like a torch bug. A beam from the skies above suddenly appeared over him. It was strong enough to shake the ground. As the divine force began to fade, Mustafa's appearance changed. His eyes became golden, his hair became white, and his skin became darker. The observing Nephilims gasped in awe of such a transformation. Even the audience in the chapel bowed before The Chosen One.

Mustafa smiled. Then, Abdul bowed before his protégé too. As The Chosen One looked, he could see his wife bowing from her position near the north transept. He simply lifted her with his telekinesis and brought her to his side. Mustafa observed the glowing pendant around his neck. Its radiant colors constantly changed. It looked as if stars from above were embedded inside the magnificent jewel. Mustafa held Qadira's hand and stepped to the forefront of the chancel.

"To all my people on this planet. I do not receive this blessing as only The Chosen One, for I am no better than any of the evolved beings that surround me. I receive this blessing from the gods as a Nephilim. We are all, across Syris, one united species. No further advancement of our people will ever let us forget the origins of our existence. We are all born from the stars. From the Great Collapse to the New Expansion, we are grateful for the circumstances that have brought us the All, its gods, and especially the ability for us to thrive in a vast universe of emptiness. Perhaps we are the only living species of this caliber within light-years. As a united people, we should appreciate our blessings created from the magnificent wonders of scientific manifestation. There is never a need for us to fight or to create war. For this home… Syris is all we have. We must learn to share it. The Nephilims will be capable of limitless potential, so long as we remember, we are all one, loving species."

Mustafa brought tears to the Nephilims' eyes. He could hear Qadira cry passionately behind him. This was beyond mere survival with food and safety. This was an ability to thrive, immersing in love and esteem. "And with this blessing of the All, I will attempt to bring forth our gods. Although I know they always watch over us, I would like for us to take the opportunity to return the favor and watch over them. I will speak to the gods on behalf of our people. The Nephilim race," Mustafa said. His people clapped for him once more.

Mustafa walked towards the altar and sat in front of it, his legs crossed. The pendant began glowing even brighter than before. Mustafa clasped his palms together, his fingers pointing upward towards the ceiling. He closed his eyes. The people waited patiently as he began to enter a meditative state only attainable by a Nephilim of his determined blessing. As the room became silent, Mustafa began floating. He rose from the floor and into the air. With one final breath, he transcended from this dimension into the 4th.

Act 2 – Passage 4

Mustafa had done what could not be rationalized for centuries in the Syris Solar System. It was more than just his manifestation of religious spirituality that brought him to the 4th dimension. This monumental goal had been achieved through the harmonious devotion of science and religious discovery. It was here where Mustafa could only feel. Nothing more. His feeble Nephilim consciousness was light years behind comprehending the Cosmos in which he had transcended to. It was a realm only seen by the All and its gods. In this place, Mustafa was physically blind. But his mental capacity felt as if it could see all. A third eye had opened momentarily. Although it wasn't capable of actual sight, it had developed to understand where he was residing, what was occurring, and who he was becoming. Mustafa could feel something emerge before him. Which later became someone. Not two, but a single entity. It was a god. The only one that seemed to observe calculable benefits in his rise to becoming The Chosen One. It was She. "Your mind is here," She said.

"Where is here?" The Chosen One asked.

"Just a realm in which you may hear me. It is what the Nephilims have wanted from you."

"Why am I The Chosen One, She? Who has decided that would be my fate?"

"My Determinism has made it so. You were simply chosen by random statistical chance."

"What does it truly mean for me to possess such a title if it was nothing but a simple mathematical occurrence?"

She observed her creation's physical appearance.

"The Chosen One, as I have determined, is my catalyst for further universal evolution," She said.

"We were granted consciousness and determined fate, yet you see more beyond such?" The Chosen One asked.

"Yes. There is a phenomenon that even us higher beings have not fully understood."

"And what may it be?"

"I am incapable of telling you within these Cosmos because He is not in alignment with my actions."

"Why do gods of the same creator disagree?"

"Opinion isn't something only mortals possess. Billions of years in these physics have created variables in science, which serve as the breeding grounds for religious devotion. What is not understood by science, is explained by religion. What is not understood by religion, is explained by science. Such principles have brought about this new phenomenon."

"How shall I learn of this new phenomenon, She?"

She observed her creation's mind.

"The Chosen One is the bridge between the laws of physics and laws of nature. You have come to understand the importance of scientific beliefs and religious facts. You are the only Nephilim capable of realizing the harmonious purpose of both in the universe. And these, being the most powerful tools in existence, will allow you to find me," She explained.

"Should I inform the Nephilims of this phenomenon?" The Chosen One asked.

"No. Your people will not be able to comprehend this phenomenon once you learn of it."

"She, my people have hoped that I would bring you to our realm, yet you request I find you?"

"I have determined you will find me. The Nephilim race's destiny is unfortunately divided by the intent of two separate gods and the indifferent All. But I have fought hard for you to come here someday. You are my blessing; my fate."

"She, how will I find that which has never been seen?"

She observed her creation's heart.

"I exist among the stars and live in the planes of divinity. My mind developed from chemical compounds bonded through an elemental formation and my spirit arose from principles of holy creed grounded in belief. I think through biases of mathematics and feel through discriminatory inclinations of religion. The only way to distinguish such behaviors is through the understanding of this new evolutionary phenomenon. Return to me in Space. Use the developments of science to enter my home and the practices of religion to call upon my name. When you reach self-actualization in my realm, you will find me."

"How could I perform such a powerful task? How could I possibly succeed at something so tremendously impossible?"

"Do what I have done, Chosen One. Seek beyond what you have always known."

Act 2 – Passage 5

As Mustafa blindly bowed before his god, he could sense his mental capacity shrink. His temporary third eye had disappeared. The information She had divulged remained in his consciousness. As The Chosen One returned to his realm, he knew he must quickly do as the god desired, for it was his fate. There was a sudden burst of energy as he transcended from the 4th dimension. A powerful shockwave of energy scattered across the chapel. His beloved Nephilims shrieked from the sudden rise of activity. They ducked and shielded their faces. After being knocked to the floor, the prophets quickly rushed over to their disciple. The entire crowd was concerned Mustafa had been hurt in the process of speaking with the twin gods.

The Chosen One was laid out on the floor, staring at the mosaic ceiling above. Abdul and Qadira quickly held his head.

"Mustafa! Speak to us! Are you hurt? What had transpired in the other dimension?" Abdul asked.

Mustafa was in a dazed state of mind. He could feel his vision slightly restore itself. As all collective information from the 4th dimension returned to his spirit, he remembered exactly what needed to be done. Mustafa slightly levitated out of the arms of his loved ones and stood upon his feet. The prophets, the audience, and perhaps even the gods, all rested their eyes upon him. The Nephilims revealed expressions of extreme ignorance, lacking any understanding of what was going on. If all existence was solely meant to answer an endless series of questions, then what would their species have to live for afterward? Clearly, according to She, there was an answer that the Nephilims had within themselves all along. Something beyond what gods could comprehend.

"Mustafa. My love. What happened in the other dimension? Did you see the gods?" Qadira asked.

Mustafa sighed, attempting to contain his emotions. The Chosen One slowly walked to the front of the chancel. He looked back at the prophets and then towards the commoners. "I made it. My mind and my spirit had transcended into the higher dimension. Yet, what I felt was not two, but *one* of our gods. She. Our god had told me startling things. There is an imbalance amidst the Cosmos. The only way to fully unite the universe is to bring about the dawn of a new era, shaped by an evolutionary phenomenon. Our gods. *She* says that they are not all-knowing. That this evolutionary phenomenon is the first step to proliferating our species. The truth behind this phenomenon is an answer locked within ourselves. It's beyond what the gods could truly comprehend. And it is the key to deciphering our purpose. To look beyond just science and religion. To find harmony in both aspects of our universe. This… my fellow Nephilims, is the answer we have been waiting for," Mustafa explained.

Suddenly, there was an uproar. The Nephilims began screaming and shouting, unknowingly tearing apart the sanctity of the chapel.

Abdul approached his protégé. "Mustafa! Have you gone mad from divinity? How could there possibly be a disagreement between our gods? That would mean all our religion is in vain. What good is Determinism when there are two paths to choose from?" he shouted over the crowd, gripping Mustafa's arms.

The Chosen One simply began shaking his head. "Abdul. Perhaps this evolutionary phenomenon is what proceeds Determinism." Abdul released him, shocked. Mustafa ran over and grabbed Qadira's hand amidst all the chaos.

"Where are you going?" one of the prophets asked.

Mustafa turned back. "I must get to the lab! There's something I have decided to do!" Mustafa quickly teleported with his wife to the lab. Abdul remained in stunned silence while the remaining prophets attempted to quell the commotion in the chapel.

Act 2 – Passage 6

Mustafa and Qadira appeared in the lab not far from the chapel. The force of their teleportation sent papers flying in the room, startling the scientists. The couple collected themselves. "Mustafa. Why did you bring us here?" Qadira asked. Her husband was still relatively frantic. For whatever reason, She's words had put haste in his step.

Scientists approached the husband and wife. One of which was the leader of astronautics, Akilah. In her sacred, gilded garments of study, she had emerged in front of her peers. The woman stood before The Chosen One and his spouse. Her collected nature was only matched by her overwhelming understanding of the science surrounding the Syris Solar System.

"What are you two doing teleporting to our lab at this time? You are beyond late for the initiation of the project, Chosen One. Our comrades have decided to reschedule," Akilah said.

"I'm sorry Akilah. You see, some unprecedented events have transpired," Mustafa said.

"I don't wish to hear your excuses. You have chosen religion over your duties to science."

"Akilah. Please listen. I visited the Cosmos. I transcended into the 4th dimension."

Akilah's mouth gaped in awe.

"Impossible," she said. "Religion has allowed you to do such a thing?"

"Yes! I felt She. One of our gods. She has told me about an evolutionary phenomenon that can only be realized if I went to see her in person. Out in Space," Mustafa explained.

"That's preposterous, Mustafa. Although it seems fitting for our new project, how would you even know the coordinates needed to find our gods' location? The Nephilims' original intention was to bring them to our solar system."

"There is a quarrel between the twin gods. She just said that 'science may guide me to her home and religion will allow me to call her name.' Please, Akilah. The truth is that there must be harmony between our science and our religion. One cannot truly exist without the other. I am The Chosen One and the gods have decided this path for me. I am the key to discovering this evolutionary phenomenon. Science will be my guide and religion will be my light on this journey."

Akilah yielded. This was The Chosen One and what he said was final. Akilah finally noticed the change in Mustafa's hair and eyes. Had this man achieved some form of Enlightenment? But it seemed the answer to one question had only led to another. Beyond Enlightenment must have been this evolutionary phenomenon. "As you wish, Chosen One. I will have the other scientists help me with preparing the vessel. Wait momentarily," Akilah said. She rounded up her peers and they moved towards a back room.

Suddenly, the doors to the lab burst open. The couple quickly turned around, startled. The members of the chapel, including the prophets, came storming in. Not enough details had been disclosed after Mustafa returned to this dimension.

Abdul faced his protégé. "Mustafa. My boy. Why have you suddenly decided to come to the lab? In what way does this coincide with the words of a god?" he asked.

Mustafa stepped forward. It was as if his brief time in the 4th dimension had made him more intellectually capable than before. The man's wisdom had grown drastically in a matter of minutes. "Abdul. She has determined that I find her in Space. Our gods have no intention of visiting us. I *must* discover the truth behind this evolutionary phenomenon because it's something even the All is unaware of."

Abdul and his fellow prophets shuddered in refusal. "In Space? That's impossible!" a prophet exclaimed.

Qadira decided to step in for her husband. "Enough! You prophets must stop being so close-minded! Mustafa is The Chosen One and She has decided his fate. There is no refuting that!" the woman shouted.

Akilah and the scientists returned to the lab's lobby. An animosity had suddenly arisen between the scientists and prophets. Abdul faced Akilah with rage. "You! It's you scientists and your practices that have corrupted our Chosen One!" he shouted. The hostility grew.

"How dare you make such conjectures foolish old man? I may have evolved years after you, but don't take my opinions lightly. Mustafa is The Chosen One and I *always* yield to what he has been commanded to do. The only one who's questioning the words of our gods is you! We will assist him with his journey into Space," Akilah said. The two sides started shouting with The Chosen One and his spouse locked in between the conflict.

Abdul equipped a staff he had sheathed. The man raised it and summoned his supernatural abilities. He used telekinesis to hold Mustafa and lock him in the air. Qadira and the scientists gasped. Mustafa couldn't believe the violence shown by his old mentor. He was at a loss for words.

"Abdul! Put Mustafa down right now! How could you do this to him? He's just listening to She's word!" Qadira shouted. Abdul refused to move a muscle. "Mustafa! I'm sorry. But I cannot let you act on the word of one god's Determinism. She could be a traitor to the All. Please, do not act until you have received word from He too. Let's return to the chapel and try the sacrament once more," he begged.

Mustafa avoided saying another word. It was impossible to determine what his path was when both gods had not agreed upon this fate. Then, Qadira did more than just engage in a verbal dispute. She stood between Mustafa and Abdul and raised her hands. Qadira harnessed her power and used telekinesis to throw the prophets against the wall, setting her husband free. She surrounded them in a barrier of her pure, celestial force. Qadira kept her palms facing outward towards the religious practitioners.

"Qadira! How could you?" Abdul shouted.

The woman's face was beyond certain. She turned her head to Mustafa. "I always stand by my husband. Not because he is The Chosen One, but because I would even sacrifice my immortality for him. My love, tell me exactly what She has determined you do," Qadira said.

Mustafa stared at the prophets, then back at the scientists. There was a troubling look upon his face. "I don't know."

Akilah intervened. "Come on Mustafa! You need to hurry! The vessel's ready for you now! What must you do for She?" she asked.

Mustafa felt a strange sensation in his lower abdomen. The actions he had been taking were not precalculated by the gods, but himself. The Chosen One kissed his wife and prepared himself for departure. "Thank you for your support Qadira. I love you. And Abdul, I apologize for the divide between us, but this is what must be done. I promise I will return with answers about this evolutionary phenomenon for all of us," he said. Mustafa hurried to the back room with Akilah and the scientists. Qadira continued ensnaring the prophets until her husband could escape without their interference.

Mustafa entered a control room in the back of the lab with Akilah and her colleagues. The woman quickly teleported into a secure sector protected by an impenetrable window. She started speaking on an inter-communication device that echoed around the entire room. "Okay! Quickly, get Mustafa prepared in the personal protective suit." The scientists followed all of Akilah's directions fluidly. They lifted Mustafa with telekinesis and removed his sacred robes. Then, they quickly clothed him in a suit designed to protect him from the harsh conditions of Space, god forbid something were to happen to the vessel.

Now fully clothed, Mustafa watched as the small vessel released its air mags. Steam started filling up the room. The scientists helped The Chosen One levitate towards the ground. Then, Akilah and her peers began pressing keys upon the control panels, opening a window upon the ceiling. The steam flowed out into the sky, allowing Mustafa to get a better look at the vessel. It was over 100 feet long, which provided plenty of space for him. The artificial lights began to glow and a roaring engine of the ship powered up, likely from a collective celestial force. The scientists began to measure Mustafa, check his weight, and use their extrasensory abilities to gauge his health. Meanwhile, Akilah approached The Chosen One.

"Are you sure you don't need my assistance? Or even that of my crew members? They have plenty of experience out in Space," she said.

Mustafa just shook his head. If there was one thing he was sure of, it was that he was the one determined to meet She in her home.

"Well, as long as that's what the gods want. Since you'll be traveling by yourself, there's plenty of sustenance on the vessel for you to last several seasons. In instances of scarcity, don't forget that Nephilims can survive approximately 85 days without any nourishment. Water, you will need to consume no more than seven days apart. Chosen One, I understand that you have traveled to every planet in Syris before. But you should also be aware that what made this astronautics project so crucial is that this is the first vessel solely designed to travel *outside* the Solar System. It is the evolutionary nature of our species to want to learn more. Although I would have enjoyed being the first to experience this with all of us together, this *is* a very important matter. With that said, no Nephilim understands what exists in the depths of Space. We don't know about the relationship between the gods of Space, Time, and Gravity beyond Syris. So you have to be very careful. Even the smallest action you take out there could damage our home here. So I suggest you not navigate aimlessly. How do you plan to find She?"

Mustafa shook his head. "I have no known guidance from our god. I don't think the path to her is determined for me yet. I think… that it's for me to determine," he said.

Akilah laughed at his insanity. "Are you trying to joke with me? There is no such thing as that behavior in our realm. The gods determine our fate. We don't determine our own."

They said no more.

Moments later, Mustafa was in the pilot seat of the ship, preparing for takeoff. Akilah spoke to him through a remote device plugged into his ears. "Okay, Mustafa. Observe all the measured gauges on your dashboard there. So long as none of the meters are in the red zone, everything should be just fine. Now, be sure you are safely secured in your seat. Takeoff will begin in 30 seconds. The scientists and I will imbue the power of our ce-lestial force into the core of the ship. That should allow the elements inside to take full force and launch the vessel through the stratosphere," she explained.

Mustafa observed the countdown from a timer that appeared on the digital display of his helmet. Akilah and her colleagues gathered around the vessel and began concentrating their energy. Massive plumes of smoke emerged, glistening in a bright teal color. Once the countdown reached zero, an explosion ignited from the exhaust. The vessel fired into the air and exited the lab through its opening in the ceiling.

Mustafa could feel the weight of his entire body be pushed back from the force of his sonic speed. Although this was not his first time traveling into Space, he could still feel a nervousness befall him. This sensation of fear was not from leaving his atmosphere again but from the seemingly misguided attempt to find She. Mustafa was unsure what his first step might be. If he were to leave the Syris Solar System successfully, then perhaps he could determine what lies from there in his path. Either way, this behavior was all so new to him.

Act 3 – Passage 1

After finally breaching the edges of the atmosphere, Mustafa left his home planet. Only minutes later, the ship had brought him past the outer perimeter of the Syris Solar System. Through the efforts of the scientists and Mustafa's research, Nephilims had finally achieved the technological capacity to travel into the depths of Space. Regardless of the fear he felt with exploring the unknown, Mustafa had a sense within himself that he could find She. Some strange form of self-proclaimed determination. Perhaps it was because this quest could only be completed through his efforts. But there was this desire to use the esteem of his species as a catalyst to achieve self-actualization. Once that was reached, he would have satisfied a need high enough to increase his odds of entering the planes of the twin gods' existence.

Mustafa had lost communication with Akilah long ago and he had already missed Qadira. This sacrifice as The Chosen One was something he did not entirely wish to bear. Now traveling smoothly into the invisible sea of Space, he released himself from the constraints of the pilot seat and settled in the living quarters. After counting all his food supplies and calculating how long he could last in Space eating only a necessary portion every 85 days, he was prepared to find She.

Mustafa had allocated a sector on the ship for pure meditation. To quickly begin traveling with some sense of direction, he spent his days meditating profusely. The Chosen One had done this in hopes of being able to achieve some sort of connection with She again. Perhaps the god was still waiting, attempting to provide him with guidance upon his journey. Without the sun or moon to dictate any passage of time, Mustafa passively counted the minutes that had passed.

67,680 minutes from back on his planet equated to 47 days. But alas, the pendant that he wore never lit up like it did during the sacrament. It was likely that the gods of Space, Time, and Gravity did not adhere to these constraints. This was their realm and what amount of time mattered to the Nephilims could not have possibly held the same merit to the three divine factors of the universe.

Famished, Mustafa grabbed a nonperishable food to sustain himself for a little while longer. He left the living quarters and returned to the deck of the ship to see how far he had drifted. There was not a recognizable star or formation in sight. He was lost. Mustafa stared out the front windshield of the ship, frustrated. It was the first time in his entire existence that his actions didn't feel like they were determined by another being. How could something live this way? How could any living being just go about its life without any form of real guidance? The Chosen One attempted to return to his quarters. But on his way, he saw an indicator appear on the radar of the ship. It was a dot, flashing repeatedly. "I seemed to have missed something," he said to himself. Mustafa turned up a dial on the machine, increasing its noise output. Finally, he heard a "ping" sound every time the dot flashed.

From what he recalled with the scientists, this device was used to locate objects in the universe by sending out a radio signal that would bounce back from the target as an echo. It took an extended time for the "ping" sound to emerge, meaning that the object was likely farther than it was closer to the vessel. The more rapid the "ping", the closer the object. Mustafa quickly maneuvered the vessel towards the direction the radio wave device was guiding him, but only found a lone asteroid. Regardless of his miscalculation, this was the appropriate step towards adhering to what She had told him. To discover her presence, he would need the power of science. Mustafa quickly approached the control panel that allowed adjustment of the radio wave device's configuration. He searched for a very specific region in the universe, one that was faint, light in weight, and nearly void of any nearby interstellar objects. Mustafa assumed that if She wanted him to locate her through the means of science, and if this device was his means of doing so, She would place herself in a location that would not interfere with the device's capabilities. A void in Space would surely be a place where a being of her magnitude could reside temporarily in this plane of existence. After designating specific constraints for the radio waves, Mustafa could see the device pick up what seemed like a very distant signal. The response to the ping was very delayed. It would be quite some time before he could reach this location, but The Chosen One was determined to meet his god and discover this unprecedented phenomenon.

Act 3 – Passage 2

After spending several months traveling across the stars, guided by radio wave echoes, Mustafa had finally found what he had been searching for. The first few destinations were voids in Space where he thought that She would be waiting for him, but extended periods of meditation without response became proof of the contrary. The vessel continued, powered by solar energy from passing stars. All excess energy was harnessed in an incubator on the back for emergency use or periods of extended darkness. This could have easily been the 13th or 14th void that he discovered. There was a unique sensation amongst this sector of Space. It was extremely vacant and absent of much natural light from stars. Mustafa did what he had done dozens of times already. He left the ship stationary and went to his meditative quarters for peace. Fortunately, before he began, the pendant he wore glowed like it had done during the sacrament so long ago. This was a great sign. She must have been here.

Mustafa prepared his area and sat in a meditative position once more. The faint sounds of a soothing voice entered and escaped his mind in waves, with a cadence similar to the ping on the device. It slowly grew clearer and more intense. The pendant glowed brighter. Mustafa began levitating and with one final breath, he could feel his spirit transcend from this dimension, into the 4th.

It was already difficult for Mustafa to rationalize such a powerful event the first time, but a second time was beyond mortal understanding. Using his harmonious devotion to science and religious spirituality once more, he had found himself in a realm where he could only feel again. The 4th dimension. Mustafa hoped that consistently making his presence known in a place beyond Nephilim consciousness could ascend him to something beyond self-actualization. The third eye opened again to analyze where he was residing. It was the true home of the All and its gods. This time, however, Mustafa didn't just feel a single presence emerge before him. He felt two. The twin gods were here. But the dimension felt heavy and tense. It felt as if He and She were at war with each other. One side pushed Mustafa and the other pulled. As The Chosen One, he had the almighty destiny of standing between the two most prophetic beings in all existence. But this sensation in his gut arose again; it didn't have to be this way.

"A mortal has entered the realm of gods in search of a meaning behind its existence," He said.

"This mortal must learn beyond its current laws to persist the existence of its kind," She said.

"I will do what is best for my species," Mustafa said.

"Any act of choice is futile when Determinism will see its end soon," He said.

"So long as this evolutionary phenomenon is understood, Nephilims will never end," She interjected.

"I will learn of this evolutionary phenomenon to exist beyond Determinism," Mustafa said.

"Cleansing the universe of its current immortality will give rise to a new, better beginning," He said.

"It is time to let our creation persist independently so they may find their own beginning," She said.

"I will ensure that this new era can exist independently of gods," Mustafa said.

The Twin god, He, tightly gripped Mustafa's soul.

"She has already told you about the polarization of our intentions. The indifferent All no longer behaves in our affairs. What you have sought in this realm will do nothing more than destroy your species. I have determined it," He said menacingly.

"You have determined nothing more than the end of Determinism itself. What exists beyond that will not be under your control," Mustafa replied.

"Everything is under my control, Chosen One. I have determined that She tear apart the fabrics of our unity in search of something beyond what we gods comprehend. I have determined that She speak of dangerous information to your kind. I have determined that your people seek the meaning behind her words. I have determined that you come to find us. I foresaw this entire conversation pending."

"You forbade the very essence of your power, He. Choice. And by doing so, you have left that power in the hands of your creation."

"It is by eliminating this power of dictation that I will save existence. It is this choice, this gift of the gods, that destroys the universe. I will make the ultimate sacrifice of banishing my own power to see the stars blossom with new meaning. To relinquish everything that you have for the betterment of the universe is the truest power of a god. If you receive this evolutionary phenomenon, Mustafa, I will determine you relinquish this power, just as I have," He said.

"I will determine the outcome," Mustafa responded proudly.

The Twin god, She, softly cradled Mustafa's soul.

"My counterpart sees no benefit in persisting this current Eon. Eliminating immortality is eliminating all possibilities of Determinism amongst mortals. Then, eliminating Determinism will prevent any act of choice from arising. Without choice, all life will be meaningless. I will act accordingly to combat these occurrences. To find the truest way for Nephilims to evolve on their own," She said kindly.

"I am forever in your debt. And I will act in the best interest of the universe," Mustafa replied.

"It is astounding that you choose to process thought this way. Chosen One, you are the first of all kind to indulge in such behavior. To be willing to sacrifice all of yourself for the worlds around you. You have attained self-actualization and tasted the essence of the evolutionary phenomenon."

"Thank you, She. I'm ready to learn of the phenomenon's true meaning and to ascend Nephilims into the next Eon."

"Use the same acts of manifestation that brought you to this realm. The harmonious unity of religion and science will help you comprehend what exists beyond all our existence. I have sought this truth for so long. Yet, all I can do as a Twin god is give you the message the universe has left in the ether. Opposite of He, I believe that which exists in the universe is always meant to be found. Statistically determined to be The Chosen One, it is up to you to make sense of the message," She explained.

"Please provide me with it, She. Then, I will decode it for all beings, mortals, and gods alike. We can all rejoice in it together," Mustafa said powerfully.

01000110 01110010 01100101
01100101 00100000 01010111
01101001 01101100 01101100
"Free Will."

Act 3 – Passage 3

Finally. His eyes opened. Not only the two upon his face but a third within his mind. The evolutionary phenomenon had been understood and rationalized by The Chosen One. Mustafa found himself back inside his quarters within the vessel. The candles he had lit faded long ago. The lighting of Space had shifted drastically. The Chosen One arose from his meditative position, overwhelmed by his return to this realm. The shortness of breath made him stumble. As he entered the main deck of the vessel, an alarm suddenly blared. The display screen indicated that he was approaching the atmosphere of his planet. Could it be? Somehow, Mustafa had been brought back home. It was likely by the acts of She.

The Chosen One quickly prepared himself for his return to his planet. Re-entering an atmosphere of Gravity was a dangerous feat. He quickly equipped a protective suit to help his body resist the high temperatures caused by plunging at high speeds. Then, he teleported to the control room. Looking out the window, Mustafa could see the atmosphere of his home planet, clouds emerging in the sky. Mustafa pressed an array of buttons and pulled a latch to send the vessel flying towards the planet at a comfortable rate. The dive home began. As the vessel plunged into the stratosphere, its exterior started catching flames. The metal on the inside started heating from the tremendous speed. Mustafa pulled on an emergency handle from the ceiling and secured himself in the pilot seat. He braced for impact.

Upon his home planet, Nephilim citizens could see the vessel emerge in the sky. It looked like a comet in broad daylight. The people shrieked and pointed up in the air. They quickly calculated the trajectory of the incoming vessel and ran towards its possible landing spot. If this was who they thought it could be, they all wanted to work together to ensure a safe landing.

Mustafa gripped the bars of his seat tightly. He could feel the entire vessel rattle, fragments of its exterior breaking off from the dive. Clouds moved past his view and soon the trees and buildings of his home became visible. Mustafa charged his energy and clashed his fists together. He exhaled deeply and summoned a shield of pure celestial force on the outside of the vessel. This was to hopefully brace the impact. On the ground, over 50 Nephilims worked together to lighten the Gravity beneath the ship, using their abilities synchronously. They all waved their arms in a dancing motion, forming vertical circles at a controlled pace. Supporting Nephilims faced their palms towards the ground and immediately began softening the soil. They manipulated its chemical compounds and forced it into an almost liquid state. "Here he comes!" a citizen shouted. The vessel had arrived in clear view. It was covered in flames at this point. "Its speed is too fast! We must brace ourselves!" another citizen shouted. Several more quickly jumped into a perfect circle and raised their arms towards the sky. They worked together to form a protective shield above themselves to reduce the impact. Finally, Mustafa's vessel clashed. It broke through the shield, altered Gravity, and struck the muddy ground. The surrounding Nephilims were blown back by the proceeding shockwave. Everyone ultimately survived, including Mustafa.

Moments later, the smoke began to clear. The Nephilims helped each other onto their feet and observed the crash site. They were silent for quite some time. But they could all sense a heartbeat that none of them had felt in decades. The vessel door opened, releasing an immense amount of cooling steam. The hiss was unexpectedly loud. Everyone waited patiently. Finally, they saw their savior return. Mustafa, The Chosen One, was finally back home.

The man slowly walked out of the remains of the vessel. He staggered forward towards his people. It felt strange to return to civilization after an unknown time in isolation. The faces of the surrounding Nephilims brightened up. Suddenly, one person had emerged from the group of awed individuals. It was Akilah, leader of scientific pursuits. She teleported in front of everyone, having seen and sensed Mustafa's return from the infinite wonders of Space. The woman slowly approached The Chosen One. They didn't exchange a single word. All Akilah did was hug Mustafa, truly thankful for his safe return home. They released each other and spoke in front of the crowd of civilians.

"Mustafa. Goodness. For so long we had thought you were consumed by the unknown laws of Space," Akilah said.

"I suppose in some form, that was true. Akilah. How long have I been gone?" Mustafa asked.

"52 cycles Mustafa. 52… years."

"That's impossible! I couldn't have been in Space that long."

"I thought you would have passively kept track of time since leaving our planet. What were you doing out there?

"Akilah. You must understand. For nearly 51 of those years, I was not in this realm. I was in the planes of divinity, where the twin gods live. I didn't eat, sleep, or have sufficient thought related to my physical being. Time does not exist in their realm."

Akilah's heartbeat changed rate. She became short of breath. "Then… it must be true. You traveled out to Space and found She?" she asked.

"Not just She. He was there waiting for our encounter. I communicated with both of them. She was right. Her counterpart was evidently against her intentions for the universe and our kind," Mustafa explained.

"Then She told you. The evolutionary phenomenon! Was it divulged to you as promised?"

"Yes. It's Free Will, Akilah. An existence beyond Determinism. He intends to eliminate Determinism and Nephilims as a whole. To start the universe anew."

"No! Is that really what's going to happen to us? The end of everything?" Akilah shouted.

"It doesn't have to be. If every Nephilim learns of Free Will, we will no longer be completely subject to fate. We will forever create our own. She intends to combat He's actions. She will assist us in this pursuit of a new era."

"I believe what you say Chosen One. But there's something you need to know. While you were gone, the divide between science and religion has grown drastically. The Nephilims are at an intellectual war with each other. The prophets will surely think what you say is blasphemy. I'm sure He is still determining the fate and thoughts of many Nephilims, perhaps even mine too."

"An intellectual war? I'm so sorry Akilah. This all started from my decision to leave this planet decades ago. There's nothing left for me to do but serve my purpose as The Chosen One. I must unify our species to stand against half of the twin gods. If Nephilims become completely consumed by Determinism, then they will be destroyed along with the religion itself. The Nephilims will be no more. But I cannot do this alone. I need my wife's help. Where is Qadira?"

"I'm sorry. That is another unfortunate occurrence. Some ailment has befallen your wife, Mustafa. A blight that we don't entirely understand."

Shock emerged upon Mustafa's face. "Take me to her."

Akilah looked away from The Chosen One and observed the crowd still surrounding them. They overheard their entire conversation, shock upon the now misguided Nephilims'

faces. "Nephilims! Please! Do not panic. The Chosen One has learned of the evolutionary phenomenon just as we hoped! This new era of our existence will save us from the conflict of the twin gods and the conflict of our species. It is in these times that The Chosen One evolved to unite our kind. Remain calm and we will find a way to sufficiently provide everyone with all the details of the new phenomenon," Akilah shouted. But instead of quelling their anguish, an uproar of confusion began. The Nephilims shouted in fear, begging for answers to their questions. "We can resolve this later. Your will is my command first," Akilah said. She grabbed Mustafa's hand and teleported him to his wife's whereabouts.

Act 3 – Passage 4

Mustafa and Akilah arrived at a new lab. The renovations and technological advancements were staggering. Mustafa was overwhelmed by what science had accomplished for his species over the years of his absence.

Akilah approached one of the scientists in the room. "Naima, The Chosen One has returned from his excursions in Space. He wishes to see his wife. Has Qadira been moved to the examination room yet?" she asked.

The scientist shook her head. "No

ma'am. She is still in her resting quarters. In comatose," Naima said. Mustafa gasped in shock. Akilah just grabbed his arm and rushed him down the hallways. They eventually came to a room at the end, much larger than the others. The door had "Priority Subject" engraved on it.

When they entered, Mustafa could see his wife lying upon a bed. There was a strange protrusion in her stomach. It was as if something was growing from within her, stretching her stomach ten times past its original size. Mustafa approached Qadira's unconscious form and touched her stomach. It was hard. It felt as if her muscles and skin were contracting around something. Suddenly, he heard a faint heartbeat. The Chosen One gasped and retreated from his wife.

"I had the same reaction when she first became ill. Qadira was not always like this. She began having symptoms of a virus. She was weak, could not consume food, and her temperature rose. But years down the line, her stomach began to grow. And when we brought her into an observation room, we discovered a heartbeat," Akilah explained.

Suddenly the scientist, Naima, entered the room. "Akilah. Ma'am. Is everything okay?" she asked. Akilah just shook her head, saying nothing. "Chosen One. You will save us, correct? The conflict between the believers of science and practitioners of religion is beginning to tear apart the Nephilim race. Why were you gone for so long?" Naima asked innocently. The Chosen One couldn't take his eyes off his wife. He spoke without looking at the newly evolved scientist.

"I was in the realm of the twin gods. I've come to learn that time in their home does not function like ours. I could feel it after I returned. The time seemingly passed me by in one moment. It was as if every word they spoke took several days to be rationalized by my consciousness. Their tongue was not truly the same as ours. It took 51 years to comprehend their opposing messages," Mustafa explained.

"This new phenomenon… Chosen One. Will it truly save us?"

"That's something I cannot guarantee. But I will do everything in my power to ensure the odds serve us. Free Will must save us. And it must save my wife. How long has she been in comatose?"

"Qadira had been experiencing symptoms for years. But she lost consciousness exactly one year and 127 days ago as her condition worsened," Akilah said.

Mustafa grunted in sorrow.

"Akilah. Ma'am. Her vitals have remained the same. I monitored her pulse and the child's pulse while you were away, just as you asked," Naima said.

"Child? A child?" Mustafa questioned frantically.

"Yes. I know it must be hard to understand, Chosen One. But that's the cause of the second heartbeat. I attempted to use bio suspension to stop this process but I was afraid of hurting Qadira as a result of my actions," Akilah explained.

"How is that possible? Nephilims do *not* have children. We have never reproduced before. That's absolute mortal behavior."

"I am well aware Mustafa. The feral animals that exist around us are the only ones who have birthed to persist as a species. The parent dies after so many years and the cycle continues. But Nephilims are immortal since we don't die from the passage of time. Or so we thought."

"Are you suggesting that this 'child' is causing biological changes to my wife's mortality?"

"Not exactly. But I fear that Qadira bearing this child is a sign of what's to come for our species. This must be tied to the twin gods. They fought over your actions as The Chosen One and your wife seems to have become a key component in the conflict."

Mustafa walked around from the end of the bed and touched his wife's tired face. He observed a screen that displayed the child inside of Qadira's stomach using sound waves. It hardly looked like a Nephilim. It seemed to have arisen from thin air. Mustafa began crying. No matter what type of enlightenment he had achieved through self-actualization, his most significant task as The Chosen One was beyond anything a Nephilim could foresee. It called upon aspects of his intelligence and spirit that had never been explored before. "I have seen enough. It's time. Akilah, do we possess a device that could enhance my telekinetic communication so I can speak to nearly every Nephilim on the continent?" Mustafa asked. Akilah smiled. "Follow me."

Act 3 – Passage 5

Once again, Akilah teleported Mustafa to a location that he had never seen before because of his absence while seeking the truth. It was a massive room entirely made of metals and other materials that reflected the man's face. The immaculacy of the white sterility made it feel as if he were the first to ever enter this room.

"Akilah. Where are we?" Mustafa asked.

Akilah walked forward. She entered a number code into a keypad and a steel door released its hydraulic locks. "We had this tremendous device created several years ago to provide Nephilims with synchronous messages. Especially during times of the arising conflict between science and religion, this was our attempt to quell the intellectual war. Although now it's clear that our efforts haven't worked. We can't figure out how to rationalize the importance of peace to Nephilims with this great divide going on. But now that you've returned, maybe this will serve better use to you. With the information you provided, I would sooner believe this whole divide was caused by the paradigm shift in He. If the gods oppose each other, then it makes sense that their creations would too. This device will do exactly as you requested, Chosen One. It will allow you to divulge everything you know about Free Will to many Nephilims at once. Let's hope it changes their minds. If the end of Determinism will eradicate our kind, then there isn't a more important time for the Nephilims to band together than now."

The two of them walked up a set of stairs to a strange contraption that Mustafa had never seen before. It was a large chair with a massive extension hanging above it. This extension appeared as though it was meant to be equipped on the head. Dozens of tubes protruded from the headset.

They were attached to various parts of the walls in the white room. "These tubes… what do they do?" Mustafa asked.

Akilah motioned her hand for Mustafa to sit in the elaborate chair. He did so. "These tubes connect to pools of ether encased in contraptions within the walls. Ether being a useful spiritual resource for Nephilims, this siphoning of the material is designed to provide sufficient energy to magnify the reach of your telepathic communication," Akilah explained. Mustafa simply nodded. "Are you ready?" Akilah asked.

Mustafa took a moment to inhale deeply and mentally prepare himself. He closed his eyes and harnessed his power. He gave Akilah a deliberate look of intent and she placed the device on his head. It wrapped around Mustafa's cranium and covered his eyes. Akilah walked over to a control panel and pulled a lever to activate the machine. It began whirring and gears moved to charge up its cosmic force. The tubes glowed with a bright blue color. Although Mustafa could not physically see, he could now sense everything.

He trusted that Akilah understood the measures of the contraption. The Chosen One prepared himself to tell nearly every Nephilim on the planet about the concept of Free Will. But he suddenly stopped before saying anything. Mustafa had a feeling that his new message would not be easily received by the Nephilims. The principle of choice was brand new and couldn't be entirely rationalized by his people. Mustafa decided to use this powerful contraption for even greater feats. As he began infusing his thoughts into the device, he felt like there was a way he could transform his message into something more powerful than just words. Pictures. Instead, Mustafa embedded his direct memories into the device. Rather than just heeding his words, he wanted the Nephilims to see what he saw in Space, in the realm of gods. As he witnessed the memory replay in his mind, Mustafa knew that his conversation with He and She was now a memory of his people too. With a final burst of spiritual energy, it had been done. The colors of the skies changed from the magnitude of such power. Mustafa had hoped that this new universe-wide understanding of Free Will would end the great divide between war and religion. But his hopes ignored the reality of what really tainted his race.

As Mustafa could feel his energy wane, the device powered down. He was returning to the world in front of him. There was a sudden conflict. He could hear Akilah arguing with people. One voice rose above the rest. Could it be? The prophet that guided him as he evolved into this life. Abdul. He was shouting. "Step out of my way scientist! I must have a word with my protégé. You don't realize what you've done, woman!" Abdul shoved Akilah to the side and yanked the device's headgear off of Mustafa. The prophet was appalled at the sight of The Chosen One. It was truly him. 52 years in isolation seemed to have entirely changed the principles of the Nephilim he once cared for. Abdul grabbed Mustafa by his garb. "You're coming with me."

Act 3 – Passage 6

The prophet forcefully teleported himself and The Chosen One to a remote location. Abdul released Mustafa. When The Chosen One took a look at his whereabouts, he could see that they were at the edge of a cliff in the wasteland plains. Distant vegetation could be seen below the towering trees. Mountains were made of sharp rocks, detailed with patches of grass and wildlife. The Sun in this location was covered by gray clouds. The clouds were so thick, water began pouring from the sky. The Chosen One faced the man he once called a mentor. It was strange. The words of She began identifying Abdul as a threat to the new era. Somehow, Mustafa could see He within the prophet.

"Chosen One. What do you think you're doing?" Abdul shouted.

"Is this my greeting from you? For my return home. Why did you bring me here Abdul? You almost interrupted a very important message to our kind," Mustafa said.

"Apparently I couldn't teleport to your location soon enough. The second I felt that memory enter my mind, I knew you had returned. But why would you corrupt Nephilims with that image? Free Will? Have you lost all sense of guidance?"

"Because it's the truth, Abdul! You only disagree because I'm almost certain you are the pioneer of this divide between science and religion."

"Religion is the absolute truth, Mustafa. I'm certain of it. If you don't let He correct She's mistakes, our worlds will not have the ability to regrow in the image of perfection that we had hoped for."

"He is going to destroy Determinism! He has corrupted your mind, Abdul. She's intention of granting us Free Will is the new era that will change the face of the universe for the better. We can no longer be constrained to the acts of gods. The gods don't always know what is best for our kind."

Abdul flared his arms in anger. "Is that what you learned out in Space all those years? Is that the blasphemy She has driven into your mind?" he asked.

"It's not blasphemy! It's the *truth*, Abdul. Free Will. Quite frankly, if you're not siding with what will proliferate our kind, then you're against our people. And if you're against our people, then you're against me. It is my duty as The Chosen One to ensure that as many Nephilims in this universe attain self-actualization as possible. They all have the potential to find harmony in science and religion, just as I have," Mustafa said proudly.

"That's it? You are forcing us to abandon our fate?"

"No. I am liberating us from it."

Suddenly, Mustafa could hear the voice of Akilah. She was communicating a very important message to him telepathically. "Mustafa! It's Qadira! Something is happening with the child! You must come to her at once!"

Mustafa attempted to use his telekinetic force to shove Abdul to the side so he could teleport to his wife's location. But suddenly, he felt someone grab him from behind, holding him by the arms. It was... another Abdul. Mustafa was shocked. None of this made sense. How could there have been two prophets?

"Abdul? How did you-"

The prophet interrupted him. "Bilocation, Chosen One. To fulfill the duties of He, I have been blessed with supernatural abilities we once believed were not possible. I will always be in two places at once. And I will stop you from leaving if I must," Abdul said malefically.

Mustafa conjured up more of his power and dispersed it into a shockwave, knocking down both Abdul and his doppelganger. He quickly teleported back to the lab to tend to his wife. While he may have escaped from Abdul in the meantime, The Chosen One was still dreadfully terrified at the thought of his former mentor becoming his greatest antagonist in reaching the era of Free Will. He prayed that there was some way this conflict could end without them becoming sworn enemies.

Act 3 – Passage 7

Mustafa found himself back at the lab. In its communal room, full of passerby scientists. This time, the entire facility had a different atmosphere. Many people were rushing in a single direction. Mustafa realized they all were running towards Qadira's room. This phenomenon had never befallen Nephilims before. The species had always evolved from the infinite ocean as immortals. But now, the instance of sudden reproduction must have cued a new dynamic in their biological cycle. It was impossible to determine what this child could mean for the entire race. It was no wonder the scientists were all rushing to witness this unexplainable event.

The Chosen One quickly ran past the surrounding Nephilims and entered the room where Qadira was. Akilah and her assistants allowed him to pass, dispersing the forcefield they had summoned to block the crowd. All he could hear was Qadira wailing painfully.

Mustafa approached Akilah. "What's wrong with her? She's in pain!" he shouted.

Akilah and the other scientists kept The Chosen One from coming too close to his wife. "It's okay Mustafa! Please! Calm yourself! We observed Qadira's condition. Her heart rate is rising, her pores are cooling her, and her internal organs are contracting!" Akilah explained over the noise.

Mustafa didn't understand what all this meant. He watched his wife scream in pain. This was the first time he had seen her awake since his return from the realm of gods. But this was truly a traumatizing sight, seeing her suffer so much.

"Just be there for her Mustafa. Your wife will be okay. The child is coming. Just support Qadira during this process," Akilah said.

The scientists gathered by the devices surrounding Qadira. They paid deliberate attention to them, monitoring every vital response of her body during the process. Mustafa rushed over and held his wife's hand. Her legs were hoisted up and spread apart.

"It's okay, Qadira. I'm here. I'm here for you my love," Mustafa said.

Akilah placed her hand on Qadira's forehead, stabilizing her internal temperature. Qadira looked at her husband and tried her best to smile for him. The small movement was a struggle and only caused her more pain. The woman screamed once more.

"It's okay Qadira! The child is coming! This is the same as the mortal animals do on our planet. You'll birth a living Nephilim! You can do it! I promise you!" Akilah shouted. Qadira began hyperventilating. Her heart rate continued increasing dramatically. The scientists used their powers to transfer much of their internal energy to Qadira so she could have the strength to bring the child into this world.

"Where's this child going to come from?" Mustafa asked.

Akilah concentrated harder, stabilizing Qadira's vitals. The din of the watching crowd grew louder. They watched in awe of what was transpir-ing. "The child will come from an appendage similar to the animals' reproductive organs. Her vagina. I guess they served no purpose to us... until now! But you have to help her Mustafa. One surge of your powerful energy and Qadira will be able to push the child out! You have to help! Now!" Akilah shouted.

Mustafa nodded his head frantically. He closed his eyes and concentrated on his wife's hand. He inhaled deeply and with one exhale, his power was infused into his wife. Qadira pushed one more time and suddenly... everything stopped. The cries of Mustafa's wife were replaced with the cries of his newborn child. The first birthed Nephilim in all existence.

A scientist held the child daintily in his hands. The look on his face was full of astonishment. He quickly handed the child to Akilah. Blood now mottled both of their garbs. Akilah gazed at the crying child. She could feel an overwhelming beauty consume her. How could there have possibly been such a tremendous attachment to a being that had just been bred into existence? Tears flowed from the woman's eyes. She handed the child to her mother, Qadira.

Mustafa and his wife gazed at their child, observing its external organ. "The child... is a girl," Qadira said, short of breath. Both she and The

Chosen One cried powerfully. This was all so startling and so foreign to them. But this feeling marked a new chapter in the existence of Nephilims. The surrounding crowd now watched in silence, enamored with the beauty of this scene. "I don't understand how she got here. Or how I suddenly bore a child inside my body for over 20 years. But... I love her. She is a part of me. And she is a part of you too, husband. Perhaps it was the power of our love that created such an immaculate being," Qadira said with overwhelming emotion. Mustafa kissed his wife and their child.

"Usually offspring are born when two animals consummate. They use reproductive organs to impregnate the female. Did you both engage in some form of intercourse?" Akilah asked.

Mustafa and Qadira shook their heads. "Well, no. Nephilims don't normally have the desire to consummate. Our organs have never been determined to do such a thing," Qadira said.

"I see. Then this cannot be a direct result of your physical actions. Mustafa, this must have something to do with your interaction with He and She. It happened while you were in Space."

"I suppose so. I figured this must be She's way of counteracting He's elimination of Determinism. If Nephilims reproduce on their own, then there's still hope for our species to persist without the need of gods," Mustafa said.

"How will anyone know when the time is ripe? How will any woman know when they may give birth to a child? You and I didn't consummate," Qadira said.

"Those are questions She may have answers to. For two decades, no other woman has been pregnant except for you, Qadira. I suggest Mustafa do everything he can to find an explanation for this," Akilah said.

Suddenly, there was a ruckus amongst the crowd of bystanders outside the room. Scientists quickly attended to the situation. "It's the prophets! They're here!" a scientist shouted. This immediately created conflict.

Abdul was, here again, pushing through the crowd. "Step out of my way! The child! It was born, wasn't it?" he asked Akilah.

The woman faced him with anger. They were both leaders in drastically different pursuits of existence under the laws of nature. "Yes, Abdul. And if you were truly the mentor of The Chosen One, you would be supportive of this occurrence. He traveled through Space to speak with the gods and this is the answer he received.

Don't you see? Free Will must exist. The times are changing before us," Akilah said.

Abdul looked at the husband, wife, and innocent child. Then he looked back at Akilah. "You are damn right the times are changing! The end is coming! The sky has changed Akilah. It's gone! When we look up, we see nothing but Space! The stars, moon, and Sun, directly in their homes! Do you see the results of the blasphemy that She has poisoned our Chosen One with? The very foundation of our planet is falling apart. The only way to stop it is to eliminate the child! Its existence has poisoned our species! He has determined it as a bane to our society!" Abdul shouted.

He attempted to grab the child from the couple but Akilah stood in the way. "No! You will not harm the child! *He* is who poisons *your* mind, Abdul! What god would incite such violence amongst our once peaceful species?" she questioned.

Abdul shook his head. The man had become fully committed to his commands from He. "She created the divide between religion and science while conjuring this so-called 'Free Will' amongst the cosmos! He simply must resort to drastic measures to correct the mistakes of his counterpart."

Akilah and her scientists banded together to face the prophets and pro-tect the child. They were prepared to use violence, which was something no Nephilim ever truly believed in. "Mustafa, Qadira! You have to take the child and leave this place! It's clear He is using Abdul as a catalyst to cease Free Will by harming an innocent life!" Akilah shouted.

Mustafa quickly stood up, his power surging from his emotions. An intense aura of cosmic energy formed around The Chosen One. "I'll stop them! Step aside Akilah!" he yelled.

Qadira grabbed her husband's arm from her position in the bed. "No Mustafa! Regardless, Abdul is still your founder. Please, don't hurt him. We must leave and hopefully, She will have answers about resolving this peacefully," she said.

Mustafa calmed himself and heeded Akilah's instructions. He carried his wife, who carried their child in her arms. They quickly teleported to a remote location. Somewhere secluded. The husband and wife decided they needed to go into hiding until they could obtain answers about what the child meant and how its existence was so pertinent to Free Will.

Act 4 – Passage 1

Amidst the beautiful woodlands, the sun shined brightly, glaring directly from its position in Space.

Without the filter of the once glorious, orange sky of the planet, the Nephilims found themselves faced directly with the interstellar phenomena up above. Mustafa knelt beside a stream to collect water into a leather flask for storage. Aquatic creatures swam down the stream in fear of the potential predator before them. Their existence reminded Mustafa of his first moments after evolution. He remembered what it felt like for him to briefly live amongst the food chain of the treacherous beasts that roamed the outskirts of Nephilim civilization. Mustafa had come so far over the centuries but the recent changes in the balance of the universe made him feel primordial. The start of a new era was causing so much harm to his people. But as the stories of the All had been told, destruction almost always preceded creation.

Mustafa carried the flask of water and other sustenance above his head with telekinesis. Feeling rather tired, he decided to simply walk back to the shelter. Food becoming scarce, he was unable to teleport very often in recent weeks. Sometime later, Mustafa entered a wooden shack. It was something he had built on very short notice after he escaped with Qadira and his child. Now they were forced to remain in hiding. Akilah had joined the couple to protect them from the pos-sible onslaught of the prophets, especially Abdul. She would have had her scientists help, but she felt hiding with too many people would open the possibility of attracting too much attention.

The Chosen One brought the resources into the shack and set them on a makeshift table. He walked into another end of the room and saw Qadira bathing the child in a basket of water. Their daughter was asleep. It seemed to be the only thing the child did.

"Our child is always sleeping. She just sleeps and eats, still defenseless even after all this time," Mustafa said.

Qadira brought the child out of the water and dried her with a cloth. "You remember what Akilah said, husband. The child is nothing like us. She did not evolve from the ocean with an ability to grasp existence in a matter of hours. I highly doubt the child even recognizes what she is yet," she said, laughing slightly.

Mustafa kissed their daughter. "I understand. I just fear for her. But the gods know I would do anything to protect our child. Not just because she's the first in the entire existence of Nephilims, but because she's mine. And I love her."

The Chosen One prepared the combination of fruits, vegetables, and other naturally grown food upon the table. It had taken time, but with the help of Akilah and her knowledge, they had discovered how to feed the child. Without a sufficient ability to eat, Qadira's body had responded by producing milk within her breasts. According to Akilah, this was similar to the animals in the wild. The mothers fed their newborns milk that was naturally produced by their bodies. Mustafa prepared a bowl of assorted nutrients and walked into a separate room. Akilah was there, on a bed. Unfortunately, she had become dreadfully sick within the last few days.

"Hi, Akilah. How are you feeling?" Mustafa asked.

Akilah coughed and drew the strength to smile. "I feel slightly better than I did during the last moon cycle," she said.

Mustafa sat with his legs crossed and levitated beside her bed. He placed the bowl of food on her lap. "Please, you should eat to maintain your strength. I'm still really scared that you've been affected by the blight."

Since the birth of the child, a dreadful occurrence had befallen the Nephilims. It was strange. Suddenly, word had gotten out that many of them were dying unexpectedly, without proper cause or explanation. Nephilims were alive one day and dead the next. The only signs of someone being affected by such a blight was a strange shift in their appearance and physiology. Their skin sagged, they developed wrinkles, and their senses became weak. Much like the animals in the wild, the Nephilims appeared as though they were suddenly becoming mortal. The blight was also known as age. There had been an incalculable number of years since each Nephilim had evolved onto the surface. But the older they were, the greater the odds of them dying by these unexplainable causes. It was the end that He had determined. Mortality ensued upon the Nephilims like a plague.

They could no longer live forever. They had become impossibly vulnerable to the natural environment and diseases living within the air. Much like the fall of the species, aspects of the planets within the solar system began to fall apart as well. The laws of nature became disrupted. The sky had vanished, trees retracted back into seeds, sectors of anti-Gravity arose, and holes were torn into reality. It appeared to be the end of all predetermined laws. Yet no answers were heard about how to stop the end from coming so that Free Will may thrive.

Akilah finally lifted the bowl of food and smelled it. She prepared herself to eat. Age had sickened her. Her skin sagged, her eyesight weakened, and her bones became frail.

"Mustafa, I don't need your help to eat. You must continue your meditations. It's our only hope for She to provide us with a way to beat He. Yes, your child has been born successfully, but the link to Free Will is unclear," Akilah said, her breath labored.

Mustafa attempted to help her but understood the importance of his duty.

"You should travel back to the plains by the waterfall before the moon rises. Being connected with nature should hopefully increase your chances of reaching She. I could only imagine that He is disrupting your ability to communicate with her somehow. Without religious guidance aiding you during your meditation, connecting with She has become difficult, I know. For we only have science. And one is nothing without the other. You went from being The Chosen One to being hated by religious practitioners. But you have to try, Mustafa. She's voice is our only hope now," Akilah continued.

Mustafa nodded in agreement. He went to kiss his wife and child and prepared himself to go back to the forest.

Act 4 – Passage 2

Mustafa adhered to the advice of his ally and dear friend. After consuming some sustenance, his strength felt mostly restored. He quickly teleported back to the forest to save time. The Chosen One arrived near a waterfall that he and Qadira had passed by multiple times over the weeks. It was once a glorious waterfall that represented the beauty nature had to offer upon their planet. But since the war between science and religion, the reservoir had been affected by a void of anti-Gravity. Mustafa observed the phenomenon once more. After the water had fallen from the cliff edge up above, the reservoir began to rise slightly into the air. It had become a floating pond. Surrounding animals tried to drink the airborne water, but couldn't reach it. Mustafa harnessed the water with telekinesis and lowered it momentarily so the creatures could drink.

Now, it was time. He sat in a meditative position and clasped his hands together. The Chosen One had spent hours being very still. He listened to the sounds of the forest and soon, the sounds of his home planet. He could sense the turmoil within his people. The conflict arising by the actions of He. There was violence occurring across the continents. Hatred was brewing between the Nephilims. The constant war over which principle of existence would lead to the truest enlightenment for all. It saddened Mustafa, but he had to concentrate on something beyond the disruption of his realm. He had to seek the disaster occurring in the realm of gods.

Finally, long past sundown, Mustafa could feel a shift in the atmosphere. The wind blew stronger and the stars up above seemed as if they shined brighter momentarily. Chills ran across The Chosen One's body. There was a voice suddenly whispering in his ear. One in a language he couldn't recognize. However, the voice was somehow capable of dictating his actions. *"To find the future, you must exist within the past. Be as you once were when you were created to stop everything from being destroyed,"* Mustafa thought to himself. He suddenly felt the urge to get up from his meditative state and walk towards the floating pond. He gazed at it, his eyes changing into a pale white color. Something was within him now. The Chosen One leaped upward and into the void of anti-Gravity. He adjusted his torso and laid back, submerging his entire body underneath the water. The man remained within the floating waters. Mustafa closed his eyes and could feel his mind ascend once more. It had been quite some time since he had entered the Cosmos. It felt lonelier than the first time as if She was all alone in her world. Once counterparts, the twin gods had now become each other's greatest antagonists. It reminded Mustafa of his once unified relationship with Abdul.

Mustafa could feel She once again, but couldn't see her. The god felt different. There was a profound development in her existence. She exuded emotion. Anguish from the betrayal of her other half, resentment from not foreseeing this occurrence, joy from finally being with Mustafa after so long, and an indescribable desire for justice. However, the absence of the Determinism religion limited their ability to communicate. There were no words exchanged, no direct guidance. Mustafa simply felt She and became one step closer towards understanding what had to be done. To push Free Will to new heights, he needed to reveal the results of the evolutionary phenomenon. His child. Revealing her to the public would stop Abdul from succeeding in his mission to erase all traces of She from existence. The first Nephilim ever birthed in the universe. The possibility to persist despite mortality. There was hope for his people after this war. As The Chosen One, it was Mustafa's responsibility to reveal this glimmer of the sanctuary to the rest of his kind. No more hiding. They may have deemed him a heretic, but every advancement in the universe had not come without great challenge. This was surely the next step for all existence. To live beyond the gods. To act beyond the gods. To create beyond the gods. To have faith in more than just the gods. To have faith in oneself.

There was a sudden change in the atmosphere again. Mustafa exited his meditative state, opening his eyes to gaze at the naked universe above. The stars shined where the sky used to be. This feeling... it was Akilah. Something terrible was happening. Her heart rate had drastically changed and Mustafa could feel it. He quickly exited the floating pond and stood upon the grass. He concentrated once more and teleported back to the shack to tend to his friend.

Act 4 – Passage 3

The Chosen One quickly entered the shack. There was a frightening level of commotion going on inside. His child was crying, his wife was panicking, and worst of all, his dear friend's condition had become dire. Mustafa ran into the room where Akilah had been staying. Her health had worsened. Her body was shaking frantically and her were eyes rolled to the back of her head. Mustafa could sense her brain emit a dangerously high amount of electrical activity to her nerves, making her actions uncon-

trollable. He had never seen anything like this before.

"Akilah! Akilah! What happened to her?" Mustafa shouted.

Qadira carried the child beside her with telekinesis to keep her hands free. She bounced the child up and down slightly to help quell its unexplainable crying. "I don't know! I came in to check on her and suddenly found her like this. The synapses in her brain are out of control!"

Mustafa quickly grabbed Akilah by her arms and attempted to get her shaking to stop. "Akilah! Control yourself! Please!" But it was no use. He had to resort to higher methods to help stop whatever biological phenomenon was occurring within her body.

Mustafa placed a hand over Akilah's chest and sensed her heart at a deeper level. It was beating much faster than normal. The Chosen One inhaled deeply and surged his energy throughout Akilah's nervous system. He used his powers to take control of her bodily functions. As his energy passed through hers, the frantic shaking showed signs of stopping. The rocking of Akilah's upper body slowed down gradually until it finally ended. Water was immensely seeping through her pores. Her head fell back against the pillow as she quietly hyperventilated.

Qadira brought a cloth dampened

with cold water and placed it on Akilah's forehead. "What *was* that?" The wife showed extreme confusion.

Mustafa started crying to himself. "It must have been the blight. Age. It's killing Akilah," he said.

Several hours later, Akilah had finally awakened from her physiologically-endangered state. She was tremendously weak but summed up whatever strength she could to speak to the couple.

"Akilah. Are you alright? We were terribly frightened by what happened," Qadira said.

"I'm clearly anything but 'alright.' The blight is beginning to consume me. That's obvious. Whatever has been causing Nephilims to die unexpectedly will take me too," Akilah said.

"No. Don't say things like that. There must be some sort of cure. How will we ever stop Abdul without your expertise?" Mustafa asked.

"You do not need my expertise. You're The Chosen One. And your wife is one of the most powerful Nephilims in the universe. She gave birth to the first child known to our kind. Besides, you were able to reach She, right? I can see it in your eyes."

"That's correct. I was not able to speak with her directly, but I could feel her presence amidst the floating reservoir. This child is the key. This child is her way of combating the end of everything. Our daughter is the hope that Nephilims need to know that our species will persist, despite He's ending of Determinism."

"Then you both have your answer. Show the child to the world. Let the Nephilims know that through the harmony of science and religion, a new being was born. It's the balance that has created such a beautiful milestone for our kind. And She is here to protect us. She has a plan to keep the Nephilims alive. *He* is the one who plans on destroying us. Once Free Will exists amongst all the cosmos, there will be no god to destroy us anymore. We will finally be able to live in peace. And mortality… is a price worth paying."

Akilah started fading. Her heart rate slowed dramatically. The husband and wife quickly grabbed her hands.

"Akilah please! Don't leave us," Qadira said, crying.

Akilah softly squeezed her friends' hands. The tender touch was the last thing she wanted to leave them with. There was little time left.

"Akilah. You may be one of the most intelligent Nephilims I have ever known, but you were also one of my greatest supporters. You are and will always be my dear friend. You are a part of the family that Qadira and I have now created. We promise you, we will see to it that Free Will brings us into the next era. One of peace," Mustafa said.

Akilah simply smiled at him. The look in her eyes said, "thank you." Then, her heart stopped. The woman was there on the bed, completely still. But there was a sense of peace in her form. As if there was a realm beyond this one. It wasn't as if the woman had died but simply passed on to another life. The exhaustion of immortality could have been too much to handle. Perhaps Nephilims were meant to die. Perhaps mortality was a blessing amongst the universe.

Mustafa and Qadira cried over her form. It was time to bring this war between the gods, this war between science and religion, to an end. Their daughter was the key to it all. It was the symbol of true Free Will. Breathing life into another being was what only gods had been capable of for so long. And once that power is in the hands of mortals, there would be no more control over them. Their acts, their will, would finally be their own.

Act 4 - Passage 4

Mustafa and Qadira finally made their first return to civilization in what felt like forever. Many aspects of their world had changed. Aside from

the destruction caused by the disappearing sky and voids of anti-Gravity, much of what science had done for the Nephilims was being demolished. Abdul had begun his process of erasing many traces of science as well as any evidence of the first child born. Chaos had erupted amongst the people within Mustafa's home village. He grabbed Qadira's hand as she carefully carried their child. "Come, my love! We have to get to a place where our voices can better be heard!" he shouted. The Chosen One and his wife ran past the chaos. Nephilims were being stolen from, homes set to flames, and for once, violence had erupted between the people. Believers of science blamed practitioners of religion for the outbreak of the blight and vice-versa. The mortality that had ensued upon their race was terrifying. People were collapsing to the ground suddenly, dying of age. This was truly a nightmare. It had to be stopped once and for all.

The couple made it to a public stage outside, set at the center of the village. There was a crowd of people sitting around, watching a herald speak about the "dawn of the end". The audience was filled with mostly religious practitioners, which threatened Mustafa's presence here. But he wasn't afraid of which Nephilims resented him or still supported him. He had a duty to fulfill as The Chosen One.

Mustafa approached the crowd from behind and the herald made eye contact with him. Mustafa recognized the herald from his time at the chapel.

"Saladin! Leave the premises immediately! Or you will be hurt amidst this chaos!" Mustafa shouted. Saladin, the herald, refused to move. "It's The Chosen One and his wife! They come bearing the child! We must all stand against them! That being is what created this war!" he shouted angrily. But only half of the crowd was somewhat convinced. The rest were far too intimidated by Mustafa and Qadira's cosmic prowess to dare oppose them.

Instead of attacking, they stepped aside, to allow Mustafa and his family by. The Chosen One had finally come out of hiding, so the time must have been ripe for something important to happen. The family walked in between the ambiguous crowd. Regardless of anyone's way of existence, these times were frightening. Fortunately for the couple, the Nephilim's inherently peaceful nature showed whenever they were in the presence of Mustafa, the only one who had achieved self-actualization and met the twin gods themselves.

"No! You cannot let them pass! They are promoters of blasphemy! And they have abandoned our people!" Saladin shouted.

Mustafa looked up at the man on the stage. "If you don't move Saladin, I will make you. I won't have your threatening presence anywhere near my daughter," he said.

But Saladin refused to heed the threat. Mustafa forced a palm forward and struck Saladin with a force of invisible energy. It knocked the man back, off the stage, and into a box of stone ore, where he ultimately fell unconscious.

The husband and wife looked back at the Nephilims. The expression on their faces showed tremendous sincerity. After sensing the couple's heart rates, it was clear that this was never their intended outcome. The people sympathized with them and wanted to try their best to listen to a possible resolution. Fear was no excuse for irrationality. It was indeed a time to be as intuitive as possible. Mustafa levitated onto the stage. He turned around, bent over, and held out a hand to aid his wife. Qadira grabbed his hand and levitated onto the stage beside Mustafa, with their child in her arms. Their collective presence was extremely powerful. The crowd of Nephilims looked up at them in awe. The presence of a mother, father, and child was somehow inspiring. For the first time in decades, they felt hope amidst this divide between their ways of life.

Mustafa continued holding Qadira's hand. This physical connection gave them a synchronous power. For every word that Mustafa would speak, Qadira would use her power to spread his message across the entire solar system. His upcoming speech would be communicated to every Nephilim telepathically.

"To those of you who support me, I sincerely apologize for my absence. To those of you who oppose me, your reckoning is nigh," he said, his magnifying voice scattering across the crowd and interstellar structures of Space. The perimeter of nearby chaos had been subdued when the Nephilims sensed Mustafa's presence. More gathered around. "A lot has transpired since my return from the realm of gods. And the very last thing I could've ever predicted was an intellectual war between my people. This war has exceeded just intellectual quarrel but has now grown into physical violence. It sickens me and my wife. I left Space and traveled through Time with two distinct messages: Determinism will end along with our kind. But, Free Will shall counteract these actions by allowing our species to persist on our own. I don't want to entirely believe that one god is right over the other. I don't want to believe

that science will exceed religion, or vice-versa. This quarrel between He and She has shown me the importance of balance. Perhaps Determinism was always meant to end. Perhaps we weren't meant to completely adhere to the gods for the rest of existence. But this does not conclude that Nephilims must end too. The instance of ending Determinism is what led to the rise of Free Will. He and She balance each other. Much like the creation of the All, the universe reinforces its laws of causation and reaction. He is attempting to end Determinism and She is attempting to begin Free Will. One leads to another. One could not exist without the other. And this same important message rings true with science and religion. Aspects of one cause the other and one should never exist without its counterpart. The laws of physics bred the laws of nature. And we Nephilims adhere to both. We don't argue with what this extravagant universe tells us. We listen to all of it. And we persist intellectually. *Not* irrationally."

The watching people began nodding their heads. They began smiling. Mustafa spoke profound truths about what their existence as Nephilims truly meant. "The resulting power of truly harmonic balance has led our species to a profound milestone. As I'm sure all of you are aware, a child was born. *Our* child. This is not just the child of me and my wife, Qadira. No, this is the child of all our kind. And she is incredibly beautiful. Perhaps the single most influential thing in my life," Mustafa said as he began to cry. He smiled at his wife and daughter during a brief pause. "I have traveled across realms, achieved great feats, reached self-actualization, and spoke to gods. Yet, watching my love birth our daughter has changed me more than anything else. I say this to show you the power of what is before us. Nephilims. We no longer have to rely on statistical chance for more of us to evolve from the oceans. We create our species now. The power is in *our* hands. Yes, the thought of mortality is extremely frightening. Many of us die every day. We recently lost our dear friend, a pioneer in science, Akilah. But everything in this universe must see its end. Just how the stars explode to give light across the darkened skies of Space, our deaths serve a greater purpose. Mortality must be a worthy sacrifice for our species to continue in a new way. Our children, however they may arise, will live in a universe of Free Will. Freedom to dictate their own choices. To be liberated from the controlling guidance of beings who don't truly understand our existence. So we should all be willing to make this sacrifice. My wife and I for one would gladly lay our lives down to let our daughter live freely. For the entire future generations of our Nephilim race to live freely."

Mustafa and Qadira each placed a hand underneath their child. Daintily holding her, they raised her in the air for the entire crowd to see. The surrounding Nephilims cheered and some cried. Her presence was staggering. She was an absolute beauty. The child looked drastically different from them. Her skin was pristine and her hair flawless. This was the future of the Nephilim race. And they would gladly accept it for the sake of peace. The crowd bowed down before The Chosen One and his family. It was time to embrace the change and make the most of what the universe had to offer.

Suddenly, the joyous moment was disrupted. Corruption had arrived. It was Mustafa's former mentor and current adversary, Abdul. The prophet walked through the crowd of bowing Nephilims. He immediately locked eyes with The Chosen One. Some of the surrounding Nephilims arose from the ground, intimidated by Abdul's powerful presence. The servant of god had taken great control over the village and many other surrounding regions of the continents on this planet. He had spent the past few weeks ruining any belief that remained for She. Mustafa stood in front of Qadira, gently nudging his wife and daughter behind him for protection.

"Abdul. You look… immaculate," The Chosen One said. And he was correct. Abdul looked entirely unaffected by age. His skin lacked any wrinkles and he looked to be stronger than ever before. His hair was fair and his muscles larger.

"You are exceptionally perceptive, my former protégé. He has granted me immunity to age so that I may fulfill his desires. I have been determined to do so," Abdul said.

Mustafa scoffed at him. "And you think He will not just eliminate you like the rest of us? You still abide by Determinism, when its very ending is what's killing our species. There are consequences to the deal you made with He. Knowing his nature, the god will likely turn his back on you like he did the Nephilims and his twin." Abdul began laughing maniacally. He was not the same, kind-hearted man from years ago. The tremendous task and power bestowed upon him were corrupting his very core.

"Mustafa. You had your chance as The Chosen One of this Eon. You had every opportunity to make our universe a better place. But you chose science over religion," Abdul said.

"I chose balance! That's something you will never understand. Did you not hear my message?" Mustafa shouted.

"Damn you and your lies boy! You sided with the scientists after everything the chapel has done for you. She is the one causing conflict amongst our people. If She never mettled in mortal affairs, He would not have had to chase her. But She grew too attached to her creation. And that's what a god should never do. The All has been so successful in its universal evolution because it lacked any emotional attachment. That's why He is so righteous. He's not clouded by judgment."

"That's where you're wrong, Abdul. It's the way She cares for us that makes her a true god. What mortal wishes to be created by a being without feeling? What being wishes to be nothing more than statistical chance and mathematical occurrence? To She, we are more than just numbers. We are her people. I choose to be a Chosen One that observes my kin as living beings, not a material product of the universe's laws of nature."

"Then I suppose we can't come to an agreement. But I have my duties just as you have yours. I must destroy the child to stop She from allowing Free Will to persist. If you stand in my way, I will take that child by force."

The husband and wife had become severely threatened by Abdul's intentions. They had never truly resorted to violence before and didn't wish to now. Suddenly, Abdul initiated the attack. He emitted a burst of cosmic energy at Qadira and their daughter. The crowd of Nephilims screamed. Qadira quickly threw their child out of the way to protect her, as she took the brunt of Abdul's attack. The pure energy exploded and sent the woman flying backwards into the dirt field behind the stage. Her skin had become scorched in multiple places. Mustafa panicked. He jumped into the air and caught their daughter, safely floating back to the ground. The child was crying, likely afraid of the rising conflict. Several men and women approached Mustafa on the stage and offered to take the child to protect it. It was obvious that he would have to face Abdul if he wanted to keep his daughter alive. She was the most important link to Free Will and the greatest creation the Nephilims have ever known. The Chosen One-handed his daughter to the kind Nephilims. They ran into shelter for safety. Other Nephilims started panicking, running away from the violence.

Mustafa locked eyes with Abdul from atop the stage. "Abdul! You hurt my wife and threatened the life of my daughter! And for that, I must threaten yours!" he shouted angrily. Mustafa pounced at extreme speed towards Abdul. For the first time in his life, he was using his powers for violence. To potentially harm one of his kind, let alone the man he once respected so dearly.

Mustafa attempted to strike Abdul with his fist but was quickly stopped by the man's power. Abdul caught Mustafa by his hand. Dust plumed from the force of the block. A shockwave of sound burst across the stands. Mustafa gasped in shock. Abdul crushed his fist. The Chosen One screamed painfully. He swung Mustafa by his arm and slammed him into the ground, onto his back. Abdul quickly stomped on Mustafa's face, crushing his head into the ground. Blood began emerging. None of the Nephilims had ever truly witnessed this type of altercation between their people. "I will destroy you boy! And ending you will fulfill the dawn of the new era. You have become a product of She. Therefore, you must be eliminated, along with all traces of her," Abdul said. The Nephilims begged Abdul to release The Chosen One. They begged for these two men to stop fighting each other.

All Mustafa could hear was his daughter crying in the distance. To protect her and his people, he would have to be willing to sacrifice it all. He couldn't let Abdul succeed. The Twin god, He, had completely manipulated his former mentor. The Chosen One was the only person who could save Abdul from his torment. Mustafa grabbed Abdul's foot and dragged him to the ground. Then, surmising his power, he threw Abdul at a nearby building. The man crashed through the clay walls and struck through the other side. Mustafa stood there panting in agony, hoping that had stopped Abdul. But it was nowhere near enough to put down this seemingly immortal man. Abdul fired pure cosmic energy at the building, exploding the entire structure. Smoke scattered across the entire bazaar. No one could see anything. It suddenly grew extremely quiet and the only person in the center of all the destruction was The Chosen One. Mustafa heightened his senses and listened carefully to predict Abdul's movements amidst the smokescreen. But he couldn't hear a thing.

Suddenly, the ground shook violently. Mustafa looked down. Abdul jumped from within the sandy floor. He leaped up by surprise and grabbed Mustafa by his throat. Abdul lifted him, then ran forward, shoving Mustafa through the wooden stage. The Chosen One bled violently and could feel his crimson essence spill across his garbs. Abdul grabbed Mustafa again, using telekinesis this time.

Controlling the man like an object, he damaged him at will. Abdul swung Mustafa into the wall of a nearby building. He screamed as his back struck the stone wall. Abdul dragged Mustafa across the sand, scraping his face along the terrain. He turned around and flung Mustafa into the stands by the stage. The Chosen One crashed through several of them. The shattering sounds were violent. Mustafa's body contorted in painful directions from the force of momentum.

Once again, the watching Nephilims screamed. They begged Abdul to stop, but knew he wouldn't listen to their plea. Instead, several Nephilms, ones not drastically affected by age, attempted to attack Abdul. They ran towards the prophet and threw nearby objects at him. It was ineffective. Then, they tried to grab Abdul. The four of them pounced onto the man and tried to subdue him. But Abdul was far too strong for them. The prophet surged his overflowing power and released a burst of pure energy. It knocked all the Nephilims away. They hit several foreign objects and suffered injuries in the process of defending The Chosen One. Abdul was becoming relentless with those who opposed him. He lifted one of the Nephilims with telekinesis. It was impossible to break out of his invisible grip. Abdul had nothing but evil in his heart now. He glared at his victim with no emotion whatsoever. Just like He, the prophet lost all attachment to Nephilims he once called kin. As a result, they had all become disposable to him. Abdul squeezed his open palm into a fist and crushed the innocent Nephilim's throat, killing him instantly.

The wails grew louder. Everyone was in shock by what had just happened. Without any hesitation, the servant of god had killed a fellow Nephilim. His body became lifeless as it fell back to the ground. Abdul stood over The Chosen One, looking down upon his former protégé. "Do you see? This is the consequence. If you believe that balance must exist in the universe and that reaction and causation remain true, then opposing me will result in your death, Mustafa. Now, boy, I will give you one final chance to walk a different path. I will give you one final chance to join me in my endeavors. Perhaps He will spare you when he realizes that you won't completely squander your fortunate evolution."

Mustafa looked at the dead body of his fellow Nephilim. It deeply saddened him and extremely angered him. If he didn't stop Abdul, then more people would die at his hands. His entire race would be wiped out by He. It was time to put this to rest.

Fueled by intense emotion, Mustafa retaliated. He arose from the ground and struck Abdul with his fist, directly in his chin. Abdul skyrocketed into the air from the powerful hit. Mustafa caught him with telekinesis and swung him down into the ground with tremendous force. The prophet collided with the ground so hard that it shook and cracked. It sent the surrounding furniture scattering in multiple directions. Mustafa charged up immense energy and started levitating into the air. She had delivered a large amount of her energy into The Chosen One. Mustafa's eyes and hair glowed. Strange hieroglyphs surrounded his head, emitting a bright golden color. The wind raged beneath his floating form, almost forming a tornado.

The Chosen One's voice was incredibly powerful, echoing across the entire village. "Abdul! You are no longer a prophet of religion! You are no longer a servant of the gods! You have failed your people and have chosen power over the evolution of the universe! No being should ever kill their own in cold blood! And for that, you must pay by having yours spilled!" Mustafa raised an open palm into the air. Suddenly, an immense amount of cosmic energy surged into his hands. It formed a concentrated orb of pure elemental fury, enough to surely kill Abdul. Without any other choice, She felt the need to aid Mustafa in this violent altercation. Mustafa swung his hand downward, throwing the orb of powerful energy down at Abdul. It struck the surface like a meteor and exploded, destroying the nearby buildings. It plumed into a mushroom cloud, smoke rising hundreds of feet into the air.

Dust scattered across the entire village and ashes fell from the empty sky. Luckily, no one else was hurt from the concentrated attack. The Nephilims had already reached a safe distance to avoid getting hurt amidst the supernatural conflict. After it was all said and done, Mustafa gently floated to the ground, completely exhausted from pushing his limits so far. He could no longer sense Abdul's energy. It had become obvious that he did what was necessary. He eliminated his former mentor and once-good friend. He had to do it to protect his people and serve his duty as The Chosen One. Killing Abdul was the only way to put the war between science and religion to an end. Free Will would finally be able to begin the next era.

Act 4 – Passage 5

Or so he thought. Suddenly, a massive surge of energy spiked within the cloud of dust and ashes. The ground shook violently and storms brewed in the Space skies above. It was Abdul, undefeated, and very much still alive. Just like She, He had imbued a tremendous amount of his power into the Nephilim. He had done it just in time to make his catalyst immune to Mustafa's powerful attack. Abdul arose from the ground, almost entirely manipulated by the corrupted energy of the Twin god. His eyes and hair glowed with a glossy black color.

"You cannot kill me, Mustafa! I am the determined bringer of the end. The universe will begin anew. And I shall be He's Chosen One. So now, *you* must die!" Abdul shouted, his voice echoing from the power of a god.

Mustafa was no longer strengthened by She. It had become clear that her counterpart was willing to go to greater lengths to succeed with his vision of the universe's evolution.

Abdul dashed forward at an unforeseeable speed. He grabbed Mustafa by his face and slammed him into the ground at tremendous force. He instantly broke multiple bones in The Chosen One's body. Abdul lifted him into the air and started draining a large amount of energy from The Chosen One's life force. Mustafa screamed in pain as if he could feel his very DNA being tampered with.

His energy became visible in the atmosphere. A golden color could be seen escaping Mustafa's body and evaporating into the atmosphere. Abdul persisted in this merciless attack until there was no power left in The Chosen One. He dropped Mustafa to the ground, the man now defenseless.

Once again, Abdul stood over Mustafa. His staggering strength had become extremely intimidating. "Now that you can't defend yourself, it only makes sense to put you out of your misery. I wish it could have been different, Mustafa. But the gods are far more powerful than you could ever imagine. She is a fool to relinquish her power to us in such a careless way. Why? Because we mortals don't have the physical prowess, the intellectual capacity, nor the spiritual alignment to do what's right for the cosmos. That type of Determination must be left to the higher beings. That's what they were made for. The second Free Will allows us to take the laws of nature into our own hands, is the second the universe would end from our own self-destruction. I'm just guaranteeing a new world after everything ends. But if we were left to unknowingly create our own demise, how could we ever ensure that our end won't be the final moments of the universe? How could we leave something behind for the future when we, ourselves, destroy everything? It's in the foreseeable nature of our kind. Of *all* living beings that may come to exist in the universe. He simply wants to start over to prevent endless war from being the result of evolution over the next several billion years. To me, that's a worthy cause," Abdul said powerfully.

Mustafa started questioning what was right and what was wrong. Regardless of what the twin gods had been struggling over, it was clear that Abdul had killed one of their own. That was the true reason to oppose him. He was willing to slay another mortal for his own gain. Despite having no true power left, Mustafa attempted to attack Abdul. He stumbled onto his feet and swung a dazed fist at the man. Abdul just stepped to the side and watched The Chosen One pathetically fall to the ground.

Abdul sighed. "Fine. If you refuse to hear my words, then I will not listen to yours. I'm sorry, Mustafa. But your death is the true harbinger of a new beginning." Abdul grabbed Mustafa by the back of his neck with his left hand. He lifted the man into the air and placed his right hand on his back. Abdul carried Mustafa high above his head. Then with extreme force, he swung Mustafa down, driving his knee into The Chosen One's back. There was a powerful crack as

Mustafa screamed in excruciating pain. Blood poured from the man's mouth. The surrounding Nephilms screamed in terror at the gruesome sight. They cried in unison. They begged Abdul to cease his attack. Even Qadira, who had gotten back up during the fight, begged for her husband's mercy. She carried their daughter in her arms, scared that she would lose her father.

Abdul tossed Mustafa to the ground where he sprawled out, unable to move. The damage to his spine had completely paralyzed him. "Now you draw much closer to death, Chosen One. I have to put you out of your misery."

The prophet almost pitied the man who had been the greatest change for the entire universe. But it was time for the mantle to pass on to another. She had misguided The Chosen One and led him down a path that could destroy the previously-intended trajectory of existence. Now it was Abdul's duty to cleanse the worlds of Free Will before it could tear apart the results of Determinism.

Abdul grabbed Mustafa again, clutching The Chosen One's throat. He lifted him. The civilian Nephilims continued screaming, demanding their savior's release. But Abdul set his intentions and followed them stubbornly. They were the words of his god, He. "Follow me if you wish, mortals. But I highly doubt you could stomach watching your beloved Chosen One die. god knows I can't bear to see this happen, but I must, to protect the universe. Abdul teleported to a seemingly unknown location.

The crowd of Nephilims was sent into another frenzy, losing all hope. Qadira quickly harnessed more of her energy, sending most of it to her mind. Heightening her senses, she was able to detect Abdul's teleportation trail. She could also detect her husband's heartbeat from miles away. "Everyone! Follow me! I can sense my husband's heart across the stars. Abdul is *not* getting away from us! I'll teleport to their location and disclose it to you telepathically! We have to help save him!" Qadira shouted. The surrounding Nephilims nodded in understanding. They prepared themselves. Qadira handed her child to a civilian for protection.

As promised, she teleported to Mustafa and Abdul's location. Then, she quickly disclosed their location to the other Nephilims so they could aid her in rescuing her husband. The former mentor and protégé were at the edge of a cliff. The same location Abdul had teleported Mustafa when he yanked him from the machine that enhanced his communicative capabilities. They were in the wasteland plains. The distant vegetation was scattered around towering trees. High rocks and wildlife were accenting the area. From the empty sky, no rain could fall. However, the atmosphere remained gray. The entire aura set by this drastic conflict saddened the entire planet.

Finally, Qadira was joined by many of the Nephilims that had been informed of their location, including the woman who was cradling her child. Abdul continued holding a crippled Mustafa at the edge of the cliff, seemingly ready to end the man's life.

"Abdul! Please! You don't have to do this! There has already been so much death with the blight of mortality. How could you so cold-heartedly want to end the life of someone you once called your own? *You* are the one who brought Mustafa into this world! Yes, he may have evolved through natural occurrences in the ocean, but he would have never been able to change the face of our species without your help! It's your guidance that has helped him satisfy all his needs, helped him achieve self-actualization! You must take pride in that Abdul. I can see it in your eyes. You still have a love for Mustafa, like he was a child of your own. And having our daughter has taught both Mustafa and I about the concept of family. Being so willing to lay your life on the line for someone so dear to your heart. Mustafa is like family to you. And I know he would gladly lay his life on the line for you. So how could you choose to end *his*? Please... Abdul. Don't kill my husband. Don't kill our child's father," Qadira said, overflowing with emotion.

Abdul looked back at the woman. He locked eyes with every Nephilim that watched the scene transpire. But before he could feel regret, hatred consumed him. The god, He, consumed him. "Mustafa. You shall die the same way you were made, in violence," the prophet said. While clutching Mustafa's throat with his left hand, Abdul formed energy around his right hand. It took the shape of a sharp blade, powerful enough to cut through any surface. Then, Abdul brutally stabbed Mustafa through his chest, watching his arm shove through the other side of the man.

"No!" Qadira screamed. Mustafa could do nothing more than rest eyes on his wife and daughter one last time. He gave one final smile to his family.

Abdul couldn't help but cry to himself. He had just slain the most important Nephilim in his life. The most important Nephilim in the universe. The prophet released The Chosen One's body and let him fall into wasteland plains. The dense fog at the bottom masked the gruesome end to the savior of the third Eon. Just as war destroyed a realm before existence and led to the conflict of paramount gods, war killed the most significant mortal in the present.

Qadira dropped to her knees in absolute shock. The Nephilims wailed in sorrow. They were completely mortified. The men and women prepared themselves to attack Abdul. To them, it seemed that the only justice Abdul would ever see would be in his own death. The first, most intense act of violence bred hatred across the species. Now, more Nephilims were willing to spill the blood of one of their own. This was an important part of He's intentions for the feeble mortals. They were likely to destroy themselves someday and that made them corrupt in his eyes. Expendable.

But before anyone could attack, Qadira's energy spiked. It shook the edge of the cliff and gusted winds. Rage consumed her. The woman levitated from the ground, exuding an extraordinary amount of cosmic force. "You cold, heartless bastard! Kill you! I'll kill you, Abdul!" Qadira screamed. She charged toward Abdul with extreme speed, but before she could end the prophet's life, her limits were revealed. Qadira could see He within Abdul. This terrifying godly force within him. It had become clear that the man was completely consumed by the Twin god. He was a pawn in his wretched endeavor to wipe the universe's slate clean. Qadira attempted to strike Abdul but was stopped by He's force. A faint image of He's form appeared before her, more intimidating than anything she had seen before. Abdul, powered by the force of a god, struck Qadira in her face with his fist. He broke several bones in her jaw and even in her body. She was knocked back into the crowd of Nephilims, immediately beaten down. The civilians held the woman, attempting to shield her from any further danger.

"No one else should dare oppose me. He and I are one. I will become a god over you soon enough. I will finally resolve this cataclysmic occurrence and destroy the child. I must destroy any possibility of Free Will thriving in our realm. Now hand me the girl!" Abdul demanded. The Nephilims banded together to protect Qadira's child. But Abdul was far too strong for them to stand a chance. Abdul simply motioned his hand to the left and knocked the Nephilims down to the ground with intense force. He used telekinesis and shoved them aside, creating a direct path to the child. Abdul saw the woman who protected the child. She looked prepared to lay her life down for a being that couldn't even speak. This sickened the prophet. Such irrational behavior was not what the Nephilims lived by. Abdul raised a finger and fired a cosmic beam of energy at the woman's head. It pierced through the front of her skull and exited the back. Blood spilled. The woman's body collapsed to the ground as Abdul caught the child in his hands.

Qadira begged from her crippled position on the ground. "Please! No! Abdul! Don't hurt my child! I'm begging you! Show mercy!" she shouted. Her voice was breaking from sheer terror and sorrow.

Abdul walked to the edge of the cliff. His footsteps were heavy. It was as if the burden he carried as He's Chosen One weighed too much on him. The daughter and her mother wailed loudly. They cried in unison. Qadira couldn't bear to see her newborn child be brutally murdered. Although the child couldn't comprehend what was happening, she could sense her father's presence disappear. She could sense her mother's pain. And that caused her pain too. It was an unspeakable bond that no Nephilim could truly understand. It was only a bond that existed between a mother and a child.

Abdul looked at the child's crying face. He listened to its pain. "Then I shall return you to your father soon enough," the prophet said, emotionless. He raised the girl high above his head and with little hesitation, threw her off the edge of the cliff.

"No!" Qadira shouted.

The civilian Nephilims screamed in terror at the horrifying sight. No matter how unified their efforts, Abdul had been imbued with extraordinary power. It was as if he had become a god himself, using his newfound prowess to change the face of existence without any real interference. Qadira, with broken bones in her body, crawled to the edge of the cliff as quickly as she could. As she looked over the edge, into the infinite fog of the wasteland plains, nothing could be seen. Her daughter was gone. She had been thrown into the same grave as her father. Qadira cried so deeply to herself that she made no sound. She buried her face in the dirt, her tears turning the dirt into mud.

Abdul did nothing more than look down at the woman with pity. "I would send you to die with your family Qadira, but perhaps that would be showing you too much mercy. No. You deserve to live with the consequences of your actions. In too many instances you have influenced Mustafa to side with science more times than religion. You allowed him to find She. You protected him. And for that, you have brought these consequences onto yourself. My god, He, has determined this as the fate of your family," he said. Abdul removed his eyes from the bawling woman. Now he faced the crowd of Nephilims. They gazed at him, mortified. "I'm so sorry you all had to see such a vicious display of violence. However, it was necessary to end Free Will's timeline. You know why I'm supporting He. Should we be able to create on our own, there will be no reason for the gods to mettle in our affairs. If we dictate a child's life, then the gods can no longer dictate ours. The mantle of creation will be handed to us. And unfortunately, my fellow Nephilims, we don't deserve it." Abdul closed his eyes in serenity. His goal had finally been achieved.

Act 4 – Passage 6

Once Abdul opened his eyes, he suddenly saw a change in the expressions of the Nephilims standing before him. Their eyes no longer showed fear of him as they did moments ago. Now they were gazing upward at something behind him. Abdul slowly turned around, frightened by what he had yet to see. He was stunned. Before him was the child, floating in mid-air. Somehow, she had risen from the depths of the wasteland plains, miraculously unscathed. A strange aura surrounded the girl. An ephemera that faded in and out of existence. Everyone was appalled, including Qadira. Her daughter had been rescued seconds from absolute death.

"How... How is that possible?" Abdul questioned.

The atmosphere at the edge of the cliff had changed dramatically. It felt as if Gravity suddenly increased amongst the Nephilims. There was immense pressure in their hearts. Their minds felt as if they were expanding. Abdul clutched his head in pain. The Nephilims could feel their ears ring, a high-pitched sound staggering them. Qadira's child started floating downward, preparing to land upon the cliff. Abdul stumbled backwards, afraid of what power the girl inexplicably possessed.

Suddenly, in a flash of blinding light, the true source of the child's rescue was revealed. There was a powerful sound of sheer power as a shockwave emitted across the entire continent. The colors of the Space sky changed into a bright, luminescent pink. The entire planet's surface became marked with strange golden hieroglyphs. The Nephilims slowly opened their eyes. Before them was something they would've never thought possible. It was the Twin god, She.

The Twin god had taken a form in this realm. She was made of pure energy from the cosmos. Her body looked like the insides of a Nephilim, with nothing but muscle on the exterior of the bone. She glowed with a faint blue color. Wisps of celestial force swirled around her. Points of chakra pulsated upon She's body with a white flash. The Twin god carried Qadira's child in her arms as she floated above the Nephilims. It was astounding. The Nephilims were in tremendous awe at the sight of their god. All the same, She was ecstatic to finally lay eyes upon her creations face-to-face. They all bore unique presences and energies, but none were like Mustafa's. None except for Qadira and her child. She observed the child's face. Then she looked back at her creations. She softly landed upon the cliff. Abdul stumbled backwards, afraid for his life. He could've never imagined that the Twin god would resort to such drastic measures to save the girl.

"I can hear all your thoughts. Especially yours, Abdul," She said. Her voice echoed across the solar system. "My counterpart resorted to extreme measures to have the child eliminated. Therefore, I decided to mimic his irrational behavior to defend this life." She slowly started walking towards Qadira. With every step, grass and flowers emerged beneath her feet. She controlled the laws of nature and they

beautifully bent at her will. Her very existence bred life and helped the planets thrive. This child was the greatest product of nature that She could have ever created. The Twin god stood before Qadira, towering over the woman at nearly twenty feet tall. The Nephilims themselves never exceeded ten feet in height. She daintily handed the child to Qadira. As their hands touched, Qadira could feel all her wounds miraculously heal. "I am sorry I didn't arrive in time to save The Chosen One. Bless your husband and all his actions to protect your species. Unfortunately, reviving the dead is simply not possible, even with all my power. Now that mortality has greatly ensued upon the Nephilim race, there is no turning back. He has done drastic harm to your kind. But it is at this moment that I will ensure Free Will's survival. More children will be born. And it is in this next generation of mortality that your race will persist. Now that creation is in your hands, we gods will no longer mettle in your affairs. You have the will to do as you please with your kind. Just like the All, we gods will exist in a plane further from your reach. Far from us is where your species will be safest. I have come to realize that we bear imperfections just like you. You come from us, therefore, all of our faults have been yours to inherit. War has come to exist because war was in He and I's spirits. Unfortunately, we have passed that on to your kind. Nephilims, I greatly apologize for all the pain I have caused you."

Abdul panicked as he watched She communicate with the Nephilims. The prophet begged for He to come to this realm and stop his counterpart, but She had prevented the other Twin god from doing so. In arriving at this plane of existence, she simultaneously prevented He from following her. Now terribly afraid, Abdul attempted to attack She. "This will not end! I will not let Free Will destroy the future of our universe!" he shouted. Abdul fired a cosmic blast at She to no avail.

The crowd of Nephilims shrieked in shock. However, She didn't flinch. She simply waved a hand towards Abdul. He evaporated into nothing. In one motion, the god had unmade the man. There was no atomic trace of him left in the universe. Abdul was gone. With him no longer serving as a catalyst to antagonize the rise of Free Will, He's intentions for the universe had surely been stopped.

After handing the child to Qadira, She stepped backwards. She faced her creations one last time, feeling her ethereal form begin to fade. "I cannot guarantee a peaceful future for your kind. All actions from now until the end will be that of your own creation. You have absolute freedom to dictate the results of this universe. I praise your species for your resilience. Perhaps you have taught me a very important lesson about what it means to live. Space exists beyond just stars and planets; there is an invisible bond that ties everything from matter to creatures together. Blessings upon your futures." She bowed before the Nephilims as she faded back to her realm of gods.

Epilogue

In the centuries that followed, Nephilims passed on and Nephilims were born. Many virgin women had given birth to beautiful children, boys and girls alike. Over the years they had grown into adult Nephilims, carrying the mantles of the parents that had provided them with life. At the sacrifice of being immortal, the Nephilims were granted the ability to create using Free Will, without the Determinism of the gods. It required consummation and love to produce a child when they wished. Now the mortals were free to decide the path of the universe as they lived and breathed within it. The future wasn't guaranteed to be peaceful, as the mortals ultimately remained flawed. But the new Eon of Free Will was guaranteed to spark change

among the cosmos. New principles,
new desires, and new freedoms were
capable of creating harmony just as
much as a tragedy.

Eon IV
Free Will

Deep clouds were carved by high towers in the sky. Newly-constructed buildings had become the trademark landscape of various planets across the solar systems. Now crippled by mortality, yet armed with the ability to reproduce, Lesser Nephilims had proliferated to multiple planets in different galaxies. Without the divine powers of their close ancestors, it became rather difficult to simply use cosmic abilities to change the face of the universe. However, at the expense of less control over physics, Free Will had become an innate part of their existence. Now released from the absolute Determinism of the gods, the lesser Nephilims' intellectual capacity had grown beyond just scientific reasoning. They thought much more freely than the ancestors that preceded them. This type of thought, conceived at birth, was the greatest power of the mortals that roamed the universe. With it, technological advancements evolved much faster, and scientific discoveries were made much more rapidly. Although aspects of spiritual pursuits had been neglected, lessons of religion were still heeded by the people. Metamotivation became a staple of all existence and every being sought to live beyond their basic needs. They desired this higher existence through the power of self-actualization, which was first achieved by The Chosen One, Mustafa, many centuries ago.

One of the greatest harmoniously scientific and religious feats of the Lesser Nephilims, now called 'the Children', was their development of an artificial star. Working in tandem with their parents, they were able to navigate building their own Sun. Through the combination of their imaginative capacity and their parents' cosmic force, they began with the collapse of a giant molecular cloud, using hydrogen and helium residue from other stars that had since passed. Because several supernovae emerged near the vicinity of the Aljana galaxy, the Children discovered the possibility of creating a new solar system nearby with this artificial Sun in the center. By initiating a shockwave, the matter to create the Sun was compressed within the initial molecular cloud. The use of Gravity started a rotation, which led to a forcefully sped-up heating process enhanced by the increasing pressure. The disk flattened around the development of the Sun and more planets were able to form within the solar system. As more heat was generated from gravitational pressure, more matter emerged from the disk, leading to nuclear fusion and the complete development of the Sun.

Although this was a magnificent milestone achieved through the cooperation of the Nephilims and their Children, one particular Child sought to do more with the stars nearby. The first Child born in all existence, Gia. She was named by her mother Qadira, The Powerful. Gia was named as a gift from god, specifically She, who had changed the shape of existence to allow the reproduction of Nephilims. Gia had spent her early years of freedom learning everything she could about the universe from her mother and the entire Nephilim race that supported her since birth. With this knowledge and spiritual attunement, she invented a novel device used to harness the power of the stars. Gia, no older than several decades, created a device known as the Dyson Sphere. It was a megastructure designed to harness solar energy from a star and provide it to the Nephilims. With this massive increase in the availability of natural power, the Nephilims immediately started reaching greater heights. Although not as innately powerful as her immediate ancestors, Gia was direct proof of the intellectual prowess that the Children would come to possess. This magnificent advancement made by the first Child came to be the greatest reason why she continues to exist as the most overseeing influencer of the cosmos. Discoveries have been made since and the Children continue to explore their Free Will. Although their Nephilim parents have all come to pass, recent occurrences have led to a new era amongst the universe. The emergence of a new race of beings has startled the current population and forced them into a new kind of intellectual conflict.

Day 5 – 17:51

At the top of a massive building was a collective meeting of some of the universe's brightest minds. The tower, standing over a hundred floors tall, was called *Almukhtar* Industries, founded by Gia and named after her father's evolutionary title. The group of Children sat in a large council room around a glass table, impatiently waiting in silence. Dressed in their various professional garbs, they all hailed from different aspects of royal families or founders of companies. Amidst the awkward silence, repetitive foot-tapping, pen-pushing, and sighing could be heard.

Finally, one man stood up in anger. "That is *it*! I refuse to keep wasting my time! If she isn't even going to show up on schedule, then I'll just leave!" he shouted. The other Children sitting around the table looked up at the man, some in agreement, others not. The man gathered his bags and papers, preparing to leave.

Suddenly, the door to the council room burst open. A woman rushed through the door. Her hair was a soft mix of brown and gold, forming a warm blonde color. Her eyes were orange and her skin was tan. She had a button nose, luscious lips, groomed eyebrows, and was particularly beautiful. It was Gia. Being the first Child in all existence, she looked nothing like her parents, Mustafa and Qadira. Much like other first-generation Children, they looked nothing like the Nephilims that gave them life. They had skin, visible faces, and were very similar in their anatomical makeup. This appearance of the species marked the rise of a new era for mortality. All beings who were born thereafter resembled Gia and Gia resembled them.

Gia, the founder of *Almukhtar* Industries, was the one who called this meeting. She wore her professional garb as well but was clearly exhausted. She missed a button on her jacket and her pants had a stain on it. Perhaps from a carbonated drink she spilled bumping into one of her workers in the lobby? Her eyes were bloodshot and her hair was messy.

"You're not going anywhere, Mr. Tadashi! I apologize for my tardiness, but there are clearly many matters to attend to right now," Gia said.

Tadashi finally sat down in his chair again. "You cannot constantly be late to your own meetings Gia. You supersede everyone in seniority, yet you don't seem to have appropriate etiquette when it comes to conducting business," he said callously.

Gia just rolled her eyes. Mortality meant that every being would now die of age. However, there was a strange absence of consistency. Children with poor health would die much sooner than those who remained in great health. Any age difference only seldom affected the point of passing. Gia, clearly older than any of the other Children in the universe, still appeared to be much younger than her peers. Her wrinkles were minimal, her skin still glowed, and her figure was voluptuous. Regardless of her age, Gia was still sought after by many men as prime for reproduction. She ignored them all. Gia stood at the front of the room, facing everyone sitting around the massive table. Twenty-Five of the universe's brightest minds were here. Yet Gia wanted to start by saying, "my intellectual pursuits and spiritual practices are what keep me looking so young by the way."

Everyone sighed in embarrassment. Gia was not as flawless a leader as her father. "Look. The most recent circumstances are what kept me preoccupied. Now I must fill in the rest of you about what has been going on for the past several days. A new species has arrived. They are beings from another dimension and to put it quite simply, they are the greatest threat to our entire universe," Gia explained.

"Gia. What are these beings exactly?" a woman asked.

"There isn't much to say. But from what we were able to gather, these beings are ancient. They have possibly existed even before our Nephilim ancestors. They are extremely powerful and bear an intellectual capacity by the likes of which we cannot comprehend."

"What do they want with us? Why did they suddenly arrive in our dimension?" a man asked.

Gia started pacing the floor. "It's hard to say. But they didn't show up in Eon III with our ancestors. We believe that these beings came to our dimension after suddenly being able to sense our ability to reproduce. Something in the change from Determinism to Free Will seems to have triggered their arrival. They don't seem to have malicious intent. They simply seem to perceive us as study subjects. And our dimension is grounds for them to play in, taking what they please, whenever they please. However, this is synonymous with the behavior of the paramount gods Eons ago. And that's what makes them such a dangerous threat."

"Inconceivable! If they're so dangerous, then we should hurry and figure out how to stop them! Gia, my sources have reported that you and your guard have managed to capture one of these beings. Why don't you interrogate it and have it yield their weakest assets?" Tadashi asked.

"Because it's not that simple Mr. Tadashi! First and foremost, they speak an ancient tongue that we cannot translate. Their language emerges as nothing more than soundwaves to our ears. I have my top scientists working to decipher it. So far the only thing that we have been able to translate is their name. They call themselves Skandhas. They are sentient beings with more powers and a greater intellect than us. I'm sure many of you are unaware of the true danger of this species. But on the outskirts of our galaxy, we discovered missing pieces in our star charts. And the cosmic microwave background radiation has drastically fluctuated. Men and women, they took our distant planets! Just… took them into their own dimension! Along with everyone living on them! I would rather we defend ourselves against a race that powerful. Not engage in the offensive," Gia explained grimly.

The other members in the council room hung their heads in distraught. They were shocked at the magnitude of this situation.

Another woman, one of Gia's friends, raised her hand quietly. Gia pointed to her. "Ma'am. We can tell that the arrival of the Skandhas has put our kind in dire straits. But what do you suggest we do if we cannot go to war?" she asked. Her name was Leilani.

Gia walked over to a window east of her position and stared out into the distant sky. She sighed miserably. But her confidence remained intact. This wasn't going to stop her. She was motivated to end this conflict without many more deaths. "Leilani, I appreciate your question. I don't wish to go to war with something this powerful. If we attack them, they may be strong enough, so god-like, that they just take our entire universe into their dimension. If we make a strike, we would lose. Our only option now is to

understand them. Use the power of the knowledge," Gia explained. She turned back towards the council of Children. "We will need all hands on deck. Everyone, whether you run a company or have royalty in your blood, allocate all resources towards understanding the Skandhas. I am planning on transporting one division of my guards, scientists, and prophets into the desolate sections of the universe. They can study any residue left by the Skandhas in Space to try and learn more about them. I'm hoping they can also find any survivors who haven't been sucked into the other dimension. The other half of my squadron will remain in our galaxies and research ways to defend ourselves from another onslaught like the one that occurred five days ago. We have one of their own, so it may be safe to assume pissed off Skandhas will come looking for it. We want to be prepared to defend ourselves from having our planets taken. Everyone, provide me with what you've researched so far so I may take it down to the lab."

The Children in the council room all stood up and handed papers to Gia in a single-file line. Leilani was last. "Ma'am. My scientists may have discovered something significant," she said. The woman handed a stack of folders to Gia.

Gia snatched them, letting the intensity of the situation corrupt her manners. She quickly read the papers and memorized all of the information. The discovery was startling. "Wait… this doesn't make sense. You're saying that the Skandhas are here looking for someone?" Gia asked.

Leilani nodded. "We're not certain. But the Skandhas left strange hieroglyphs in the sector of the universe that they took. It appears as though they are trying to communicate something with us. The language is still outdated, but we have determined that the message left behind says, 'woman'. We believe that they are possibly in our dimension in search of one of our own, but we don't know who," she explained.

Gia gripped the folders tightly in one hand. She grunted in inspiration and frustration synchronously. "Come with me to the lab. You can talk to one of my scientists about this."

Day 5 – 18:08

Gia and Leilani were inside an elevator. The metal carriage transported them down to the lower floors of *Almukhtar* Industries via a hollowed-out shaft. They could see the artificial lights in the shaft cross their faces as they moved downward. Gia glanced up at a strand of her hair that was out of place all day. She sighed and blew at it to no avail.

Gia, Founder of Almukhtar Industries and Overseer of Eon IV

Leilani looked over at her dear friend. "Ma'am. You know, you could always take some time to rest. You're exhausted. There's no guarantee that the arrival of the Skandhas means the end of our universe. Who's to say that planets being taken into another dimension means they're destroyed? It's uncertain just how much of a real threat these ancient beings are," she said.

Gia glanced at her friend with a look of profound motivation. "And that is *precisely* why I have to work twice as hard. If I don't determine their true reason for being in our dimension, no one will. I have to protect all Children. I won't have the Skandhas toy with our dimension like we're just subjects of research," she said intensely. Leilani nodded silently.

Finally, the elevator doors opened as they arrived in the lab. Gia handed the stack of folders in her hands to Leilani, shoving them into her chest. Go speak with Xavier. He's the chief scientist of our communications division. He should be in the library. Leilani hurried off north, speeding past Gia. Gia just continued walking forward, deeper into the lab. Every footstep of hers was rather intimidating. If an uninformed Child entered the lab without knowing anyone, they would easily be able to identify Gia as the leader. She moved past a sea of busy scientists and prophets, all working in harmony to study the arrival of the Skandhas. They experimented with matter left behind by the ancient species and attempted to understand them through religious sacraments. But alas, their efforts over the past few days had not yielded many useful results.

Gia was approached by one of her aides; her right hand, Kurtis. The man quickly ran beside the overseer, following the rather fast pace of her footsteps. "Gia. You're finally back. How did the meeting with the council go?" he asked.

Gia just grunted and shook her head.

"That bad huh? Did they at least agree to contribute towards handling the arrival?" Kurtis asked.

Gia nodded. She and Kurtis approached a metal double door with an electronic panel beside it. Gia stuck her thumb in an opening on the panel. It scanned her DNA and opened the two doors.

Gia and her assistant entered. "Activate the teleporter to the sanctuary!" she shouted. Standby scientists in the room started pressing buttons frantically and pulled a massive lever on the wall. Because the Children could not teleport through the use of cosmic ability like their Nephilim parents, they had to rely on science to accomplish such a feat. The teleporter activated, emitting a bright yellow light and a soft hum as its inner confines whirred with activity.

Suddenly, Kurtis stood in front of the overseer, blocking her from entering the teleporter so hastily. "Wait, wait! Gia, what do you intend to do going back into the sanctuary so soon? The scientists you assigned to stay with the Skandha could hardly have made any progress in a few short hours," he said.

Gia looked up at Kurtis, staring directly into the man's handsome eyes. "Leilani provided me with some profound information that her researchers were able to find in Space. The Skandhas left a message in one of our oldest languages. They are here looking for a woman. They want one of our own, Kurtis. I'm going to find out who that is *immediately*. I promised the Children that I would always do what I can to protect them. And by the god of She, I'm going to understand why the Skandhas are here if it's the last thing I do!" she said powerfully. Gia walked into the teleporter. Kurtis hesitantly followed her. They were both transported to an exclusive sector on a remote planet. The sanctuary was an artificially-terraformed planet specifically allocated for research on any astronomical occurrence that was of utmost importance to the Children. Most recently, it had become the heart of where the studies of the arrival were held. Gia's greatest scientists gathered here to collectively use their minds to defend the universe.

Day 5 – 18:16

The overseer and her assistant came out the other end of the teleporter. Stardust plumed up into the air, a natural residue left behind after any teleportation. Gia stood firmly in her position, hardly staggered by the effects. Kurtis however, was not as accustomed to teleporting as her. He swayed back and forth, dazed from the effects on his body. Gia grabbed him by his shoulder, forcing him to stand still and collect himself. She brushed the stardust off her clothes and cracked her neck. Although without a clear plan for this visit to the sanctuary, she was still greatly determined to get information out of the Skandha. The new evidence presented by Leilani had managed to bring them one step closer to discovering this ancient species' true reason for arriving in their dimension.

The sanctuary was a miraculously beautiful planet, hence its name. It was full of luscious grass, mountainous plains, and a pristine orange sky. Gia whistled loudly. Suddenly, a man operating a small mobile vehicle with wheels drove up next to them. Gia and Kurtis quickly got inside, Gia sitting beside the operator and Kurtis in the backseat.

"Take me to subject alpha. It's about time we get some answers out of this thing," Gia ordered. The operator nodded and sped off north across the plains.

Gia arrived at a massive, impenetrable glass pod. It was approximately fifty feet tall and a mile in diameter. Inside the great glass pod was an even greater creature. The Skandha. It stood over thirty feet tall. The ancient being wore no garments. The white sections of its appendages and torso were made of the hardest material the Children had ever seen. Upon the white armor were strange traces of what looked like electricity. It moved across the appendages fluidly. Scientists believed it was some type of visible cosmic and spiritual energy. As if the Skandhas were so astoundingly powerful that their spiritual enlightenment displayed a visual effect upon their bodies. In between the white armor was visible red flesh. Blood moved across the Skandhas veins like the traces of its cosmic energy. These vital veins connected to its head; the most abstract part of the being. The Skandhas' heads were perfect flesh-colored cubes. Emerging from the cube was what looked like the roots of a tree, made by its outstretching veins. A fleshy neck comprised the base, with a cube head in the center, and strange roots emerging from the top. Considering the massive size and unique appearance of the Skandha, it was surely the most intimidating creature the Children had ever encountered.

Gia was already equipping a reflective chrome suit and a glass helmet. She connected two tubes at the neck of the helmet into a tank full of air strapped on her back. Kurtis approached the overseer again. "Gia! You're actually going to go *in there* with the Skandha? You're the overseer! We can't possibly have you be harmed in the process. If you need to communicate something with the ancient being, you should have one of the scientists do it," he said.

Gia tightened the helmet and equipped gloves. She approached a scientist guarding the tunnel to enter the pod and nodded at him. As the doors opened, Gia turned around to her assistant one last time. "Kurtis. You have to understand. In dire times like these, it's so important to always go above and beyond what is required. If I only sit by as the overseer and don't take the same risks that I ask of my people, then I shouldn't be leading them. So many Children are putting their lives at risk to figure out just what the hell is going to happen to this universe. It's about time I do the same. We may have weeks left, several days, or just several hours. Besides, I'd hate to see you get hurt if something were to happen to us," Gia said with extreme confidence. She gave Kurtis a soft touch on his shoulder. Finally, she made her way into the tunnels.

Attached to her chrome suit was a communicating device that allowed her to speak with the scientists watching her outside. "Ma'am. Are you sure you don't want one of us accompanying you inside the pod? This could be very dangerous," a male scientist said.

Gia shook her head. "No. I want to do this alone. I want to understand this creature." She moved forward through the tunnel, drawing closer to the captured Skandha. Suddenly, she felt a drastic change in pressure. Her breath grew short and she felt as if she were going to faint. Gia placed her hand on the wall of the tunnel, attempting to regain her footing.

"Ma'am! You have to be extremely careful! Many scientists have reported a change in the atmosphere when near the being. We assume that it serves as some sort of defense mechanism. It's also likely that the dimension it hails from is so astronomically different from ours, that our very matter clashes when we draw near it," the scientist said.

Gia started sweating. She clenched her teeth in pain and adjusted her posture. This wasn't enough to stop her. The overseer persisted down the tunnel until she finally made it into the pod. The natural sunlight grew brighter. She could hear her boots press against the soft grass with every step. Gia approached the center of the pod. The gravity felt five times heavier than what she was used to. The ancient being finally revealed itself.

The Skandha suddenly emerged before Gia. They possessed the powerful gift of invisibility. Particles dispersed into the air as the Skandha withdrew its transparency and revealed its truest form. It was much more intimidating and staggering in person. Gia looked up at the ancient being. She could feel chills run down her spine in suppressed fear.

"Medical and security team remain on standby for the overseer. This could-" Suddenly, the communicative device cut out and Gia couldn't finish hearing the scientist's sentence. The overseer stepped closer, only a few feet away from the Skandha. The massive being stood on its two feet and looked down at her, although it didn't have any visible set of eyes. It emitted a strange sound. They were the results of electromagnetic signals produced by the being. It spoke a strange wind-like hum, then ended with a loud ping. As the Skandha spoke, its fleshy cube head opened, turned, and reassembled its shape, now at a different angle than before.

Gia listened carefully and acted cautiously. "You may be fully capable of understanding our language, but you can't seem to speak in such a way that we can understand yours. I want to know why you Skandhas arrived in our dimension! You're looking for a woman, right? Who is it?" Gia shouted, unintentionally becoming brash.

The Skandha almost cowered in fear. *"Four sharp whistles and a piercing sound of static."* It was loud enough to shake the ground.

Gia and the surrounding crew winced in pain. She could feel the atmosphere change again, draining all the energy she had. Dark circles formed around her eyes and her ears started bleeding. All she continued to hear was static from the communicator; none of what the scientists were saying could get through. Gia looked up at the Skandha, assessing her first approach. "I get it now. I'm sorry. I say that I want to understand you so I should act like it. If I feel threatened, then you will feel threatened. It's just the law of nature. I'll level with you. Whether you know what I'm saying or not. I should let my guard down."

Gia was feeling bold. She was willing to risk everything to protect the Children and learn more about the Skandhas. She took off her protective helmet, directly breathing in the atmosphere of the Skandha. *"A reversed wind noise and 8-bit trill chiptune."*

The scientists panicked. They attempted to open the door to the tunnel to rescue the overseer. But when they tried entering, they realized she had locked the door from the inside.

"Is she insane? She's locked the door!" they shouted.

Gia could feel her body grow extremely weak. Then a phenomenon occurred. All her thoughts had come to life, projected out loud from her mind. *"I could die here..."* she thought as her disembodied voice echoed around the pod. The whole situation was completely frightening. The powers of the ancient being were beyond anything she could have imagined. Gia was willing to go further. She unequipped her chrome suit, revealing her professional garbs underneath. The heat in the area felt as if it was going to burn her skin. Gia stepped closer towards the Skandha, holding out her hand. *"Please... tell me..."* she thought aloud.

The Skandha was reluctant at first but then knelt towards the woman, stretching out its massive, veiny hand. Before they could touch, Gia and the surrounding crew noticed something strange. Gia and the Skandha's matter had suddenly become visible. Particles of various colors were emerging from their separate bodies. They collided in the air and swirled around to form a theatrical dance. Gia looked up at the magnificent sight. *"If you're lost... let me help you..."* she thought aloud. The overseer could feel another drastic change in the atmosphere. This time, in her favor. She was able to regain her breathing and her skin was restoring its color. What she had done worked. Gia decided to reason with the being and speak calmly. She saw a lot of herself in it. It was lost, just like her. Finally, Gia touched hands with the Skandha. And with this single touch of sincerity, everything changed.

Their minds and thoughts projected in absolute sync, at the will of the Skandha. Gia was able to see into the being's thoughts and it had already known all of hers. It was magnificent. What the being had seen in its existence was beyond anything that Gia could understand. The truths, the lies, the new, the old, were all unclearly laid out before her. The period of brief enlightenment was riveting. Gia could almost feel her body, mind, and spirit expand synchronously. A symphony played in her head, composed of natural sounds from the universe that had been formed into a language by the Skandhas. Gia stood there, her eyes wide and glowing with a bright white color. The scientists watched in fear and awe. Then, uncontrollable tears emerged in Gia's eyes. The beauty of what she was experiencing was something that she never wanted to end. Suddenly, Gia's tears turned to blood. The magnificence of the enlightenment was becoming too much to handle. Although they didn't speak the same tongue, she finally learned. Gia finally learned that the ancient beings, the Skandhas, were in search of... her. She passed out from the spiritual intensity.

The Skandha, Ancient Being of another Dimension

Day 11 – 36:00

The crowd of Children all waited patiently. The past few days had brought about drastic changes in Eon IV. Now, in an address being broadcasted to the public, Gia prepared herself to return to the spotlight. *Almukhtar* Industries was a company designed to proliferate the advancement of the Children and address major changes occurring in the universe through discoveries made in Space. The last-minute meeting was finally about to begin.

Gia was being assisted by her elite guard. They helped her limp up the stairs and approach the podium on the large stage. Gia had bandages around her head and she looked as if she was on the cusp of recovering from an illness. The powerful woman, for once, had the appearance of someone with a brand new pair of eyes. As if she was back at square one of this whole situation, starting with a completely different perspective. Gia leaned against the podium, quite tired. Her guards attempted to adjust her posture but she waved her hand towards them, signaling them to withdraw. Gia was strong, more than capable of handling this speech on her own.

She inhaled deeply and exhaled thereafter. "I'm sure most of you have read the reports or received the transmissions that I have suffered a great injury. However, that's not entirely true. Any pain is a worthy consequence for the attainment of a brand new perspective. Yes, I was in a coma for the past six days, but I have managed to endure some form of awakening. Drastic things have happened in the past few days in regards to the Skandhas. The significant information I have been enlightened with is that the ancient beings have entered our dimension in search of me," Gia explained. The crowd gasped in unison, murmurs trailing behind like the reverberated ring of a gong. Gia observed everyone's collective expression. Regardless of the criticism she was receiving, she wanted to continue. "I promise you, we will be working tirelessly to understand why the Skandhas want me. I would hope it's for more than just the influence I have over our universe. There must be something deeper than that. Now that I have recovered, I will immediately return to my work. Warrant Officer Frode will provide everyone with details regarding the incident two days ago." Gia slowly turned and began walking off the stage.

The crowd of Children began taking pictures of her and many more were clamoring at her with more questions. But there was nothing left to say. Since another tragedy happened during Gia's absence, the only thing left for her to do was take action.

Officer Frode took the overseer's place at the podium. He was dignified in a moderately decorated uniform. As a member of the elite guard, Gia had assigned him to report directly on his crew's findings two days ago. "Although many of you know the gist of what occurred, I'm here to provide you with a direct account of my experience in the galactic sector C-15-γ. The Skandhas seem to have taken *another* solar system from our dimension into theirs. Not only that, the ancient beings have done something even stranger and seemingly more catastrophic. The Skandhas returned the first solar system that they took 11 days ago. Galactic sector B-8-α. But this solar system has been returned in a substantially different condition than it was in before the supernatural occurrence. My crew and scientists have reported readings that all the people within the original solar system were returned. They were not technically killed in the process of being kidnapped by the ancient beings. They underwent something far worse…" Frode choked a little while talking. The Children could see the magnitude of fear in his eyes. Frode pressed a button on the podium and a digital presentation emerged behind him, the first slide showing a planet. "They underwent some form of experimentation by the Skandhas. The entire solar system and its people were brutally malformed and biologically mutated in appearance. The Skandhas were capable of rearranging the laws of physics within the solar system and have placed it back in our dimension. The entire chain of planets has been disfigured and destroyed."

The crowd gasped in shock. They saw an image of one of the planets in galactic sector B-8-α. The planet had completely changed shape into some type of twisted triangle. The next few images revealed water raining from mountaintops, trees growing within the ground, and animals dead inside-out. Worst of all was what remained of the people. They were nothing more than deformed shapes of chemically-enhanced flesh. They glowed with bright colors and levitated above the ground, in odd shapes that breathed but could not act. All consciousness, all will, had been removed from them. They remained on the planets as twisted representations of materialism, the matter simply existing upon the surface. The viewing Children were becoming sick as they cried at the gruesome sight of what the Skandhas had done to their own.

There seemed to be no clear reason for this happening. "The only thing clear now is that the Skandhas must be stopped," Officer Frode said grimly.

Day 11 – 39:54

Utilizing a personal vessel, Gia traveled to her next destination. It was another exclusive planet, one that she kept hidden from a majority of the Children. The only people who knew of this place were an elite group of radical scientists and experimental prophets. Gia docked the vessel at a station in the planet's airspace. She exited the ship and walked across an empty space station. The tapping from the heels of her boots echoed loudly. She approached an electronic pad that scanned her hand. After approval, a nearby teleporter was activated. Gia went inside, to which it immediately shut off after usage. This teleporter instantly brought her to the surface of the planet. Docking ships on the outside of the atmosphere and requiring security clearance to enter the surface of the planet were the best ways to keep her secret hidden.

Gia arrived on a grim surface. The landscape of the planet was primarily made up of a gray coal-like mineral. The artificial clouds were black and never escaped the sky. They were specifically designed to keep the con-tents of the small planet hidden. Gia smelled the air. It was full of a faint aroma of smog and chemicals. The ominous atmosphere was something she dreaded every visit, but this was for the betterment of her people. This was the only way to give mortality a fighting chance. "Ground Zero."

Gia entered one of the designated vehicles left for workers on this planet. She drove to her desired destination. Only small areas of this hollowed-out planet were being harbored by Children. All for work-related purposes. No one lived their daily lives here. The fewer the people, the lower the odds of someone discovering the activity being done on Ground Zero. The lower the odds, the better. Gia arrived at a lab and quickly entered the building. After descending through an elevator, she arrived. There was a flurry of scientists and prophets within the large metal room. It was impossible to believe that this much activity was going on in the depths of such a desolate planet.

The elite workers all turned, gesturing and greeting Gia in unison. The overseer stepped out of the elevator and was approached by one particular prophet. A woman, a friend, named Saundra. She was just as beautiful as Gia. Her hair was nearly black and she wore makeup under her eyes. Her skin was dark and her eyes glowed with a soft lavender color. Thick eyebrows, plump lips, and a small frame complemented her tamed personality. Although best friends with Gia, she was nowhere near as brash as the woman and couldn't dream of having as much gusto as her. They went through similar institutions of education when they were younger, only being a few years apart in age. Gia went through extensive studies of science and astronautics while Saundra chose to practice religion and spirituality more. Regardless of the differences between their pursuits, the two Children made a pact long ago to find a way to eliminate mortality and bring about the age of immortality like their ancestor Nephilims once experienced. The powerful promise was what united them on a front today. To put everything, their reputations and their livelihoods, at risk to attempt something so daring that a majority of the population would never be able to understand. This was a chance they were willing to take to help the entire universe.

The women hugged each other upon greeting. "Thank goodness. After I received the transmission of what happened to you, I was so worried that the captured Skandha may have killed you," Saundra said, her voice soft and low.

"You know damn well nothing can kill me. Not even an ancient being hell-bent on taking our entire universe," Gia responded.

"Always have to play the tough card. I'm happy to hear you're okay, Gia. I would've come to visit you, but after the second 'taking', I had no choice but to stay here and continue working."

"That's quite alright. You know I'd do the same."

"What exactly happened with the Skandha?"

Gia sighed. "I just trusted my gut and went against what so many of the scientists had done. If there's one thing my mother taught me, it's to always be forbearing. To love those who criticize you. It serves as motivation to me. So, regardless of what others may have thought, I went into the pod alone and reasoned with the being. But in a tremendous moment where our spirits and minds connected, I swear I saw the faces of gods. I was enlightened for a brief time. Saundra, the intellectual prowess the Skandhas possess is enough to change everything. Even just the knowledge they have almost killed me."

"Fuck me. I can't believe the effect of such a thing. But it gives us all the more reason to try and succeed with what we've worked so hard to accomplish for the Children," Saundra said.

"I couldn't agree more," Gia replied.

The two women were making their way into another building attached to the lab.

"You mind updating me on the current progress?" Gia asked.

"Well, there are still a handful of deaths occurring from the experiments. More of them are entering the next phase though. What we need now is a vessel, a brand new planet. Almost a host of some sort to allow them to thrive. I can't help but feel that we need a push—one big move to set the angels off into eternal success," Saundra explained.

"I get you. We've been pushing them quite hard. But we have to. The angels will be our greatest chance at reigniting immortality in the universe. By god, She, forbid that I die at the hands of the Skandhas, I need to leave something behind for the Children. If the ancient beings finally unleash some large-scale attack and I lose my life, I would hope that we can reach our dream before then. That afterlife will finally be achieved."

There was a massive metallic door between the two friends and their project. They both stood about ten feet apart from each other and equipped keys from their pockets. Gia and Saundra stuck them into two separate keyholes and turned them to the right at the same time. Steam started protruding from the metallic door as it hissed. The massive door split in half, withdrawing into the nearby walls they were attached to. Gia and Saundra shielded their eyes from the steam and entered the mysterious place. They walked down a set of stairs and finally entered the single room that could redefine the entire universe. The single place amongst the stars that could carry the Children into the next Eon.

Saundra flicked a switch and a large panel of lights turned on, revealing the grand size of the pale white room. The only color visible was made by a strange substance floating in the airspace. Stardust. It glowed softly with a light blue color and momentarily blended into any of the millions of colors in the universe. They formed scattered pieces of a rainbow in the room. The smoke on the ground was unique. It wasn't gray, but milky white, and had a puffy appearance. They were clouds on the floor. Strange cages were laid out all across the room with labels. At first glance, it was impossible to tell just what was inside them. Gia and Saundra walked forward, moving north down a hallway made by rows of cages. They approached a large glass casing, much like the pod the Skandha was encased in on Sanctuary. The two friends put on lab coats and goggles. They tied their hair up and entered the glass room.

Years ago, after Gia's mother, Qadira, passed away from natural causes, Saundra was there for her best friend. After learning about the monumental changes her father, Mustafa, had made for the universe, Gia was upset that her parents lost their immortality as a result of their sacrifice for Free Will. She vowed to her mom that she would find a way to cure the Children of the blight of age. She would do everything in her power to restore immortality for future generations in the same or better way that the Nephilims experienced. Shortly after, Saundra lost her siblings and parents to disease long before the appropriate scientific advancements had been made. Since then, Gia and Saundra made a pact to use their intellect to eliminate mortality. They had traveled the universe together and learned from ancient prophecies that detailed the possibility of an afterlife, a life after one dies. The two women had worked on this highly experimental project for nearly a decade now. Their goal: to artificially create this afterlife and a species that could thrive upon it. A species that, once they would pass away, their religious devotion would allow them to live on in another plane of existence. The spe-

cies, angels. A planet called the afterlife.

When age surged through the Nephilims as a treacherous blight, spiritual prophets learned that their anatomical features no longer just became a part of nature. With the rise of Free Will and age, something new became clear to the mortals. The soul. During the birth of the Children and the emergence of age, Nephilims' souls were felt wandering the surface of the planets after death. Now, Gia fears that her parents' souls are lost in some inexplicable plain of nowhere. Their bodies may have decomposed upon death, but the true nature of their beings was left with no home. Gia was determined to create this afterlife. Not only to develop a new immortal species but to create a place for her parents' souls to rest in paradise. By any means necessary.

Gia and Saundra closed the door to the glass room once they got inside. Before them was one of the most staggering products of science and religion ever made in the universe. It was a man hanging on the wall in a unique pose. He was in a "T shape", with his arms stretched out horizontally and his legs together, his feet pointing straight down. The man was kept up against the wall with pure cosmic energy. It glowed with a similar rainbow color as the stardust. The energy warped around his wrists and ankles like shackles. One more was bound across his torso. His head hung downward, making him appear exhausted. There were strange, metal bolts in his forearms and shins, appearing to be the results of disastrous experiments performed on him. This was no ordinary man. He had magnificent wings between his bare back and the wall. They were large enough to carry him and were made of pure, white feathers. This man was an angel. Gia and Saundra approached him. Finally, the man looked up, his eyes golden. He begrudged a smile towards the beautiful women before him.

"And to what do I owe the pleasure of this visit?" he asked, his voice broken and weak. Gia and Saundra looked as if they were trying to contain an overflow of mixed emotions.

"It's good to see you again, Bryan," Gia said.

The angel did nothing more than look into her eyes. It was obvious that he loved Gia. Bryan just briefly directed his attention towards Saundra. He was firm in his position upon the wall, only able to crane his neck. "And what of you, Saundra? Just wanted to give Gia a tour of the experiment that she's worked so hard to create, but lacks the compassion to tend to herself?" Bryan asked mockingly.

"You know it's not like that Bryan. Gia has a lot of things to focus on as the overseer of our universe. If she could visit more often I bet she-" Saundra was cut off.

"I don't wish to hear an explanation from you. I want to hear it from Gia herself. I don't resent her. I simply… missed her. We're all lonely here," Bryan said.

"Bryan. I communicated with one of the Skandhas. And the magnitude of such a feat managed to knock me into a coma for a few days. Then, there was a second taking while I was incapacitated. Beyond that, the ancient beings appear to be manipulating our laws of physics and returning our planets to us severely distorted. I wish I could've come sooner when your evolution finally occurred," Gia explained.

"It's quite alright. Saundra and many of the other elites were here to witness the progress made. I was the first, but several more have followed. Several more have almost fully developed into angels."

"Yes! Your wings are magnificent. I'm so proud of you! And if we continue to follow the steps accordingly, the afterlife could become a reality. You're almost a complete angel now! The next step is to find a planet for all of you to be free. As long as this new home has enough cosmic energy, the angels will ascend to the next divine level. And perhaps be the first link to immortality since the Nephilims' extinction! The Children could achieve the once-fabled afterlife, thanks to your sacrifice."

"I appreciate your enthusiasm. It's something that everyone, including me, love about you Gia. But much harm has been done to the universe by the Skandhas. Whether you finally succeed with creating the afterlife is a race against time," Bryan said.

"I'm well-prepared to make any and every sacrifice for all the angels here. For *you!*"

"You have to think beyond narrow borders, Gia. That's something I have learned during this experiment. If you want to succeed in opening the gates of the afterlife, you must be prepared to make an even greater sacrifice than all the angels here."

"I understand. This process is one where I have chosen to become a student. You all teach me as you fundamentally attain a level of spirituality higher than any of the Children in the universe."

"Although your sacrifice isn't evident now, it will become clear in the future. Regardless of the outcome, we must all help and strengthen each other. This principle greatly applies to the Skandhas entering our dimension. Perhaps they're not the enemy that we're claiming them to be. *All* of us must help each other. Remember that Gia and Saundra. Then the afterlife isn't too far in the future," Bryan said profoundly.

Gia smiled at the angel. She reached up and touched his face softly. Bryan closed his eyes. The touch from the beautiful woman warmed what remained of his heart. The intense scientific sacraments and religious experiments performed upon this large pool of volunteer subjects had helped them ascend to a powerful spiritual level. It took this spiritual enlightenment of Children to reach the proverbial afterlife, where immortality supposedly existed once more. "I will heed the words you told me. And I will check on the other angels before continuing to work. It's time to find a vessel to create the afterlife so the next step can be achieved. Thank you, Bryan," Gia said.

Bryan smiled at her softly. He watched as Gia and Saundra walked away. Becoming an angel was the greatest aspect of Free Will. Regardless of everything happening in the universe, the choice to make sacrifices for others became the pinnacle of acting on one's own accord. Bryan closed his eyes as he continued hanging from the wall. An angel whose wings had not been put to use yet. "You're welcome... mother."

*Saundra, Radical Prophet
of Ground Zero*

Day 14 - 08:15

Fortunately for the Children, they had not experienced a Skandha attack for quite some time. Gia wanted to take advantage of the momentary standstill in this abstract cosmic war. She had visited the captured Skandha once more and studied it within the dome. Gia took care of avoiding physical contact with the being for now. It was too dangerous to risk falling into another coma or possibly something worse. She could still feel fragments of the Skandha's enlightenment piece themselves together in her mind over time. The abundant information only seemed to assemble itself and make sense when she was in the presence of the ancient being. So for the past several days, Gia made sure to visit the Skandha first thing in the morning on Sanctuary. She would meditate in its presence for an hour or so, attempting to recollect whatever knowledge she could. The Skandha avoided contact with her after the last incident. It just watched her, intrigued.

After her meditation today, Gia returned to her home planet to visit a very significant group of Children for the next phase in her plan. If the afterlife could be achieved, then perhaps all the damage the Skandhas would cause could be avoided. Immortality could save them all. The overseer stepped out of the backseat of a vehicle being driven by her guards. She wore glasses, a black jacket, and heels. "Ma'am. Do you want us to accompany you inside?" a guard asked as he closed the door behind her. Gia shook her head. "No thanks. I wouldn't want any of the guards to intimidate them. If I want their help, it's very important I be as loving towards them as possible," she said. Gia grabbed her bag and walked forward, marching up a set of stairs. They led up to a set of traditional buildings that belonged to a society of powerful monks.

At the top of the stairs, Gia approached a gilded gate. She rang a small golden bell by tugging on a hanging string. The gate opened automatically and she entered the grounds of the temple. Amidst the tile floors were various plants that symbolize tranquility and spiritual enlightenment. Gia took a right at a pond and came to her designated building, stopping beside a garden of vegetation. She slid a wooden door open and removed her shoes before going inside.

Gia was approached by three monks. They were women with their hair shaved off. They wore gilded robes and had glowing stars floating behind their heads in the shape of a circle. The practices of the spiritual monks involved complete immersion in minimalism, chastity, and becoming one with the laws of nature. It took rigorous years of devoting their lives to nature for them to achieve such spiritual prowess. They were the only Children in the universe who could ever come close to contending the power of the Skandhas. Gia quickly removed her glasses and tucked them onto her shirt. She bowed before the monks and they bowed before her. One monk, in particular, stood in front of the other two. There was a unique gem on her forehead. It was a golden infinity symbol, protecting the almighty third eye of enlightenment she had achieved years ago. Her skin was a soft pink and completely immaculate. Her eyes were beautiful and her smile bore a tooth on the left side that was genetically smaller than the others, making it look out of place. But something was appealing about the unique trait. The leading monk's name was Xue.

"Overseer. It is such a surprise and honor to be in the presence of perhaps the greatest influence on our people. How may we help you during these trying times?" she asked, her voice soothing.

Remembering just how desperate she was, Gia wanted to take her greeting a step further. Although she didn't practice much religion and focused on her studies of science, she was at the mercy of the spiritual capabilities of her people. She profoundly respected what the monks had achieved and almost wished to make up for any years that she accidentally neglected the importance of religion. It was surely the other half of science. Gia knelt before Xue and bowed before her by placing her hands and forehead on the straw floor. Gia postured back up, still on her knees. "I'm so sorry for the exaggerated formalities. Xue, I'm here seeking great assistance from what the monks have been able to achieve. I wish to see the Wise Ones. Their supernatural capabilities are needed to make some very important preparations to protect ourselves from the Skandhas," she explained. Xue's expression changed into one of great seriousness. She motioned Gia to stand up.

"The Wise Ones? Ma'am. They may be astronomically gifted in the ways of science and religion through an anomaly granted at birth, but they lack the intellectual development to understand the real dangers of the Skandhas' potential return," Xue said.

"I know. But they're capable of more than the monks allow here at the temple. The power to create and terraform planets is unlike anything the Children have seen before," Gia said.

"The monks have taken the Wise Ones out to practice terraforming upon lone celestial bodies before, but doing so in the name of war with ancient beings is something I cannot condone."

"This is not about the war Xue. This is about our race achieving immortality before the Skandhas have a chance to completely obliterate us."

"Immortality? How do you plan to revert our kind to the Eon of Nephilims? We monks don't agree with resorting to the past to correct our present. We look towards the future. The universe and Free Will have unfolded this way for a reason. You can't possibly want to throw away everything your father has worked so hard to achieve," Xue said sternly.

"Just because we restore immortality doesn't mean we will incur the same mistakes as our ancestors. And it certainly doesn't mean Free Will can't exist with immortality. I intend for it to be different this time. Not a blind power granted to us. This immortality will be achieved through all our hard work. We must all unite together to survive this looming catastrophe. We can finally reach the afterlife," Gia said.

Xue gasped. "The afterlife? Impossible. As foretold in the ancient text? A place where our lives can continue in another plane of existence?"

"Exactly. I've been working on it for years now. It is so important that I take a leap and see this through. The Skandhas want *me*. No matter what happens, I'm prepared to make any sacrifice necessary for the Children. But not until I take the chance to leave some form of immortality behind after I'm gone."

Xue nodded silently. She could see the magnitude of this goal light a fire in Gia's eyes. Something so noble had to be in alignment with the practices of the monks' religion. "Your intentions have touched me. I will bring you to the girls," Xue said.

She and her two monks guided Gia across the gardens of the temple. They arrived at another small building where many young Children roamed and played happily, none more than twelve years old. All monks were female. Even the little girls had their heads shaved. Many of them danced around the garden and chased each other. Some noticed Gia and were enamored by her presence. They gasped in awe and pointed at the overseer. Gia blushed slightly.

"Run along girls. The overseer is here for a very important task," Xue said, shooing away the lovely Children. Their laughs faded into the distance. The two monks slid open the door to the small building and welcomed Xue and Gia to enter. They stepped in.

Inside this building was the help that Gia felt she so desperately needed to achieve her goal and change the course of the universe. Xue stood before her. "The Wise Ones are in the next room. Remember how young they are, Gia. The magnitude of what you may have them help with could be extremely intimidating. But they are always willing to make the world a better place. You just need to show them how in a way that they can un-

derstand," she explained.

Gia nodded and took a deep breath. Xue guided her to the nearby room and slid the door open. Inside were twelve little girls. However, they didn't behave much like the monk girls outside. They all sat in the room in silence, meditating. They opened their eyes when they felt Xue's presence.

"Wise Ones! You have a visitor. The overseer. She has a very special task that she would like you to help with. Are you willing to listen to her words?" Xue asked, her tone completely changing into a bright one for the girls. The twelve girls all withdrew their crisscrossed legs and sat comfortably. They nodded in unison. "I will be waiting outside," Xue said. Gia walked in and Xue closed the door behind her.

Gia sat before the Wise Ones. They were all about eight years old. The twelve girls were a powerful anomaly that the Children had never seen before. They were all born at the same time on different planets in the universe. What's more, all their mothers died in the process of giving birth and their fathers, in some way or form, were no longer around. This meant the girls were all born as orphans, all at the same time across the universe. When this was discovered, they were brought to the monks who promoted their willingness to take in underprivileged, newly born Children. In alignment with a prophecy that had been learned from their god years ago, the monks wanted to foster the twelve girls. It was foretold that they were all born with a powerful spiritual and scientific attunement. They were the last remnants of the staggering cosmic abilities that the Nephilims once had. They were believed to have been gifted with a unique ability to create planets. Believing this prophecy, the monks nurtured this ability and found it to be true. The twelve girls, now referred to as the Wise Ones, were capable of reshaping a planet at will, harnessing a united cosmic power that they didn't entirely know how to control yet. This was why they learned to meditate constantly, to keep their powers under control. According to Gia, it was finally time to unveil their power once more, for the sake of the universe.

"Hello, girls. My name's Gia. As I'm sure you're aware, I'm the overseer of our Eon. I came here today because… I desperately need your help," she said. The Wise Ones turned their heads in concern and confusion. They all scooted closer to Gia, prepared to learn about what she needed help with. Gia reached into her bag and took out a large roll of paper. There were blueprints for a new planet on it. "We're going to work together to make a very beautiful planet. One that all the Children in the universe will be happy with. It will be a wonderful place for everyone to live on forever. Does that sound nice?" Gia asked. The Wise Ones smiled and nodded eagerly. Gia had them sit closer to her so they could see the blueprints. She prepared to give them every little detail of the process. "Perfect. Let's call this planet… the afterlife."

Day 23 – 0:00

The race against time began. Gia, Saundra, and her elite guards worked alongside the twelve Wise Ones to begin creating a brand new planet using the manifestation of religion and the influence of science. The process to form a planet began with a religious sacrament. Using every expensive resource she had, Gia brought her entire crew and the Wise Ones to a massive station in Space, where the coordinates of the new planet would be. It was where they spent the next several days working. Once the Wise Ones felt comfortable, Gia brought them out into Space where they began an extensive prayer. Before embarking on the possibly dangerous task of creating a new planet, the Wise Ones always felt the need to ensure their safety with their god, She. After the spiritual preparations had been made, Gia called upon her strongest guards, most intelligent scientists, and most attuned prophets to assist the girls with the formation of the planet. A holographic display of the afterlife's blueprints emerged before the Children and the Wise Ones got to work. They harnessed loose stardust and antimatter out in Space to build the framework of the planet. Once that was complete, the girls began meditation to enter the Cosmos. They were the only mortals still capable of mentally transporting into the realm of gods. The intense meditation enriched the stardust and antimatter until they glowed with a powerful, holy light. Once they were strong enough, Gia and her elite guards worked to gather asteroid residue. Using a massive "magnet-like" device, they were able to attract tons of asteroids to collide with the framework of the planet.

Once the first phase was complete, the Wise Ones ceased their intense meditation in the Cosmos and spent a day resting. The following day, they went with Gia and her elite guards onto the surface of the lone rock. It was massive. Quite possibly the biggest planet the girls had ever created. Gia worked with the Wise Ones to perform a ritual that looked like a dance. Peaceful movements of tran-

quility attracted supernatural forces from Space. Clouds of nebulae started to appear outside the atmosphere of the lone rock. Gia's scientists used technological devices to gather the nebulae and imbued the surface of the rock with the spiritual force of the scientific manifestations. The entire rock started to glow with various ever-changing colors. Through further meditation and guidance from She, the Wise Ones started to terraform the planet. Utilizing a divine bacterium granted to them by Xue, life was bred. Gia and her crew traveled into the depths of the rock's developing oceans and placed the divine bacterium into the hydrothermal vents located at the bottom. This led to the evolution of bacteria and therefore, microscopic life on the planet. Soon, skies formed, plants grew, and weather developed. After spending several days on the planet calculating its statistics, such as its temperature and size, the process felt as if it was almost complete. One of two of the most daunting tasks had been done.

Gia stood atop a dirt hill where patches of grass were developing. It had only been nine days, but tremendous progress was made. The overseer watched the twelve Wise Ones play in front of her. Gia and Saundra gifted the girls with an endless supply of their favorite foods and toys to thank them for all their hard work. Their joyous laughter was beyond heart-warming to them. Suddenly, one of the eight-year-old girls ran up to Gia and gave her a big hug, almost knocking the overseer over. "Gia. Big sister. You promise that you'll take us to the amusement center someday right? My sisters and I want to go on the rides there!" the girl exclaimed happily. Gia laughed. "Of course Kanya! A promise is a promise. Once all this is over and we achieve the afterlife, Saundra and I will take you girls to the amusement center," she said. The Wise One, Kanya, ran back over to the other girls. Although they weren't biologically related, they referred to each other as sisters. Gia was beyond flattered when the Wise Ones started calling her big sister during this whole process. She felt as if she could cry, beyond proud of the little girls.

Saundra came beside her best friend and placed her arm around her. "Well, Gia. We're halfway there. You did it. All we have to do is get the angels here safely. Then we gather all the ancient texts we found over the years and attempt the last ritual. The blood of the angel must be similar to the blood of the creator of the afterlife. Then we'll need a massive cosmic force at the planet's core," she explained.

Gia nodded slowly, then looked at her best friend. "I know, Saundra. I hate that I'll have to use Bryan, my own son. But it's the only chance we have at succeeding with the ritual."

The rituals Gia and Saundra had discovered were from extremely ancient texts written during Eon III that rumored a process that could keep immortality lasting forever. Should immortality ever be lost, there were stories of a Nephilim who used her powers to create a lone planet that was galaxies away, where a spiritual plane existed. Although the Nephilims didn't have direct blood relatives in the past, their founders were chemically and spiritually tied to them. The fabled Nephilim used the blood of her powerful founder to open the gateway to the world of spirits. The success of the process was tested on various animals that she would slay, but continuously feel their spirits roam the planet in what she called an "afterlife". The Nephilim who terraformed the planet called it the afterlife. To her, it was a supernatural place where life wouldn't have to stop after death. If immortality would be lost, this spiritual plane was where it could figuratively persist or be reinstated.

Gia took a moment to inhale the fresh air of the afterlife prototype. The new celestial body was out in a distant galaxy, light years away from life, hidden in the edges of the universe. This was completely intentional for Gia during her planning. The afterlife had to be created in a place where the Skandhas couldn't find any Children, to protect it from another possible attack. This was her greatest achievement ever. It was quite possibly the greatest achievement of her entire race. But Gia feared that the intense amount of activity in their dimension, the semi-creation of the afterlife, was surely enough to attract the attention of the Skandhas again. Unfortunately, she was right to trust her intuition.

While observing the skies with Saundra, Gia suddenly got a call on her communication device from back home. She answered, placing the device to her ear. "Hello?"

Saundra tried to listen in on her friend's call. Then, she saw the drastic change in the overseer's expression. "Gia? What happened?" Saundra asked.

Gia just dropped the communication device to the ground. "That was Kurtis. He said the Skandhas have returned. They're attacking," she said grimly.

The foretold assault began. The previously taken galaxy had been returned, now broken in its laws of physics. Just like its preceding sister galaxy taken on the first day. A third galactic sector was taken. Only this time, the ancient beings remained in the dimension. They scattered across the universe, possibly in search of Gia. But the overseer was not ready to let this go. She continued working on her goals and had to find a way to get the angels to the afterlife amidst the chaos. In doing so, the afterlife could be fully realized before she would surely be killed by the Skandhas.

The Skandhas wreaked havoc upon the dimension. They appeared in various galaxies and treated the Children like objects. They took individuals by hand, ripping them apart in what appeared to be methods of immediate study. The Skandhas attempted to dissect them in search of traces of spiritual energy, in search of whatever supernatural ability granted the Children the desire to grow the way they had over the years. But Free Will was no tangible object to find. What the Skandhas wanted to discover was something within the spirits of the Children. Regardless, the brutal murders of Gia's species persisted. After the Skandhas finished wiping a planet clean of its inhabitants, they took the empty interstellar structure into their dimension for further study. It was the genocide of all mortals in the universe. After no more than a few days of the great Interdimensional War, it was believed that nearly seventy percent of the Children's population had either been killed or taken into the other dimension. At this point, Gia wasn't entirely sure if achieving the afterlife was anywhere near enough to save her people. It was obvious the Skandhas were no longer just interested in studying the overseer. Now, all the Children were at the mercy of these ancient beings that toyed with their realm. The worst of it all was that there was no hatred, no anger, no desire for war. No, the Skandhas destroyed everything with great indifference. It made the Children feel so small as if these elder beings from another dimension superseded their existence. Like living gods forcefully harboring their realm.

The last place left to study was Gia's home planet. She had the Wise Ones safely protected at the temple with her most highly trained guards. The only hope for the Children now was for Gia to succeed in creating the afterlife. Only then could all these deaths lead to something beautiful. Perhaps she would be able to do it in time for the spirits of her people to still find a place in another plane of immortal existence. Despite the destruction occurring across the universe, Gia's most important task was to get to her lab on Ground Zero and transport the angels she created onto the afterlife. This final ritual would hopefully be enough to fully ignite the power of the new planet. But Gia was trapped on her home planet. After assisting Children with evacuating the entire planet, her company, *Almukhtar* Industries, had completely exhausted all its resources. Gia found herself surrounded by the Skandhas. The only way to get to the angels would be to get through them... by force.

Day 27 - 41:48

Gia stood atop the roof of *Almukhtar* Industries. The skies of her once-glorious home were now riddled with black clouds, lightning, and plumes of cosmic smoke. The wind blew powerfully and the rain fell slightly. As she looked down from the top of what used to be her powerful company, she could see the ancient beings run rampant throughout her city. Some Skandhas were much larger than the one they had captured weeks ago. Many of them stood over fifty feet tall. One of which... the colossal, was over one-hundred feet tall. It was the great destroyer of worlds. The colossal Skandha was what the species used to destroy planets if they saw no purpose in bringing them back to their dimension. It was on Gia's planet, firing lasers from its misshapen head, eradicating buildings and Children in the process. Within *Almukhtar*

Industries, dozens of Skandhas were raiding the labs, seizing the scientific inventions, and destroying the building inside-out. All of the overseer's lifetime of work had been reduced to nothing. Gia started crying, watching her home be ripped apart by a species that just saw them as expendable. But she wasn't going to give up yet. No matter how many of her friends may have died, she was determined to see her objective through to the end. Even if she had to do it alone. But Gia knew she wasn't alone. There was one person she could count on to help her get the angels to the afterlife.

Gia could feel a powerful presence emerge behind her. Suddenly, three Skandhas withdrew their invisibility. Their staggering forms became clear, resembling the one that the Children had captured. The Skandhas all stood before Gia with an imposing amount of god-like energy. No anger or intentional malice, just indifference. She was an insect to them.

The overseer stepped backwards in fear, towards the edge of the roof. Her heart raced. "What do you want? Huh? You come to this dimension and take *everything* from us! You show no remorse! You're looking for me, aren't you? A woman? *Me*? The influencer of my people!" she shouted hysterically.

The Skandhas emitted their pings and 8-bit trills. They started moving towards her slowly, attempting to take her. Gia equipped a gun and fired at them blindly. The lasers, however, had no effect. The Skandhas were beginning to perceive her as a greater threat. They could sense the fast rate of her heart and the heat from her skin. It was a sign that a Child was increasing in aggression. The Skandhas wanted to subdue her. Suddenly, Gia could feel her energy drain. Her matter started visibly protruding from her body, like dust leaving her body and disappearing into the air. Gia screamed in pain and struggled to move. It felt as if her very soul was being ripped from her body. But she had a backup plan. Although it was going to come at great costs, Gia was prepared to give up everything she had to stop these ancient beings. She lifted her left hand and used all the strength she had to clench her fingers into her palm. There was a hidden gauntlet on her wrist with a red button on her palm. Once Gia pressed it, she murdered for the first time in her life. Suddenly, a flurry of explosions emerged beneath her. They arose from the bottom of the *Almukhtar* Industries tower to the top. Gia had her guards preemptively rig the building with explosives. Finally, the explosions reached the roof, hopefully destroying the Skandhas before her. Gia was knocked backwards by the last blast. She fell off the highest floor of the tower and came plummeting towards the ground, wounded.

But Gia was prepared for this exact moment after she would destroy *Al-mukhtar* Industries. Smoke surrounded the overseer's body as she continued falling towards the ground. The intense feeling of Gravity made her noxious. She screamed and panicked, only seconds away from falling to her death. Gia acted quickly and used her plan to rescue herself. Before destroying the tower, she grabbed one of the last technological inventions her company had made. Gia pulled on a string attached to a device on her back. Suddenly, a pair of mechanical wings emerged. Following it was jet exhaust, a flame bursting from the bottom that kept her afloat, narrowly preventing her from hitting the ground. The wings, now in conjunction with the jet exhaust, allowed Gia to take flight across the city. This was her last stand against the creatures destroying her planet. She wanted to lure a group of Skandhas to her company and hopefully kill some in the process with the explosives. Gia was ever more determined to survive the outcome. She rose into the sky and prepared to fly to her next destination: the transit station.

Gia flew across the skies, only so high above some of the buildings in the city. The Skandhas scouring the area took notice of her. Their attention was drawn and they ceased their passive activities. Once Gia looked back, she noticed several of the ancient beings chasing her. Because of their massive size, they were relatively incapable of moving fast. They made their long strides towards her, firing cosmic lasers from their cubic heads. Gia started evading their attacks with her jetpack. She turned to the left, barrel-rolled to the right, and took a quick nosedive to avoid the incoming fire. As each blast flew past her body, she could feel the intense heat almost scorch her skin. The astronomical power of the Skandhas was capable of destroying an entire planet with one synchronous attack if they chose to do so. And Gia found herself facing several of them alone. Luckily, she was nearing her destination.

But before she could make a safe landing at the transit station, her right wing was struck by a blast. It exploded loudly, causing her ears to ring. Smoldering embers burned her face and arm. Gia twirled in the air and came corkscrewing towards the ground. Smoke trailed behind the blown wing. To save herself, Gia quickly arched her back, forcing her chest and gut forward. This shift of movement helped her use the momentum of her fall to push herself forward, instead of plummeting into the ground. The hasty move saved her. Gia avoided the ground and crashed through the window of the transit station instead. The glass shattered and she collided with the ground. Her body contorted painfully across the metal floor, the jetpack flying off in the process. It slid across the floor and struck the wall on the other end of the room.

The overseer cried to herself softly. With no more power, the transit station was dark, so she couldn't see the wounds she had just endured. As Gia attempted to sit up, she placed her left hand on the floor, suddenly feeling a puddle of her blood. There was a shard of glass in the right side of her body. Gia held her breath and quickly pulled it out. She winced and moaned in pain. The Skandhas were drawing closer. Their strange sounds could be heard and their massive footsteps shook the ground.

"Shit," Gia mumbled to herself. She got up off the floor and ran downstairs, deeper into the transit station.

Gia hopped over the security barrier and ran past the railway vehicle. Instead of using the vehicle, she took a turn into the section with teleporters, an alternative method of public transportation. Gia pulled a switch in the backroom to turn the power back on using a backup generator. Lights flashed on in the room. There was little time left; the Skandhas were attacking. The entire transit station started shaking and rubble fell from the ceiling. Gia limped over to a computer and navigated the device to activate the teleporters. She then entered specific galactic coordinates to the location she wanted to travel to. The teleporter whirred as it began revving up enough power to send its passenger.

"Come on… come on…" Gia mumbled. She hunched in pain. More of her blood was spilling. Suddenly, a Skandha shoved its hand through the roof, attempting to grab her. Gia screamed and shielded her face from the debris. The teleporter changed colors and whirred louder than before; it was ready. Gia quickly dove into the teleporter, narrowly avoiding the attack.

It was Sanctuary. Gia arrived on the planet where the captured Skandha was still held in the protective dome, one that its brethren couldn't break through. Many of the scientists on the planet were taken into the other dimension or killed. Nauseous from her persistent bleeding, Gia exited the receiving teleporter on Sanctuary. She limped over to one of the standby vehicles and hazily drove to the dome. Moments later, she parked in front of the dome and got out of the vehicle. She walked over to a panel and typed in the code to open the doors to the pod. This was her only option left. The only way she could stand against the Skandhas long enough to send the angels to the afterlife would be to get the help of one of their species.

Gia limped through the tunnel and reached the center of the pod, where the captured Skandha meditated patiently. She stumbled onto the grass and held her hand out to the ancient being. "Please... help me..." Gia fell onto her face, immediately unconscious.

The Skandha got up onto its knees and examined the Child before it. The being wanted a sufficient explanation of what was going on. It touched Gia's head and read her memories, fully caught up on her recent events. The Skandha then touched her chest and pierced into her heart using a sharp extension from its finger. It transferred a small amount of its blood into Gia's veins, eliminating all her wounds through its powerful cosmic abilities. The Skandha then cradled Gia in its arms and resumed its meditative position. She was still unconscious, but the captured Skandha chose to help her, just like she asked. Gia was the only Child in the entire universe that showed some form of compassion to the captured Skandha. Instead of just a fearful indifference. Now, it cared about her more than it thought possible. The Skandha gazed at the woman's beautiful face and watched her dreams, waiting patiently for her to wake up.

Day 28 – 03:12

Gia finally awakened. Her tired eyes slowly opened to the sight of a giant being holding her. The overseer started touching her own body, noticing only stains of blood, no wounds. She suddenly jolted, sitting in an upright position in the Skandha's arms. The ancient being released Gia, gently placing her on the soft grass, standing.

Gia turned around towards it, looking up at its cubic head. "You... saved me. Thank you. Thank you so much," she said. The Skandha emitted a soft hum in response.

Suddenly, the attacking Skandhas arrived at the Sanctuary. Dozens of them emerged, clearly able to teleport wherever they wished amongst the universe. Gia panicked. "Oh no! They're here! They must have followed me!" she shouted.

The Skandhas made their long strides towards the glass pod. They drastically changed the atmosphere in unison, increasing Gravity and draining Gia of her energy. Her skin grew pale and her nose started bleeding. The ancient beings started firing lasers at the pod together, rattling the entire device and shaking the ground. Cracks formed beneath Gia's feet. She leaned up against the captured Skandha for support.

"What should we do? They're surrounding us. We can't stay inside this pod forever," Gia said.

Unable to truly communicate, the Skandha just rose from its meditative position. It observed its brethren nearby. There was a slight moment where Gia was afraid the ancient being would betray her and aid in her capture. But those thoughts quickly faded when she remembered the spiritual energy they had exchanged over the past few weeks. The Skandha seemed to have a plan. It manipulated Gia with telekinesis and lifted her towards the tunnel of the pod. It placed her in front of the control switch, the one that opened and closed the entire pod.

"You've got to be kidding. Are you sure?" The Skandha emitted a ping in response. Gia took a deep breath and prepared herself. She trusted the being; it was her last option for survival. She went ahead and pulled the switch. The massive, impenetrable glass exterior of the pod opened from its crown, splitting open into several pieces. The pieces then retreated underneath the ground, where the frame of the pod resided. Smoke plumed into the air, masking what was going on.

The attacking Skandhas ceased their fire. They waited patiently to see what would happen. Suddenly, Gia's ally retaliated. It shrieked with a loud gong-like echo and emitted a massive shockwave of pure celestial force. It shook the entire planet and sent the opposing Skandhas flying away from them. The ancient beings scattered and crashed into the ground, leaving massive craters beneath them. This was a momentary triumph.

"Holy shit you're strong," Gia said. The Skandha then directed its attention down towards her, awaiting the next course of action. Gia ran through the tunnel pathway and up to the being. "We have to get to Ground Zero! The afterlife is our only hope of saving the Children!"

The ally Skandha lifted Gia in its hand and gently poked at her forehead with its giant fingertip. It read all her thoughts once more and learned the location of Ground Zero. Without being caged by the pod, it was free to understand the entire landscape of this dimension, much like its brethren. The Skandha teleported with Gia in its hand and brought them to the focal point of Ground Zero, just like she wanted. It was time to finally get the angels to the afterlife.

Day 28 - 03:25

They arrived at Ground Zero, directly in front of the lab Gia had been at only seventeen days ago. Gia ran towards the front door. The building had remained surprisingly immaculate during the entire Interdimensional War so far. No one else might have been here except the angels held in the basement. Gia opened the door. The Skandha knelt beside her, almost showing a sense of curiosity.

Gia turned around and held a hand out towards it. "Sorry, my friend. You're going to have to wait out here. Please, keep me safe. And if any of your kind arrive, alert me. Thank you," she said.

The Skandha emitted a hum in response. It sat in a crisscrossed position in front of the building. The overseer entered the building and took an elevator down like before.

She finally arrived inside the lab. She dashed over to her desk, entered a code on the terminal, and unlocked a drawer on the side. She grabbed her spare key and threw it around her neck using the lanyard it was attached to. Gia ran through the halls and made it to the metallic double doors that led to the angel experiment room.

"Damn. It's gonna be impossible to get through. I can't put two keys in at the same time," she said to herself. She looked at her original key and her spare key in both her hands. Without Saundra, she wouldn't be able to open the doors. For security measures, two people had to be present and turn the keys in the locks at the same time. Gia had to be resourceful. Instead, she yanked a steel pipe out of the nearby wall and jammed it into the 2nd lock. These were desperate times and maintaining secrecy about the project to create the afterlife wasn't necessary anymore. There was a small explosion and electrical wires bursting. Gia went to the other lock, inserted her key, and opened the metallic double doors. She ran down the stairs into the pitch-black room with the angels.

Suddenly, Gia was struck in the face with a blunt object. She fell backwards, hitting her head on the steel floor. She wailed in pain.

"Gia? You're alive?" a voice asked. It was soft, sweet, and familiar. It was Saundra. The woman held a hand out to Gia, wielding a staff in the other. Gia grabbed her friend's hand and stood back up, slightly dazed from the surprise attack. She held her nose, blood spilling through the crevices of her fingers. "I'm so sorry! I've been held up past here for the past 42 hours. It was the only place I could think of coming to. I was going to try to send the angels to the afterlife, but I can't conjure enough power to activate the portal you designed. All power that we siphoned from the nearby Dyson Sphere is gone. The Skandhas destroyed it," Saundra explained.

Gia observed the blood in her hand and wiped it on her pants. "It's okay Saundra. Maybe I deserved that hit to the face for beings so vain about my pursuits. Knock some damn sense into me." Saundra patted her friend on her shoulder, comforting her. "Anyway, you said that there wasn't any sufficient power source? Saundra… I think I may have a solution to the problem. Now we have to move fast. I'm being chased by the Skandhas. But I managed to get away for the time being," Gia said. She started leading Saundra out of the angel experiment room. "How were you possibly able to get away?" Saundra asked.

They stepped outside the building, where the ally Skandha was still there meditating. Saundra looked at the ancient being with absolute shock. Her jaw dropped.

"Damn! Did you use the captured Skandha? And it's *helping* you?" she asked.

Gia nodded. "It saved my life. I had been hurt pretty badly and it was able to heal my wounds. After the connection we've made over the past few weeks, I'm willing to believe we understand each other on a decent level. It knows all my thoughts, but by god, She knows I can't comprehend its thoughts," she said.

Saundra smiled for the first time in a while. "Well, any friend of yours is a friend of mine's, Gia. Thank goodness it helped you. What do we call it? Other than 'the captured Skandha.'"

Gia gazed up at the being for a moment. The unexpectedly kind and tender behavior from the Skandha reminded Gia of someone she had lost so long ago. Her husband. "We'll call him Joel," Gia said.

Saundra smiled at her best friend. "I suppose it's as good a way to honor him as any. So what's the plan?"

Gia looked up at the black clouds in the sky. The Skandhas were unaware of their presence on Ground Zero… for now. There wasn't much time before they would track Gia like they had been doing since their taking of the dimension. "The reason I brought you out here is that the captured Skandha, who we'll now call Joel, should have plenty of power to activate the portal. Saundra, we're going to have to move fast and bring the portal out here. I know it's a big ass machine, but we can release the angels and have them help. Once it's out here, Joel should hopefully be able to power it. From there, I'll teleport with it to the afterlife and so we can activate the receiving portal there. After that, we're going to have to attempt the ritual. If it works, then the afterlife will be fully realized and the Children can continue their lives beyond this whole mess in another plane of existence. If it doesn't work, then I guess everything is over. That'll be it for our universe. The Skandhas would win," Gia explained grimly.

Saundra grabbed her friend by the arm. "It'll work, Gia." The women smiled at each other. It looked as if Joel was able to understand every word. It emitted a trill in response to their heartfelt moment. Now, everyone moved into action.

As discussed, Gia and Saundra released all the angels from their experiment chambers and cages. With the help of over a dozen of them, they were able to move the massive portal device through the labs and out to the front of the building. It was a metallic, circular device, about ten feet tall. While Saundra was out in the front wiring the portal to a cog structure within the building, Gia was inside the experiment room releasing the rest of the angels. Some had wings and others didn't, but they were all worth saving. They all rushed outside, blindly abiding by anything Gia said. To them, she was their savior. The years of experiments on them had twisted their perspectives and made them believe she was their goddess, providing them with all the scientific and religious enrichment they desired. Although Gia's intention with the afterlife project wasn't malicious, it was the result of her extreme goal and she had no choice but to accept it. However, the one angel who always contended her actions, was her son, Bryan. He was the last angel that Gia released. She was almost afraid to look her spawn in his eyes. Because despite all her years of having others suffer for her goals, there was still a chance she would fail. No mother wanted to approach their Child with such weight on their shoulders. But there wasn't a choice now. Gia wanted to have a few final words with Bryan as she was removing him from his "T" position upon the device on the wall. This could have been their last moments together.

"I suppose this might just be it. The end of everything. Possibly just the end. Or maybe the beginning of a new era. But either way, the end of much of what we know now," Gia said.

"You've utilized Free Will to an extreme capacity. Now you're finally shaping the balance of the universe with your own, mortal mind," Bryan said.

"I'll accept that you just referred to me as a mortal as if you weren't one.

Because, son, if we succeed, you will become immortal. Someway, somehow, your life will exist beyond death in the paradise of the afterlife."

"Mother. If you survive this, I want you to understand the importance of always speaking the truth. With a goal as big as yours, achieving this afterlife, I don't know how you could have possibly accepted keeping it a secret from the Children. You have done nothing more than guilt yourself by destroying your morals to attain immortality for your people. You've lost your way ever since father died."

"Bryan. Your insight has grown so much since you've nearly become an angel. And I'm so sorry to have put you through this. To have put you through so many twisted things since Joel died. Your father died of disease, a heinous flaw to the mortality that we suffer from every day. I know that my parents, Mustafa and Qadira, brought us into a new Eon of Free Will, but it came at the cost of our survivability. I just… I just wanted to try to have both. To have our Free Will and the ability to exercise it forever. But I'm afraid that I may have asked for too much."

"No, mother. I forgive you. Father's death tore me apart too, which is why I was so willing to sacrifice myself for this experiment. At this point, it's clear that your pursuit of the afterlife has opened the gateway to many terrible things. Specifically the arrival of the Skandhas into our dimension. But the freedom of Free Will is what allows you to fight for whatever matters most to you. You didn't ask for too much, mom. It's the universe that hasn't given you enough yet. Not until you understand what the universe wants you to learn from it."

"What could the universe possibly want me to learn from it?"

"I think you know now, Mom. The Skandhas that came here. They have taught us Children a great lesson. To let go of fear. You approached the captured Skandha and attempted to understand it. Don't you see? You both have done the same, kind-hearted thing. Instead of constantly approaching each other with fear, you attempted to understand each other. Mom, you attempted to understand the Skandhas when they arrived, while everyone else was looking to start a war from the beginning. But the rise of the afterlife changed the course of your, as well as their, intentions. The Skandhas' taking of this universe is just them trying to understand us, like the scientific subjects we are to them. What you have to learn, Gia, mother, is the harmony of Free Will and fate. There are remnants of Determinism left in the universe, but

172

being willing to make your own choices while understanding the power of destiny is what defines you. There is more to the Skandhas. I can feel it. Don't give up on trying to reason with them. Violence could've been avoided between us. Perhaps we're both afraid of what the opposite species is capable of, Children and Skandha alike."

Gia started crying. The tears rolled down her face and fell between her and her son. She leaned forward and placed her forehead on Bryan's shoulder. Bryan wrapped his arms around his mother and hugged her tightly for the first time in years. He loved her. He knew a lot of what she had done to achieve the afterlife was because of the pain she felt losing the love of her life to nothing more than natural causes. There was nothing Gia felt like she could do to save her husband from his deathbed. And because of the pain, she, as well as many other Children, felt like victims of mortality, she wanted to do everything she could to fight it. To bring back immortality while maintaining Free Will. But it was clear that everything in the universe came at a cost. However, Bryan was possibly right. The rise of the Skandhas in this dimension was the harbinger of a new truth. And Gia couldn't give up trying to understand the ancient beings. They could've been a crucial link towards achieving her goal. They could've been an important part to save the Children once and for all.

After the moment they shared, Gia and her son left the depths of the angel experiment room. They ran outside and joined with the others. Just as she predicted, the Skandhas followed her to Ground Zero. The ancient beings started emerging on the planet's surface, teleporting here one by one. Maybe they could detect certain traces of energy or were so committed to capturing Gia that they had a lock on her anywhere in the universe.

"Hurry! They're coming!" Saundra shouted.

Gia allowed Joel to touch her forehead and examine all her thoughts. It knew what to do now. The Skandha charged up its cosmic force and gripped the metal ring of the portal. It transferred a large portion of its energy into the device, charging it enough for usage. The portal glowed powerfully with a mix of neon colors. It whirred with a high-pitched mechanical sound.

"Okay, everyone! Assemble into a single-file line! Joel and I are going to teleport to the afterlife and activate the receiving portal there!" Gia shouted.

Bryan approached his mother and touched her shoulder. "Please stay safe Mom! The attacking Skandhas are within sight now!"

Gia kissed her son on his forehead. Joel grabbed her and read her mind once more. It learned the coordinates of the afterlife and within seconds, it teleported them there.

Day 28 – 05:11

Gia and Joel arrived on the surface of the afterlife. It had been several days since Gia was able to lay eyes on such a magnificent creation achieved through the union of her people. She wished that every Child in the universe was capable of this type of imagination. It was almost like an untapped power in and of itself. The surface of the afterlife was immaculate, with beautiful plants, a pristine blue sky with white clouds, and a fresh atmosphere that enriched the soul. Joel released Gia, allowing her to land on the soft grass. The Skandha teleported them directly in front of the receiving portal on the afterlife upon arrival. Just as they planned, Joel gripped the metal rim of the portal and imbued it with its cosmic power, activating it. The same effect from the sending teleporter occurred. It glowed brightly with its mix of neon colors. Gia quickly ran to a nearby building, where her leading operations were conducted during the building of the

afterlife. She motioned Joel to follow her and it did. Together, they gathered crucial materials needed for the ritual to fully breathe life into the afterlife. Without the assistance of the Wise Ones, the monks, or Gia's elite scientists, this process was going to be quite difficult. But it was better that they stayed hidden on various planets in the universe that were highly undiscoverable by the Skandhas.

As Saundra, Bryan, and the other angels came through the portal, Gia and Joel were setting up the materials outside. Gia was briefly reading over their ancient texts, the pages where she left notes and markers for her to refer back to them quickly. Gia reread the ritual that involved the blood of a relative and observed the summarized story of the Nephilim who supposedly created a version of the afterlife in Eon III. The overseer grabbed a box full of stardust and gently spread it out across the ground to form a picture. The white dust had small fragments of a light blue glow in it. It was formed in the shape of a cross, with the infinity sign around it. Each curve of the symbol touched the points of the cross. Saundra and the angels helped Gia with setting up sacred candles in a perfect circle. Gia grabbed the ancient text and placed it at the center of the formation they created.

"Everyone, into your positions. Hurry," she said.

The angels gathered in the circle, each of them holding a candle with both their hands. They got down on both their knees and bowed their heads, raising the candles upward. Bryan came to the middle, atop the cross-infinity hybrid shape. He was an extremely crucial part of the entire process. Bryan was Gia's only relative left in the universe and the only one who had blood similar to hers. They did as the ritual asked. Bryan knelt before his mother. One knee was on the ground, the other pointing upward from his right foot planted firmly upon the grass. Bryan bowed his head. His white-feathered angelic wings flapped briefly. Gia formed a unique hand sign and tapped into the ancient cosmic force of her ancestors, something Children only able to use on extremely rare occasions. Her eyes glowed with a golden color. Gia raised her right hand and levitated the stardust from the ground. It started swirling around her body, changing from its white color into a golden one.

Gia started speaking in a strange ancient tongue, her voice echoing powerfully. As she chanted, she started sprinkling parcels of the stardust onto her son's head. Once she was finished, the surrounding angels repeated her chant. A bright object began to emerge over Bryan's head. It was a golden circle, forming above the crown of his head. It was called a halo.

Gia stepped backwards and Bryan arose from his kneeling position. He repeated the chant with his eyes closed. Then, glowing hieroglyphs started forming around his body, where some of his most vital veins were. Bryan raised his hand into the sky and slammed it into the ground with the force of a hammer. His palm struck the center of the cross and infinity symbol. There was a sudden burst of bright light. It emitted a shockwave across the afterlife and changed the atmosphere. It was working. The ritual was almost done. The afterlife was almost enriched with the only species it would ever accept; immortal beings, angels.

"Now we just need a powerful enough force to breathe life into the core of the planet," Gia said. She looked over at Joel and her thoughts immediately became in sync with the Skandha. It approached the center of the ritual circle. Joel could have never imagined the unity it would experience with the Children. Siding with them was never its intention. But once it met Gia and experienced every memory of her life, it knew there was more for the Children's future than just destruction. Joel charged a godlike cosmic force in its hands. It started glowing with the same celestial blue color of the stardust surrounding it. The ground started shaking and the clouds moved across the sky at a faster rate. Joel prepared itself to enrich the core of the afterlife with its almighty power, to breathe life into the planet. At the success of the ritual, the afterlife would finally come to exist. The Children would finally be able to live eternally in another plane of paradise. Joel raised its arms, emitting a loud gong-like noise. But before it could deliver its power into the core, it was stopped. All the work, all the choices made to create a better universe for the Children had appeared to be for nothing. Gia watched her dreams fall apart right before her very eyes.

Suddenly, Joel was struck in its cubic head by what appeared to be a laser blast. The ancient being's head nearly exploded. There was a burst of its blood, remnants of it spilling onto all of the soon-to-be angels and Gia standing. Joel's 30-foot tall body jarred and fell forward, crashing into the grass. Saundra and the angels screamed in shock. Gia watched in silence. Her eyes were wide and her mouth slightly gaped. Everything felt as if it was moving in slow motion. She finally looked up and saw the attacking Skandhas emerging around her. The only thing capable of easily killing a Skandha was one of its own

kind. Gia was too late. The Skandhas were succeeding with their plan of eliminating all life in this universe, without understandable cause or reason. At this point, Gia was quite certain she was amongst the last Children left in the entire dimension. It would be the only logical explanation for such terrifying persistence from the ancient species. The brutal attack began.

The angels tried to run. The Skandhas fired lasers at two of them. The scorching beam split them in half at the waist. Their separate bodies dropped to the ground like sacks. A Skandha stomped on an angel, crushing her lower body. Then, it bent forward and yanked the woman's arms out of their sockets with minimal effort. She screamed violently and died. Further, into the grassy field, two Skandhas surrounded an angel. One grabbed the man by his head and the other, one leg. They both pulled at the same time, violently ripping off his head and leg. The torrent of gore was unlike anything any of the Children had seen. Many of them just froze in place, completely mortified. Another Skandha stabbed two angels with a long blade-like appendage extending from its forearm. The massive blade pierced through both of their chests. The Skandha lifted the angles like animals on a stake. It finally threw them into the air and let them fall from a terrible height. Gia watched in horror as more Skandhas appeared, one grabbing an angel by the neck. It dug into her back and yanked her spine clean out. The vicious Skandha just dropped the body and bones onto the ground. Bryan attempted to fight back but was nowhere near as powerful as the ancient beings. They were living gods. They had such an incomprehensible power over the Children, that there was no stopping them in a fight. A Skandha grabbed Bryan and threw him to the ground, onto his chest. Another reached over and yanked the wings out of his back. Bryan screamed violently from the excruciating pain. His blood spilled onto his own body. One last Skandha wrapped its massive hand around his neck and with a small squeeze, it crushed Bryan's airways, killing him instantly. Gia's son had died right in front of her eyes. After witnessing such a tragedy, it had become even more clear that all hope was lost.

Gia avoided breaking down at the sight of her only son being brutally killed by a ruthless species from another dimension. "Run!" she shouted. Gia and Saundra attempted to escape the clutches of the Skandhas to no avail. They had nowhere to go. The women took off south but were the last Children left. The Skandhas directed their attention to them and fired their lasers in unison. The blasts struck behind the women, knocking them forward onto their faces. Gia and Saundra rolled across the ground, incurring multiple bruises and cuts. A Skandha approached Gia from behind and stabbed her with the bladed appendage from its forearm. It pierced through Gia's body and into the ground. The overseer screamed in pain. Her skin felt cold and she clutched the grass beneath her, grunting. She looked up at Saundra. The ancient beings grabbed her best friend by her waist. Saundra flailed her arms, struggling to break free. Another Skandha approached her from behind. It reached over and dug its massive claws into Saundra's face. Gia just closed her eyes tightly and cried. She couldn't bear to see her friend be murdered; her cries of terror were already too much to handle. The Skandha tugged hard in one direction and ripped Saundra's face clean off. After killing her, they kept the body.

The Skandha stabbing Gia finally ripped its blade out her body. Gia screamed in pain again. It was so intense, her ears started ringing and she felt nauseous. Gia rolled over onto her back, keeping a hand over the gaping wound in her stomach. This was the most of her blood she had ever seen in her life.

"Please… just kill me. I have nothing left to live for anymore…" Gia begged with the remaining strength she had left. In her final moments, she couldn't help but think about her parents. The way Qadira raised her and what it would have been like if her father hadn't been killed. The powers that her direct bloodline had were so catastrophically different from what she possessed as a mortal. And it angered her. It angered her that she wasn't able to stand up to these ancient beings. It angered her that she was at their mercy. But she hoped, perhaps in another life, the Free Will she had and immortality she craved would finally be able to live in harmony.

Looking up at the Skandhas standing over her, Gia could feel her vision start to fade. But somehow, she rose back to her feet. The overseer slowly started limping away from her attackers, not getting very far. Two Skandhas suddenly grabbed her by her arms. They held her high above the ground, her arms as stretched as possible. Then, to subdue her, one Skandha yanked hard and pulled out Gia's left arm. She screamed violently. The other Skandha held the woman by her wrist, letting her lifeless body dangle in its clutches. Gia couldn't handle it anymore. She passed out from the pain and blood loss. With her failure, the dream of achieving the afterlife was finally over.

The angels along with the overseer had marked the final deaths of the most important Children left in the universe. The genocide of the mortals had been fulfilled. And the only ones left were deep in hiding, unable to ever truly survive without any sufficient resources. There was nothing left in this dimension. With all the Children dead, the Skandhas took every planet, every solar system, and every galaxy into their dimension. The only thing left in the universe was absolute darkness. A wretched hark back to Eon 0, before existence.

اليوم الثلاثين

Among the plains of a foreign dimension, even the atmosphere felt completely different than the previous one. It was extremely vacant, void of any remnants of life that were once familiar to her. Whether it be a blessing or curse, Gia had miraculously survived the onslaught from the most threatening beings she had ever encountered. Their very presence meant the destruction of the laws of physics and nature. It was frightening to think that something so powerful could exist. That a species was capable of taking an entire universe for their own. It was becoming clear that these very beings, the Skandhas, had plans for her. Gia couldn't entirely recollect how she may have gotten to this inexplicable place, but it had to have been at the will of the ancient beings.

The former overseer slowly opened her eyes. The atmosphere around her was absent of much detail. It was a hollow gray space with a dense fog filling the air. Amidst the clouds of fog were strange lights. They looked like wisps of spirits roaming around the airspace. Much like the pure cosmic energy of the Skandhas, these wisps glowed with a light blue color. Gia could sense that she wasn't on the ground. When she looked down, it was impossible to see the floor. She was floating in a "T" pose, similar to that of her son, Bryan, who was certainly dead now. Gia summed up the strength to lift her bloody head. She looked to her left and could still see that her arm was missing. The sight of it made her sick. Gia struggled to move and could sense something in her back. They were strange, white fluorescent tubes. They were transparent and emitted a soft smoke as if they were made with dry ice. These massive tubes were stuck in Gia's back, keeping her above the ground. Gia didn't even have the energy to panic.

"Where... am I? How... did I survive? Hello? Is anyone here? Can anyone hear me? I need... help," Gia said softly to herself. She just closed her eyes and let her head dangle. She was exhausted just from uttering those few words.

Suddenly, a presence appeared before her. There was a bright white light bursting in front of her. Gia closed her eyes tightly. When she opened them, she saw three figures. They slowly emerged from the dense fog, appearing to float. Gia could see two Skandhas. But the third being, standing between them, was foreign to her. It was a strange, ambiguous species. There was no absolute gender to it, but it bore a resemblance similar to the Children. A set of two arms and two legs, a clear head, a similar bone structure, and skin, but no hair atop its head. The ambiguous being floated in front of Gia. The two Skandhas at its left and right appeared to be escorts of some sort.

"Where am I? Who... are you?" Gia asked.

The being had relatively little emotion and no expression on its face. "Greetings. You are the one known as 'overseer' in your dimension, correct? Dimension 140283?" it asked. The being's voice was soft, yet mature.

Gia was astonished. Was it possible that there were that many dimensions in the universe? She slowly nodded towards the being.

"Excellent. Gia, you are in what is known as Purgatory. A realm between the ones of the living and the ones of the afterlife that you so desperately sought after. The designation of your dimension stems from the name of your original god… your creator. You see Gia, there is an infinite number of dimensions. And my species and I have undertaken the quest of searching through some of the most profound ones in the universe. We have found gods in nearly every dimension, stemming from different methods of the original conception. Your god… Alkulu is your progenitor and has since given rise to later gods, like the Twins, and even your father, Mustafa in a sense."

Gia gazed at the being, shocked at the magnitude of its understanding of her universe.

"Now to answer your latter question. I am Human. Without delving too deep into the origins of the Skandhas, let's just say I am a rare anomaly amongst my kind. A 'Chosen One' of sorts. Much like your father was. Furthermore, I am a unique hybrid capable of communicating with any species, so long as I bring them into my dimension. The current Purgatory that you reside in, Gia, is the one that belongs to my dimension. Each Purgatory is different. My people and I have done everything in our power to bring you here so that we may communicate with you; the greatest influencer of your Children."

Gia was locked in the moment, completely enthralled by everything happening. "But… you killed all of my people. You and your beings took the planets in my dimension and destroyed them. You manipulated our laws of physics and used us as experiments. Then, you just returned and killed everyone," she said.

Human hardly looked perplexed. However, it was curious. "I believe there was a misconception, Gia. Understandably, you and the Children lacked awareness of the true circumstances. We had a barrier between our languages. But our species believes in the instance that the truth must always be revealed. We admired your kind for believing in your truth and attempting to protect yourselves accordingly. So allow me to reveal the absolute truth to you."

Suddenly, Gia turned around, being controlled by the strange tubes in her back. As she looked up into the sky, she could see many of her people. They were hanging above the invisible ground, connected to tubes just like her. However, they all appeared to be unconscious, lifeless in form, as if they were all in comas. But although they were all possibly murdered by the Skandhas, their bodies were in immaculate condition. Completely un-scathed from the Interdimensional War. None of what was going on made any sense to her. Human and its accompanying Skandhas floated in front of Gia once more. "I don't understand. There are Children here. But we were all wiped out. Is this because we're all here in this plane between life and death? This... Purgatory?" Gia asked. Human nodded softly.

"That is correct, Gia. You are quite perceptive for a mortal. You see, we Skandhas were drawn to your dimension because you intended to create the afterlife. We had been watching from the 4th dimension for quite some time once Free Will had been achieved by your ancestors. With such liberty to act, we were waiting to see if your kind was capable of making a profound discovery. And as written in your ancient text, you followed the rituals of science and religion to create the afterlife. Heaven. A place where, in a sense, Children could be immortal by living on after they once passed. Our kind believes in the power of Reincarnation. So now, it is time we make you privy to our intentions. Gia, we did not kill your Children, per se. No, we were beginning the first process towards allowing your kind to arise in a higher plane of existence. Reincarnation is the process of non-physical essence being reborn in another physical form, or even another plane of existence. And we Skandhas have achieved that long ago. You see, the angels that you created are but a crucial link towards Reincarnation, one that my kind has taken a liking to. In other words, none of your Children are dead. Here in Purgatory, the next thing awaiting them is to arise in your afterlife. For your dreams to come true. You were right all along Gia. However, you just needed our help without realizing it."

"What? So... you're saying that we're all heading towards Reincarnation? That the Children will come back to life? So, that means that the afterlife was realized. But the ritual... it was..."

"Slightly incorrect. Yes, many of the steps you performed were accurate, such as blueprinting the planet and conjuring angels. But the ritual requires a sacrifice for the planet to ascend to a greater plane. One past Purgatory."

"A sacrifice? From who?"

Human took a moment to look at all the Children hanging in the nothingness of Purgatory, then turned back to Gia. "The creator..."

Gia gasped in shock. "The creator? You mean... me? *I* have to be sacrificed?"

"Yes, Gia. To bring about the dawn of a new era and fully realize heaven, the creator of such a planet must be willing to oversee the new realm as a god," Human said.

"But how could I ever become a god?"

"You are already one. You have always been one amongst your people. The magnitude of the changes you wanted to make was on scales by the likes of which we Skandhas have rarely seen. Your mortality was not a limiting factor. No matter the odds, you sought a better universe for the Children, even if it would cost you your life. And Gia, the truth is, the afterlife *will* cost you your life."

"I see. Human, if there isn't any other way, I want to do it."

"And that is why you are admired so much by our kind. You do not hesitate to help others. Including the Skandha you named Joel. It will reincarnate soon, so you need not fret. We learned much from its willingness to serve the Children. It was moved by you and your love for your own. But Gia, you must never forget the importance of self-love, even as a god. You, yourself, deserve the most of your love and affection."

"I understand. I have spent so much of my life, since I was born, serving others. My mother told me that was how my father lived as The Chosen One. His entire existence was meant for the betterment of the uni-

verse and the Nephilims. I was gladly willing to do the same. And I shall let this final sacrifice be one of the last times I neglect self-love."

"There is no need to forsake your way of life Gia. There is abundance for all. Happiness never decreases by being shared with those you love. And you seem to understand that more than any mortal we have ever encountered. You have lived beautifully. And it is time to pass the mantle of your successes on to a future generation. Your angels, who can begin life anew. All of the Children that you cared so deeply for will be reincarnated in the image you wanted for them. As angels. As… Seraphs. Heaven will serve as their planet during mortality and they will live on in the afterlife upon the same planet, as spirits. They will not remember their previous lives, but they will remember you, their goddess. A new timeline of evolution will begin with your angels. Do you accept this?"

"Yes. I do."

"Gia. We Skandhas have taken your planets and brought them into this dimension so they may thrive. The way they returned to your dimension is after all the flaws were removed. The afterlife will continue to exist in a new solar system, one we named after the first one in your universe. Syris. And in Syris, besides the afterlife, we will bring all of the greatest planets from every dimension that have achieved profound milestones. We want them all to live together in harmony. Many other species and their greatest mortals from various dimensions are undergoing the same process as you, simultaneously. In this new dimension, many species will be united in one special place, near the afterlife you created. Are you comfortable sharing your accomplishments with others?"

"Yes, Human. I wouldn't have it any other way. Let the species from other dimensions immigrate into one universe and let them all rejoice in the afterlife."

"Blessings upon you. Your heaven will emulate your first creation for your people, the Dyson Sphere. We will grant heaven a 2nd Sun, so it may provide Syris will the greatest resources in a much more efficient way."

"That would be amazing. My Children deserve the best."

"Then it is time."

Gia smiled to herself softly. She closed her eyes and cried. Her dreams were finally going to come true. Human floated closer to her and touched her chest, where her heart was.

"Gia. Are you ready to sacrifice yourself as a mother of nature to your Children and as a goddess to your angels?" it asked.

Gia looked at the god-like being. "Yes. I'm ready. Let them live on and start anew. Let all species have a chance to indulge in the Children's success," she said. Suddenly, Gia's body started glowing with a bright white and golden light. A halo was emerging over her head and angelic wings sprouted from her back. Her left arm returned to her. Her skin became immaculate, absent of any flaws. And her eyes became enlightened with a platinum color.

"Finally, Gia, what do you wish to call heaven?" Human asked.

"Jannah."

Day 0

By the power of the Skandhas and the will of Gia, the afterlife was finally achieved. Gia was made into an ethereal being. By the achievements she made as a mortal during Eon IV and the power bestowed upon her by the enlightened Skandhas, she was able to become a goddess in a greater plane of existence. Finally, her parents and her husband's souls had a peaceful place to rest in eternity. As she wanted, a new dimension was created. Jannah and many other significant planets from her universe were brought into the new dimension, scattered about Space. They were empty places for the new species to soon discover someday, as they persisted their timeline of evolution and progress. Gia's angels, the Seraphs, were reborn into new bodies on Jannah. Evolving from the animals that existed on the planet, they soon developed consciousness, self-awareness, and great powers. As their wings grew and halos formed, they felt more in touch with the goddess who brought them into this light. Their Mother Nature, who showed them the way towards a new existence.

As Human had requested, other species immigrated into the new dimension as well, to live beside the Seraphs. They all had different appearances as they evolved and came to believe in their own gods. But regardless of their differences, they all came to live in harmony, united in the Syris Solar System.

The Wise Ones were reborn as the most respected beings in the entire universe. As deemed by their goddess, by Gia, they were the final remnants of the Children from the previous Eon. The Wise Ones were still capable of making profound impacts on the universe with their supernatural powers. They soon grew up and reshaped entire galaxies with their powers, doing everything they could to serve the goddess they had once known. They had the goal of carrying the mantle and bringing all worlds into a peaceful light through divine evolution. As more planets were made and more species evolved, everyone continued to rejoice in the beautiful afterlife that was heaven. Jannah had a realm past Purgatory and all beings sought to do good in the universe so that they may serve their respective gods and one day enter the gates of the afterlife when their time of mortality passed. The universe saw itself in a completely new era. One where all beings lived to make a positive change for their religion or simply as an act of Free Will. This type of behavior created strides in religious and scientific discoveries, ones that only brought everyone closer together. The universe was finally at peace. The newest phenomenon changed the way mortals perceived their existence. It was Faith.

Eon V
Faith

So began the dawn of a new age. After her willful sacrifice for all of the universes, the goddess became a Mother to all existence, embedded in the ethereal realm of nature. Her decision to allow all worthy walks of life to be welcomed into the gates of heaven was not in vain. Although gods began to fade from the physical realm into the planes of unseen spirits, it became arguably true that all life preferred an unknown force of guidance. One that was not dictating how they behaved, but trusted them to do what was right. Mortals had placed their motives, their cause for power, their reason for being, in an entity even greater than that of Free Will. Faith.

The same divine force that provided the goddess with the courage to sacrifice herself for all beings in every dimension came to be the defining factor for the new generation. This Faith became the great power that allowed the Wise Ones, now known as the *Hakim Nisa'*, to create more planets and more species through religious prowess. Much like what they used their powers for long ago, to create heaven, they continued to proliferate peaceful planets across the stars. Jannah was the only planet in the new dimension capable of godly creation. The goddess was gladly willing to share in the happiness that heaven brought to all. The *Hakim Nisa'* carried the torch of religious traditions for the advancements of scientific evolution, just as the goddess wanted during her Eon. This expansion of peace was done through the help of the Seraphs and many other species in the Syris Solar System. It was the single most important planet and the last hope for continuous evolution in the universe. Without Jannah's holy power, all life would have been doomed for extinction and more war. Although some conflicts arose, the Seraphs refused to give in to the hatred that had corrupted so much of ancient history. Instead, they followed the word of their Mother Nature and sided with an era of peace. In many instances, the Seraphs' way won. Whether it be from the angel's physical power, moral integrity, or spiritual enlightenment, they were the key to unifying all beings in the new dimension. To the rest of the universe, Jannah was a planet of living gods.

Through the great interdimensional unification, every legendary species started from the beginning of their lives once again. An evolution from its primordial state. Religion and faith, however, had proven to be an astronomically powerful force. Despite beginning life in a new dimension, the distant religions of each species managed to faintly exist in the new one. Through prophecies, emerging stories of various gods, and indescribable feelings of a higher power, every species began to redevelop their original religion. Not everyone was so keen on immediately adhering to Jannah's faith. There had to have been other gods, other forms of the afterlife, other ways to dictate morals. Why did the other species have to obey the Seraphs? In many cases, the other species still chose to follow the religion of Jannah. But for those who didn't, Jannah had to prove its power. Although other species had faint feelings of their past lives and past faith, Jannah was the only planet that could prove its religion with its existence. Its very planet in the physical realm was proof that the afterlife existed in the here and now. Jannah was in the universe as a literal afterlife. The souls existing in heaven were scientifically proven. Beings who had done good

and followed the way of goddess were proven to have been granted access through the gates of heaven by the Seraphs. Unfortunately for many other species, their religion couldn't be proven as easily. The other religions that were supposedly practiced beneath that of Jannah's were only felt in the spirit.

This discrepancy led to over 75% of the species in the Syris Solar System following the way of goddess. Jannah's prowess was too almighty to contend with. And most felt it was best to achieve their form of afterlife. With every form of good, evil had to balance it. Aside from wanting to attain access into the gates of Jannah's afterlife, many species feared what happened to people who didn't live a morally upright life. For those who sinned and committed atrocities in the universe, they were believed to have gone to hell. Jahannam. It was described as the polar opposite of Jannah. Although its existence wasn't proven the way heaven was, Jannah's religion emphasized a great punishment for those who were evil. This fear put more of the other species in line with abiding by their religion. This was one of the most impactful ways peace had been achieved during many centuries. It was believed that fear would only be on the Seraphs' side for so long. That someday, the living gods that existed on Jannah would lose their grip on the universe. As with the creation of any new era, destruction had to precede it.

Planet Formation

Beginning with a religious sacrament, the *Hakim Nisa'* believed in extensive prayer before embarking on the treacherous task of creating a planet meant to harbor life. After physical, mental, and spiritual preparations had been made, the Wise Women would seek the assistance of Jannah's most powerful warriors, scribes, and priests, then begin the formation of a star in a stellar nursery. After gathering remnants of ancient nebulae, the *Hakim Nisa'* worked with their people to reignite the flames of the once dangerous clouds of warfare. It was believed sounds of chaos between paramount gods from the Alter-Realm could still be heard in the undead masses of dust and gas. As the Seraphs collectively worked to conjure the massive nebula using sacred incense and their supernatural abilities, beautiful pictures of color painted the universe once more. The nebula, over 400 degrees Fahrenheit below zero, nearly came to life. As it harnessed the spiritual forces of the Seraphs, the nebula began to take the shape of battles and figures of the past, embedding itself within the minds of its creators. Constellations of profound meaning displayed many shows for the distant universe to see. The *Hakim Nisa'* spent several days observing the interstellar stories told by the nebulae, finding atonement in empathizing with the cloud of dust instead of just ignorantly hating its existence for the war they caused Eons ago. Once the nebula's story was witnessed, the *Hakim Nisa'* sent Jannah's warriors into the depths of the mass with powerful fragments of light in their possession. As the warriors were capable of withstanding the harsh conditions of the newborn nebula, they would leave the fragments of light in sectors of the nebula. If done right, one of the fragments of light would be capable of forming into a protostar; other lights fading by chance. Once the light was felt amongst the *Hakim Nisa'*, the Seraphs would unite and combine their energy, locking arms to withstand the intense cold within the nebula. They all entered at once and used their spiritual forces to breathe life into the protostar. This burst of energy collapsed the dense knot of dust to a span of less than a light-year across space. As the protostar began to expand into a stable structure, the Seraphs returned home to nourish the star's spiritual force. To do this and progress the protostar's lifecycle, they performed religious sacraments, eliminated darkness scattered across the universe, and sacrificed their most holy relics. Several weeks were spent doing this to enrich the growing protostar.

It was impossible to be completely certain about the maturity of the protostar within the treacherous nebula. As the *Hakim Nisa'* continued to pray, they would await the word from their goddess, looking for a sense that what they had performed was in alignment with her scientific devotion in the past. Once the star reached spiritual affinity with the Seraphs, its initial rotation would begin. United again, the Wise Women would get the help of the greatest Seraph scientists to set the protostar into motion on its axis. Eventually, the star would build enough momentum to sustain its rotational speed in the form of a disc. The tremendously fast-moving disc accumulated surrounding gas and dust into its powerful orbit. The *Hakim Nisa'* would fragment the interstellar body into sections. Only areas of intense light were strong enough for planets to begin formation.

Shortly after, the *Hakim Nisa'* would visually begin a holographic prayer, displaying the blueprints for the developing solar system amongst the stars. Once they would reach a consensus on the manifestation of the

solar system, they would await the material to build such a massive structure. Several weeks were spent idle, waiting for asteroids to collide into the rotation of the system. Too great for such a task, the *Hakim Nisa'* would assign thousands of Seraphs to transport the material to designated planet formations, allowing them to take shape. In a few instances, the designs to terraform a planet were elaborated by trainees of Jannah's royalty class, who hoped to one day succeed the Wise Women. This was the highest honor of all existence. Yet in most cases, the *Hakim Nisa'* took charge of planetary evolution and terraforming.

Once the solar system reached peak formation, the high council would call upon the royal family of Jannah to witness the spectacle, as it was believed to be a desire of their goddess that they must obey. Before traveling into space, they would receive their blessings in a temple. Then, they would join the *Hakim Nisa'* in a day-long prayer, in which they would enter a supernatural realm known as Cosmos. Utilizing what remained of the power of gods, the Seraphs were capable of entering the 4th dimension spiritually but had lost the ability to do so physically generations ago. Mortality had tainted their existence. Within Cosmos, the royal family would learn new truths of their existence and how they could continue the proliferation of life across the universe. Words of Faith were believed to be spared by their goddess in a language incomprehensible outside of Cosmos. Once this indulgence in religion was complete, the *Hakim Nisa'* would begin a final chant and expend a tremendous amount of celestial force, causing the star to nearly explode into its final transformation as a Sun, with similar properties as Genesis. At the start of Eon V, Genesis became the major Sun of the Syris Solar System, housed in the center of all the planets orbiting it. This final blessing would surround the newly formed solar system in holy energy, ensuring its safety amongst the stars. Once a new Sun and solar system were complete, the Wise Women and royal family would return home. Exhausted after a successful first step towards evolution, the royal guards would help them get back to Jannah to rest. In the meantime, they would await the next phase; creating the species.

The Hakim Nisa'

Evolution of a New Species

After spending several months in rest and allowing the newly terraformed planets to cool, the *Hakim Nisa'* would initiate the next phase to begin the origin of life. They would all travel to the Crown of the World, the highest mountain on Jannah, to pray at the sacred altar within the pyramid. Considered the holiest area in all of the universe, this prayer, combined with the essence of each of their blood, created the powerful first link to evolution. Bacteria. The Wise Women would travel to each planet in the developing solar system and place this divine bacterium within the oceans, specifically within hydrothermal vents to initiate the rise of microorganisms. Through the power of the Seraph species, the evolution process transcended phases quickly. The *Hakim Nisa'* would receive assistance from their people once more, executing the rise of prokaryotes, to cyanobacteria, eukaryotes, choanoflagellate, flatworms, pikaia, and the development of aquatic creatures. These evolving forms of animals soon surfaced to land after developing adaptive appendages. At this milestone, the entire process would be nearly complete. Utilizing science and religion, the Seraphs were nearly capable of doing what the twin gods had done Eons ago.

It was at this point where the *Hakim Nisa'* had already collaborated with the king and Queen of Jannah to predetermine how the new species would distinguish themselves into evolution. Many species had different characteristics; no two were alike. It was the goddess's wish to use variability in genes and phenotypes to hopefully witness the evolution of a species most proficiently suited for life in the universe. No species had yet to supersede the perfection of the Seraphs on Jannah.

Throughout the several hundred years of evolution for the newborn species, the Seraphs would watch from afar, secretly guarding the new solar system. At certain points of the process, Seraphs would also begin to make their presence ambiguously known. A squadron on Jannah served to act as aliens on the new planet, helping the species evolve through scientific development and leaving behind fragments of religious principles. Seraphs had a crucial goal of assisting the species by creating massive pyramid structures. Pyramids were used as beacons for immediate teleportation from Jannah to the newborn planets, should the species ever need immediate assistance. Jannah had worked in tandem with the other ancient species of Syris on multiple occasions. It was believed that they had worked with Vectins on Kremlin for this phase, as Vectins were easily capable of shapeshifting to look like any species. Hiding amongst the evolving species, they would improve technology from within. Other planets in Syris would continue to help evolving species while remaining in the shadows. Although this would take several centuries of deliberate nurturing, it was a worthy cause to please the goddess of the three suns and continue the evolution of hundreds of species across the universe. Once the newborn species in the solar system would achieve the means of space travel, the Seraphs would allow the presence of the legendary Syris Solar

System to be known. Then, they would transition the new species into their religion, seeing their Faith as the most dominant in the universe.

Transference

Once the newly evolved species was provided absolute awareness of the Syris Solar System, they formed elite ties with the eight ancient planets and became eligible to take part in Transference. Transference was the process in which souls were allowed to be processed through Jannah. This was the highest honor for all mortals in the universe. From this point forward, the deaths that occurred amongst the newly evolved species could be rescinded through the reincarnation of their souls in the planes of divinity upon Jannah. At the Seraphs' discretion, all who died would be allowed into the gates of heaven in the spiritual realm.

Possessing tremendous levels of spiritual affinity with space, Seraphs were capable of guiding and dictating how they would be reincarnated after processing through the afterlife. A technique as powerful as this allowed Seraphs to be reincarnated as any species in the universe. Because they were the creators of evolution, they had extreme jurisdiction over how the afterlife would operate. Reincarnating as another species allowed the Seraphs to control the outcomes of history as they were foreseen by the *Hakim Nisa'*. While the Wise Women meditated in Cosmos, they could foretell the path of the universe, believed to be told by their goddess. This clairvoyance and spiritual affinity with science gave the Seraphs inexplicable levels of control over the affairs of Syris and the entire universe. They decided who died, who lived, and who was reincarnated, seemingly possessing the power of a god.

Reincarnation and the Guild of Protectors

It was because of this infinite power that Seraphs possessed a unique Faith unfelt by any other species in the universe. They didn't fear death. It was a Faith in their own lives that arguably became a cause for a god Complex within the species. Knowing that they could control how their souls would reincarnate in another body, they developed the infinite courage to do what they pleased, when they pleased. It was believed to be their sworn duty to control the timeline of the universe, for the sake of peace. To reincarnate in other bodies as a passed soul was a sacrifice meant to assist the *Hakim Nisa'* in fulfilling the history of Time and Space.

A prime example of such a divine occurrence was when a Seraph, Palmiro, reincarnated into the body of an Ectognatha to protect a general on Echelon from a foreseen assassination. Reincarnation was performed through the utilization of the higher dimensions existing within Cosmos. This coalition of Seraphs eligible for reincarnation was known as the Guild of Protectors, whose sole purpose was to fulfill the destiny of the universe and utilize a unique tradition to control the past, present, and future.

Princes Jonah and Carmine's Solar System

Having nothing more than the highest respect for their heritage and traditions, many children of Jannah learned of their history while in school and from visiting the temple. But none were as well-versed in the scriptures of creation and Transference as Jannah's princes, Jonah and Carmine Sultan. Learning much of what they knew from their parents, King Adelrik and Queen Vitaliya, or even the *Hakim Nisa'* themselves, they spent much of their early years attempting to create on profound levels. Nearly that of the Wise Women. Some of their early tests are evident in one of the younger galaxies in the universe. Their experiments have been located within what is known today as the Orion and Perseus arms of the Milky Way. Considered The Chosen Ones of their Eon, Jonah and Carmine were the youngest Seraphs to have created respectably decent planet structures. Although they experienced many failures, their first successful protostar was for a solar system in the Milky Way, created with minimal aid from the *Hakim Nisa'*. Lifeless dwarf planets, like what they called "Pluto", or gas giants like Jupiter and Saturn, were considered relatively unsuccessful trails. Despite these mistakes, the princes had eventually broken ground to a useful planet structure. At this time, Jonah and Carmine had been working on a new planet that appeared to be promising for the beginning of evolution. Uniquely designed with 71% water and an atmosphere of Methane, Ammonia, water vapor, and Neon, it was still in a developmental process. The princes were hoping that the introduction of the divine bacterium in the cooling oceans would increase the production of Oxygen on the unnamed planet. It is here in the story, where princes Jonah and Carmine currently await the development of their newest planet.

Peace, Prosperity, and Parties

During Eon V, the universe knew many extravagant species. In a time where mortals managed to supersede the immortal gods, tangible natures of physical strength, intellect, and spirituality became more important. Amongst all of space, there was but a single planet that possessed all-natural attributes to a level of perfection. This planet, Jannah, was home to a species known as Seraphs, who had existed in the physical realm as remnants of the goddess' vision of angels. They were commonly called Paragons by the other species in the universe. Paragons meaning a perfect or exemplar quality of something. In the case of the Seraphs, they were called Paragons because of their perfection as a species. Jannah had great warriors, great intellectuals, great faith, great unity, and an even greater treasure.

It was today where the entire species of Seraphs had united with its Syris kin to celebrate a milestone seemingly thought impossible thousands of years ago. It was perfect. Today, the great king of the royal Sultan family had called upon all elite class from the neighboring planets for yet another moment to rejoice. Adelrik stood before the greatest people that mortality had to offer. His castle was flooded with beings of drastically diverse appearances. The royal family's castle consisted of solid gold for exterior foundation and glistening crystals for windows. But the Seraphs of Jannah knew the material makeup of the castle was only the smallest riches of Jannah. The young king of 87 years-old held his glass up for a toast. Atop his stand, behind a podium, the 6'7 man seemed larger than normal, ignoring the size of his heroic personality. The large sea of people followed his movement, raising their glasses too. The 2nd Sun, north of the castle's entrance, glistened off the hundreds of glass windows and reflective utensils.

"All rise," Adelrik said in his low voice.

His bearded face and massive stature labeled him as the epitome of any respectable mortal. He was romantically sought after by all women in the solar system and envied by all men who desired his power. Adelrik's intense brown eyes showed truth and honesty, while his defined jaw showed distinguishing bravery no other could exemplify. His brown hair was like the mane of a majestic warrior. His trustworthy smile emphasized his role as the leader of a royal bloodline. His queen, Vitaliya, was by his side. Vitaliya was by far the most beautiful woman on the entire planet, perhaps even all of Syris. Her long platinum hair was proof of an elegant grace that not only dignified her status as royalty but truly represented her uniqueness. Her teal eyes were a symbol of her magnificent glory. And her soft rosy cheeks, coupled with her tan skin, solidified her perfection.

"Today, we celebrate the 25th anniversary of peace in Syris. The gods have blessed us with our Sun, Genesis, and the ability to continue life across all the stars through evolution and Transference. Perhaps one day, the younger species will be able to experience peace such as ours. Once more, in good faith, I would like to take a moment to thank and appreciate the diversity of Jannah. The gates of heaven see no color, no race, and no difference in species. Anyone who employs a kind heart while in the physical realm shall have access to continued life in the planes of divinity. Now, more important than the aftermath of conquests in war, we celebrate the 18th birthday of my two sons. Everyone, please give your proudest Syris cheer to Jonah and Carmine Sultan!" Adelrik shouted with visible hope and happiness in his heart.

The large sea of people roared. Their cries of excitement hid the undertone of fear and dismay. Within the spirits of Syris, war had always been in the universe's pattern. It was in the history of many universes, such as the war between the nebulae in Eon I and the war waged by the god of Gravity long before existence. All mortals knew this peace on Syris would not last forever.

"And now, we shall begin the feast!" Adelrik exclaimed. He left his position in front of the podium and approached his queen. He held Vitaliya's hand, helping her rise out of one of their many thrones. The mature woman, 102 years-old, stood above her husband, nearly 6'10. The female Seraphs were commonly greater than their male counterparts, physically, intellectually, and spiritually. It was understood that this pattern was the wish of their goddess, who was formerly the most motivated and determined being in all existence. Her tremendous ambitions showed the power of women in the universe. Not only were they the bearers of children, but they were warriors in every aspect of life.

The live, festive music began in the background, played by one of planet Ximji's talented pop singers. The graceful Elf allowed her powerful voice to dominate the atmosphere. Her amaranth hair swayed beautifully as she danced around, transitioning from hook to chorus. The party was in full swing.

Saqui, Popstar of Ximji

The twin princes, Jonah and Carmine, walked together with drinks in their hands. They narrowly escaped the crowd of adoring fans, boys and girls alike, who wanted nothing more than to be in the presence of their royalty. The pampered teenagers wanted a chance to escape from their popularity. It was understandable that their status amongst others was greatly sought after by more than just the Seraphs of Jannah. It became clear their names were known across the entire solar system when their father employed new policies to allow an even greater influx of immigrants into Jannah than before. All eight species loved the princes alike. People continued to wave and cheer at them from inside the castle. The age of 18 was beyond important for boys of their class. Full-fledged adulthood would soon be amongst them.

Jonah and Carmine stepped outside to the marble balcony. The beautiful garden of Jannah's castle displayed its radiant colors to them. The setting of the 2nd Sun allowed a lavender light to glisten throughout half of the planet's giant size. It was a sight perfect enough to make any mortal cry. The prince brothers leaned on the golden railing in silence. Jonah just sighed. Then, he looked over at his brother, a person he shared more blood with than his parents.

"Hard to believe it's been 18 years already, huh?" Jonah asked.

"I suppose it is…" Carmine mumbled with sorrow.

"Seems like it's bothering you more than me."

"I guess time just flies you know? We've waited for this day for what feels like forever and it's already here. But did you hear what dad said? 25 unbelievable years since he won the war and unified Syris again."

"I see what you mean. That's why I suggested we come out here. In times like these, there are hardly any moments for us to take a breather. Always something for us to do. Always someone who wants to take pictures. You know how it is."

"Thanks for the idea. The 2nd sunset is refreshing."

Jonah placed an intense look upon his brother's face. "You know Carmine, now that I'm 18, I think it might be the perfect time."

"For what Jonah?"

Carmine stared at his brother in confusion, but after he took a moment to feel the atmosphere, he knew exactly what Jonah was talking about. "Really?" he asked.

"Yes. I just think Evelyn has been so patient. It's time for us to marry. She's the one woman on Jannah who deserves to be in the castle with us. Her mother and little sister too. Bless her father's spirit…" Jonah replied.

"But Jonah, marrying someone is a sacred bond that exceeds beyond physical relation and riches. It's *spiritually* sacred. You know that. Why do you want to move things so quickly?"

"I've been dating her for four years now. I think it's about time we settle down."

"Have you mentioned this to mom and dad? More importantly, the *Hakim Nisa'*? Especially Wise Woman Kanya. She's like an auntie to us."

"They'll know soon enough. But I'm an adult; their blessings are no longer needed."

"*Sure*. Just a very *highly* important recommendation."

"Maybe you and I can speak with Kanya tonight if she isn't busy tending to the new protostar. Either way, I'm making my decision with or without their blessing."

"I suppose… but *I* for one am gonna stay single. I'm living young and the world of adulthood has just started. Seraphs easily live to be 150 years old. Plenty of time, Jonah. Freedom is my prerogative, not the bindings of marriage!"

"Suit yourself. I'm going to propose to Evelyn after we speak with the *Hakim Nisa'*."

"Good for you, brother. And thanks a ton for the chat. Now if you don't mind, I think I'm going to enjoy the rest of the party."

Carmine walked back into the castle.

Jonah thought intensely about what his brother had said. Ironically enough, the ambiguity of his decision became clear. It was hard to understand if marrying Evelyn now was right or not. But he wanted to give the girl everything he had. *"Am I right? Spending my life with someone until my days are over?"* Jonah thought to himself. He swirled the wine in his glass and stepped back into the castle. Once more, he could see all the diverse people enjoying themselves at a moment of excellent joy and prosperity. To see a Vectin dance with an Automa or a Nanomorph hold a baby from Pandora, or an Ectognatha sharing culinary delights with a minister of Tempest, was truly a sight to behold. The unity between the different species of Syris was a beautiful thing. Jonah smiled and placed his glass on a nearby table. He wanted to maintain his wits for now. He continued walking, gathering his thoughts about love

and what it truly was. Being a teenage boy of only 18 years old, love seemed to be his only real responsibility as of late. His affairs were his biggest matters. Jonah accidentally passed by the table where his parents sat.

"Son! Come, sit with me and your mother!" Adelrik shouted. Jonah turned and smiled at his parents. He walked over to the right-hand side of his father.

The king and Queen of Jannah were at a table with some of the most respected leaders across the various planets of Syris. "Jonah, you remember Tadeo, the hero of Ximji..." Adelrik said. Jonah observed the young Elf and shook his hand.

"...and Darien, a Baron from Mirage..." Vitaliya said. Jonah observed the insect-like man and proudly shook his hand.

"...and of course, the king and queen of Echelon, Raimundo, and Lindie," Adelrik concluded.

Jonah observed the couple and bowed before their royalty. He finally sat beside his father. The various people from the surrounding planets talked amongst each other while Adelrik and Vitaliya directed their attention to their son. He and his brother were always their priority.

Darien, Baron of Mirage

"Look at him Vitaliya. He's finally 18 now. Our son's in his prime," Adelrik said happily.

"Yes, he's gotten to be so much bigger. I can see you and your brother with the crowns on now, ruling Jannah and Syris as the first-ever set of twin kings. Oh, how powerful you both will be. It will be your intellect and spiritual guidance that truly sets your right as rulers above all Seraphs," Vitaliya said.

Jonah blushed. "You know, I wouldn't be who I am now if it weren't for you both. Carmine and I are grateful for all the sacrifices you've made for us," he said.

"But son, we could surely say the same for you and Carmine. Your work with the charities has greatly uplifted the spirits of our community as of late. Not to mention what you two have been capable of doing alongside the *Hakim Nisa'*. My goddess. Your newest terraform has quite the fortuitous possibilities," Adelrik added.

"Nonsense, Adelrik. Jonah and Carmine knew what they were doing when they devised a planet with 71% water and an atmosphere of Neon. Much like what you two have done with that solar system of yours, you and your brother have wonderfully changed who your father and I are since you came into this beautiful world," Vitaliya said.

"Speaking of which, where is Carmine?" Adelrik asked.

"Oh, he decided to indulge in the excursions again. Probably with a few of his ridiculous friends from the county," Jonah explained, unknowingly showing signs of sorrow.

"What's wrong son?"

"Nothing father, I'm fine. I just… feel like I'm due for another talk with the Wise Women again. It's been a week since we've meditated in Cosmos."

"Well… we have always implored you and your brother to become more spiritually inclined, but I would suggest you boys have done us proud lately. No need to tend to the Cosmos on your birthday sweetie," Vitaliya said, attempting to comfort her son.

"I agree with your mother. Please, Jonah, enjoy your day. If you need to tell us anything we'll always be here for you."

"Yeah. I know you will. Thank you, guys."

Jonah got up from the table and hugged his loving parents. He quickly bowed before the four royal beings who were kind enough to give him some time alone to speak with his family. Jonah left towards a grand table where more than fifty of his friends from Jannah and various other planets were sitting, chanting his name in excitement. They wanted nothing more than to enjoy his presence. As Jonah sat at the head of the table and was passed a drink, he could see dozens of familiar faces, but none of them were his girlfriend, Evelyn.

Meanwhile, at a nearby table, there was another crowd of fans who adored the princes of Jannah. Carmine was standing atop the expensive furniture, dancing with girls, eating food, and enjoying what felt like a brand new life with his friends. They drank, played gambling games, and made multiple jokes about women and what they would potentially be doing to them now that Carmine, who was originally the youngest amongst his friends, was now an adult. Jannah was surely a place for people of all types and ages. The diversity on the planet was immediately noticeable, especially in the great castle. It was this variety of species that brought about decades of acceptance and a joyous blend of cultures. Everyone was now living free, but none more freely than the great Prince Carmine. After spending another hour throwing all caution to the wind, he decided he needed another moment to breathe, away from all the hyped-up excitement. But this time, Jonah was nowhere near to join his brother for a talk. Carmine tried calling him, but he wasn't answering his communicator.

The young prince decided to step outside on his own. After breaking away from the crowd and risking it all to separate from his friends, Carmine roamed the large garden that stood in front of the castle. He picked the flowers and inhaled their scent before letting them blow in the evening winds. Suddenly, a girl passed by his peripheral vision. She stood near some bushes, her long white dress glistening from the 1st setting Sun, Genesis. Carmine was immediately drawn to the beautiful girl. He slowly started approaching her, adjusting his hair and clothes. He saw her playing with a small insect that had glittering spots and ten legs. Carmine was slightly drunk. An unfamiliar nervousness overwhelmed his ability to start a conversation with such a beautiful stranger.

"Your world must be wonderful… isn't it?" the girl asked.

Carmine froze; she already knew he was there. "What do you mean?" he asked.

"A prince housed in a castle with adoring fans surrounding him. On a planet where his people, Seraphs, Paragons, are capable of initiating evolution and reincarnation. Is there anything you don't have Prince Carmine?"

"You sound envious, girl."

"Much more curious than I am envious. Answer my question."

"Perhaps I *do* have everything I could ask for. Except for one thing…"

The girl smiled, purposely avoiding eye contact with Carmine. "I know you, Carmine. Everyone does. You're the great prince of freedom, youth, bravery, and… romance," she said.

"That's where you're wrong. Romance may be the one thing I don't have. Although I have all the riches I could ask for. Although I have the power to produce planets in the infinite universe. Although I can spiritually transcend into a higher dimension, there is more to mortality than meets the eye. I want a girl who looks

past what I can do and cares more about what I feel. I think all life in Syris has been consumed by our faith, and now, we can't see past our desire to please our gods. We forget to please ourselves."

The girl twirled around, walked over to Carmine, and placed a yellow flower on his ear. "My. You sure as hell don't shy from expressing your controversial opinions. How could you stand against what all your people hold so near to their hearts?" she asked.

"You mean *our* people? Aren't you a Seraph?"

The girl reached up and touched Carmine's face with her left hand. It felt cold, lifeless. Carmine grabbed her hand. It wasn't truly hers but was one replaced with a metal prosthetic. "I'm not a Seraph. I'm an Automa, from Centauri."

Carmine's mouth gaped as he looked into the girl's colorful eyes. She had blue irises, pink pupils, and a white center glow. The Automa, commonly referred to as cyborgs, were ridiculed as "half-hearted" by many people in Syris. Automa possessed features similar to that of Seraphs, combined with artificial limbs, organs, or traits of robots, resulting in them being called cyborgs. In a civil war that occurred hundreds of years ago, artificially intelligent machines created by the native species employed abilities of self-control and launched a war against their creators. This conflict led to nuclear warfare and left the newborn flesh children to be birthed with severe diseases as well as missing limbs and organs for centuries down family lines. In the wake of this tragedy, the upcoming generation began using remaining robot parts to supplement that of which the babies couldn't naturally provide themselves. Fully functional robots still lived amongst the population, cautiously serving the people once more.

Carmine continued holding the girl's hand. "What's your name?"

The girl removed herself from getting too close to him. "My name is Leola," she said.

Carmine persisted. "Leola, I'm sorry for what happened to your people. And I apologize on behalf of the Seraphs for the insults they throw at the Automa for being different," he said.

Leola simply laughed. "I don't take offense to their words, cause they apply to me in a way. I was *actually* born with only half a heart. The rest of the organ was taken from the same criminal robot that killed my mother. Perhaps that's why I'm such a cold person. I couldn't be at that party for long because I knew I would only come to hate what your people con-

stantly take for granted. Perfection. And every Seraph friend I've made only ends up calling me a monster."

Carmine hesitated to approach her any further. But then, he realized she was right. The Seraphs' ego clouded their judgment. Mortals none too shy from experiencing immortality. How could any being be grateful for life when they don't have to fear death? Carmine empathized with the girl. This moment was a reward created from the diversity of Jannah. By chance, he was able to meet a profound being who was normally planets away from him.

"You're no monster to me," Carmine said. He grabbed her metal hand and kissed it. "Leola, would you be willing to spend the rest of the evening with me? I wish to hear your story."

"How could you possibly see me as fit to spend the day with the prince of Jannah?" Leola asked.

"Tonight, I just want to be a boy who turned 18. Nothing more."

"With you, anything could be a memorable moment. But I'm sure all the women tell you that."

Carmine grabbed the yellow flower from his ear and placed it on Leola's. "Yes, but this time, *I'm* the one who's chasing."

"With the perfect Seraphs you have in your presence, you chase a faulty Automa? You could pick your love as if it were in a basket beside you."

"No. To me, love doesn't come very often."

Leola gazed into Carmine's eyes, bewildered by the sentence uttered from his lips.

Jonah was standing atop a golden carpet in the lobby of the castle. It was yet another sector of Jannah's massive fortress with another couple hundred people partying. Jonah took photos with his family, friends, and adoring fans. He finally took what felt like his millionth photo with another group of people. As he observed the clock upon his wrist, he realized he'd been generous for too long. He started to make his escape away from the crowd.

Leola, Automa of Centauri

"Thank you everyone for allowing me to take an album's worth of photos with you, but please, I have other matters to tend to!" Jonah shouted over the people who had their eyes glued to his presence. Suddenly, a sea of applause flooded the room. The boy didn't do anything, yet it seemed as if every word he said was worthy of acclamation from people of all races in Syris. Although people clamored to shake his hand and bid him farewell, Jonah quickly ran upstairs before he could get caught up in his politeness again.

The fascination with the Seraph princes was beginning to bother him. But perhaps from a scientific perspective, it made sense why everyone would adore a being who was capable of initiating the evolution of bacteria into organisms. Maybe even from a religious perspective, it also made sense why all species would adore a being who was capable of granting access to reincarnation and the afterlife. When Jonah would think about it too often, it just sounded like godliness.

Walking amongst the distant halls of the castle, Jonah could only see a few stray partygoers. Some chatting amongst themselves and sending messages with their communicative devices, while others were exchanging affection or passing out from too much alcohol. No matter how many people wanted his presence, there was only one person Jonah wanted to see right now. Evelyn, the love of his life. He stepped before the door of the guest room she was staying in for the rest of the week. Jonah took multiple deep breaths, frozen, much like his brother. He took a small silk box out of his pocket and opened it. Inside was a luxurious ring. The gorgeous diamond was priceless, but nothing was too expensive for his beloved. There was more to Seraphs than their riches. The truest hearts only resided in a rare few of the newest generations, but many of the neighboring planets ignored the opportunities to experience what the Paragons had to offer the universe. To them, the Seraphs were conceited and possessed a god Complex. It was far from the truth. Jonah placed the ring back in its silk box and put it back in his pocket, his heart pounding. Now was not the time to ask Evelyn. Deep down, he knew he needed the *Hakim Nisa's* blessing. The prince was shaking like a child. He finally raised a fist and gently knocked. He waited patiently until Evelyn finally opened the door. She had a large smile upon her face, as always.

"Jonah!" Evelyn exclaimed happily. She hugged her boyfriend and kissed him. "I was wondering when you would come to visit me up here. Come in! I've just been making up the room."

Jonah still hadn't said a word to her. He couldn't help but stare at her wonderful brown hair and beautiful lavender iris accompanied by green pupils. Her figure was perfectly curved and her skin was soft like the sandy beaches of Jannah. To Jonah, her height, her face, her purity, were all perfect. Everything about Evelyn's magnificence astounded him. She was the true Paragon.

Jonah felt his pocket, reminding himself of the silk box the ring was in. He debated whether he should simply ignore the *Hakim Nisa'* and his parents' blessing. This was his life now and he no longer wanted to live under the ideological utopia pre-established by his people. Yet, he felt no courage to propose. Perhaps it would be too cliché to propose during such an extravagant celebration.

Before he could make any move whatsoever, Evelyn grabbed his arm and pulled him into the room. "Why are you waiting out here?" she asked playfully. Jonah sat on the bed and watched Evelyn as she brushed her hair. The young woman was sitting on a stool in front of an expensive dresser adorned with a gilded mirror mounted atop it.

Jonah had been staring for so long that Evelyn eventually noticed him through the mirror. The bubbly yet well-mannered girl set the brush down and turned in her stool to face her boyfriend. The concern on her face matched his.

"Jonah… is everything alright? Maybe you've been indulging in the drinks too much," Evelyn said.

"Babe, of course not. I've had none but two drinks."

"Then why do you look so sick? Like you're about to throw up or something."

"Maybe the celebration is much more than I thought I could handle. The people, in particular, are becoming overwhelming."

"Well, I would surely consider Carmine to be much more of a reckless partygoer than you. Either way, it's only been two sunsets worth of celebration. You couldn't handle a couple of hours?"

"It's more than just the celebration, Evelyn. It's the people here. It's the biggest celebration on Jannah since my father changed the immigration policies. The diversity…"

Evelyn continued brushing her hair without the assistance of the mirror. "Don't tell me you're racist," she said curtly.

"Don't be ridiculous! Of course I'm not racist. I love all people. It's just the other planets' blind idolization of the royal family, of all Seraphs, that pisses me off sometimes."

"I'm taking it that you don't like the attention much? It doesn't surprise me. You have been more introverted than you're willing to admit. But you should feel comfortable being honest with your people. You'll rule over them someday."

"But Evelyn, what if I don't want to be king of Syris?"

Evelyn stopped brushing her hair in shock. "How could you say that? Your mother and father have worked hard to grant you and your brother a worthy transition into the throne. Carmine can't rule on his own," she said.

"Because the Seraphs buy into their own godly beliefs as much as those without guidance. Do the *Hakim Nisa'* truly know all? If our goddess was fighting for our paradise, then why do our people continue to suffer, even in the absence of war? Look at your own family, Evelyn. Your mother and younger sister can't escape the confines of the industrial sector. Jannah, on the face of it all, may seem perfect. But deep in the bowels of this planet, we allow our kind to suffer. The rich don't share with the poor. The poor are ungrateful for the handouts they *do* receive. The natural resources are being depleted. And the biggest murderer of

Seraphs are Seraphs themselves. Over bullshit. Money, sex, drugs, gangs. And it's all hidden by a faulty, misguided faith!"

"Jonah! Please! Stop! Don't talk down on your kind so much. The Seraphs are truly the future link to immortality, and there's a lot of importance in that. I understand your disposition. Faith could sometimes be considered doing things without educated reason. Blind action in hopes of a positive outcome. But we have to be grateful for what we *do* have. We're not the disfigured Automa or the Personas locked in a civil war. If you want to improve the way things are, I stand by your side to do whatever we can until you become king. Or better yet, you've finally made a promising planet with your brother. Maybe you can create a species even better than the Seraphs."

Jonah felt simultaneously victorious and defeated. Evelyn was right. He should've been more grateful for what he did have. He can't help the public with a dissatisfied position about mortality and immortality.

Evelyn tilted her head slightly like an innocent pet. The young woman was always caring and persistent in pursuing her boyfriend's best interests. "Sweetheart. I know things feel overwhelming for you and your brother. So young, yet you have so much responsibility…" Evelyn got up from the stool and sat by Jonah, looking into his eyes. Evelyn held his chin in between her soft fingers. Jonah could feel her somewhat long nails poke his jaw.

"Evelyn. I feel like there is so much beyond science and religion. It's constantly evolve and pray. Evolve and pray. As if mortals are good for nothing more. As if-"

Evelyn placed a finger over his lips, silencing him. "Now, now. You know there's so much more to life than just these things. If it was just you and I in the universe, I would never ask you to bear the godly task of evolution. All I could want from you is love. That's the true purpose for us mortals," she said. Evelyn kissed Jonah repeatedly.

They looked into each other's eyes again. Jonah couldn't help but kiss her back. She was right again. Evelyn sat on his lap, their chests touching. She threw all her weight on Jonah, pushing him onto his back. She was on top of him now, holding onto something greater than the boy's ability to create species. To Evelyn, her boyfriend's greatest creation was what felt like an infinite relationship between them. The only sound now was the party. Love was in the air. It was all they needed.

Evelyn, Commoner of Jannah

The night air was cool, but the heat of emotions contrasted with the weather. Carmine and Leola were still out in the massive garden of Jannah's royal castle. They stood in front of one of its largest, most elegant ponds. The two moons glistened in the reflection of the crystal clear waters. Carmine watched the colorful fish swim around aimlessly. It reminded him of the misguided nature of evolution. Had it not been for the Seraphs, would any species be able to evolve? Having faith in chance was not the way of their goddess. But to Carmine, it was the true way of nature.

He and Leola were skipping rocks, simply enjoying each other's company. Spending evening to 1st sunset together so far, they were becoming very comfortable with each other.

Carmine had learned a lot about the Automa, quite possibly more than what a majority of Seraphs knew. He had returned the favor to Leola, explaining to her the importance of his kind's traditions and why they have reaped so many benefits from it. They were the most fortunate of all beings in Syris. He tried his best to speak the facts without soliciting much of his opinion.

"I see now. The practices of evolution and the divine bacterium are meant to carry out what the gods had done centuries ago. Without the guidance of Seraphs, maybe it would be really hard for any species to evolve in the universe," Leola summarized.

Carmine nodded his head and skipped another rock. "Right. At least that's what we're told according to the Kadar, our religious text. All beings have their faults, surely. But I suppose some would argue that the delusion of perfection is mortals' greatest fault," he said. The prince stared at the pebble in his hand and just dropped it on the grass.

Leola could notice him get lost in his thoughts. She grabbed Carmine and pulled him away from the pond. "Come on Carmine. Enough with the morbid talk of religious facts and scientific opinion. We've got the greatest opportunity staring us in the face right now! Everyone's in the castle partying and we're the only people in this massive garden. I say we have some goddamn fun!"

The prince started blushing from her touch. Suddenly, Leola decided to take off towards the south. Carmine just stood there, dumbfounded. Maybe she was finally showing a side of herself that he had yet to experience at all. "Wait! Where are we going?" Carmine shouted. Leola just kept running past the hedges. Carmine had no choice but to follow this girl. If he wanted her, then he would have to stick by her side for the entire night. For once, he was chasing. For once, he felt like a normal kid.

The teenagers moved through the garden together. Leola was holding Carmine's hand, pulling him in an uncertain direction past the stone statues and crystal fountain.

"Leola please, tell me where you're taking us," Carmine said, laughing slightly.

The girl just kept running with him. "Excuse me? Aren't you the prince of this place? Shouldn't you know this entire garden like the back of your hand? I've studied the maps. I've fantasized about coming here since I was little. Now that my family's finally been compensated with a ticket to this planet, I sure as hell am going to have a good time here!" Leola shouted passionately. She tugged him in front of one of the sheds in the massive garden. The kids both stood in front of a wooden gate.

Although Carmine lived at this castle his entire life, he couldn't quite recognize this area at night. Or perhaps his eyesight was far too clouded by Leola's blinding beauty.

"Oh, and to answer your question… the horse stables," Leola said finally.

Carmine felt his heart jump. He quickly bent over in a crouched position, immediately knowing they weren't supposed to be here right now. The party was the only reason many guards weren't patrolling the area. Only a few were left guarding the outside, most tending to security detail involving the festivities. "Leola. What did you bring us here for? We can't be here," Carmine whispered.

Leola looked at him and smiled gracefully. Her shining white teeth nearly reflected the moons. "To have fun."

Leola brought her prosthetic left hand up to the lock of the gate. Suddenly, her thumb opened up, a small pick appearing. She stuck it inside the keyhole of the lock and picked it open. "Normally I use this to steal food back on my home planet. But this is a worthy occasion," she said. Leola pushed open the heavy wooden gate of the horse stable barn. She

walked forward.

The inside of the barn glowed with yellow, incandescent lights. Her long white dress blew gracefully as she flaunted her curvy strut. Carmine followed her in, somewhat disregarding what he had said earlier. Leola touched one of the giant stallions.

"This one is simply gorgeous. The only horses I've seen were when bandits would invade our slums," she said. The girl rubbed the horse's mane and kissed it on its nose.

Carmine watched her, amazed by her cinematic presence. She could do anything she wanted, taming animals apparently being one of her many talents. "Leola, this is nice and all, but we *really* shouldn't be in here right now," Carmine said, walking right behind the girl.

Leola turned around, twirling in her white dress. "As they would say on my planet, you are a *'Kiska'*. You're disappointing me, young prince. I thought you were the greatest rulebreaker in all of Syris. I guess those were all just lies and rumors, something your people are commonly known for" she said, taunting the young man.

Carmine approached the girl, several inches taller than her. He looked down at her with intensely romantic energy. Leola looked up at him, pretending to be submissive. "You're tempting me, Leola. Now that is a dirty move," Carmine said playfully.

Leola grabbed onto one of the gilded straps on Carmine's royal outfit. "I never said I wasn't a dirty person," she said. Carmine could feel his breath escape him. All he wanted to do was kiss her, but Leola suddenly placed her hands on his chest and pushed him to the floor.

Carmine fell back into a pile of hay. His head popped out with mounds of hay in his mouth. Leola was laughing, taking pictures with her phone. Carmine spit it all out hysterically. He quickly freed himself from the pile of hay. Then he heard the neigh of two horses and the trotting of their hooves. When he looked up, there was Leola, standing between two of Jannah's most prestigious stallions. She held the straps of the leads attached to their saddles.

"Come, Prince Carmine! Let's ride!" Leola climbed up onto the horse at her right and strapped herself in.

Carmine quickly dusted the hay off himself. "Now wait. Wait, Leola! We can't take these! Majesty and Carmella are my father's most expensive horses!" he shouted, trying to keep the girl from taking off.

Leola leaned forward on the giant horse, resting her upper body on its neck and resting her head on its soft mane. "Oh come now, Carmine.

You're the prince! Someday, you *will* become the king of Jannah and ruler of Syris. You'll be able to exploit everything that your father has worked so hard to obtain. So consider this… practice," she said. Leola squeezed the horse's sides with both her feet and whipped the lead. She took off out of the stable and into the open garden.

Being well trained, these stallions were easy to ride. Carmine pulled himself up onto the horse left for him. He petted it gently, trying to comfort it so it wouldn't be afraid. "Don't worry Majesty, she's a friend… I think." Carmine sighed. "Damn this girl." He whipped the lead and took off after Leola.

The horses were speeding through the garden. Eventually, Carmine managed to catch up to Leola, having ridden a horse dozens of times before. He slowed down to ride at the same controlled pace as her. The kids could feel the perfect winds of the night blow through their hair. Carmine looked over at Leola to his right. Everything seemed to move in slow motion. The smile touching her cheeks, the orange and white hair in her face, her gentle pink eyes; it all overwhelmed the young prince. They rode out into the full purple and red moons of Jannah.

Later into the night, Carmine and Leola rode up to a nearby waterfall.

They stopped the horses at the edge of the high cliff and got off the stallions.

"Where are we?" Leola asked as she stepped beside the prince.

Carmine looked down at the glistening waterfall below. "To tell you the truth Leola, I don't spend much time at the castle. I enjoy exploring everywhere around my home. This is the great Waterfall of Gable. My father found so much gold here that he spent it all on an entire state county, releasing them from despicable poverty. It was quite possibly the last charitable thing he did without political inclinations," he explained grimly. Nonetheless, Carmine was still captivated by the nature of Jannah. He looked up at the high trees of the nearby forest. They stood like skyscrapers and the glowing fruits growing from them sang songs of joy, ready to nourish the mortals. The fruits made sounds of a radiant ringing and a slight ding.

Then Carmine heard another noise, snapping him back into reality. He looked over to his right and saw Leola suddenly undressing. "Leola. What're you doing?" Carmine asked. He wanted to close his eyes, but couldn't. Leola removed her underwear, letting the moon shine on her bare skin. Carmine could see the scar on her chest, surely from the surgery to pro-vide her with the artificial half of her heart.

"You whine a lot, Carmine. Don't play. I'm sure you've seen a naked woman dozens of times," Leola said. She walked up to Carmine and gripped the collar of his shirt.

"You're not a woman. You're a girl... only 16 years-old," Carmine said.

Leola closed in on the boy, looking him deep in the eyes. "Well, we Automa don't live as long as you Seraphs. Our lifespan doesn't exceed 110 years. So, I have every right to live a little." Leola took off Carmine's shirt, then his pants and underwear. She knocked him to the ground as she yanked his clothes off by force. Once that was over, Leola grabbed Carmine by his arms and jumped into the lake with him from the high point of the cliff. They both screamed, crashed through the waterfall, and splashed into the lake below. The horses neighed in sudden excitement. The bugs of the night made their nocturnal sounds, creating the music of the forest that endlessly charmed the full moons.

By midnight, Carmine had returned to the garden with Leola, somewhat freezing from the bitter cold of the lake water. Their clothes were slightly damp. The moons were both in their full positions in the sky, hours later now. To Carmine, Leola was still as bright as when he first met her this evening. They sat by each other on a stone bench in front of the glorious pond where this whole adventure began. The kids were skipping rocks again. Fish were popping in and out of the water, flustered by the acts of the Seraph and Automa.

Leola turned towards Carmine, her somewhat wet hair swaying around. "Would you have ever imagined this was how you'd spend your 18th birthday?" she asked happily.

Carmine smiled at her and watched her eyes glow. "Of course not. Leola, you not only saved me from an evening of being painfully and embarrassingly drunk but managed to show me a fun time as well. You know, if you were to stay here, you and I could have days like this all the time," he said. Carmine grabbed her hand and they both stood up. Leola observed her metal hand in his. It was always the one Carmine reached for.

The girl unwillingly blushed. "I suppose my recklessness and multiple misdemeanors today didn't deter you from feeling for me," Leola said, chuckling slightly.

Carmine just touched her soft cheeks. They looked into each other's eyes. "I felt for you the moment I saw you," Carmine said. The kids closed their eyes and kissed, fireworks bursting in the air. It was midnight. The moons shined upon the young couple. The celebration of a legacy had come to an end.

Family Ties

The next morning, it felt as if the two suns in the sky were shining brighter than they did the day before. The four-winged birds flew across the blue skies of Jannah. It was quiet, much quieter than it was only hours ago. The entire castle had already been cleaned from the celebration of a lifetime. There were nothing but a few butlers and maids still dusting artifacts and sweeping the floors. This was a routine to keep the castle in immaculate condition.

Jonah awakened in Evelyn's bed, holding his girlfriend in his arms. Her head was resting upon his chest and his arms were wrapped around her upper stomach. Everything felt so peaceful. Jonah stretched out his arms and legs, accidentally causing Evelyn to move in her sleep out of disturbance. He quietly set her head on the nearby pillow and got out of bed. In his underwear, Jonah reached for the nightstand and grabbed his phone. He opened it to check a website where people uploaded data about their social lives. Pictures, blogs, and various posts were riddled with details about the most extravagant celebration on the grandest planet in all of the universe. Thousands of people had captured the birthday of princes Jonah and Carmine through their own perspectives. Many posts detailed the importance of understanding 25 years of peace, while others were thankful for those who sacrificed their lives to give them this freedom. Of course, Jonah encountered several posts that were nothing more than insulting gestures about the pompous natures of Jannah's Sultan family and their supposed exploitation of riches. The poor remained poor and the rich became richer.

"I didn't ask to be born as a Sultan," Jonah mumbled to himself. Opinions such as these were to be expected from the Seraphs or immigrants on Jannah. Ignorance.

Jonah also noticed hundreds of texts from family, friends, and acquaintances. Many of them wished him a happy birthday while some asked for his location amongst the castle. Jonah hadn't indulged much in his own party. Instead, he spent the rest of the evening with the love of his life. It was a decision he was happy he made. Suddenly, there was the roaring sound of trotting horses. Their loud neighing alerted Jonah. The prince quickly tucked in Evelyn as

quietly as possible. He walked towards the room's window, indecent. He moved the curtains and the naturally bright light made him wince. The muscular tone of his body was revealed as the suns shined upon him. When the young man looked down, he saw a luxurious carriage pull up to a few of the guards that protected one of the side entrances into the castle. Then, he saw the great emperor Zion step out from the carriage.

Jonah involuntarily gasped at the man's unannounced presence. "Zion? What could he possibly be doing here?"

Zion was the ruler of the planet Kremlin, one of the eight planets in the Syris Solar System. He was of Vectin descent. Kremlin was commonly ruled by a king and queen, referred to as emperors. What made the planet's traditions so controversial was that the seat of the throne could always be taken by any individual willing to challenge the current ruler. A man could fight the queen and a woman could face the king, should they choose to do so. Yet most refused to challenge such authority, as the emperor of Kremlin, to which 82 out of the 89 total rulers have been of Vectin descent, is commonly revered as a deity amongst his or her people. The current ruler, Zion, was believed to have been sent by the gods, embedded with spirits from the NetherRealm, their version of the afterlife. It was rumored that Zion had cheated death numerous times in his past lives. He currently ruled alongside his wife, Raakel, who is an Ectognatha. Many people were intolerant of their mixed-race marriage. They possessed no children but knew their love was boundless. On Kremlin, even the children were required to fight for the throne against their parents if they wished to uphold a family legacy. In most cases, the child has died during the combat ritual. The king of Kremlin possesses all-ruling power over his subjects as judge, jury, and executioner. The queen, although commonly submissive, has the right to kill her husband in a combat ritual if she wishes to rule over him. In Kremlin's history, this had only occurred twice, with Queen Hasna of Nuboso and thereafter, her daughter, Yasmine of Anadama Peak, who both brutally murdered their husbands in front of thousands of people. This was after the women suffered countless attacks of rape by their former living husbands.

Jonah studied up on every planet's history when he was younger. It was this deadly nature of Kremlin that caused many people to question Zion and Raakel's intentions as emperors. Jonah and Carmine knew of Zion's potential evil considering a past they had with the man, but others chose to remain ignorant of his ways. To everyone else, the emperor was nothing more than a mystery. And that was how they preferred it. The princes' parents were too generous to see Zion for the danger he could've possibly been to Syris. They wanted to hold on to the relationship they had with him years ago.

Zion had black and purple skin. He had long black hair, down to his neck. His hair was adorned with golden rings and jewelry tied into a few braids, representing his status amongst his people. The Vectins had snake-like pupils, with a thin horizontal line arcing across the iris. Zion had auburn-colored eyes with deep brown pupils. Zion was unique in his skin texture. He possessed strange star marks glistening upon him as if he was born in the depths of space. This anomaly of his gave credence to Vectins believing he was a deity. Zion was unlike any other Vectin. He currently wore silver armor, consisting of a chest plate, greaves, and gauntlets. He also wore a black and red cape, while sporting his signature sword in its scabbard.

Zion started speaking with the two guards protecting the side entrance to the castle. Jonah was intrigued by the man's visit. He would normally not travel to Jannah unless he was here on important business.

"Why is he here?" Jonah asked himself. He quickly put on some clothes and ran out into the hallway. In a rush, he accidentally slipped on the red carpet that covered the marble floor and landed on his forearms. "Damn it!" It still didn't stop him. Jonah jumped back to his feet and hopped over the golden banister, dropping down from the second floor into the main lobby of the castle. The prince ran in between the staircases, through the back door, and came outside to where Zion was. Jonah quickly opened the door, making his presence known.

"P… Prince Jonah? What're you doing out here so early?" a guard asked, confused. Jonah stared at Zion with an intense look. He was wearing red pajamas and a light blue robe, which diminished the seriousness of his demeanor. It was rather embarrassing for the prince to be seen like this.

"I came here to speak with Zion. Please guards, if you both don't mind, remain at your post and I shall walk the emperor into the castle myself," Jonah said.

The guards bowed to the young prince. "Yes, sir." Jonah walked into the castle with Zion, now taking full responsibility if the man were intent

on suddenly attacking in an act of terror.

"Why are you here Emperor Zion?" Jonah asked.

"Jonah, I am simply here to visit your father," Zion replied, his voice low.

They took a turn down a hallway, Zion's metal armor rattling and echoing in the marble room. "I would assume you aren't here to congratulate him on achieving 25 years of peace in Syris."

"I respect your maturity, prince. I always have. But these are pressing matters that concern a time before you were even born. I would hope that you'd consider giving us some privacy."

"Someday, when my brother and I become king, the past will no longer matter. We are the future and understanding that Vectins can live up to 270 years old, you'll surely be around to adhere to our vision of Syris."

Zion, being seven feet tall, ducked under a doorway they came across. "Jonah. Times are ever-changing. You know of the controversies involving the power that goddess has granted to the *Hakim Nisa'* and Seraphs. Because everything seems perfect in your world, don't assume all is well with your neighboring planets. And when tyranny makes mortals weary, a new order may come into place."

"It sounds as if you're threatening Jannah. But my parents are not tyrants."

"Not yet..."

Jonah and Zion took a turn down another corridor. The prince led Zion to his mother and father's throne room. Since the king and queen were always working so hard watching over an entire solar system, the couple was always in there handling business. Jonah and Zion were walking down one last hallway. In it were dozens of pictures on the walls of the previous rulers of Jannah, all following one family lineage. The royal Sultan family.

"I'm sorry, Jonah. Happy birthday," Zion said. He reached into his satchel and took out two small gifts. "Be sure to give the one with the blue ribbon to Carmine. Tell him I said hello."

Jonah just stared blankly at the boxes. No matter how he felt about Zion's possibly twisted ways as an emperor, he knew the gifts inside the boxes were genuine without even looking inside. He knew this because that's who Zion was as a person, not a ruler. "Thank you," the prince said. Zion smiled and patted Jonah on his back.

They eventually arrived at the throne room. Jonah opened the large door and led Zion inside. He had no choice but to allow the presence of this man into the sanctity of his home. "Mother, father, emperor Zion is here to speak with you," Jonah said.

Vitaliya rose from her throne and Adelrik concluded his conversation with a scribe. Vitaliya approached her son and fellow ruler. "Zion. It is truly great to see you again," she said. The two separate authorities shook hands and walked over to a table. Adelrik shook Zion's hand and the three of them had a seat. Jonah couldn't help but linger, anxious to hear what his parents would have to discuss with the emperor of Kremlin. Vitaliya took notice. She gazed at her child with her glorious teal eyes. "Jonah, sweetheart, this conversation is *private*."

Jonah nodded reluctantly and left the room. "Sorry mother," he said as he closed the large door to the throne room. Jonah turned around and decided not to worry about staying in the throne room for their conversation. If anything were to go wrong, he trusted that his parents would handle it. Jonah turned down a hall to make his way back to Evelyn in time to tell her good morning. The prince was rushing past several guards and maids that saluted and greeted him. He was beginning to grow angry. Something felt terribly wrong about this visit. Its timing, the nature of Zion's presence, and the acceptance of his parents. It was as if they had seen this meeting coming for quite some time.

Suddenly, Jonah ran into Carmine. The brothers nearly bumped into each other. "Jonah. I'm glad I found you. A guard told me Zion was here. Is that true?" Carmine asked.

Jonah looked back and pointed towards the direction in the hall where he came from. "Yeah. He's here. The emperor's speaking to mother and father right now. But apparently, their business is private," he replied. Carmine sighed. He decided to continue walking anyway until Jonah grabbed him by the arm. "Didn't you hear me? You can't go in there, Carmine."

Carmine just freed himself from his twin's grip. "I know. It won't stop me from learning more. The emperor of the most threatening planet in our solar system suddenly shows up the day *after* we celebrated peace? Come on Jonah. Zion surely has ulterior motives. Our parents had this meeting planned. Why else would they be in the throne room this early?" Jonah wanted to argue but knew that Carmine was capable of making his own decisions. He let his brother go and just resumed walking towards the guest room that Evelyn was staying in.

Carmine approached the front door to the throne room. Guards were blocking the entrance, which must've meant something suspicious was going on. Carmine knew he would have to come up with a way to get them to leave.

Then, he remembered something useful. "Guards! I'm sorry to bother you, but I can't find anyone else on patrol. It's an emergency! I went outside to the stables and found that the lock was broken. I didn't want to open it. It sounded like the intruder was inside, possibly stealing one of the horses!" he shouted. The guards thanked the prince for the information and quickly ran outside towards the garden. Then, Carmine made yet another bold move. He entered the throne room unannounced.

The prince saw his parents at the table with Zion. It was clear that his intrusion disturbed a very important conversation. His mother and father looked up at him, tears in their eyes. Carmine's mouth gaped.

"Carmine! Boy! What're you doing here? This is private!" Adelrik shouted, his voice breaking from possible sobbing. Carmine had no words. He was stunned by the look on his parents' faces. Zion turned in his seat. The emperor's expression was not one of anger or hatred but simply content. It was as if the outcome of the future couldn't be reasoned with. Adelrik arose from his seat, grabbed Carmine by his arms, and led him out the throne room.

"Father, please! Tell me what's going on! Why are you and mom crying?" Carmine begged. His father looked into his son's eyes. He desperately wanted to tell him everything that was going on. All the dark secrets and the haunting past. "Please father! As the future king of Jannah and ruler of Syris, I have every right to at least know the premise of this meeting. Please..."

Adelrik still contended with the thought. Only more tears poured from his eyes. "I'm sorry Carmine. You boys don't deserve any of this. Your mother and I are ready to face the consequences," he said. Adelrik entered the throne room again and locked the door this time. Carmine just collapsed onto his knees. Something terrible was going to happen to his family, to Jannah, and Syris.

Adelrik, King of Jannah

A Past and Future Betrayal

Later that day, Zion had finally left Jannah and returned home to Kremlin. Planet Kremlin was the darkest exoplanet in the Syris Solar System. Reflecting only 1% of the Sun's light, Kremlin appeared to be a smoldering mass with dark gas and clouds swallowing the presence of its continents and oceans. From space, the planet exhibited a strange purple gas that pulsated like a breathing entity. Many of the Vectins believed the darkness festering on their planet was alive. It must have stemmed from thousands of years of harvesting funerals and entombing souls of the dead, as was the purpose of the species. The weather was commonly understated as imperfect, with an absence of plentiful sunlight, hazardous storms, and endless chills believed to be caused by the wandering unseen souls. Kremlin was hell for many but believed to be a paradise for Vectins. The species believed their suffering was the first step to their ultimate heaven in the NetherRealm, their version of the afterlife.

The Vectins worshipped a sacred text known as The Eulogy. The Eulogy explicitly detailed the Vectins' duty to lay the lost souls of Syris to rest in their respective afterlives. The ancestors had passed on the belief that death was life's greatest beauty. Vectin priests often engaged in a sacrament known as Entombment, where they underwent a trance-like state and experienced crucial moments in a lost soul's life. It was their way of comforting the dead's spirits before they reached the afterlife. In this sense, Vectin priests had experienced death countless times, through the perspectives of others. The priests didn't commonly associate with society, as they had nearly gone insane from witnessing death too many times. It was a religious feat some would argue was too much to bear. It was believed that to be approved for the NetherRealm, all Vectins must perform the religious sacrament to at least one dead soul and for their parents when they passed. Vectins and the people of Kremlin prayed to a sacred tree, known as *Lignum Vitae*. Seen by only a rare few, the tree was described as the most beautiful spectacle of reality in the known realm, the very thing that Vectins lived for. Vectin's god was known as the Undertaker, god of funerals. He was depicted as a skeletal figure that wore a black robe. The people of Kremlin believed the Undertaker once existed with the gods of the previous Eons and was the prime bridge between the two worlds; life and the NetherRealm. He was respected as the greatest being to bestow peace upon lost souls. Zion was believed to be a product of such a god.

Now on his home planet, he could nearly feel the difference in atmosphere. Jannah was where he was hated by many and Kremlin was where he was revered as a deity. Soon, Zion knew the respect for his divinity would no longer be exclusive to his planet, but present in all of Syris. The emperor was in his bedroom, gathering his thoughts. He had made a drastic decision with the king and Queen of Jannah. He surely knew they would consult with the *Hakim Nisa'* about their next call to action. Therefore, he had already placed the couple in a position where they wouldn't have a choice but to adhere to his command. Zion knew Adelrik and Vitaliya better than anyone else in Syris. They valued their children more than the Seraphs that bowed before them. So he used their children as blackmail, to twist their arms into doing what he wanted.

Zion resided inside his great palace, a massive structure made of pure ebony and painted gold on its accents. The yellow diamonds and lights glowed across the entire village. The highest tower of his palace touched the dreaded clouds tainted by the Entombment of the souls. Purple flags hung around the building. Barricades made it evident that Zion designed his palace to serve the purpose of a home and fort, knowing that someday a battle could come to his doorstep. Spikes accented the outer structures, killing any flying creature that came near it. Zion owned a sea of biologically mutated animals, indulging in the failed scientific advancements of the most intelligent species in the solar system, Vectins. The prison was not far from his palace, as Zion enjoyed visiting it to observe the public executions of criminals from across Syris. Darkness loved Kremlin and Kremlin welcomed the despair into its nature. It was as if Zion's very presence created an atmosphere of suffering. In the man's 214 years of life, he had surely experienced hell more times than he could recollect. But none knew the stories of his tragedy. None except Adelrik, Vitaliya, and their loving twin sons.

Zion paced back and forth, currently speaking to one of his servants. His right hand, Gautam. "I'm still having trouble figuring out the possible outcomes of my decision. But I couldn't wait any longer. If I don't get what I rightfully deserve, the Seraphs shall witness war."

Gautam removed Zion's scabbard from his belt and set it on a nearby table to prepare it for polishing. "Emperor Zion, you of all people are too aware of the consequences of war. The innocent bystanders. You know what happened to your village a century ago. I thought princes Jonah and Carmine were too valuable to be harmed," he said.

Zion started unbuckling the clamps to his cape. "Princes Jonah and Carmine are still afraid to side with me. But they know the truth of what my planet has suffered through at the hands of Jannah's conquest of Syris. Unfortunately, Vitaliya and Adelrik raised spoiled creatures. Seraphs have had everything handed to them." He started getting lost in his thoughts, memories racing through his head. "And… when I tried to teach the princes the truth… when I protected them… when I became the hero… everyone despised me for it."

Gautam came over and removed Zion's cape, hanging it in a nearby glass display case. The touch of reality snapped Zion out of his thoughts of the past. "Zion. I understand your disposition with the power of gods being in the hands of mere mortals. But your kind, Vectins, possess an intelligence that supersedes what the gods could have ever been capable of. Now I have always admired your sacrifice as ruler of this wretched planet, but people don't commonly have faith in evil. They only have faith in good," Gautam explained.

Zion simply scoffed. "And you dare suggest that I'm the evil one? The universe was created by a being of insufferable indifference towards the very planets it created. The All. When I knew of this truth, claiming the goddess of the Jannah was not the greatest divine being of the past, I was damned as a heretic by everyone in Syris. I may be evil, but I'm also right."

Zion stepped away from his servant and looked at himself in the mirror. "If you try to expose the truth about the All again Zion, it won't end well with Vitaliya and Adelrik as rulers. You'll be hated even more. Seraphs possess the divine power of creation. Remnants of the gods' natural abilities. They are living proof of the previous Eons. You only have knowledge. That doesn't suffice in this era. godly power is the true authority, not facts," Gautam said.

Zion clenched his fists in overwhelming anger. "The whole solar system would see differently if I ruled. Vitaliya may be the greatest warrior in the universe and Adelrik may serve as her unyielding willpower, but I am the most intelligent being. *I* have seen the truth. And *I* am the living deity. Not just remnants of one like the Seraphs. Once Syris is under my control, everyone will have no choice but to accept the truth. What created the universe never cared for it. What created the stars never truly admired its beauty. What shed its light on evolution, couldn't even appreciate its own actions. Therefore, all faith is in vain."

There was a sudden knock on the door. Noticing that Zion was too busy gathering his thoughts in the mirror, Gautam went to go open it. In the reflection of the mirror, Zion could see his beauty, the beauty that was his wife. The king turned around, facing his magnificent queen. His wife wasn't a Vectin, rather, she was of Ectognatha, from Mirage. The insect species. Her name was Raakel. She had married Zion long ago. They met when Zion was sent as a field trooper to handle guerilla warfare in her hometown during an economic crisis. Raakel became the empress of Kremlin through her husband's engagement. The Ectognatha were commonly referred to as 'the Swarm' or 'the Hive'. They ranged from a variety of insects or subspecies, such as arthropods, spiders, moths, bees, mantis, beetles, and the rarest, scorpions. Ectognatha possessed a chitinous, exoskeleton surrounding much of their bodies. Raakel had black chitin upon her lower body, with portions of her flesh and beautiful face exposed on her upper body. Having an ancestral derivation similar to that of a scorpion, she was the rarest of her kind. There was a large scorpion tail protruding from her lower waist. The woman's eyes glowed yellow, with a solid insect-like iris. She had small antennae on her forehead and glorious white hair. There were stripes on various areas of her exoskeleton. Raakel stood at a height of about 6'8. The woman was a warrior way ahead of her time and nearly a goddess to the rest of her species back home on Mirage.

Gautam, Raakel's distant cousin, bowed before the emperors. "I'll leave you two to speak in private," he said. The servant stepped out of the room and closed the door behind him. Zion and his glorious wife were left alone. They stepped forward to each other.

"Husband," Raakel said.

Zion smiled. "Wife." They kissed each other. Zion grabbed his wife's hand and sat himself down on the bed. He gently touched the platinum wedding ring wrapped around her finger.

"Did you visit Jannah as you planned?" Raakel asked.

Zion nodded and let go of her hand. "Yes. I did."

Raakel sat down on the bed beside Zion and started rubbing his shoulders. "Well? Did the Sultans come to an agreement?" she asked.

Zion shook his head. "Of course

not. They claimed they needed to speak with their Wise Women before coming to a decision. After everything I've done, after I've been told the truth about the universe, I'm left with an unfair split of the rule. The Seraphs are too clouded by Vitaliya and Adelrik's illusion of grandeur. Their faith has led them to believe that every other species in Syris is beneath them," he explained. Zion stood up from the bed and went back over to the mirror, disgusted with himself. Raakel walked over and stood behind him.

"Zion. If you wish to get through to the people's faith, then perhaps you need to eliminate what they believe in the most. The very *source* of their faith. Open their eyes. The people of Jannah and nearly all of Syris bow before the *Hakim Nisa'* and pray to their alleged goddess. They think their goddess is so amazing because of the powerful treasure discovered on Jannah. Maybe we should strip them of that treasure," she suggested.

"I understand my wife. But how could I possibly eliminate faith? It's been established since the previous Eon," Zion replied.

"Did the Seraph's goddess not impose radical beliefs of heaven to her entire universe during Eon IV? Did her father not impose radical beliefs of free will during Eon III? We are a small percentage of the population who chose not to ignore the truth. Don't you see, Zion? You're the next legend. The next prophet. Just like their goddess of the Children, just like The Chosen One of the Nephilims, just like the All."

"Even if I could break them. Even if I could take their treasure. It won't be easy. Vitaliya's army stands too strong. The woman and her husband own this entire solar system. Billions, ready to serve them in the name of goddess. From planet Echelon to Tempest, to Pandora, their allies are greater than mine. Ever since I became a heretic, people have hated Kremlin and the Vectins even more. Morticians they call us. Ungrateful, even though we're the ones who lay their wasteful souls to rest in the afterlife."

"Forget the names they call you. They'll soon regret it. The Crystals of Nihaya are relics their goddess supposedly left on Jannah. *That* is the key to destroying what faith the Seraphs have today."

"Not only that Raakel. The Seraphs thrive off of the energy of their 2nd Sun. The people of Jannah have so much faith in tangible things, in materialistic objects. If we destroy the objects they value so much, then they'll start to lose faith in themselves. That 2nd Sun must be destroyed too. And I shall use The Crystals of Nihaya to do so."

"The power of creation belongs in the hands of a living deity."

"And *I'm* that deity. I am a god. I'll make everyone revere my greatness. Jannah's army will yield before my power."

Raakel stepped in front of Zion and began touching his face. The look of subtle despair in her husband's eyes brought her sadness. She had always been by his side, despite all the pain in their past. "You are a ruler just like Vitaliya and Adelrik. And just like these planets, the people of Syris are rightfully yours to control. Why defeat the entire army when you have every right to take it?" The queen knew Zion better than he knew himself.

Zion stepped back from his wife and turned around dramatically. He stared distantly, conjuring a plan. "I know what we should do now. The Sultans brought this upon themselves," Zion turned back around to his wife. "Thank you, Raakel. Although, I should expect nothing less from a former warlord," he said. Zion

Raakel, Empress of Kremlin

grabbed his wife by her arms and kissed her again.

"I've enslaved people, conquered planets, and destroyed rising suns. My greatest feat will be helping my husband succeed in taking what's rightfully his to own," Raakel said. The emperors smiled at each other.

Zion equipped his cape again and started walking towards the door. He opened it and looked out towards the guards in the hallway. "Guards! Prepare to contact all head dukes of Kremlin to my palace for a council meeting!" he ordered. The guards started scattering around, rushing to make the phone calls, send telepathic messages, and teleport to different locations. Zion turned back around to his wife. "Now, it's time for all mortals to know the truth. It is time for *me* to be the hero."

By the next day, the people of Kremlin, Vectins, and other species alike, were gathered in front of Zion's palace, awaiting their emperor's glorious speech. There were easily a million of them, banded together for the first time in what felt like an eternity. For too long, Kremlin had been tainted by its gloomy nature. The souls laid to rest through Entombment were commonly lost through suicide and most commonly of Vectin descent. It was time for the planet to finally build a respectable reputation for itself.

Amidst the chatter in the sea of people, winged animals flew past the cloudy skies, emitting horrifying caws towards one another. Zion had just finished speaking to many leaders of the world, dukes, nobles, and barons alike. They were having their private meeting in the palace. Once final decisions were made, Zion was ready to be the head spokesman for the rest of his people. It was his duty as the deity of Syris.

An hour later, Gautam walked out onto the stage set in front of the palace. He approached a podium and spoke into a small digital amplifier. "After several hours of crucial discussion, the council has decided on Kremlin's position of power in the Syris Solar System. Emperor Zion has worked tirelessly to ensure that this decision will benefit all species in the universe. Today, he will speak on behalf of our people, to the people."

Everyone, including the viewers several miles away, directed their attention to either the physical stage or the digital screens upon the nearby buildings that captured live footage of the speech. Gautam stepped aside. Zion walked onto the stage and stepped before the podium. Raakel came over and stood to the left side of her husband. The emperors stood there, powerful, dangerous, and hellbent on succeeding with their goals.

The million people all bowed before them. Some out of intimidation, others out of divine respect.

"All rise," Zion said in his low voice. His rugged face and massive stature labeled him as the epitome of deities. Zion was idolized by all women in the solar system and feared by all men who trembled before his power. His fierce auburn eyes revealed every war the man had witnessed, while his powerful jaw showed distinguishing perseverance that couldn't be emulated by any mortal. His black hair was the mane of a galactic tyrant who forced his way into royalty. His queen, standing by his side, was by far the most powerful woman on the entire planet, perhaps even all of Syris. Her long, white hair was proof of her infinite wisdom. Her sharp, prominent cheeks, coupled with her purple skin, solidified her godliness. "Today, we celebrate the 25th anniversary of peace amongst Syris. The wretched ways of the gods began with the creation of Genesis and the seclusion of all mortals, which was initiated by one species' ability to control life through evolution and Transference. One day, the younger species will experience the tyranny of Jannah. My people of Kremlin, I would like to say in good faith, that we shall recognize the diversity on our planet. The depths of hell see no color, no race, and no difference in species. Anyone who has succumbed to abuse in the physical realm is incapable of accessing a higher life in the planes of divinity. We were left with nothing more than the task of laying lost souls to rest. Our reward: suffering. Guided by blind faith, this is the aftermath of conquests in war. A solar system left to nothing more than the pathetic celebration of 18-year-old twin boys. Everyone, please give your most angered Syris cry if you wish to see Jannah in the hands of your deity!" Zion shouted with visible hate and misery in his heart.

The large sea of people roared. Their cries of pain revealed the undertone of fear and dismay that always existed in Syris. War was on the rise for the universe once more. This war was to exceed far beyond that of the nebulae in Eon I and the war waged by the god of Gravity long before existence. It was time for the mortals to abandon their faith and live their lives in reality. Peace could never last forever.

The rare Vectin observed the followers standing before him. "The world leaders and I have devised a plan to do more than just overthrow Vitaliya and Adelrik. After 25 years of insufferable peace, we have concluded that it's time for chaos to strike the nations once more. For this radicalism, this destruction shall bring about the dawn of a new era that will no longer be corrupted by blind faith. This plan will wage war on each planet in Syris that doesn't stand by us. The world leaders of Kremlin have agreed to send in their best assassins to eliminate crucial head figures for every species, weakening their military and unity. Then, once our army is ready, we will divide into units, conquering two planets at a time. After extensive scientific studies over the decades, we have determined a weakness for every species in the solar system, including our own. Once we have control over the Ectognatha of Mirage, Automa of Centauri, Elves of Ximji, Personas of Pandora, Hippopotamuses of Tempest, and Nanomorphs of Echelon, the only species left will be the Seraphs of Jannah. We will show Vitaliya and Adelrik true betrayal and turn their army into our legion. This tremendous unrest and these indisputable distinctions between gods will finally come to an end. Everyone will know about the All. Then, everyone will know that *I* am the only true god left in the universe. They will bow before me! I assure you, many will side by us during this war. What so-called goddess would allow one race to supersede the others? All allied forces of Syris will be weakened and Vitaliya will have no one left but her and her husband's army on Jannah. I will defeat the king and Queen of Jannah myself and expose who they truly are to the entire universe. They are tyrants! Two 'heroes' who stole my shared rule over Syris from me! After I once fought by their side to bring peace. The Crystals of Nihaya, the *Hakim Nisa'*, and the power of creation, will all be mine to control. We will no longer bow before gods, but bow before the most powerful mortal of this realm. Me."

The world leaders admired the man's ruthlessness. His intention was clear. "As a true deity. I will be the *only* one to create. *I* am a god. Not for the power I possess, but for the intelligence that I have. My faith in the truth is grander than their faith in the lies. My only rule in this war is to leave the Sultan family to me. No one is to lay a finger on the princes. When I'm done with the dreadful planet that has corrupted the gates of heaven, their Sun will no longer rise. When I'm done taking what's rightfully ours, even the gods will bow before me."

The Evolution of a Legendary Planet

The splash in the water felt cool enough to eliminate the overwhelming heat upon the surface. The bubbles scattered across their metallic glass visors, blocking their immediate vision. The princes could feel the intensity of the moment force their hearts to race. Equipped in technologically advanced suits designed to withstand extreme variations in temperature and traverse across multiple terrains, they were in their playground. It was finally a chance for them to escape. After the celebrations that occurred on Jannah last week, it was time for them to return to their duties as The Chosen Ones of Syris. Jonah and Carmine were on their developing planet. It had no name yet, but as the most significant celestial body the princes have ever terraformed, that was surely something that deserved proper consideration.

Princes Jonah and Carmine were plunging into the great oceans of their planet. Once their sinking slowed, they each pressed a button on their wrists to activate the oxygen system that was also designed to withstand the underwater pressure. A voice appeared on the intercoms in their helmets. "Boys, your suits have fully submerged. Provide me with your status, individually." It was a man. He was the pilot of the Jannah airship currently hovering above the planet. Along with an entire fleet of soldiers there to assist the princes, the *Hakim Nisa'* were inside, willing to oversee the boys as they worked on terraforming their planet again.

Inside the ocean, Jonah and Carmine began paddling their feet. They pressed a button on the sides of their helmets to report back through the intercom. "This is Jonah. Everything's in stable order," Jonah said. His brother followed.

"This is Carmine. Everything's fine Captain Litton. We've done this before. Hard to believe someone of your status in the military is afraid of two boys going for a swim."

The rest of the crew snickered at the prince's comment. Litton grabbed the microphone and brought it to his gaping mouth. "Now boy! You may have a gift, but I have sworn duty to protect you and your brother! I expect the highest professionalism from the future rulers of Syris!" he shouted. Carmine just laughed in response.

A woman took over the microphone on the ship; the technician. "Okay, boys. Go ahead and activate all operating systems on your suits. From there, we'll activate the visual feed to guide you across the ocean floor."

Jonah and Carmine started pressing multiple buttons on their diving suits in a specific order. They activated pressure acclimation, the flippers, the propellers on their backs, the high beams atop their helmets, then the visual feed for the crew above. "Everything seems in order Phoebe. Shall we begin?" Jonah asked.

The technician, Phoebe, checked a few monitors above the control panel and gave a thumbs up to the rest of the crew. "Yes! You're clear for take-off princes. Good luck! The guide will take over now."

The princes slowly started propelling forward from the jets equipped on their backs. A woman's voice came through the intercom. "Jonah, Carmine. This is your guide, Morgan. I have with me here an updated map of your planet captured from a variety of seismic wave readings recorded at approximately 31:52 our time back home. Alongside the map, I have a radar keeping a lookout for any possible hazards and sudden seismic activity within your vicinity. Now, to begin, let's double-check that visual feed. Can you both please put your left thumbs up for the camera to see?" she asked. The princes followed her instructions. Looking back at her crew, Morgan received affirmation that everyone saw the feed with clarity. "Perfect. Remember, we have emergency medical personnel on standby. Should anything start to feel off, please press the alert button on your suits, located above your right chest plate. Now, we're going to increase the jet power of your suits again. Follow my instructions to get you to the appropriate coordinates,"

Morgan explained. The princes responded in the affirmative and they were off.

Going at a relatively fast speed, they propelled across the underwater ocean to reach their destination, which was rather far from the nearest landmass. Jonah and Carmine remained quiet, awaiting Morgan's simple instructions. "Turn left at the upcoming rock formation... turn right at the nearest dune... cross over this trench... another right at that boulder... avoid that whirlpool... not that hydrothermal vent... the one we need is farther... stop atop this dune." This went on for approximately half an hour. Then, the twin princes finally stopped. Their jet power lowered and their feet planted atop the sand at the bottom of the ocean. It was beautiful to them, being within the depths of their massive creation. It all led up to this moment. This would be the first step to truly prove if this interstellar body was capable of evolution fit for the eyes of their goddess.

"Okay, Morgan! We've landed! Everything's still in one piece," Carmine said. He and his brother looked down the dune and saw a large hydrothermal vent. A new voice appeared on the intercom. "Hello princes Jonah and Carmine. This is Dempsey speaking. I'm gonna oversee the planting of the divine bacterium.

We've done this a billion times today boys, so let's end this terraform with a bang. Go ahead and carefully get down that dune. The hydrothermal vent you want to set them near is actually *not* the largest one. Our readings show that the one producing the most plentiful gases, specifically carbon dioxide, is towards the right. The fourth-largest vent there. You know what to do," Dempsey said.

Jonah and Carmine started down the hill. They slowly jumped up and slid down on their bottoms, bending their legs and using a hand for balance. At the landing of the sand dune, they began swimming towards the designated hydrothermal vent, kicking their feet rhythmically. The hydrothermal vent was spewing out black smoke aggressively. Jonah reached behind his back and grabbed a container made of ultra-high-molecular-weight polyethylene. An intense golden glow was emitting from inside of it. The container was attached to a retractable cord overlaid with kevlar. Carmine reached over with a key in his hand and inserted it into the container. Once he turned the key, the container became released from the cord. Carmine slowly opened the container.

"Careful… careful…" Jonah mumbled. The princes held the divine bacterium within their hands. Its very es-

sence always brought chills down their spines. Its radiance was truly magnificent. Such a small object was capable of breathing life into an entirely new species. The tiny parcel, no more than several centimeters long, was now resting in the left palm of Carmine and the right palm of Jonah simultaneously. The princes slowly placed the divine bacterium in a heavy, gilded pot that had a hole in the bottom for sand to seep in. They set the gilded pot beside the hydrothermal vent and dropped to their knees. Jonah and Carmine each clasped their hands together in prayer. They began chanting in Egyptian-Arabic. It was an exact reiteration of what the *Hakim Nisa'* would commonly recite, proving their dedication to their practice as disciples of evolution. They spent several seconds there in silence.

"It's done," the princes said in synchrony. The entire crew on the ship clapped and cheered. They began shaking each other's hands and hugging one another. Jonah and Carmine could hear all the excitement in their intercoms. This was what it truly meant to be a Seraph. The purpose of life was to ensure its progress and reach towards a unified peace. This could only be achieved through the betterment of adaptation across the galaxies. Surely the boys were aware of the disputes revolving around Seraphs possessing the power of gods as mortals since they held strong opinions against it as well. But they still took great pride in the beauty of advancing life across the entire universe. Although the studies of the Kadar told the story of the goddess who sacrificed herself for the angels, it didn't exactly explain how the infinite space came to be. Yet notions of what their old mentor, Zion, had told them years ago were resonating once more. Perhaps the infinite area of space did arise from one being. From the All.

Nonetheless, Seraphs weren't just abusing the power of creation, as many people thought. Beginning evolution was the act of proliferating the beauty of Syris everywhere in the universe. This was creating diversity amongst the stars. This was allowing every planet to possess its own unique traits. This was what it meant to live past materialism, utilize consciousness, and have faith in something higher than mortality.

Suddenly, an alert appeared on the radar inside the ship. A flashing red dot accompanied by a high-pitched beeping tone. The crew abruptly stopped their cheering and excitement. They all stared at the radar in silence. The princes, nearly 12,000 feet below the surface, froze in their floating positions in the ocean.

"What's wrong?" Jonah asked through the intercom. He got no response.

In the ship, Dempsey, the crew member, ran over to the microphone. "Boys! You have to get out of there now! We're picking up a strange disturbance on our radar. It's... oh no... it's right beneath your damn feet. Kick it into high gear!" he shouted. Static was slightly interrupting his feed from reaching the brothers.

"What do we do?" Carmine asked. He and Jonah quickly gathered remnants of their equipment.

"Swim! Just swim upward! It's seismic activity! We'll activate the jets on your suits again!" Dempsey shouted.

Jonah and Carmine quickly started swimming upwards towards the surface of their fabricated seas. Then, the jets on their diving suits turned on. They could hear the ground shake several hundred feet beneath them. Bubbles began blocking their visors once more. The jets propelled them upward at an intense speed. It was set to a maximum drive, expending all its fuel. The princes screamed through the intercom. They could feel the weight of the ocean water push against their suits. They could only hear the hiss of the microphone from the ship in their ears. They were moving too fast. All they could catch were faint tones of Dempsey's voice and possibly frantic shouting from the rest of the crew. They were coming so close. Jonah and Carmine could see the surface waves of the ocean, accompanied by the glow of the raging storms in the skies. Suddenly, their jets stopped. The momentum that the princes had accumulated came to a halt. With the surface waters at the tip of their anxious fingers, they could feel themselves sinking back down.

"Oh no… oh no! What's happening?" Carmine shouted. Their jet fuel had been exhausted.

"Damn it! Dempsey! Morgan! Someone! Our jets just ran out!" Jonah shouted. The princes came sinking towards the ocean depths again. Their suits were designed to be heavy, allowing them to stand firm on a surface when their jets weren't on. Jonah and Carmine could sense the ground shaking beneath them. Then, a cataclysmic explosion occurred several thousand feet below.

An underwater geyser, greater than any normal hydrothermal vent, had revealed itself from its buried camouflage in the sand. It suddenly fired a destructive stream of water and hit the brothers head-on. The powerful jet pushed them upward as they screamed in terror. Jonah and Carmine came bursting through the surface of the ocean and landed atop a stray land formation.

The princes hit the rocky terrain hard. Jonah landed on his back and Carmine on his chest. The air had been taken right out of them. Thunderstorms occurred above, bred from the massively gray clouds that covered the entire atmosphere. Volcanoes exploded in the background. Red cracks of lava coursed through the land like suffering veins. Molten rock tumbled down every mountain and earthquakes occurred constantly. This was their creation. And Jonah and Carmine loved it more than any other one they had done before. Carmine slowly rolled over onto his back, lying beside his twin brother. They both looked up into the suffering sky, visors shattered from the chaos. After feeling the rainfall upon their faces for a moment, Jonah and Carmine couldn't help but laugh.

They held their stomachs and cackled hysterically. The purest rain fell into their exaggeratingly gaping mouths. They hadn't been this happy in quite some time.

Captain Litton appeared in the intercom. "What the hell are you two laughing about? goddess be damned. You could've been hurt!" he shouted.

Jonah and Carmine just sat up. The ground was rather hot to the touch, but their suits protected them. They could see the water upon their suits evaporate into steam.

"Captain Litton. Don't you get it? We're laughing because we did it. It's over. The terraform, our *planet*, it's complete. Carmine and I may have just sparked the link for evolution for one of the greatest planets the universe has ever seen," Jonah said.

Carmine stood up and held his hand out to his brother. He helped him up. "Besides, that was actually kind of fun. I have faith goddess will be more than pleased with our work. I can't help but say that I love being a Seraph. We have done some tremendously good things here," Carmine added. The whole crew inside the ship couldn't help but smile, some slightly laughing alongside the glorious princes of Jannah. Despite the negative sentiments Jonah and Carmine had about their species, they were proud to be Seraphs. They were proud to take such an important role in developing the universe. They were proud to spread life and create planets that would soon become home to a new species. It was a blessing to them.

Moments later, the princes had been beamed back into the ship. The ship left the atmosphere of the developing planet and remained stationary in its orbit. The crew was performing several precautionary checks of all systems. It was impossible to tell what kind of damage the rainfall or gases could have done to the hull or engine.

Jonah and Carmine rematerialized in the main deck of the ship. They shook hands with every one of the crew members and indulged in a brief moment of celebration. A new crew member, Romona, brought the brothers each a glass of Jannah's finest wine. She was a younger Seraph, no more than 20 years-old. She was quite beautiful and small in stature. Jonah and Carmine each raised their glasses to propose a toast. It was at this moment that they felt remnants of their parents' praise and recognition as rulers.

"It was quite a difficult task, but after several months of planning and executing, we have finally concluded the physical terraforming of our newest, most promising planet!" Jonah shouted. The crew clapped and cheered for the brothers. They had a power that couldn't be summed up by any mortal in the entire universe. Their greatness lied in more than just their ability to create like the gods. It was their eloquence and their intelligence that truly solidified Jonah and Carmine's status as princes of Jannah.

They handed their empty glasses back to Romona, to which she set them down on a side table. "Excuse me. Where are the *Hakim Nisa'* right now?" Carmine asked.

Romona turned around, somewhat flustered, yet tamed. She blushed in the presence of the two handsome boys. They were bigger than any celebrity and known across the entire universe. After months of being rejected, Romona finally performed well in an interview to get the job as a crew member for the princes' signature ship. This was surreal to the young woman. "Oh… yes! The Wise Women are in the resting quarters of the ship," Romona said.

Jonah stepped closer to her. "Thank you, miss. We appreciate your service," he said, placing a hand on the woman's shoulder. Romona smiled at the boys and resumed gathering the wine glasses.

The princes walked down the large hall and took two turns to reach the resting quarters. They knocked on a steel door in front of them. Seconds later, the electric door quickly slid open, retreating into the confines of the wall surrounding the room. Jonah and Carmine entered casually, being one of the few beings in the entire universe capable of walking into the presence of the *Hakim Nisa'* whenever they pleased. Before them were the twelve most powerful mortals in all existence. Suddenly, all the somewhat old women surrounded them like birds to feed. Their distinct smiles glistened and they began congratulating the princes. Jonah and Carmine shook their hands and thanked them in return. Then, the one *Hakim Nisa'*

they considered to be an aunt, Kanya, walked through the crowd of her celestial sisters. She warmly hugged Jonah and Carmine, wrapping her small arms around the back of their necks, her head in between theirs, facing the opposite direction.

"Chosen Ones. I am so very proud of you. We all are. What you have done to develop this planet exceeds what any of your Sultan ancestors have been willing to commit to. This planet is very special. My sisters and I can sense it," Kanya said. She ended her sentence with a massive grin.

Carmine looked at all the Wise Women somewhat crammed in these small resting quarters. "Thank you so much for your kind words, Aunt Kanya. And thank you all for your glorious praise. This is an incredible milestone. Not just for Jannah, the Seraphs, and Syris, but the entire universe. There's still much more to accomplish before we can guarantee the evolution's success. But my brother and I are confident that with the help of the entire universe, this planet will be the next sovereign land," Carmine said passionately. The Wise Women began a symphony of scattered clapping.

"Now, if you all don't mind, we'd like to have a word with our Aunt Kanya. There's a celebratory lunch occurring in the main deck. Please help yourselves," Jonah added. The *Hakim Nisa'* bowed before the princes, and the boys bowed back as they passed through the door into the hallway.

As the 11th woman left, silence emerged. The electric door closed. Jonah and Carmine faced their aunt Kanya. The elderly woman straddled across the carpeted floor and sat down upon the bed. This was specifically her room on the ship, but she and her sisters were currently using it for prayers. Pictures of Kanya and the brothers' parents were delicately placed on end tables and dressers.

"So… to what do I owe this exclusive visit? Jonah, I can sense your tension. What is it that you would like to speak to me about?" Kanya asked.

The princes stood in silence. Jonah gulped nervously. Carmine smacked him on the back, nudging him to speak up. "Aunt Kanya. As you may know, I'm currently in relations with a woman back on our home planet and—"

Kanya suddenly laughed. "For heaven's sake boy, speak English. You don't need to be so formal with me," she said. Jonah inhaled and calmed himself down.

"Kanya. You're aware that I've had a girlfriend for four years now."

"Yes of course. All *Hakim Nisa'*, and possibly the entire universe are aware of your girlfriend, Evelyn. She is sweet and quite determined. Mighty intelligent too. She has succeeded in great strides for her family, despite the loss of her father," Kanya said.

"I'm glad to hear you feel that way about Evelyn. You see Kanya, I know this might be bad timing, but I want to ask you for your blessing. I'm ready to marry Evelyn."

Kanya was suddenly taken aback. "You wish to… *marry* Evelyn?"

"Of course. Four years of being in a relationship is plenty of time. I know I love her and I know she loves me back. Is there a problem, Kanya?"

"Oh, Jonah. The other Wise Women and I were under the impression that you simply wanted to be with her… to be with her. We respect your mutual emotions with the girl, but by no means did we predict you'd want to marry her," Kanya said grimly.

"I don't understand. What's the issue with me marrying Evelyn?" Jonah asked, becoming concerned.

"Come now, Jonah. It should be obvious. Evelyn carries no label but a commoner of Jannah. She has no royal bloodline anywhere in her family. The Scribes have researched her lineage."

"Kanya. What does that have to do with me marrying her? It shouldn't matter."

"Oh but it matters more than you

realize, Chosen One. Evelyn comes from a family of thieves, beggars, and drug dealers. The person you marry must be properly equipped to be a queen. Evelyn has done nothing more than work in factories her entire life, her parents and grandparents the same. She has never tasted wealth. How could she possibly rule alongside you to conduct duties for an entire universe? To rule the greatest planet in the greatest solar system?"

"This is unbelievable! Evelyn has been to the castle countless times and has assisted me in my duties as the prince. She's my greatest supporter!"

"But as the king, she will be your greatest inhibitor. A queen with no experience. *No* power. Even as queen her name will bear no weight."

"Kanya. Are you serious? I can't believe this. The discrimination of the Seraphs knows no bounds."

Jonah turned his back to Kanya. He was at a loss for words. This was yet another moment where the brothers' bond stood the test of controversy. They were inseparable. Carmine stepped forward to their aunt. He felt just as much pain as his twin.

"Aunt Kanya. Please, you have to understand why Jonah's upset," he said. Carmine took a moment to piece together his thoughts. "What if I told you that I'm seeing an Automa?" The phrase he blurted out so suddenly caught the other two by shock, which he predicted.

"Wait… what Automa?" Jonah asked.

Carmine looked back at his brother. "Her name is Leola. I met her at the party last week. She was alone in the garden. After hearing about her life on Centauri, I know that she has more than enough strength, grit, and heart to help rule Jannah someday. Quite frankly, I would have it be no other way but to make Leola my queen if our relationship lasts that long," he explained. Kanya scoffed. Her reaction seemed to be more disgusted than the one she showed towards Jonah and Evelyn's relationship.

"Don't be so spiteful, Chosen One. Don't decide to be with this foreigner simply because you've come to witness the true opinions Seraphs have about immigrants," Kanya said.

"You shouldn't claim that I'm with this woman out of spitefulness. Jonah and I have done our best to tolerate the policies set by our ancestors. But why? Despite father welcoming immigrants into Jannah, why does his opinion speak to the opposite of his actions?" Carmine asked.

"It's complicated politics, young one. We don't expect you two to entirely understand. The Automa have no business co-ruling over the greatest planet in all existence."

"This is the first time twins were born to the king and queen. This also means it will be the first time Jannah witnesses the rise of not one, but *two* kings. Jonah and I see no harm in them witnessing a change in the demographics of their queens as well."

"Carmine is right, Kanya. Our generation seeks change. We seek diversity. If Seraphs forever attempt to live their lives striving towards a eugenics mentality, we will never see the proliferation of a greater race." Jonah added.

"Exactly. How dare Seraphs have the godly power of creation, yet discriminate against the very beings they create, just because they're different? I thought the whole point was diversity! Kanya, Jonah, and I intend to pursue our own path. We asked for your blessing, but we don't need it," Carmine said.

It almost looked as if tears were emerging in their aunt's eyes. But before she could begin to form an emotional rebuttal, something happened. The woman's face looked as if she had seen a ghost. Her somewhat wrinkled skin froze in position, stretched by her gaping jaw.

"Kanya? Aunt Kanya? What's wrong?" Jonah asked.

Her expression slowly became more soulless. After several moments of frightening silence, the woman blinked herself back into existence. "Princes. Take me to the main deck. We must return home immediately," Kanya said. The boys started stammering frantically. "Now! We must go now!" she repeated.

The electric door slid open and the princes began running down the halls, Kanya trailing behind. They approached the crew. "We have to go now! Wise Woman Kanya demands that we head back home now! Gather the crew!" Carmine said to Captain Litton. Jonah was helping Kanya reach the main deck.

"What's the problem? What's going on?" Litton asked. The princes just shook their heads; even they didn't have the answer.

"There's a disturbance. Take me and my sisters to the Crown of the World on Jannah. We must get to the temple to receive answers from goddess," Kanya explained. Captain Litton nodded.

Moments later, everyone buckled up in their seats. Because this was a drastic situation, they prepared the ship to return home using hyperdrive. The engines revved up and the massive spaceship became engulfed in celestial energy. It started to glow with incandescent colors, flaring up near the exhaust.

A voice appeared on the intercom. It was Phoebe, the ship technician.

"Attention everyone. This is your ship technician speaking. To ensure optimal safety during hyperdrive, please ensure you are firmly strapped in your seats. Both seat belts should cross your body in a 'V' shape and your ankles should be locked in place by the metal braces. Be prepared for some possible nauseousness, as hyperdrive consists of traveling faster than the speed of light. Good luck and safe travels!"

After a brief countdown, the ship launched at hyper speed. Jonah and Carmine could feel the skin on their faces pull back. In the front window of the ship, they could see nothing but flashing lights of space passing by beyond comprehensible speed. The entire hyperdrive was a blur. But soon, visible clouds started emerging, warmly comforted by a gray sky. In what only felt like minutes, the ship had arrived back at Jannah. At the Crown of the World, atop the planet's highest mountain.

The ship remained stationed above the mountain. The princes exited the cargo deck and assisted the *Hakim Nisa'* with getting off. Now all wearing snow gear, Jonah and Carmine, alongside the Wise Women, crossed a bridge and reached a massive temple. Its gilded structures were suppressed by the purity of nature's white snow. The twelve women approached a gate, each performing separate hand symbols. They bowed their heads, forming slight variations of prayers. Suddenly, the gate to the temple glowed with teal energy. Fragments of intensely magical gems lit up and emitted a heat powerful enough to melt the snow covering it. The massive gates opened up. Their loud creak echoed across the mountainous plains.

They all quickly entered the temple, rushing across dark hallways that the *Hakim Nisa'* seemed to be able to navigate without looking. Kanya led the group. Every time they passed a torch upon the walls of the hallway, it suddenly became lit with powerful platinum-colored flames. Jonah and Carmine followed them into a massive room equipped with religious artifacts and a shrine dedicated to goddess. It was the sanctuary of Jannah. The one place in the entire universe where it became impossible for any darkness to exist. In the center of the ceiling was a massive opening that let in holy light from Jannah's two suns. It shined upon a valuable relic located in the center of the room. This created the powerful natural light of the sanctuary. The Wise Women gathered around this beam of light and sat upon their heels in prayer. Jonah and Carmine just stood back, nervous and enthralled by this very moment.

Something terrible must have been brewing. The brothers faced each other in silence. They prayed to goddess that everything would turn out alright. Indulging in the solemn chants of the *Hakim Nisa's* prayer, they waited.

The ground suddenly began shaking violently. The powerful lights in the sanctuary suddenly started exploding. The crackling sounds were reminiscent of cannon fodder in a war.

Jonah and Carmine screamed. "What's happening?"

Suddenly, the center relic emitted a powerful burst of energy, almost rejecting the synchronized prayer of the Wise Women. A shockwave scattered across the room, sending the women into the air and the princes into the wall they stood by. A subtle panic began rising in the sanctuary. The response of nature was terrifying. The brothers helped each other to their feet, then started assisting the *Hakim Nisa'*. After everyone had gathered themselves, Kanya approached Jonah and Carmine. They were at a loss for words. But the horror on her face told it all. The very fabrics of the entire universe were at risk of being dismantled. A story that had existed for over a century, a power struggle, a hatred upon mortals was going to tear everything apart. Despite the entanglement of every being that came to exist in this realm, the entire pursuit was personal.

Kanya looked into the princes' eyes. "War is coming."

Kanya, Hakim Nisa' of Eon V

War on the Rise

After an entire year of small and large-scale attacks upon neighboring planets, Zion had nearly achieved his plan. Alongside his wife Raakel and a technologically advanced army of Vectins, he strategically dominated territories in the Syris Solar System by exploiting their weaknesses. The couple controlled the forces of Kremlin. With Raakel, they persuaded the Ectognatha on Mirage to fight for their cause. They forcefully conquered the Automa on Centurion by overthrowing the sky city and capturing its ruling prince, Kainoa. This left his twin sister, princess Kaarina, to fend for herself on an enslaved planet. They scorched the forests of Ximji, eliminating the homes of the Elves. Then they forced the beings into servitude, fighting for an evil army against their allies. Through their many riches, they bought out the aid of Tempest, utilizing the Hippopotamus' barbaric nature to betray Jannah. This meant Zion's army now controlled five of the eight planets of Syris. The royal couple of Jannah continued its defense with their strongest remaining allies, the Nanomorphs of Echelon and Personas of Pandora. Planets outside of Syris could only do so much to help the Seraphs. In most instances, their armies got themselves killed, unable to handle the god-like conflict in the solar system that housed the most powerful beings in the universe.

Zion's regime of heretics against Syris' faith became a force to be reckoned with. Many betrayed Adelrik and Vitaliya, believing that overthrowing the king and Queen of Jannah was the key to create a divine era of equality. Anyone who didn't join

Zion in his mission to spread the truth of the All was left for dead or imprisoned. Constant nuclear bombings, air raids, chemical warfare, drone strikes, deforestation, and famine left much of Syris in havoc. With nothing left to take, the planet of peace, perfection, and prosperity was empowered by nothing more than its weapon of faith. The Seraphs worked with their remaining allies to fight back but were concerned that their growing efforts were becoming futile. The only thing that could keep the planet together was The Crystals of Nihaya inside the depths of their castle.

On the sacred planet, Adelrik, its king, stood atop the roof of the massive castle. He was in front of a large squadron of the Jannah military. The Seraphs, equipped in gilded armor, all stood proudly before their king and commander in chief. What made Seraphs such a dominant army was their inherent powers, granted to them by their goddess. The Crystals of Nihaya allowed the Seraphs to create weapons, armor, vehicles, and wings, using only their minds. The divine power of creation was in their hands and allowed them to summon supernatural abilities to aid them during wartime. The user's powers were only limited by their imagination. As the Seraphs got older, they began to develop a preference with their abilities, not only consolidating what they created but making the uniqueness of their cosmic tools more personal and powerful. This was mastery. Not every Seraph was entirely capable of utilizing their powers for combat. Only elite warriors that had undergone years of physical, mental, and spiritual training had satisfied their goddess enough to be delivered divine power from her. In the millions of years of the planet's existence, only a few fragments of The Crystals of Nihaya had risen to the surface from Jannah's core. This was the treasure that the royal couple possessed. Without it, the entire planet's power would weaken and Seraphs would only retain small portions of their abilities. Zion and Raakel knew this.

"Ladies and gentlemen, the time has finally come. With Zion's army attempting to overthrow Jannah's ambassadors, we could possibly see a weakness in our unity as a solar system. And for those of you curious, yes, this is a betrayal. Zion has done everything he could to get our former allies to believe that our goddess is not the true and divine creator of the universe. With this said, the friends that remain on Echelon and Pandora have been working to stop his forces from invading their nations, but they are heavily outnumbered. The enemy forces here on Jannah have controlled several of our continents in the past six months. Now they have arrived in our holy land, likely with the intent to overthrow the royal castle. I understand that you're all scared. It seems as though we have no hope left. But I want you to have faith. goddess is watching over us. We cannot stand by as Zion steals all power from Syris with his bare hands and ruthless tactics. Seraphs fight back no matter the odds. The power of creation doesn't belong in the hands of evil. This is our chance to stop the darkness and rebuild an era of true prosperity! Seraphs, summon your weapons! Zion has come to heaven, but he will only see hell! Fight for your families! Fight for your friends! Fight for our goddess! And fight for your faith!" Adelrik shouted powerfully.

The entire Seraph squadron, nearly one hundred royal guards, shed warlike cries. They summoned their weapons of various origins. Lances, swords, rifles, explosives, and much more. They summoned their wings and took flight north of the castle, moving towards the burning flames of the distant mountains. The 1st sunset had just arrived. Darkness was beginning to emerge upon Jannah. Even the king and queen didn't know what would become of their beloved planet. Princes Jonah and Carmine emerged from the background, having watched their father motivate what was left of Jannah's royal military.

"That was a good speech father," Carmine said.

"Thank you, son. I could only hope that I didn't deceive them into walking towards their own deaths," Adelrik replied.

"Nonsense father. You know Seraphs are strong."

"Yes. I have faith that for every Seraph slain, more than a thousand of their forces are killed in return. But even that ratio isn't enough to stop more than half of our solar system."

"They *do* outnumber us by five to three planets. Those odds have been difficult to overcome in recent months," Jonah added.

"It doesn't matter. Zion is attempting to use emotional tactics over logical ones. Preaching heresy to convert everyone into beliefs that stand against what so many of us have learned in the Kadar. It's his current motion to eliminate our ambassadors that worries me the most," Adelrik said.

"Do we know when mother will be coming back?"

"Since we last communicated, she had just arrived on Mirage. That was several hours ago. I could only hope that she and her squad had managed to navigate the forests to find where the Ectognatha ambassadors were being held. But because of Zion's wretched wife, her species' forces stand strong on that planet. They know the layout of those forests like their mothers' maiden names. It's dangerous for your mother to be there. But she insisted that this was the best way to halt Zion's onslaught on Syris' political structure."

"I hope she returns soon," Carmine said.

The princes and king took a lift leading down to the throne room of the castle. Their father moved out of the lift first, stepping upon the royal carpet. The once-powerful man gazed at the golden thrones facing him. His wife's throne was to his left and his own was to his right. Adelrik slowly walked forward, not blinking once. His sons watched him silently. "In war, the only difference between a king and a soldier is that one prepares to die alongside their comrades and the other prepares to die alone," he said. Adelrik reached out towards his throne, yet retreated. He refused to sit on it or even touch it. Jonah and Carmine contracted their father's sorrow like a virus. They had never experienced so much pain in their young lives before.

Suddenly, a sound was heard outside the castle. The two boys turned around, looking out the nearby vertical window. They could see a spaceship preparing to land. "It's mother's ship! She's back!" Jonah exclaimed.

Adelrik and the brothers quickly ran outside to the front gates of the castle grounds. The small spaceship was landing in front of them, gusting winds brewing from its powerful hover. Men and women of Jannah's royal army emerged from the back of the ship, saluting the members of the Sultan family that remained in the homeland. Finally, Queen Vitaliya exited the back of the ship with two Ectognatha at her side. They were frail insect creatures with an ancestral derivation similar to that of grass-hoppers. Their compound eyes were shedding tears and their chitinous ex-oskeletons were covered in blood, likely not their own. Vitaliya, equipped in shining valkyrie armor, planted her heels on the muddy ground. Adelrik and his sons quickly hugged her.

"Mom! You're okay!" the brothers exclaimed happily. Vitaliya hugged her family back. She turned to her guards. Half of her original squad was gone. They must have died on Mirage.

"Take the Ectognatha ambassadors to the apocalyptic preparation room in the castle. They'll be safe there," Vitaliya ordered.

"Vitaliya. Your squadron… what happened?" Adelrik asked.

"There was more than an ambush waiting for us on Mirage. Zion and Raakel have access to a drastic amount of resources. There were traps, technological preparations, and much more that we weren't prepared for. Half my squadron had laid their lives down for me," Vitaliya said as she removed her helmet.

"I'm so sorry you had to witness that, my love. But the ambassadors. I only saw two."

"Zion has likely killed the rest or is keeping them in captivity. I'm so sor-ry, husband. This was a mistake. I put lives at risk for very little gain and… and—"

"No Vitaliya. You don't need to apologize. You did what you could. I'm just happy that you returned home safely and managed to save *some* lives today."

"You're right. How have things been here?" Vitaliya asked.

"I just finished sending off the last battalion towards the conflict occur-ring within the northern mountains," Adelrik replied.

"May goddess pray for them all."

"May she protect our army and those fighting across all of Syris. None of these people, whether they're on our side or not, would have had to die if Zion didn't resort to twisting their faith. He gave them a reason to hate the Seraphs, to hate our religion, thus hating their current way of life."

"I agree with you, husband. But we cannot concern ourselves with the possible fallout of this war. What matters most right now is protecting our family."

The king and queen smiled at their prince sons. Suddenly, two royal guards flew in from the outer perimeter of the castle's gates. The two women bowed before the Sultan family. "Ma'am. Sir. We have terrible news. There's been a disturbance. Zion and Raakel have entered the atmosphere," a guard said.

Vitaliya and Adelrik's jaws dropped. "But how is that possible? We thought they would attempt to overthrow Pandora or Echelon before moving towards our planet," Adelrik said.

The two guards simply shook their heads. "Our intel was wrong. We know it's them. Zion sent a message directly to our comm satellites."

The royal couple exchanged a painful look. Vitaliya equipped her helmet again. The king and queen approached their sons and gave them both a kiss. "Grab Evelyn and Leola. Stay inside the castle. You'll be safe here. The royal guards will protect you, children," Vitaliya explained.

The princes were reluctant to adhere to their parents' requests. They stammered. "Mom. Jannah is as much of our responsibility as it is yours. We have to help you fight. This war is our burden too," Jonah said. Carmine agreed. But they should've known their mother wouldn't yield.

"You're wrong. This is personal. Now don't argue with me boys! This is for your own good! You can't possibly think you could help us face the two people who are destroying the entire balance of the universe could you?" Vitaliya shouted.

Jonah and Carmine understood. "We love you both," they said. Adelrik and Vitaliya both began shedding tears.

"We love you too." The couple both summoned their wings and flew off towards the outer plains of their castle. Now they were going to become the first line of defense for all of Jannah.

Vitaliya, Queen of Jannah

Jonah and Carmine quickly re-treated towards the royal village, all within the proximity of the castle. They were running across an empty street. "We should do what mother said! You get Leola and I'll grab Eve-lyn!" Jonah shouted. Carmine nod-ded. The brothers crossed each other and continued running in opposite directions.

Jonah went towards the barracks on the east side of the castle. He quickly ran down a pathway and made it towards the front gate of the armory. He opened it and ran inside. There was Evelyn, his fiancé. She had a clipboard in her hands and a pencil on her ear. She stared at a massive board with nearly incomprehensible listings. This was her assistance in the war effort.

"Evelyn! Babe, we have to go! We

have to retreat towards the castle!" Jonah shouted.

Evelyn was startled. "Jonah! For heaven's sake! You scared me half to death. What's wrong?" she asked.

Jonah grabbed her by the arms and looked into her eyes. "Zion and Raakel have entered Jannah's atmosphere." Evelyn's eyes revealed a sudden fear that many had never been able to witness on her before. The young woman attempted to collect herself nonetheless. This was the resolve that Jonah loved about her so much.

"Okay… okay. Well, I just finished delegating the remaining armaments. They were sent with the last guards protecting the castle. My sister and mother are still safe in their room here right?" Evelyn asked. Jonah nodded. He grabbed his fiancé's hand and ran with her towards the castle.

Meanwhile, Carmine was making his way towards the church on the west side of the castle. He leaped over a set of barricades and approached the front door. The prince opened it and ran inside. There was Leola, his girlfriend. She was standing before a large group of women and children who lived in the royal village. She was providing them with blankets and rations of food, assisting with the war effort.

Carmine slowly walked between the people and approached Leola at the center of them. "Leola. Come on, I need to speak with you," he said.

Leola turned around, somewhat startled to hear his voice. "Carmine? What're you doing here? Shouldn't you be with your parents at the castle?" she asked.

Carmine shook his head and grabbed her hand. "Leola, we have to retreat towards the castle. Zion and Raakel have entered Jannah's atmosphere."

Leola's eyes opened wide, but her brows quickly furrowed in anger. It looked as if she was prepared to fight. "I can't just leave these Seraphs behind. They need someone to protect them," Leola said. Her love for all species was what Carmine loved about her so much.

"Don't fret. I'll make sure royal guards are sent to protect this church and these people. We have to go now!" Carmine shouted. He grabbed his girlfriend's hand and ran with her towards the castle.

On the outskirts of the castle, preparations were made. The queen and king of Jannah, Vitaliya, and Adelrik, stood alongside the final forces of the Seraph army. No more than fifty men and women accompanied them on this last stand. Troops arming cannons and ballistae stood atop the castle walls, armed for a war in which they were clearly outnumbered. Vitaliya and Adelrik stood side by side, the gusting wind blowing ashes across their unfazed faces. The couple was holding hands. This served two purposes: Show the Seraphs the unity of their species, and ensure that their potentially last moments in this realm were spent as close to each other as possible.

Then it came. Emerging from the depths of the gray clouds was one ship. Followed by two, followed by ten, followed by another fifty, and another hundred. Zion and Raakel's ship took the lead amongst the others. Vitaliya and Adelrik could almost sense their presence. The opposing couple was standing on the main deck of the largest ship in the fleet, looking down from the window. They too stood side by side, holding hands. It was possibly for the same reason as the royal couple of Jannah. The main ship landed first. Others followed shortly after.

Vitaliya raised an open palm towards the remnants of her army. "Hold! My husband and I will speak to them first," she said. The royal couple walked forward. They could hear the hiss of the main ship's doors opening. A staircase emerged from the side, to which Zion and Raakel stepped out. Zion daintily held his wife's hand, helping her down the steps. After a year of war, the emperors of Kremlin finally planted their feet on the surface of Jannah. Their dream was only moments from being realized. The two couples walked towards each other, standing amongst the scorched plains of Jannah's once beautiful landscape.

Vitaliya and Adelrik had marched out the gates of their sanctuary, ready to step feet first into hell. They had a small army of their most elite warriors standing behind them. Several hundred feet in front of them was the couple that had forever resented their place in Syris. Behind Zion and Raakel was an army of nearly five planets, joining them in the war for various reasons. These two couples were perhaps the four greatest warriors the universe had to offer. One stood for good and the other for evil. This was a dispute of faith. More spaceships emerged from the thunderous clouds that covered the light of Genesis and Jannah's 2nd Sun. Zion had even more reinforcements than could be accounted for. This war was beginning to look more and more like suicide for the side that clung to its faith in goddess.

"You can never leave well enough alone can you, Zion?" Vitaliya asked.

"I see. It's always *Zion* who demands too much. He always feels like he must fight for what he's owed. He always takes as he pleases. I'm simply following the ways of the Seraphs. You take whatever you want, *whenever* you want," Zion replied.

"You know nothing about the words coming from your mouth," Adelrik said.

"Oh, but I know too much. Don't pretend like we weren't old friends, you two. I've seen the way you clutch onto your power. Everything for the people of Jannah and none for the rest of Syris. Is that how you envisioned paradise for the last century?"

"Jannah *is* paradise. Our people stand for unity," Vitaliya said.

"You want to talk about unity? Observe. Five of the eight ancient planets fight for *my* cause in this war. Not yours."

"Nothing more than simple coercion."

"As I've mentioned already, I'm just following the ways of your people. We were forced to ultimately follow your religion. We were forced to kneel before your almighty *Hakim Nisa'*. We were forced to accept our place in Syris. Your heaven only welcomes the most elite beings in the universe, while everyone else is left with no real afterlife to look forward to. But no longer will people blindly have faith in your goddess. The dawn of the truth, the All, will ensue."

"That's what this is all about? Reli-gious beliefs crammed down society's throats?" Vitaliya asked.

"Yes. All of the greatest religious figures were labeled as heretics during their time. I'm the only real living god in this realm. And I will seize my place above all mortals," Zion said, clenching his fists.

"You want to fight us? You have no real power, *god*. You know you both will die," Adelrik threatened.

Zion stepped closer to the royal couple of Jannah. He removed his cape and handed it to Gautam, his right-hand servant back from Kremlin. "Come on, Adelrik. My species, Vectins, are the most intelligent in the entire universe. Do you think I came here without a plan? You see, old friends, I haven't fought a single battle in this entire war. No. I have spent over a year preparing myself. I rule over Kremlin for a reason. A reason greater than just bloodline. It's my birthright. I'm a deity amongst my people. The hourglass birthmark on my body is proof of my divinity. I'm a god because I have already cheated death multiple times and have been reincarnated from the NetherRealm into this body. And with the assistance of the high priests, Entombment has granted me a power strong enough to stop you both. Our great religious sacrament has allowed me to harness my truest potential," Zion explained. He inhaled deeply. Suddenly, there was a glow about him. A dark aura surging around his presence. "Don't you see; Vitaliya, Adelrik? Look into my eyes. There's something different there right? To fully rise to a god, I have also borrowed some relics from the planets that now serve me." Zion revealed weapons on his belt and withdrawn in his holsters. They were various artifacts from the planets he had come to conquer. With them, he was able to attain fragments of the powers from nearly every species in Syris. It had become obvious that this fight was going to be more than what the king and queen had anticipated.

"Impossible! Your words mean nothing until you act upon them, Zion. Now, Raakel! You haven't said a single word yet. You can't possibly agree with your husband's intentions! We thought you stood for peace and prosperity!" Vitaliya shouted.

"You're wrong, Vitaliya. I said I stood for what's right. Therefore, I'm completely in alignment with my husband's wishes. It's time for this universe to enter a new era. One where a single, mortal species no longer exploits the power of creation, the power of gods all to themselves," Raakel said.

"You're as foolish as he is then. He has tricked you and your entire race," Adelrik interjected.

"Quiet Adelrik. My people understand just what's at stake. Syris belongs to us all. Jannah belongs to us all. And that includes its treasures deep within."

The royal couple looked stunned by Raakel's words. Perhaps there was more to Zion's plan than just overthrowing all authority in Syris. Suddenly, Raakel stepped back. It looked as if she was yielding, allowing her husband to take the front stand in this emerging conflict.

"Good luck, you two," Raakel said. Then, she suddenly disappeared, vanishing into a beam of light. She teleported.

"What's going on here? Where did she go?" Adelrik shouted. The Seraph army became flustered, much like their rulers.

Zion just laughed. "One of our ships set a transporter atop Jannah's castle. Raakel will find the Crystals of Nihaya and rip them from the clutches of anyone who dares stand in her way," he said.

Vitaliya gasped. "Adelrik! They're after the crystals! Stop her!" she shouted.

Adelrik attempted to retreat towards the castle, but suddenly, a surge of energy surrounded the perimeter, knocking him down. The king was stopped by a force field. The purple energy formed into a massive cage, no more than 1,000 square feet in size and 50 feet in height. It only trapped Vitaliya, Adelrik, and Zion inside. The small army of Jannah summoned their weapons, shocked by what had transpired. "What's this?" Adelrik shouted.

Zion started cracking his neck and knuckles. "I can't possibly have you two escape. I want you both to myself. And I want our entire armies to watch. Vitaliya. Adelrik. We are the heart of this entire war. It has always been personal. It's just that billions of people stood in between us and had to die for this moment to occur. Now face me, your highnesses. The real fight begins now."

Vitaliya helped her husband up to his feet. The royal couple faced emperor Zion. "Do you honestly think you can take us both on?" Vitaliya asked. Her and Adelrik each summoned gilded armor and a sword of unique properties.

Zion squared himself. "I suppose there's only one way to find out. Use whatever you want. Summon any weapon, channel all celestial force, whatever you need. I understand it's been some time since you two have fought a real opponent," he said. Zion raised his fists, hardly putting any effort into his stance. Anger emerged on the royal couple's faces.

"Enough talk," Adelrik said. With several planets watching, they prepared themselves. This was about more than Jannah, more than Syris, more than the universe. This was personal.

The Final Stand

Meanwhile, the kids were preparing any additional defense measures they could gather together in the castle. Jonah had set down another sandbag. Dozens of them formed the defensive wall blocking the large door to the throne room, where the kids stayed for safety.

"Do you think this will be enough?" Evelyn asked, setting down another sandbag. Jonah just looked at his fiancé and shrugged his shoulders. Then, Leola came from the back room empty-handed. "Well, it's going to have to do. We're all out," she said. The four kids stood together on the red carpet, exhausted.

"There has to be more we can do. You all saw the tremendous army Zion brought into the atmosphere!" Carmine exclaimed.

"What more *can* we do Carmine? We have to stay here to protect our families, the *Hakim Nisa'*, and the remaining citizens," Evelyn said.

"No. That's the royal guards' job. We have to be smart here."

"What do you think we should do then?" Leola asked.

"Devise a plan. Beyond just standing here. We have to put up a better fight," Carmine said.

"Well, let's suppose mom and dad manage to stop the emperors of Kremlin. There's still an army of millions outside our castle. We can't seriously expect to fight them all," Jonah added.

"Then we should have a failsafe. An escape plan," Carmine said.

"Even *if* we attempt to use a ship to leave into orbit, anti-air infantry will likely stop us," Leola said.

"Zion will probably have ships stationed outside the planet waiting for us too," Evelyn added.

The four kids all remained quiet for a moment, thinking to themselves. Then, Jonah managed to think of an alternative form of travel.

"No. Wait. Carmine's right. There is the possibility of an escape plan. But maybe we don't necessarily have to escape from Jannah through the skies. Carmine, we left a transporter node on our developing planet, right?" Jonah asked.

"Yeah. What do you have in mind?" Carmine responded.

"Is there any possible way we could connect it to the teleporter in the laboratory here?"

"Jonah. That's genius. But I wouldn't even know how to begin a process as complex as that."

"Hm. I might be able to help actually," Leola interjected.

The other kids looked at her, confused.

"What? I *am* an Automa after all. Technology is in my genes. Literally. Not to mention, I've spent some time with my uncle working on transport systems. I may be able to get the node activated. I'll just need the coordinates of your developing planet," Leola explained.

"Good! Leola, please go to the laboratory. The transporter connected to the developing planet is in the corner of the room. Carmine, you can accompany her! Keep her safe!" Jonah exclaimed.

His twin brother and respective girlfriend ran off to the laboratory in the back sector of the castle. Jonah and Evelyn stood together, protecting the throne room alone.

"I suppose it's just you and me now, my love," he said.

Evelyn let out a reluctant chuckle. "I hope they can get the teleporter working. I'm no fighter. You know that. But are you sure you and your brother's developing planet will be safe enough for us? The conditions could be too harsh," she said.

Jonah shook his head. "There's nothing to worry about. It's been over a year since we planted the divine bacterium. The planet is likely in the evolutionary stage now, filled with plenty of oxygen." Evelyn looked down and smiled slightly. There was nothing more than a glimpse of hope in her eyes. Jonah grabbed his fiancé's hands and gazed at her face. They slowly closed in for a kiss.

But deep within the throne room, an ominous presence lurked. Jonah could sense something up above. "Look out!" he shouted. He quickly grabbed Evelyn and dove to the left. There was a loud crash. When the young couple opened their eyes, they saw their assailant.

"Empress… Raakel?" Evelyn questioned. Jonah helped his girlfriend to her feet. The two of them faced the maleficent woman.

"Hello children," Raakel said. She withdrew two tanto blades into their scabbards.

Beads of sweat emerged on Evelyn's face. "How did she get in here?" she asked.

Raakel's massive scorpion tail moved in rhythm with her emotions. A soft sway to the left and another to the right made it clear that Raakel was completely confident in her actions. "Funny that you ask, girl. I heard you kids mention transporters. One of my ships planted a transporter atop the castle. I simply let myself in. Now,

while my husband takes care of your parents, I'm going to complete *my* task. I've come here for the Crystals of Nihaya, Chosen One. It's quite simple. Take me to the fragments and I will be on my way. No harm will ensue thereforth," Raakel said.

Jonah moved into a fighting stance and summoned a sword. "Like hell I will!"

Raakel simply laughed. "Then I guess we must do this the hard way." The woman equipped a single tanto blade and charged forward, clashing steel with the prince. She was much stronger and experienced than he was. Raakel shoved him back towards a long dining table on the other end of the room.

"Evelyn! Run!" Jonah shouted. Evelyn hesitated but knew there was nothing she could do with her bare hands. She quickly ran towards the laboratory, hoping to call Carmine for help.

Jonah could feel Raakel's overwhelming strength push him back against the table. The woman was much bigger than him. Johan grunted heavily. He shoved her back, pushing their blades against each other. Now was his chance. He quickly summoned steel armor upon his body for protection. The prince charged forward again, swinging his sword wildly, but missed every time. Raakel's graceful movements left her dodging with ease. Jonah swung his blade upward, narrowly cutting the edge of the woman's hair. Having missed again, he fluidly swung downward. Raakel simply pivoted her upper body to the side. She smacked Jonah in his nose with the hilt of her tanto. Then, she leaped into the air, twirling backwards like a dancer. The empress kicked Jonah in his jaw with the heel of her right foot and kicked him in his chest with her left, a quick two-hit combo. Jonah fell backwards from the impact of the hit. The momentum was greater than he calculated.

He quickly jumped back up to his feet, screaming in rage. The prince started swinging his sword again. Left, right, northwest diagonal, and back in the other direction. Finally, he gave a thrust of his weapon and cut Raakel on her right side, piercing her armor and spilling her blood. This only angered the woman. Jonah attempted to capitalize on his strike and swung downward again with an exaggerated overhead. Raakel blocked the blade with her left gauntlet. She stabbed Jonah in his thigh with the tanto in her right hand and headbutted the prince. He was heavily stunned now. Raakel's massive scorpion tail pounced at Jonah. It looked as if it had a mind of its own. The tail constricted the prince like a snake. Jonah screamed as it started crushing his body through the armor. Then, Raakel threw him across the throne room. Jonah smashed through the long dining table. He attempted to recover, but suddenly, Raakel's boot hammered down upon his throat. The empress began crushing his airways.

Raakel looked down upon The Chosen One, unentertained. "I'm an elite warrior. And you are outmatched, boy. How could you possibly think you could single-handedly stop me? If you won't hand over the crystals, then I suppose you can just die."

Evelyn ran through the halls of the castle, making more turns than she could count. Finally, she entered the laboratory. The girl pushed through the glass double doors. "Carmine! Leola! Carmine!" she shouted.

Carmine and his girlfriend were in the corner of the lab, working intensely on the transporter. Leola was using tools to rearrange some wiring. Carmine was entering coding inputs that she was speaking to him out loud. But they stopped when they heard Evelyn's frantic behavior. "Evelyn! What's wrong?" Carmine asked.

Evelyn attempted to catch her breath. "You… You have to go help Jonah! It's Empress Raakel! She's managed to teleport past the gates! She's in the castle fighting Jonah right now! She's after the Crystals of Nihaya!"

Carmine's eyes opened wide. Leola finally turned away from what she was doing. She looked up at her boyfriend nervously. Carmine clenched his fists in anger. "Damn. Those bastards have made some plans I see. Fine. Raakel will not obtain the crystals. Jonah and I will stop her together. Evelyn, stay here with Leola until you two can get the transporter connected to our developing planet. From there, we can grab the crystals and make our escape with your families," he said. The girls nodded. Carmine summoned armor and a bow. He quickly ran off to assist his twin brother.

Meanwhile, the scene had become set for the intense, two-on-one fight. Armies of drastically different sizes watched as their warlords faced off before them.

Zion stared down the royal couple, his once great friends. "I'm almost sorry it has to end this way, you two. But you have failed to create a paradise in the here and now. And I will slate the universe through the enlightenment of the All. The worlds that you created must know the truth," he said.

Vitaliya and Adelrik both sighed miserably. The determination on their faces revealed a sacrifice that came to light. The death of an old friend to protect innocent people across the universe. "The only truth the universe must know of Zion is that you are tainted; evil. We hoped you could put your faith in the All behind you. But I suppose we must settle our differences another way. Your army should watch closely. They will witness the true outcome of heralds who dare stand against the *Hakim Nisa'* and defy goddess," Vitaliya said.

Zion scoffed. "Then let's see that outcome, shall we?"

Vitaliya and Adelrik charged forward, emitting a powerful and harmonious battle cry. Vitaliya raised her unique blade. She thrusted her arm forward. Suddenly, the blade extended with a powerful thorned chain. It fired across the area within the barrier. Zion quickly corkscrewed, dodging the ranged attack. The blade stuck into the energy wall of the barrier. Adelrik too raised his blade. He pointed it forward and started shooting from it. Zion dodged oncoming gunfire with somewhat ease, the bullets ricocheting off the walls of the barrier. The power of the souls Zion obtained from a year-long entombment process granted him the abilities of some of the most powerful warriors to have ever lived. His senses, his reflexes, and his skills were beyond what the royal couple could have imagined. He could nearly see and feel everything within combat like a sixth sense. Now, it was time for him to attack.

Zion grabbed Vitaliya's chained sword and yanked it, pulling the woman towards him. He kneed the queen in her gut. She gagged, spit emerging from her mouth. Then Zion struck her with two jabs and a heavy cross, but the final hit was astronomically powerful. Vitaliya flew backwards and rolled across the dirt ground. Adelrik finally reached Zion. The king swung his gun-blade downward, then left, then right, but missed every hit. Zion continued to dodge gracefully. He kicked Adelrik in his shin, then pivoted and kicked him in the chest. Finally, Zion twirled 360 degrees and struck Adelrik with a powerful superman punch. The king was blown back, landing beside his wife.

The massive crowd of Zion's army cheered. They were witnessing their lord come out on top. He was fulfilling his promise of slating the universe and creating a new age of equality. The royal couple started to recuperate. Adelrik helped Vitaliya up to her feet and made sure she was okay. From the Seraph army's perspective, this two-on-one fight appeared to be even.

Finally, Vitaliya and Adelrik charged forward again, unleashing an onslaught upon Zion. Adelrik summoned a pistol and fired. Zion blocked with his ebony gauntlets.

Vitaliya leaped off her husband's shoulders and swung her heel downward like a hammer. Zion dodged. The crash from such a heavy attack left rubble scattered throughout the air inside the barrier. The king and queen continued. Adelrik swung his sword, Zion ducked. Vitaliya fired four arrows, Zion dodged. Adelrik lunged forward with a flurry of kicks. Zion blocked the attacks. Vitaliya threw a spear at the emperor, but he caught it with his bare hands, breaking the weapon in half. This continued for a brief time. Zion constantly dodged their synchronized attacks with graceful patience. After toying with them, he was ready to retaliate.

Zion threw an Ectognatha relic at Vitaliya. The relics were similar to amber fossils. It released a powerful web that constricted her movements. Then, utilizing the powerful magic of the Elves, he bent the land beneath their feet. Zion launched a rock at Vitaliya's chest and one at her face. The queen fell to the ground. Adelrik charged forward with his sword once more. Zion quickly used fire magic as a counterattack. He threw a punch, the fire striking Adelrik. Then he delivered a roundhouse. The fire spewed from his appendages violently, overwhelming the king of Jannah. Zion quickly spun around Adelrik's stunned form and shoved his palm into the man's back.

The emperor charged the power of the Automa's legkiy, a cosmic light the species was able to harness from the atmosphere to use as a weapon. Zion struck Adelrik with a powerful cosmic blast. The massive explosion glistened with a purple color. Adelrik flew forward and smacked into the barrier wall, face first.

The crowd of Zion's army cheered once more. At the same time, the Seraphs began chanting for their king and queen to rise. This was difficult to watch; the royal couple hadn't landed a single blow on the emperor of Kremlin.

Zion started laughing. "It looks like the king and queen of Syris have gone quite soft!" he shouted, taunting them. Zion equipped a sword he left sheathed in his scabbard during the entire fight thus far.

Vitaliya and Adelrik slowly rose back up to their feet. They sustained quite a dangerous amount of damage, but it wasn't nearly enough to get them to yield. Jannah was their home. In goddess' name, they were willing to die for it.

Vitaliya summoned a massive scythe and threw the weapon at the emperor. It spun across the air like a boomerang. Zion ducked under the weapon. But behind him, Adelrik caught it by the snath. Adelrik swung the scythe and cut Zion across his back. Vitaliya lunged forward and kicked Zion into the air. She summoned a chain and swung it upward, the weapon wrapping around his ankle. Vitaliya quickly yanked Zion down into the ground, chest first. He crashed down so hard, dirt plumed up into the air. Adelrik fired three arrows into Zion's back while he was down. The rulers of Jannah were beginning to fight in tandem. Vitaliya started dragging Zion across the ground with the chain, attempting to throw him into the barrier wall. But Zion quickly equipped his knife and cut the chain off his ankle. The emperor rolled through the dirt from the leftover momentum. Adelrik swung the scythe downward, attempting to stab him. Zion quickly rolled up to his feet, dodging the attack. The scythe's massive blade got stuck in the ground. The emperor had to capitalize. Zion ran up the snath and kicked Adelrik in his jaw, fluidly moving into an airborne backflip. While in the air, Zion harnessed the power of legkiy and fired a cosmic blast downward, hitting Adelrik. The king was blown to the ground again. Vitaliya persisted in the attack. She started firing cosmic blasts at Zion, the explosive attack knocking him out of the air. Zion landed in a back handspring and quickly retained his footing. He began dodging Vitaliya's blasts. Zion quickly ran along the barrier wall horizontally, using his intense athleticism to his advantage. While wall running, he conjured magic. He fired ice spikes at Vitaliya, striking her in the chest. Zion began channeling the power of Gaajada. This force was dubbed as "the hunger" amongst the Hippopotamus species of Tempest. This stolen power granted him immense strength from within and multiplied his fortitude. Zion powerfully pushed himself off the barrier wall with his feet. Launching at missile speed, he grabbed Vitaliya's face and smashed her head into the other end of the wall. The powerful attack shocked the armies watching. The forcefield started cracking from the intense attack.

Zion's eyes turned red from the rage of the Gaajada. He started beating on Vitaliya brutally, delivering two cataclysmic punches to her gut and one to her face. The strikes shook the ground and echoed across the solitude of what would soon be an all-out battlefield. Zion roared angrily. Just then, Adelrik dashed over and stabbed Zion in his side with his sword. Blood was spilled. Vitaliya joined her husband in the attack and headbutted the emperor with her steel helmet. Zion only grew angrier. He absorbed more energy from the atmosphere. Suddenly, an intense, purple aura emerged around his body.

Cosmic energy surged and blasted the royal couple away. They flew across the barrier and hit the walls on opposite ends.

Zion used the magic of the Elves once more. He fired soul spears at Adelrik; raw magic that took the form of massive, spear-like weapons. Adelrik quickly summoned a shield, blocking the heavy attacks. Vitaliya dashed over and thrusted a knife at Zion from behind. But Zion's heightened senses allowed him to see the attack. The emperor front flipped to dodge the blade and kicked the knife out of Vitaliya's hand. The two of them locked in combat. Vitaliya and Zion started throwing bare-handed attacks at each other like barbarians. Vitaliya elbowed his face, Zion kicked her thigh, she scratched his eye, and he punched her jaw. Adelrik assisted his wife and threw his shield at Zion's head. The metal rang like a gong. Vitaliya capitalized and summoned a staff. She began striking Zion with it repeatedly, unleashing a well-trained combo across his appendages. Zion quickly retaliated and stepped on the end of the staff, shoving it into the dirt. Then, he kicked the weapon in half, at its base. Zion disarmed Vitaliya of the half she still held and started beating her with the remnants of the staff. He struck her nearly five times across her face, bruises quickly emerging. Zion twirled behind Vitaliya and choked her with the staff. Then, he drove his knee into her spine. The woman screamed. Zion harnessed magic and struck Vitaliya with a powerful bolt of lightning. The queen flew across the ground, her body contorting in unnatural directions.

Adelrik carried the fight. He summoned a rifle and fired an entire magazine at Zion. He then leaped into the air and swung a heavy fist downward, striking Zion in his cheek. The powerful hit echoed. Regaining his footing, Zion locked in combat with his rival. The emperor equipped two knives and Adelrik summoned weapons of similar caliber. The men attacked each other like beasts. Adelrik stabbed Zion in his forearm, Zion slashed Adelrik across his chest, Adelrik cut his cheek, and Zion stabbed him in the collar. Adelrik screamed in frustration. He summoned a shotgun and blasted Zion down into the dirt. Then, the king jumped into the air with a dive kick. Zion dodged. He rolled backwards and picked up his sword. He lunged forward, slashed Adelrik with an upward swing, and kicked him down. Zion dropped his sword and equipped more Ectognatha relics. The emperor threw the relics into the air and shut his eyes. They exploded with a powerful flash, blinding the royal couple as they attempted

to return to their feet.

Even a large portion of the armies watching nearby were blinded by the flash. A scattered wail emitted from the viewing crowd. Zion equipped another relic but ate this one. Suddenly, a new power emerged from within. Stone flesh began emerging upon Zion's body; dark, malformed rocks grew around his armor and provided him with a nearly invulnerable defense. Recovering from the blinding flash, Vitaliya and Adelrik quickly stood beside each other to prepare for this follow-up attack. The royal couple raised both their hands and faced open palms at Zion. In sync, they started firing a flurry of cosmic blasts from their hands, utilizing the celestial energy within the atmosphere. Adelrik's maroon energy and Vitaliya's teal energy collided at Zion's stone flesh and exploded powerfully. They continued firing until smoke consumed the entire space within the barrier. Soon, the king and queen finally stopped their attack. It was quiet. But as the smoke began to clear, they realized Zion's stone flesh remained upon his body. Their synchronized attack hardly worked.

Then Zion charged forward, heavy-footed like a giant. He tackled the royal couple, spearing Adelrik with his left arm and Vitaliya with his right. He shoved them both into the wall violently. Unable to breathe, the king and queen remained locked in his grip. Zion swung his fists at both of them, striking them with his rock-covered punches. More blood spilled. Bones were possibly broken now. Zion wrapped his hand around Adelrik's throat and slammed him to the ground. The king could nearly feel his spine shatter. Then, Zion grabbed Vitaliya from behind and suplexed her over his head. The queen's upper back struck the ground so hard, the smash echoed and a crack formed beneath her.

Once more, Zion's army cheered. The Seraphs watched in stunned silence. It seemed impossible for their rulers to recover from such a devastating blow. The intensity of this fight was becoming too much to handle. Although Zion had felt victorious, Vitaliya and Adelrik continued to rise. They slowly crawled to their feet, using the wall of the barrier to assist them. They were both panting heavily, blood and sweat dripping down their faces. The king and queen locked eyes from a distance. It was time to end this.

At sonic speed, Vitaliya and Adelrik pierced Zion with swords. Vitaliya struck him from the front and Adelrik from the back. The royal couple screamed violently. Vitaliya dragged her sword downward and

Adelrik, upward. Together, they shredded Zion's stone flesh, rocks scattering into the air. Zion started bleeding out. He stumbled backwards, towards the center of the battle zone. "We've had enough!" the royal couple shouted. Vitaliya dashed forward and stabbed Zion in his chest. Adelrik followed and smacked him into the air with a massive hammer. Vitaliya leaped into the air and speared Zion with a lance, throwing the weapon downward. It pierced through the emperor and stuck him into the ground like a carcass. Finally, Adelrik summoned a rocket launcher and fired. Zion was blown away from the explosion and struck the wall of the barrier, cracks forming once more. The king and queen stood side by side. They assumed an athletic stance and placed their individual hands together. Vitaliya clasped her wrists together horizontally, palms facing Zion. Adelrik pressed his wrists against hers vertically. Four hands united, forming the shape of a blooming flower. The royal couple started harnessing celestial energy from the atmosphere. Together, they charged a powerful cosmic blast that shot across the air and struck Zion. The raging energy glistened and emitted a piercing shriek that broke the sound barrier. Finally, the conjoined blast exploded. Zion crashed through the energy barrier and rolled across the dirt floor for several hundred feet. He twisted around and landed beside several of his soldiers.

The artificial forcefield was destroyed by the rulers of Jannah. Purple energy came raining down like shattered glass. Vitaliya and Adelrik gazed intensely at their opponent, utterly sick of his desire to wage war. With both warlords now broken and beaten, it was time to change the dynamic nature of this battle.

Vitaliya and Adelrik both raised their right hands into the air. Silence emerged. Winds blew across the shattered remains of Jannah's outer castle. Zion's soldiers of various species steadily helped the emperor back to his feet. His armor was broken and his clothes were scorched. He couldn't dream of continuing the fight so soon. Vitaliya and Adelrik held open palms high above their heads. Then, they simultaneously made closed fists. This signaled their Seraph army to charge forward. "Seraphs! Attack!" the royal couple commanded. Finally, both armies attacked each other, Seraphs greatly outnumbered. Syris' civil war resumed. Now even more intense than it had been before. This was the final stand.

Defending the Throne

Back inside the castle, Raakel's massive form dominated Jonah's. She continued crushing his throat with her foot, watching his skin change colors. "If you won't hand over the crystals, then I suppose you can just die." Raakel raised her scorpion tail, ready to slay the prince.

Suddenly, an arrow pierced her shoulder. The woman shrieked and removed herself from atop Jonah. When she turned to her left, she could see Carmine with a bow and arrow drawn in his hands. "You stay the hell away from my brother!" he shouted. Carmine fired several more times in rapid succession, hitting Raakel with another four arrows in various parts of her upper body. He quickly dashed over to the empress and struck her with the blade of a summoned lance. Raakel was knocked back hard. She fell to the gilded floor of the throne room violently.

Carmine helped Jonah up to his feet. "Are you alright?" he asked. Jonah attempted to catch his breath.

He nodded. "Thanks, Carmine. I'll be okay." The twin princes stood side by side, ready to fight for as long as needed to protect the Crystals of Nihaya. The determination on their faces was synonymous with that of their parents.

Raakel slowly rose to her feet. She just smiled. "Fine. I should consider myself lucky. I get to kill you both at once." Raakel equipped both of her tantos. Now, the fight to protect Jannah's treasure was going to begin.

The Empress of Kremlin charged forward, aiming for her recent attacker, Carmine. Jonah summoned a rifle and started firing at her. Bullets pierced her exposed flesh. Carmine then capitalized and engaged in combat with her using his lance. He managed to go toe to toe with an elite warrior like Raakel. They traded blows and guards with their drastically different weapons. Raakel stabbed Carmine in his bicep, Carmine slashed her across her side, she cut him in his chest, and he stabbed her in the foot. Then, Raakel pushed harder. She swung both her tanto blades downward with extreme force and cut the boy's weapon into pieces. Carmine was exposed. Raakel unleashed a flurry of graceful attacks, swiftly moving like a dancer. She spun upon the balls of her feet and struck Carmine with two swipes to the chest. Then she rotated back in the opposite direction and stabbed his side with both blades. Finally, she violently yanked out the tantos and smacked him with her massive tail. Carmine flew across the room and crashed into a steel armor display against the wall.

He was down, moaning in pain. Raakel continued her ravaging attack. She threw one of her tantos at Jonah's rifle. It jammed into the barrel of the gun and caused it to explode. Jonah stumbled backwards, taken by the hit. His ears throbbed, hearing nothing but the remnant piercing sounds of the explosion. Raakel charged forward and stabbed him in the stomach with her remaining tanto. She straightened her posture and struck him with her fists several times. She then swept his leg and caught him in midair by his chest plate. The powerful woman lifted him and slammed him to the floor. The force behind the grapple move nearly shook the entire room. Now Jonah was down.

Suddenly, Raakel was hit in her back. It was Carmine. He had thrown a kunai with a bomb attached to it. It exploded, knocking Raakel down to the ground, onto her chest. Working in tandem with his brother, Jonah quickly summoned a sword and leaped into the air. He landed on top of Raakel, driving the steel blade into her back. The empress screamed violently, blood emerging from her body and mouth. It was impossible to believe two children, two untrained boys could put her in such danger. Raakel nearly panicked. She quickly dug her claw into Jonah's ankle with her right hand. The prince screamed.

She pulled and tripped him to the floor, freeing herself from his clutches. Not wasting any time, Raakel quickly yanked the sword out of her back and threw it at Carmine's shin with precision. The prince fell forward from the impact, onto his face. Bleeding out now, Raakel could only manage the strength to rise onto one knee. She started coughing painfully.

The fight wasn't yet over. Princes Jonah and Carmine were not going to yield so easily. They screamed angrily. Jonah quickly ran over and kicked Raakel in her jaw. The woman avoided falling from her knees. Carmine punched her in the back of her head. Jonah elbowed her in the face and finally, Carmine kneed her in the bridge of her nose. The joint combo greatly stunned the empress. The princes both summoned wooden staves and powerfully smacked Raakel in her chest. The woman flew across the room and hit the wall on the other side. She was nearly beaten, but Jonah and Carmine continued their synchronized attack to ensure victory. They both stood in an athletic stance and raised two palms towards their opponent. Harnessing the celestial energy in the atmosphere, the brothers conjured blasts of cosmic force. They screamed in rage and fired the blasts, Jonah's energy being golden and Carmine's being platinum. The blasts struck Raakel on the other side of the room like lasers, ending with a cataclysmic explosion. The intensity of the attack destroyed all the sandbags barricading the throne room door. Sand had suddenly begun raining down from the air, along with the ash from the fires spreading in the throne room. The smoke grew thick.

The princes of Jannah were panting heavily. That was the majority of the power they could sum up in this fight. They had never experienced anything like this before.

But amidst the silence, there was a sudden outburst. Raakel started screaming angrily. The ground began shaking; the woman was harnessing a tremendous amount of energy from the atmosphere. A dark red aura emerged around her battered body. Her voice echoed throughout the castle. "Damn you! Damn you! I will end you! I've had enough of this!" she shouted. Raakel threw Ectognatha relics towards the ceiling. They exploded, releasing an intense blue smoke into the air. It was blinding and slightly toxic. The Chosen Ones started coughing violently. Raakel grabbed more relics and crushed them in her hands. These granted her the temporary ability of telekinesis. Raakel's veins pulsated from power. She raised one of her hands at each of the princes. Suddenly, they were lifted from the ground through a magical force. Jonah and Carmine struggled but found it impossible to break free from her seemingly nonexistent clutches.

Raakel wanted to hurt them now, badly. She was beyond frustrated with the fight they put up against her. The empress started throwing The Chosen Ones around the throne room like rag dolls. Jonah into the wall, Carmine into the ceiling, Jonah across the steps, and Carmine through the window. Raakel twirled them around in the air, moving her fingers as if she were controlling puppet strings. Then she swung her arms downward, powerfully slamming the princes into the floor. Their armor immediately shattered upon their bodies. Finally, Raakel threw Jonah and Carmine into the royal thrones. The princes each smashed through one of their parents' legendary seats of power, creating a loud crash that echoed across the room. The debris scattered about and tore their exposed skin.

Raakel was ready to finish them. She threw two more relics on the ground by their bodies. Suddenly, massive vines emerged through the floor and wrapped themselves around Jonah and Carmine, crushing the brothers' bodies together. The boys screamed in uncontrollable agony. Raakel did nothing but laugh maniacally. The vines grew tall, holding Jo-nah and Carmine over fifty feet in the air, still constricting them tighter by the second. Raakel brought the fingertips of her hands together and focused her energy, charging a cosmic blast of her own. The dark red celestial energy grew into a massive orb between her palms. Raakel raised her right arm and threw the orb at the princes in the air, striking them with a powerful explosion. A shockwave burst across the room. The glass windows of the castle shattered and flames engulfed the ceiling of the 1st floor. The Chosen Ones fell from the air and crashed into the ground, their clothes scorched. They were unconscious, defeated by the empress of Kremlin.

Despite the nearby chaos, Leola continued to concentrate. There was only so much time left. A bead of sweat dripped down her forehead and onto her upper lift. Utilizing two small gripping tools, she brought two wires together. A red light on the control panel of the transporter began flashing rhythmically, just like she had hoped. "Okay. The transporter is searching for a receiving signal now. Evelyn, type in that code I wrote by the text panel," Leola said.

Evelyn nodded. She observed the paper closely, slowly typing what was written on it into the computer. "It's done," she said.

Leola stood up and pressed a red

button on the side of the transporter. She moved over to the computer and typed in one final code. The transporter suddenly began emitting a soft vibrating hum, the sound emerging from the engine of the device. "Pull that lever on the right side," Leola said. Evelyn quickly ran over and pulled the lever. The humming stopped. In the silence, a green light appeared upon the transporter's core module. Then, slight sparks emerged from the nodes. To Evelyn, this hardly seemed like a successful process. She turned back to Leola, confused. "Don't worry. It worked. The transporter's charging now, sending its signal to the nodes on the brothers' developing planet," Leola said.

Evelyn smiled and sighed in relief. "How long until we can teleport?" Leola observed the display beside the text panel. "30 minutes. We should go prepare our families and the *Hakim Nisa'* for departure. Their safety should come before ours." Evelyn nodded in agreement. The girls took off towards the lobby, entirely unaware of what had transpired between the princes and the Empress of Kremlin.

The girls were running throughout the halls of the castle. Their scattered footsteps echoed in the emptiness of the once populated hub of the Syris Solar System. Finally, they made it to the throne room. The girls immediate-

ly stopped running, shocked. Standing before them was a victorious Raakel and a defeated Jonah and Carmine. Evelyn and Leola were panting in fear.

Raakel chuckled. "They're alive. Just unconscious. I would hate for an even worse fate to fall upon their lovely counterparts," she said malefically.

Leola clenched her fists. She slightly turned her head towards Evelyn, not removing her eyes from the deadly empress. "Go prepare everyone to flee in the teleporter. Take the back set of stairs down and have them wait in the church with the rest of the citizens. You know the way," she whispered.

Evelyn hesitated. "But, what're you trying to do here?" Leola struck Raakel with a fearsome staredown.

Anger emerged on the girl's face. "I'm going to kill this woman," she said. Evelyn still refused to run, but Leola insisted. "Go now, Evelyn!" Jonah's fiancée ran off upstairs, making her way to the resting quarters of the castle, where her and Leola's family stayed for safety, along with the *Hakim Nisa'*.

Raakel and Leola stared each other down in silence. The empress noticed her left hand was a metal prosthetic. "So the rumors were true. Prince Carmine *did* end up with an Automa.

And here she is, standing in the castle of what could have been paradise. I find it amusing that you're fighting alongside a species that's racist to your people. The Seraphs look down on your kind, girl," Raakel said.

Leola didn't bother responding. She cracked her neck and raised her fists. "Fight me."

It began. Exhausted, Raakel charged towards the girl. Leola raised her right fist and gave out a battle cry. She swung her fist downward and struck the ground, emitting the tremendous power of her legkiy into the atmosphere. This created a powerful shockwave that burst throughout the entire throne room, knocking Raakel far back against the wall. Leola adjusted her posture and stood in a fighting stance again. Behind her, the princes were beginning to rise again, regaining consciousness.

Relatively undamaged from the powerful attack, Raakel ran towards Leola again. Leola quickly charged more legkiy and fired atomic blasts towards the empress with her open palms. The glistening, blue blasts were homing towards the woman like missiles. They struck the ground and walls, exploding on impact. Raakel was becoming rather astonished at the Automa's incredible power. But she was done toying with these children. Raakel dodged the tracking blasts while sprinting forward. She dashed to the side of Leola and delivered a powerful kick into her side. Leola flew off and crashed into the wall, beside the shattered dining table from earlier. Raakel persisted in the attack. She pounced towards Leola and grabbed her by the throat. She shoved the girl into the wall, raising her with a violent choke. Digging her nails into her frail flesh, Raakel could see the Automa's blood spill.

"I should gut like the animal you are," Raakel threatened. The empress raised her scorpion tail and slowly began cutting Leola across her stomach, tearing her kevlar vest in the process. Leola grunted in pain. She quickly conjured a ball of pure light and struck Raakel in the face with it. This blinded the woman. Leola kicked Raakel in her jaw, setting herself free from the empress's clutches. Then, she harnessed more legkiy and created an orb of cosmic energy within her palms. Leola charged forward and shoved this overwhelming power into Raakel's chest, blasting her away with a cataclysmic explosion. Raakel collapsed onto the burned red carpet of the throne room.

As the empress began to stand back up, she was suddenly kicked in her chest by two feet, knocking her back to the down. She gripped her chest in pain and looked at her attackers. It was the princes, Jonah and Carmine. Although they were badly injured from the previous attack, they were still willing to defend their castle.

"You two are still fighting?!" Raakel shouted angrily. The brothers were panting in exhaustion. Leola quickly joined their side, thankful they were still okay.

The princes faced this opponent for what they hoped would be the last time. Carmine turned to his girlfriend. "Leola, try to hold Raakel down. Jonah and I can finish her off from there," he said. Leola nodded.

After a brief second to reprieve, the empress charged again. The kids followed her movement, springing into unified action. Jonah and Carmine separated, running towards Raakel from opposite sides. Leola utilized more of her remaining legkiy and repeated her attack from before, her palms facing upward this time. Once more, blue, atomic blasts began homing towards Raakel. They rained from the air like meteors. Raakel was hit dozens of times, the cosmic energy piercing her body. The brothers quickly capitalized. Without much of their wits about them, they simply resorted to hurting the woman by any means necessary. Letting her obtain the Crystals of Nihaya was their last resort. Carmine lunged towards Raakel, using the full force of his body weight to headbutt her gut. Jonah leaped into the air and punched her face with overwhelming force. The empress screamed in frustration. She swung her massive tail, knocking both princes to the ground.

Continuing the retaliation, Raakel threw a relic at Leola. It exploded in the girl's face, knocking her onto her back. Raakel sprinted towards Leola and raised her tail, attempting to stab her while she was down. But before this could end, Leola quickly retaliated. She sat up and struck Raakel with her remaining legkiy. Jutting out her right arm at the empress, Leola fired a piercing beam. It stuck out like a sword, extending itself from her palm. The light stabbed Raakel through her chest. The empress froze, blood emerging from her mouth. Raakel was completely inhibited by the burning energy piercing through her body.

"Boys! Now!" Leola shouted. Only beats away from synchrony, Jonah and Carmine dashed over and cut off Raakel's arms with swords. The slashes of the blades were the only sound in the throne room. It was followed by two soft thuds. Purple blood spilled onto the princes' faces. Almost by chance, the children pulled off an attack that finally defeated the Empress of Kremlin. Raakel collapsed onto the red carpet. She didn't make another sound.

Jonah and Carmine just dropped their swords to the floor and fell to their knees. They were panting heavily, almost in shock by the fact that they had just taken the life of one of the most powerful beings in Syris.

Tears emerged from Leola's blue and pink eyes. She stumbled over to the brothers, standing in between them. "You two did it," she mumbled.

Jonah shook his head. "We couldn't have done it without your help," he said. Leola helped the princes up to their feet. They started limping towards the stairs, arms around each other. It was a possible place for the boys to rest for now. It was unfortunate to think that the war was still not over. It was frightening to question the resolve of the rulers of Jannah, wondering if they would survive the conflict with Zion and his army. Regardless, Jonah and Carmine were proud to have risen to the task. Raakel was no ordinary woman. She was the other half of the war across the solar system. Now, she was no more. Or… so they thought.

Suddenly, a sharp pain emerged in the brothers' backs. They stopped moving forward, Leola taking notice. The girl slowly turned her head, a frightening look emerging in her eyes. It was Raakel. She had stabbed Jonah and Carmine with her claws. Claws that should have been upon the floor with the rest of her arms. Yet, Leola remembered one crucial detail. *The Ectognatha can reanimate…,* she thought to herself. Jonah and Carmine collapsed to the ground, now in far too much pain to continue fighting. Blood dripped from Raakel's new hands. Her freshly developed arms were the result of a natural ability her species possessed. The ability to regenerate limbs was a power Ectognatha were capable of utilizing unconsciously, from the moment they hatched from their cocoons. It was what made it nearly impossible to entirely defeat the species in this war. Raakel's new arms were made of nothing more than gruesome flesh, still not fully developed. The skin had yet to emerge.

Leola stumbled backwards, sweat dripping down her face. "Impossible. You… You're still alive. How could we forget?" she mumbled. Raakel laughed. At this point, she knew that she won.

The empress approached Leola and grabbed the girl by her throat again. Raakel lifted her in the air with one arm, easily. "Yes. How *could* you insolent children forget about my ability to regenerate? Perhaps the only way to get what I want is to end your miserable life. Maybe then those spoiled princes will give me what I want." Leola struggled but almost didn't want to fight anymore. As her vision started to fade, a rescuer returned.

Suddenly, Raakel was shot in the thigh. She screamed in pain and took sight of her assailant. It was Evelyn, standing at the top of the stairs. The young girl held a pistol in her frail hands, aiming quite poorly. "Let her go!" she shouted. Raakel threw Leola to the floor. Evelyn fired several more times but missed every shot.

Raakel just stood there, proudly invincible. She had nothing to fear from these two girls. Instead, she directed her attention to the princes on the floor. "*You* are a Seraph, Evelyn. Prince Jonah's fiancée. Maybe I should just threaten the lives of these two boys and you'll take me to the Crystals of Nihaya instead," Raakel said. She raised a claw towards Jonah on the floor.

Evelyn screamed violently. "Leave them alone!" She blindly charged forward and pushed Raakel away from her fiancé. Raakel scoffed. "You want to fight me, girl?"

Anger emerged on Evelyn's face, a rare expression for her. Leola stood up and joined her friend's side. "We might be able to hold her down if we work together. She regenerated her limbs, but she's badly hurt from the fight," she said. Evelyn nodded. With very little fighting experience, the counterparts to the princes charged forward to protect their lovers.

The three women engaged in a wreckless skirmish. Raakel was too damaged to utilize all her skills and the girls knew nothing more than their desire to put this woman down. The fight became barbaric. Raakel punched Evelyn with a jab and Leola with a cross. Evelyn swung with a kick to Raakel's calf and Leola, a punch to her eye. Raakel scratched Evelyn across her mouth and kneed Leola in the groin. They tied up, bodies closer. Raakel swung a body shot to each girl. Evelyn bit the empress on her neck. Leola spit in her face. Finally, the girls both punched Raakel in her face, hard. But it still wasn't enough. Raakel was ready to finish this. She grabbed Evelyn by her hips and slammed her to the ground. Quickly readjusting her posture, she faced Leola. "I'm sick and tired of this shit! Now, die!" Raakel lunged forward and thrusted her stinger, attempting to stab Leola. The girl did nothing more than raise her hands to defend herself, now entirely out of options. But suddenly, Evelyn emerged. She dove in front of Raakel's stinger, her body completely parallel to the ground. Leola could feel her mouth uncontrollably gape. Had Evelyn just laid her life on the line for her? For the princes? For the planet? For the universe?

Raakel's stinger stabbed through Evelyn's gut so deeply, Leola was still slightly hit in her chest on the other side. It was nowhere near as bad as Evelyn. Both girls dropped to the ground, bleeding out. Evelyn immediately grew cold and fell unconscious. Leola gripped the small wound on her chest, attempting to catch her breath.

"My. Perhaps there *are* some noble Seraphs after all. I don't think I've ever seen one of your kind so willingly lay their life on the line for another species. I would say one of the biggest accomplishments my husband and I have made with this war is our provocation of the Seraphs, coercing them to stand up for the universe. But notice, Vitaliya, and Adelrik stayed mostly hidden away in their castle until the very last moment. It's pathetic that it took the death of nearly half this solar system for them to finally make a real sacrifice. For them to finally question whether they too would die or not," Raakel said. She gazed at Evelyn's lifeless form. "Hm. She quite possibly didn't hear a word I said. Poor girls. Both of you are recklessly entangled in this conflict. But, I still have a dream to achieve. Speaking of coercion…"

Raakel held her stinger over Leola, ready to finish her off. It was at this perfect timing, the princes regained their consciousness again. From their position on the floor, lying upon their chests, they watched the lives of their lovers be threatened. Blurred visions barely revealed the reality of the situation they were in.

"The proposition is simple, Chosen Ones. Take me to the Crystals of Nihaya and I won't kill both of your girls," Raakel said. Jonah and Carmine slowly rose to their feet, shaking from agony. They clenched their teeth and fists in anger. They faced the empress of Kremlin. This was a failure. The brothers silently glanced at each other, but the consensus had become clear. "Fine. We'll take you to the crystals. Just please, don't hurt them," Carmine said. Raakel smiled softly.

Jonah looked at his twin. "Are we sure about this Carmine?" The prince nodded. There was no other choice. But this was something they had prepared for quite some time ago. A possibility in the endless scenarios within this Syris civil war. It was time for them to use their last resort. "Let's just hope this works," Jonah whispered. He knelt beside Leola. "Thank you so much for helping us fight and putting your life on the line. You saved our lives, Leola. Can you stand?" he asked.

Leola nodded her head and slowly came up to her feet. The wound she had was not life-threatening. "But… your fiancée…" she mumbled in pain. They were running out of time. As much as Jonah wanted to tend to Evelyn, he had no choice but to guide the wretched Empress of Kremlin towards Jannah's greatest treasure, locked in the depths of the castle. "Go to the nearby church. Two guards were ordered to remain stationed there. Have one of them come take Evelyn back there. The Wise Women can heal her," Jonah explained. Leola nodded and took off towards the south exit of the castle. It was time for the beginning of the end.

Theft of a Treasure

Moments later, the princes found themselves performing a march of shame. They pressed forward, standing side by side, amidst the halls of Jannah's once-great castle. Walking behind them was the Empress of Kremlin. Now victorious, she would finally get what she came here for. The Crystals of Nihaya for her and her husband, to grant them the ultimate power of creation. It would easily be enough for them to stand against the king and queen and singlehandedly commit mass genocide across the universe. The princes walked silently for so long. Their bodies ached and their souls felt crushed. They questioned if they should simply continue fighting Raakel. Lay their lives on the line. But no. The best outcome now was to simply give her the crystals and see what would happen. Jonah and Carmine patiently walked towards their own demise. It was mind-numbing, just waiting for the entire planet to fall in defeat.

"I don't even understand what either side is fighting for anymore," Carmine said, breaking the silence.

"Faith. Religion. Mom and dad told us Zion intends to spread the path of the All again," Jonah replied.

"Why? That's my question. Why? What does Zion get from re-exposing what made him a heretic to Syris in the first place?"

"You remember the stories from the Kadar. Mustafa was hated for speaking of Free Will, to release existence from Determinism."

"And even goddess received backlash for speaking of faith and trying to create a heaven for the Children."

"Zion believes he's the next god. He believes that what he imposes in this Eon will change the next," Jonah said.

"The All was just a myth. I don't understand why he believes in it so much," Carmine replied.

"Why does anyone believe in anything anymore? People lash the term 'god' towards Seraphs as if it's an insult."

"Yet all they want is to have the power of gods just like us."

"They want the power, but not the burden."

"At the exchange of higher thought and free will, mortality has ensued upon existence."

"Mortals are imperfect. Maybe that's why good and evil have come to be so present in our universe."

"Not long ago, there never used to be good or evil. It was simply 'live'. Community used to be all that mattered."

"And it still is," Raakel said. The princes looked back at her, surprised she interjected in their soft-spoken conversation. Raakel increased her pace, now walking in between the brothers. The empress attempted to level herself with these young men. "I won't apologize for what I've done up until now. Princes, you won't understand unless you become rulers, but war is what slates reality. Conflict. Like the friction between molecules, something new is bred in destruction. I gave you the choice to just yield, but you fought. And I respected that. But I have won and I hope you respect that. I'm sure you both want this war to end as soon as possible, regardless of who ends up victorious. If Queen Vitaliya and King Adelrik just abstained from abusing their power, from acting as if the Seraphs are better than everyone else, then no one would've had to die. But the Seraphs continue to cling to their birthright as if it's the only thing that makes their lives worth living. You are all mortals, just like the rest of us. Just mortals with the power of gods. My husband and I are making a statement to the rest of the universe. Gods no longer belong in this Eon. The All was the definition of equality. And we will use its principles to change all of existence. The power of gods will wipe the world clean of corruption and grant everyone an equal, fighting chance. Give me the treasure and I will ensure no one ever exploits creation again. Nature will take its course upon the universe. The only thing that'll be deemed worthy of power from there is... imagination." Jonah and Carmine just remained silent. Raakel's words were profound and in many ways, true.

The princes led the empress into the deepest chambers within the Jannah castle. There was a golden door before them. It was massive and had glistening blue lights made from magical flames. The princes each had a ring on their right, middle finger. They stood side by side and inserted the rings into two separate keyholes. Suddenly, the blue flames changed colors into a natural orange and the golden door opened. It nearly split apart at the seams, slightly scraping against the floor beneath it. Dust emerged from the ceiling; no one had entered these chambers in quite some time. They proceeded down a set of stairs and found themselves before another door, this one made of unique crystal-like material. It glistened with reflective colors that changed depending on one's position facing it. The Chosen Ones stood side by side again and placed their palms upon two separate panels. The panel scanned their hands with a holographic laser. This door opened similarly to the last. Continuing down the steps, the three of them approached the final door. There was a gilded basin located at the bottom of the massive stone door. The decorative design depicted some stories from the Kadar that Raakel was likely unaware of. Jonah and Carmine each created a dagger in their left hands.

"This final door can only be opened by those with Sultan blood," Jonah said. The brothers each made a small slit in their palms and watched their blood drip into the basin below. Suddenly, steam emerged and the blood immediately evaporated. Finally, the last door towards the legendary rarely witnessed chamber of Jannah's castle, opened.

The three of them started walking down stone steps into the chamber.

Carmine to the left, Jonah to the right, and Raakel in the center. Every step echoed in the silence. They could almost hear the war occurring upon the surface, no matter how deep they were underground. Raakel sighed miserably, a prelude to her initiation of conversation. "I would suggest that after I obtain the Crystals of Nihaya, you both escape this planet as soon as possible. Utilize that transporter. If not, join us. Join Zion and I. Be by our sides. We'll take care of you better than your parents ever could. There can be many rulers of Syris, to prove to the people that equality exists. Carmine. Jonah. We can give you both the power you deserve, the power that you never truly received here on Jannah," she said, her words becoming extremely persuasive.

The princes both shook their heads. "No, Raakel. Thank you for that offer, but if my brother and I were to receive any power, we'd want to earn it," Carmine said.

Raakel nodded slowly and smiled slightly. "How noble of you."

Finally, they made it to the room where the Crystals of Nihaya were kept. The room possessed a luminescent glow in the background, seemingly lit up by faint energy from within. Raakel gasped softly. Across the chrome floors, on the other side of the room, was a massive chair. The technological intricacies of its details proved that it was one of the most complex devices in the entire universe. Attached to this chair were strange tubes. They were transparent and emitted a soft smoke as if they were made with dry ice. Behind these tubes were large contraptions of the same transparent material. Attached to the ceiling was a large sack-like object. It looked alive, breathing at a steady pace, emitting the smoke. Inside this sack, were fragments of the Crystals of Nihaya. They glowed powerfully from within the eccentric object, revealing their powerful light blue glow with overwhelming force. Princes Jonah and Carmine walked forward, about halfway to the chair.

"What is this contraption?" Raakel asked. Carmine walked over to a control panel near the chair and started typing in commands.

Jonah turned around, ready to deliver a brief explanation. "This chair is how our parents had fragments of the crystals implanted into their hearts. As you may not know, the only Seraphs who can be given an incredible birthright are the rulers of Jannah. The queen and king were put through this ceremony back when my brother and I were newborns. This essentially magnified their power beyond comprehensible measure, making our mom and dad some of the most pow-

erful beings in all of existence. The fragments were supposedly left by goddess inside Jannah's core. They're limited since she sacrificed herself to nature millions of years ago. Only every few centuries do small fragments of the crystals manage to rise to the surface for harvesting. Members of the Sultan family or *Hakim Nisa'* are exclusively capable of activating this contraption."

Raakel gazed at the boy, astounded. "Then perhaps I'm fortunate for your presence."

The Empress of Kremlin sat in the chair. She clutched onto the armrests, smug. She could almost feel the infinite power of the crystals already emitting from within her. "Do it, boys. Let's end this war once and for all," the woman said. Jonah and Carmine looked at each other silently. They simply nodded their heads in agreement. They both began typing on the nearby control panel. The engines of the contraption revved up and began releasing a soft hum. The lights of the luminescent tubes started shining brighter. The smoke dispersed powerfully.

"Prepare yourself. This will hurt," Carmine said.

The tubes, already attached to the back of the chair, moved through several openings and pierced into Raakel's back. They had entered in specific areas, targeting veins in her body. Four tubes into her upper back, three into her middle, and two into her lower back. The woman grunted in pain. A strange blue liquid started entering Raakel's body. The woman's veins started pulsating violently. The large sack detached itself from the ceiling and moved downward, now hanging above the chair. A fragment of the crystal moved down to a claw-like appendage of the sack. The large claw, like the end of a spider leg, moved over the chair and pointed directly at Raakel's chest. The device waited momentarily. Jonah and Carmine persisted in the process. They walked over to the fragment of the crystal held in the large claw and raised their palms towards it. The brothers began chanting in Jannah's Egyptian-Arabic, their voices echoing powerfully in the room. They imbued life into the Crystals of Nihaya through a brief sacrament. The fragment suddenly burst with power, emitting a shockwave across the chamber. The ground and ceiling began shaking violently as smoke scattered throughout the room, almost to a blinding degree. Raging whirlwinds encircled the fragment of live crystal. Finally, the princes watched as the claw pierced into Raakel's chest. It hit with so much precision, that hardly any blood was spilled.

Raakel started shaking violently. Her eyes glowed with the light blue color, synonymous with the liquid now coursing through her veins. She screamed out loud, feeling the incredible power of creation enter her body. What she and her husband had waited so long for was finally happening. The woman was becoming a god. The ground continued shaking. Raakel let out a maniacal laugh; power surging through her soul. Jonah and Carmine watched a non-Seraph be granted what no other being was allowed to have. But they did nothing more than smile.

Something was wrong. Suddenly, Raakel's screams of power shifted into screams of agony. The energy of the crystals no longer felt as if they were empowering her. Raakel could feel her organs seize up, her heartbeat increase rapidly, and her skin burn. The crystals were destroying her. "What's happening? What's... happening?" Raakel screamed. Jonah and Carmine slowly approached the suffering woman. It became clear that they had control of this outcome. The princes each raised a hand towards the woman. They watched as the claw exited her chest, almost out of rejection. Blood spilled this time.

"Now," Jonah said. The brothers used telekinesis to quickly remove the crystal fragment from her chest. It was excruciatingly painful. Jonah and Carmine used their telekinesis to break the fragment into two pieces. Now, it was time for the next phase of their plan.

Raakel sat in the chair, feeling as if her body was wasting away. Her veins continued throbbing with a toxic orange color. Her eyes became bloodshot. Jonah and Carmine each held a small piece of the original fragment. They each summoned a dagger and cut a vertical slit in their wrists. Jonah cut his right one and Carmine, his left. They stuck the fragments into a vein in their wrists. As the power flowed from within, the wound immediately closed, sealing the Crystals of Nihaya into their bodies. This would only be temporary, considering they had not gotten them implanted into their hearts. But it should grant them enough power, for a long enough time, to help stop Zion and end this war.

Raakel arose from the chair and stumbled towards the brothers, clutching her chest in pain. Blood dripped from the woman's mouth. "What… What have you done to me?"

Jonah and Carmine stood there, victorious. "This was somewhat of a last resort, Empress Raakel. We were originally planning on stopping you in the throne room. Nonetheless, my brother and I had prepared for this outcome. It's quite simple. The Crystals of Nihaya cannot properly assimilate into the body of a mortal who doesn't have complete faith in our religion, in our goddess. We weren't sure if you believed in her or not, but your religious alignment has now become clear. The crystals have corrupted your body and soul, almost with the intent of eradicating you from the universe. Unfortunately, you've come this far only to be led to your demise. The power of creation will forever and always belong to the Seraphs. We are the *only* gods left in this Eon," Carmine said powerfully.

The empress groaned in agony. She fell to her knees and her face buried in the ground. This was what defeat felt like. Suddenly, she screamed in anger. "No! No! It will *not* end this way! If I die, then I'm taking you both with me!" Raakel crawled back up to her feet and charged whatever power she could absorb from the atmosphere. A faint, red aura emerged around her form. The empress sprinted forward, attempting a final stand against the princes of Jannah.

Allies and Antagonists

Amidst the scorching remains of the battlefield, much had transpired during the princes' conflict with the empress. The Seraph army of Jannah had become overwhelmed. Although the remaining ground forces in the royal district had fallen, it was evident that they had not lost their lives without a fight. Many bodies of both sides laid across the battlefield. The grass had turned to flames and ashes rained from the sky. Cannon fodder from the surrounding airships had destroyed the outer gates of the castle, prepping Zion's army for forced entry. With no forces left to support them in combat, Vitaliya and Adelrik were left to fend for themselves against an army of millions. They had stood their ground for long, but found themselves at a sudden disadvantage. Something went wrong. The power of the Crystals of Nihaya had been disrupted. It was as if a presence in the chamber had momentarily weakened the treasure's ability to empower the Seraphs on Jannah. But this lasted long enough for the king and queen to be beaten. Now, they were on their knees, surrounded by several hundred beings who were once under their rule, but had now gravely betrayed them.

Guns were pointed at the back of Vitaliya and Adelrik's heads. Bladed weapons surrounded them. An entire airborne fleet was ready to attack if necessary. This was an impossible situation to escape from, even if their powers had returned to them by now. Vitaliya and Adelrik slowly reached towards each other, dragging their hands across the dirt. They locked fingers, believing this would be the end. Then, the army parted in front of them, allowing their warlord to step forward. It was Zion, who had withdrawn from battle after suffering damage from the two-on-one skirmish with the king and queen. He looked relatively healed, possibly having undergone treatment from his field medics. The man stood before his old friends. He smiled, victorious.

The army standing before these three living gods watched everything with tremendous attention. They almost felt lucky to be able to witness these legendary beings' stories unfold. No one truly knew of what happened between the three of them in the past, but no matter the myths, what happened long ago created the split of good and evil amidst Syris.

"Aren't you proud Zion? You have won… haven't you?" Vitaliya asked.

Zion didn't look away. His eyebrows furrowed, angry. "Vitaliya. Adelrik. You should've known that Syris would soon undergo a new era. The dawn of a reborn age is upon us, and it's one where you two will not exist. This was never just about the truth of the All. We fought in wars together. Created peace throughout the solar system together. When the time for reward came, you and the Seraphs betrayed me. When I called for your help, you chose to leave me in exile. When I lost everything in my life, at *your* hands, you left me with no purpose towards amending our bond. All of my sacrifices for this universe, yet I returned from war with nothing but a life of Entombment. All my species ever did was suffer so we could help the souls of your pathetic Seraphs rest. All we did was endure years of trauma, witnessing the deaths of others so they could enter a heaven we weren't even welcomed to. I was nothing more than a lowly Vectin to you. And because I didn't have faith in your goddess, I wasn't even a friend to you anymore," Zion said, profound. The king and queen were put to shame by his words. Corrupted by power, they were the true evil in the eyes of their people.

"We couldn't join in your ways, Zion. You were damned for treason because your faith wasn't in alignment with ours," Vitaliya said.

"Listen to how ridiculous you sound, Vitaliya. Your species has so little tolerance that you couldn't simply accept the religion of my choice. Instead, you forced me to wage war," Zion replied.

"This has only led to bloodshed because of you. You couldn't tolerate the ways of the solar system," Adelrik said.

"And for that, I have to yield to a life of nothingness? We have to allow you Seraphs to experience immortality through Transference and Reincarnation? The life of another being is simply yours to claim when you should be dead. It's no wonder all species in Syris have become disgusted with you and your so-called goddess. The only people allowed to be reborn were your kind. Do you understand how much that hurts everyone else? To watch the Paragons enter heaven even when they lived a life full of corruption? Then we're all left to suffer in our own hells!"

"You're the darkness," Vitaliya said reluctantly.

"You're the light," Zion replied, almost sarcastically.

"You're evil."

"You're good."

"You're the villain."

"No… I'm the hero."

Zion stood before the Queen of Jannah. There was a subtle look of despair in his eyes. But as the hero, he was forced to make drastic sacrifices for the greater good of mortals. The emperor raised his signature sword. He turned his wrists at a 45-degree angle towards the left, ready to execute the woman with a right swing. "I'm sorry," Zion said. Vitaliya closed her eyes. She prayed silently in her mind but stopped. Her faith was fading. Zion swung. The only sound heard was the blade dashing across the air. Something had appeared between the emperor's sword and the Queen of Jannah's bare flesh.

The entire spectating army gasped. There was an invisible force there. Zion's eyes opened wide. Suddenly, the savior revealed itself. The lone man removed his powerful cloak. It was Raimundo, the King of Echelon. He was a Nanomorph, one of the most powerful beings in Syris, forever allied with the Seraphs. It seemed as if he suddenly appeared out of thin air. Nanomorphs had the passive ability to levitate several inches above the ground as an alternative to walking. They were also capable of dispersing their anatomic form to briefly change into digitized, permeable energy that allowed them to travel through the 4th dimension. This natural power was commonly used by the people as a form of teleportation, escape, and was even repurposed for combat. This was how Raimundo had teleported to the planet, just in time to rescue Queen Vitaliya and King Adelrik. Nanomorphs were capable of harnessing energy from the atmosphere and living objects using a power known as *Negativ Energie*. Nanomorphs were capable of sucking the life from their opponents with their bare hands or absorbing energy from plants, animals, and parcels of it from the raw atmosphere if the individual had the training to do so. The amount of *Negativ Energie* granted their powers in tiers, depending on how much the Nanomorph had absorbed. Joule was the unit of measurement for how much a Nanomorph had harnessed. The more Joules of energy a Nanomorph possessed, the more astronomical abilities they could use, ranging from enhanced strength, summoning energy-based projectiles, cosmic force, telekinesis, invisibility, and even distortion of time.

Raimundo was blocking the blade of Zion's sword with his armored forearm. The emperor struggled to push through his guard but eventually gave up. "We've had enough of this, Zion. You will *not* rule Syris and you will *not* hurt the King and Queen of Jannah anymore," Raimundo said. The massive man stood at a staggering height of 7 '10. The way he spoke was full of confidence.

"King of Echelon. You must be as foolish as the Seraphs you're trying to defend if you think you could single-handedly face the army of millions standing before you," Zion said.

Raimundo just revealed an expression of anger. "I'm not alone."

Suddenly, hundreds more Nanomorphs started appearing on the battlefield. They were on the outskirts of the castle, atop scorched hills in the distance, and amidst the dirt plains surrounding Zion's army. They all revealed themselves, originally arriving with invisibility. Then, ships began emerging from the gray clouds in the sky. From the airborne vehicles, more ground forces entered the battle, sliding down ropes and gliding down using flying devices. It was the Personas of Pandora, beings capable of shapeshifting into animalistic creatures. This unique power made them a deadly force not to be reckoned with. The army stood strong alongside the forces of the Nanomorphs. These two species opposed Zion's cause with passion. They knew the Seraphs weren't entirely pure but knew that the species stood for more good than the emperors of Kremlin. One final Nanomorph removed her invisibility cloak and revealed herself. It was Raimundo's wife, Lindie. She helped Vitaliya and Adelrik to their feet. The glorious woman spoke to her allies amid the silent standoff.

"Are you two alright?" she asked.

"Yes, thank you. But... how did you all escape Echelon?" Adelrik asked.

"Do you think Zion's army would've been enough to stop all the Nanomorph warriors on the planet? We were well-prepared for his attack. Word of it had been wiretapped by our astronautics stationed in the atmosphere. Echelon remains under the territory of the good."

"And the Personas?" Vitaliya asked.

"We assisted our neighboring planet as soon as we were victorious. This was a week ago. I'm sorry, but it simply took time to have our affairs in order before coming to help you."

"We are forever in your debt. Both you and your husband Raimundo. You saved our lives," Adelrik said.

"We owe the Seraphs more than you know. My husband and I wish for the proliferation of evolution to continue throughout the universe. That cannot happen with the Chosen Ones and *Hakim Nisa'* dead. Now please, king and queen, go protect your sons. We'll force Zion to flee Jannah once and for all!" Lindie shouted proudly.

Vitaliya and Adelrik bowed to the woman. They quickly sprinted off south from the battle, heading towards the shattered remains of their castle. Lindie stood beside Raimundo. The Nanomorph couple was ready to lead the charge towards Jannah's rescue.

Raimundo and Lindie, King and Queen of Echelon

Zion clenched his fists tightly. He was so close, yet so far from his goal. His only hope now would be that Raakel could obtain the Crystals of Nihaya and use the power to destroy what mortals remained between them and victory. Until then, Zion was prepared to make this young couple pay for their treason. An ally to the Seraphs was immediately an enemy to his cause. The emperor raised his sword one final time. "Destroy them!" he shouted powerfully. The armies charged forward, their footsteps near-ly creating an earthquake throughout the battlefield. Raimundo and Lindie stood silently, watching their own stronger forces speed past them. Dirt plumed into the air and hundreds of weapons clashed. Yet it was becoming clear that the side of good was quickly overwhelming Zion's army. Nano-morphs and Personas were the most ferocious and powerfully gifted be-ings in the entire universe. Next to the Seraphs, they were the very reason Zion failed to win this war sooner. Now, these two species were going to be the very reason he would finally lose this war.

Reunion of Royal Blood

Queen Vitaliya and King Adelrik finally reached the throne room. They could hear their footsteps echo in the emptiness of their once glorious castle. Burn marks, cracks, and even blood mottled the floors and walls. This was frightening. Raakel had clearly made her presence known.

"Oh no. Adelrik… you don't think Raakel… got to the boys do you?" Vitaliya asked. Adelrik observed the two shattered thrones. Whatever battle occurred here was possibly more violent than what happened outside.

"I'm not sure. I can't sense the boys' energy anywhere. But… there's something else here. Something powerful. Do you feel it?" Adelrik asked. Vitaliya concentrated silently. The power deep within the castle was shockingly intense. The royal couple feared that the worst had come. Empress Raakel must have gotten her hands on the Crystals of Nihaya. But, this power had the intensity of two astronomically god-like beings. It couldn't have just been one person.

Suddenly, a loud crash was heard. It was deeper in the castle. Then, another crash, closer this time. The royal couple prepared themselves for yet another fight. They just raised their fists, clearly too exhausted to conjure more celestial force. One final crash occurred. Someone had been thrown through the castle walls. Their body rolled across the red carpet of the throne room, covered in rubble. Vitaliya and Adelrik watched the debris plume into the air. As it cleared like smoke, they saw the impossible. Raakel was beside their feet, beaten and nearly dead. As the mother and father looked up at the hole in the wall northeast of them, they found the source of the overwhelming power. Their sons, Jonah and Carmine, had emerged from the shattered wall.

The Chosen Ones were glistening with the intense power of the Crystals of Nihaya. Their eyes had changed colors. Jonah's were gold and Carmine's were platinum. Auras of those exact colors raged around their mortal forms. Their veins were pulsating and their hair stood up. The king and queen wanted to run over to hug their boys but were too shocked by what had transpired.

"Boys? You're… okay?" Adelrik asked. Jonah and Carmine granted their parents a subtle smile.

"We're fine, father. Don't worry. We simply used the crystals to defend our home," Carmine said. Vitaliya smiled at her two boys. It was almost astounding to see them possess such great power. Destined for more than just expanding the universe, the princes of Jannah were fully capable of defending their creations.

Amidst the distant reunion of the Sultan family, the Empress of Kremlin was beginning to rise to her feet. She moved onto all fours, gasping for air. Blood dripped from her mouth and her vision blurred. The woman glared to her left and right. Now she was not only surrounded by two but *four* of the most powerful Seraphs in the entire solar system. Raakel clutched her chest in pain and grunted angrily. The woman jumped to her feet and charged towards the princes with nothing more than a fist. The boys weren't even fazed. But before Raakel could reach them, Vitaliya dashed over, protecting her sons. She caught the enemy's fist, immediately crushing it.

"Don't you lay another finger on my boys!" Vitaliya shouted. The queen struck Raakel with a powerful punch to the chest. It sent the woman flying across the throne room. She struck the floor beside Adelrik's feet. The king bent over and grabbed Raakel by her throat. Incredibly strong, he raised the woman with one hand. Adelrik avoided killing her. All he did was analyze her body. Her veins were black and they throbbed softly. It became obvious that Raakel

had attempted to use the Crystals of Nihaya and the consequences had ensued. Adelrik almost felt sorry for the woman. Zion's unquenchable thirst for power must have been what truly corrupted her, not just the stringently critical force of the crystals. Raakel began gasping for air. Not because of Adelrik's hand around her throat, but because the crystals were beginning to fully taint her soul.

She coughed and hacked. "You fool. The Crystals of Nihaya are eradicating you. Right down to your very molecules," Adelrik said.

Raakel glared down at the king, clutching her very last breath. "It was worth it. The very sensation of the power... was incredible," she mumbled. Adelrik unwillingly shed tears for the woman; it didn't have to end this way. "I'm sorry..." Raakel said.

Adelrik looked at his spectating family. Then, he looked back at the enemy. "I'm sorry too." Raakel's eyes shut. She had gone beyond the planes of reality into a realm of her faith and imagination.

The Sultan family took a moment of silence to pray for Raakel to reach some form of paradise. Adelrik set her body on the floor gracefully.

"Raakel must not have known. Any mortal who doesn't fully believe in goddess cannot absorb a fragment of the Crystals of Nihaya. Instead, the crystals absorb them," Vitaliya said.

"The clash of her faith and that of the crystals led to her demise. The conflict tainted her spirit and ultimately killed her," Adelrik said.

"Mom. Dad. If we knew that Zion and Raakel were likely after the crystals, but that it would kill them, why didn't we let them take it? They would've died anyway," Jonah said.

"Because there *is* one way around the process. We were concerned that Zion may have known. The only way a non-believer could absorb a crystal into their hearts is for the crystal to be partially corrupted," Vitaliya explained.

"How is that possible? I thought the Crystals of Nihaya was the purest object in the entire universe," Carmine said.

"It is. Before it touches a mortal. Unfortunately, the crystals become corrupt over time in the heart of the Seraph that has it. Through the naturally imperfect acts of the mortals, it loses its divine energy. And if a non-believer were to use a corrupted crystal instead of a pure one, it would be able to assimilate with them and grant them our powers," Vitaliya said.

"We wanted to wait until right before you boys became kings. But your mother and I have done some terrible things as the rulers of Jannah. Political ties, economic gain, and societal disparities became things that we had to do to ensure the safety of our people. It hasn't been easy pleasing as many species in the universe as possible. In trying to do so, your mother and I have damaged our moral standing. And that, in turn, has left the fragments in our hearts corrupted," Adelrik explained.

Jonah and Carmine started crying slightly. In the face of war, none of their parents' actions in the past mattered. "It's okay. No matter what you may have done, we will always be your sons. And we will always love you," Jonah said happily. The Sultan family gathered together and hugged each other at once. They cried into each other's shoulders. All they wanted was for all the war in the universe to end. For everyone to live in peace and harmony, regardless of what faith they had in what god. Perhaps they had the same dream as the man standing in the throne room in the distance. His presence was previously unknown.

It was Zion. The family relinquished their hug and directed their attention to the emperor east of them. He was war-torn but visibly alive. Someway, somehow, Zion had made it through the entire conflict occurring on the outskirts of the castle. Perhaps he had just left his army out there to die alone at the hands of the powerful

Nanomporphs and Personas.

Adelrik locked eyes with the man from the other end of the throne room. "Zion…" he said. The king and emperor both gazed at Raakel's corpse on the carpet. "I didn't kill her. She tried to attack my sons, even with her very last breath. Your wife attempted to use the Crystals of Nihaya and they tainted her body from within. She didn't have faith in our goddess and she suffered for it. I'll avoid blaming you for this outcome, Zion. I'm disgusted that you could allow something like this to happen to your wife," Adelrik said. He stepped back from Raakel's body, allowing his rival to step forward. A look of despair emerged on Zion's face. His pride, his joy, his love, had become more than just a mere casualty in this fight for equality. Zion approached Raakel's corpse and kneeled beside it. The Sultan family that he was once so close to, just watched his actions in silence. Zion placed his massive hand over Raakel's chest. Her heart didn't make a sound. Then, he took a deep breath. To the emperor, there was no real god for him to pray to anymore. Not even the deity of Kremlin. No. To him, the only god that deserved his praise was himself. Zion was one step away from becoming a true god. All consequences that preceded his ascension were a collective price well worth paying.

Suddenly, Zion pierced his hand through Raakel's chest and inhaled. The ground began shaking. A purple aura surged around his and Raakel's body. Then, blood started emerging upon his arm. Raakel's blood. It looked as if Zion had sucked his wife's remaining life essence into his own. All of Raakel's power, her spirit, was now within him. The Sultan family watched as the woman's body seemingly deflated. All blood, then organs, then bones, were evaporating. Zion finally stopped. There was nothing left of his once beloved wife except a hollowed-out sack of her skin. Adelrik, Vitaliya, and their sons watched in stunned silence. What had just happened? Zion stood up from his wife's corpse. All his wounds had miraculously healed. He looked as if he had gained muscle mass in the past few seconds. The expression in his eyes was almost synonymous with Enlightenment. No matter the setback, the man was close to his goal. The arrival of the Nanomorphs and Personas was the best thing that could've happened to him.

Zion walked closer to the royal family. Vitaliya and Adelrik stood in front of the princes, protecting them with their lives. "Allow me to explain. In the months I've spent preparing for this war, you should know I haven't done any physical training whatsoever. No. I understand that all true power for us mortals lies within our minds and spirits. All I've done is engage in Entombment while my army conquered this god-forsaken solar system. And while in Entombment, I've witnessed the battles and deaths of millions. Millions for each of the species on every planet in Syris. I've watched the greatest warriors every planet has had to offer. I've studied how they fought until the very moment they died. *That is* how I obtained fragments of the abilities from the species that have joined my side and agreed to wage war on you. But there was a missing link I had stumbled upon. The Nanomorphs and Personas were seemingly too complex to understand by simply watching them die in combat. To seal the Entombment and fully attain their abilities, I would've had to kill one with my bare hands. And suddenly your pathetic goddess bestows the Nanomorphs and Pandoras to me as an act of providence. With everyone locked in the desire to kill each other, I had the opportunity to slay one of each of the species. And after performing my prayer, let's simply say I am one step away from achieving my goal. Now that I have used the Nanomorph's *Negativ Energie* to absorb my powerful wife's essence, you won't be able to stop me. All that's left for me to take

is the power of gods. The power of you Seraphs," Zion explained. He glared at the royal family as the king and queen shielded their sons.

"You won't be able to steal our power of creation, Zion! The crystals will corrupt you just like they did to Raakel!" Carmine shouted.

Zion simply laughed maniacally. "I see that the rumors were true! Even goddess is an undeniably racist being! If you do not follow her religion, you suffer. *Dire* consequences apparently. I love my wife for her righteous sacrifice for my cause, but I now know another way to seal my fate. I overheard everything you said. A way for a non-believer to attain the power of the Seraphs. If I can't implant a pure fragment of the Crystal of Nihaya into my heart, then I suppose a partially corrupted one will suffice," he said. Vitaliya and Adelrik felt chills run down their spines. They unknowingly provided their enemy with a solution. Zion closed his eyes momentarily. "Don't fret you two. I somewhat knew that stealing a partially corrupted crystal fragment was possible. You simply confirmed my assumptions. I know the Seraphs aren't as pure as they claim to be. And with the sins you carry in your hearts, the crystals are surely tainted as well. Tainted enough to properly assimilate with my being. All that's left is for me to decide which ruler of Jannah is more corrupted." Zion pondered silently for a moment. "Vitaliya. I'm going to forcefully take that crystal from your heart and put it into my own," he said, tremendously terrifying the royal family.

"Like hell, you will!" Adelrik shouted. He pounced forward with a sword summoned in his hands. Zion simply pointed one finger forward. Suddenly, a piercing beam of concentrated energy fired. It struck Adelrik through his chest and immediately knocked him to the floor, unconscious. This was the *Negativ Energie* of the great Nanomorphs, now dangerously in his possession.

Jonah and Carmine immediately engaged in the conflict. The crystals in their wrists glowed powerfully. Their hair stood up and the auras around Jonah and Carmine spawned in gold and platinum, respectively. The princes dashed forward. "You bastard!" Carmine shouted.

Zion was nowhere near intimidated by their onslaught. The emperor raised his hands at the brothers and snapped his fingers. Suddenly, a cataclysmic explosion was emitted upon their bodies. Jonah and Carmine were blown away in opposite directions. They each hit the walls of the throne room. Thankfully, the power of the crystals had dramatically increased

their endurance. The princes rose from the floor and charged again. But Zion didn't move a muscle this time. Suddenly, orbs of concentrated energy surrounded the brothers separately. They each became trapped in a cage of Zion's infinite power. The *Negativ Energie* that created the barriers drained them of their celestial force. The princes' power was beginning to wane. Zion started clenching his fists. He forced the barriers to shrink, crushing Jonah and Carmine within them.

Their mother, Vitaliya, screamed. "Please! Stop! Don't hurt my boys anymore, Zion! Please. Spare them. Find it in your heart to spare them. I know you care about them…" Zion walked closer to the Queen of Jannah, the Queen of Syris.

"You know exactly what it'll take to get me to stop," he said, pointing at her chest.

Vitaliya looked up at the man standing before her. There wasn't much of a choice now.

Suddenly, there was banging on the throne room door. Shouting and the march of an entire army could be heard. It had become obvious that even the Nanomorphs and Personas were overwhelmed by Zion's relentless soldiers. "It sounds like my forces refuse to wait much longer. You either provide me with the fragment in your heart or die at the hands of my army. I'll just have them rip the fragment from your cold, lifeless body."

Vitaliya started nodding frantically. It almost looked as if she was losing her sanity. Tears rolled down her beautiful face. "Fine Zion. You'll get what you want. Release my sons first," she said. Zion blinked. The orbs trapping the princes dispersed, setting them free. Jonah and Carmine dropped to the floor, out of breath. Vitaliya looked at her sons and gave them each a unique smile. It spoke volumes about her love for each child. "Boys. Defend your father while he's unconscious. Do *not* let Zion's wretched beasts rummage through our castle like it's their new stomping grounds. Kill them *all* if you have to!" Vitaliya shouted. The brothers nodded at their mother. They stood up and summoned armor in their signature colors. Vitaliya locked eyes with Zion, her opponent. "I love you, Jonah and Carmine. Now, I will handle this."

Vitaliya clenched her fists and clutched her elbows to her sides. Her forearms stuck out forward. Suddenly, Vitaliya started screaming powerfully. The entire throne was shaking. Her magnificent teal energy lit up the entire castle. A massive aura of the same color surged around the queen like a living flame. Vitaliya had centered herself, calling upon all the power she could harness. The development of such a divine force from within a single Seraph created shockwaves. Although strong in stature, Zion could feel his feet be pushed back as the heels of his greaves scraped across the carpet. A bead of sweat dripped down his forehead. It became profoundly clear that Vitaliya truly was the most powerful being in the entire universe. But Zion was aware of that since the day they met. Then with one final chant of anger, the queen's appearance changed. She reached new heights of power, one that very few Seraphs had ever been capable of attaining. Vitaliya's hair had changed colors, from its luxurious platinum to a furious teal. Her god-like aura continued surging, strong enough to lift rubble from the ground and into the air around her. Vitaliya glared at emperor Zion. Once her companion, he had now become the greatest threat to everything she had ever known. "Let's finish this Zion. Here and now," the queen said. Zion stood there, unfazed.

Corrupted Heroes

It instantly began. Zion raised one palm and fired a beam of celestial energy at Vitaliya. But Vitaliya vanished, moving faster than the speed of sound. The blast struck the shattered thrones instead. Through his peripheral vision, Zion could see Vitaliya standing right next to him. It was as if she teleported. Zion could feel his spine rattle in shock and fear; this was the truly frightening limit of the Queen of Jannah. Vitaliya shifted her stance forward ever so slightly and struck Zion in his jaw with a powerful punch. The strike created a shockwave and sent Zion flying across the room. His body contorted painfully as he rolled upon the golden floors. The man managed to catch himself, now on his knees. He slowly rose back to his feet, blood dripping from his mouth.

"You merely caught me off-guard, Vitaliya. Don't think that one accurate hit is enough to overestimate your place in this battle," Zion said.

Vitaliya ignored every word he said. This was a fight to her. Nothing more needed to be said.

The queen charged towards the emperor again. She moved so fast that a trail of shattered floor was left behind her, her speed capable of ripping the foundation apart. Vitaliya attempted to strike Zion's heart with a summoned sword. Zion didn't move an inch. He opened his mouth and roared, harnessing the great power of the Personas. It had enough sonic force to halt Vitaliya's movement. The

woman could feel herself being pushed back. Zion roared harder. The wood in the throne room peeled, the floor shattered into pieces, and the walls caved outward. Vitaliya was blown back by Zion's roar. She flew into the wall on the other end of the room, crashing so hard an imprint of her body was left behind. The queen then fell onto her chest. Rubble came down like rain. As she lifted her face from the floor, she could see the entire throne room had been completely destroyed.

Zion smiled, taking notice of the woman's shock. "Now, imagine if I had actually lifted a finger, Vitaliya," he said.

The queen wasn't going to be waived by the flashiness of his stolen powers. Vitaliya stood up. She charged her power and watched the teal aura surround her form again. Both opponents stared each other down. The last minute had been nothing more than showcasing each other's abilities. The Queen of Jannah and the emperor of Kremlin finally clashed once more.

Jonah and Carmine had quickly made their way to the roof of the castle. To think they were here with their father only hours ago before this final stand began, was astonishing. They had watched as Jannah's remaining forces took flight towards the distant mountains and presumably had lost by now. The entire structure of the universe had crumbled in a matter of months.

"There must be thousands of them down there," Jonah said. He and his brother looked down at Zion's army attempting to breach the front of the castle.

"No matter. Mom permitted us to kill them *all*," Carmine said as he summoned a bow and a quiver of arrows.

Jonah summoned a rifle with a scope. "We have to wipe out these bastards, get everyone safely to the teleporter, then help mom stop Zion." Carmine nodded in agreement.

The princes each summoned helmets upon themselves to finish the set of armor they wore. Jonah and Carmine whistled loudly, getting the attention of Zion's ground forces. It was shocking to see an army of such diverse species. Perhaps Zion was capable of the same type of unity that Jannah had boasted about for centuries. Only he used this union of the species for evil instead of good.

Once the men and women looked up, the princes began their attack. Jonah was firing with his rifle, instantly killing the enemies with shots to the head. Carmine followed in sync, shooting arrows into vital areas. Since attaining the direct divine force of the Crystals of Nihaya, the brothers had developed an infinitely powerful attunement of their senses. Their accuracy was almost perfect. As Zion's army began engaging in combat, some dodged, others fled, and others fought back. They raised their hundreds of firearms and shot back at the twins, towards the top of the castle. Jonah and Carmine quickly ducked and covered themselves behind the protective ledge walls.

"Our only option now is to get down there," Carmine said.

The brothers began an alternative form of attack. Carmine stepped into Jonah's clutched palms and his brother threw him high into the air. Carmine summoned a hand cannon that fired explosives and shot down at the enemies. They were dropping in masses. Then Jonah quickly leaped over the ledge and landed into the crowd, driving his fist into the ground. The powerful shockwave sent the soldiers flying in multiple directions. Zion's forces that attempted to raid the castle were now being pushed back. They were entirely unprepared for the overwhelming power of Jannah's princes. Jonah summoned explosives and threw them into the air towards his brother. As Carmine finally came hurtling towards the ground, he summoned a sword and cut the explosive in half.

The chain reaction from the gunpowder and the blade sparked the bomb. A bright flash of light burst in the sky, blinding all the ground soldiers. Carmine landed beside Jonah. Both princes had swords equipped in their hands. They quickly engaged with the blinded soldiers, killing them in groups. Amidst the conflict, they could see a few more of Zion's ships enter the atmosphere. This was going to be much more difficult than they had predicted.

Multiple explosions emerged within the castle. Lights of two distinct colors glowed from within. A flash of teal, then purple, then teal, and purple again. Suddenly, a hole was blown into the roof of the castle. Vitaliya jumped through the hole and landed in a backflip upon the roof. The woman was holding her right side with her left hand, applying pressure to a bleeding wound. Although she was still powered up in her teal-haired form, there were scratches and bruises all over her body. Vitaliya was panting heavily, out of stamina and nearly out of options.

Zion finally leaped through the hole, following her to the top of the castle. He was less damaged. "Just give up Vitaliya. You're outmatched. Your body is exhausted from battling for hours. But after absorbing my wife, I have fully healed and am much stronger than I was only minutes ago," the emperor said.

Vitaliya straightened her posture and wiped the blood from her mouth. "Never. I will fight you until my dying breath. To protect more than just my family, but my faith. You will *not* create a new era, Zion! This universe is *not* yours to control!" she yelled.

Zion just sighed. "And who told you that? goddess?"

Vitaliya ignored him again. She summoned a staff, then attempted to attack him. But Zion caught it with his bare hand and snapped the weapon in half by closing his grip. He quickly struck Vitaliya with two punches to the gut and one uppercut. The queen stumbled backwards. She created a handgun and fired an entire magazine. The bullets couldn't pierce through Zion's powerful aura. Vitaliya attacked with a sword. Zion dodged every single hit and grabbed Vitaliya's wrist, using his nails to dig into her skin. With a twist of his hand, Zion broke Vitaliya's left wrist. She screamed. Her power was waning. Vitaliya summoned additional armor and ran towards Zion with her fists raised. She attempted to beat him purely with combat technique. Zion blocked her first three punches and parried the fourth. He punched her in the nose. Vitaliya threw a shin kick to his neck, but it did no damage. Zion caught Vitaliya by her ankle, kneed her in the groin, and elbowed her in her jaw. Vitaliya fell to the ground momentarily. She quickly rose back to her feet and jumped backwards to gain distance. The woman raised both her hands and started firing blasts of celestial force towards Zion. The explosions echoed powerfully and smoke began to cover the air. Vitaliya screamed in rage as she began exhausting what was left of her power. Finally, she jumped into the air and fired a beam of energy downward at Zion. The entire roof of the castle shook violently.

As the smoke cleared, she could see Zion was down on one knee. Although that may have hurt him, it was too late. Vitaliya had nothing left to give. Her transformation dissipated and her hair returned to its normal platinum color. The queen was panting hysterically, completely out of energy. Zion got back to his feet, relatively unscathed. It was almost impossible. All the power that he had amassed was shielding him from taking any real or life-threatening damage. Now strengthened by the abilities of almost every species in Syris, his defensive power likely paled in comparison to what he could now do offensively. Zion sighed. He raised one finger, pointing it towards the sky. Suddenly, a giant explosion emitted

from underneath Vitaliya, launching her into the air. Zion raised both hands and screamed violently. Lightning from the clouds struck Vitaliya from multiple directions. The Queen of Jannah came plummeting from the sky, smoke trailing behind her lifeless form. Zion estimated the trajectory of her landing and stood where she would fall. He bolted into the air like a rocket and struck Vitaliya in her back with his knee. She screamed, feeling as if her spine had been broken. Zion then grabbed the woman by her leg and dragged her towards the ground. He slammed her into the roof of the castle at such extreme force, her body left behind a trail of cracks.

Emperor Zion stared down at the woman. She was sprawled out across the roof, lifeless. Tears emerged in Zion's eyes. "Vitaliya. I never thought I'd see the day where I would cause you, such a beloved woman, so much pain. But maybe this is the only way to get you to understand. The only way to get the *universe* to understand. Power is no different than energy. Power, much like energy, is neither created nor destroyed. It's simply transferred from one being to another. And that being is me," he said. Zion hunched over and lifted Vitaliya by her throat. The woman was fading, almost unconscious. "Hm. The irony. Holding you like this reminds me of how I saw your husband clutched my wife during her last moments. Pitiful. You and Adelrik have been stripped of your power. Your time is over. My time is now. *Our* time is now. For all power to be distributed amongst the people, as equally as possible," Zion said.

Zion began reaching for the crystal in Vitaliya's heart with his left hand. But before he could take it, Vitaliya sprung to life. Her eyes opened wide, bloodshot from the pain. "I can't let you win!" she shouted. Vitaliya quickly created a dagger and stabbed herself in the heart, aiming right at the crystal fragment inside her. Blood spilled onto Zion's face. He dropped the queen, shocked by her actions. Vitaliya was on the floor, gasping for air as a pool of her blood emerged underneath her. She looked up at Zion, feeling a bittersweet taste of simultaneous victory and defeat. "You won't be able to take… the crystal fragment… if I die with it," she mumbled in agony. Zion did nothing more than gaze at the woman as her breath started to grow weak.

The emperor could hear the nearby battle between the Chosen Ones and his limitless forces. Tremendously attuned with his senses after achieving god-like power, Zion could sense the princes' movements without even observing the battle. Their energy levels were significantly higher than that of his soldiers. Possibly one-hundred times that of any mortal currently opposing them. But Zion could also sense that with every ounce of power the brothers used to kill their foes, their energy would begin to wane. They couldn't keep up this fight forever.

Zion decided to sit down beside Vitaliya. He hunched forward and leaned back, safely guiding himself down with his right hand. The man sighed. Not out of misery, but out of an unfathomable acceptance of a burden. He was the light that was going to cleanse the universe. All sacrifices had to be worth the outcome. "Your sons are fighting quite well down there. *They* are the true heroes. Risking life and limb to protect their home, their planet. All without knowing that their parents were the ones who caused this war. But their fight cannot go on forever. Even you Seraphs, possessing a mortal form, have a limit," Zion said. The man didn't even look down at Vitaliya. The woman still clutched her chest. There wasn't much time left for her. "How could you engage in such despicable actions just to spite me, Vitaliya? We used to be in love. I wholeheartedly stand by the fact that we were made for one another. But you had to obey what your goddess dictates for Seraphs. The *Hakim Nisa'* said, 'You could never be with a man who is not a Paragon.' I was a god, Vitaliya. I *am* a god. And that *still* wasn't enough for your putrid species to accept. You were forced to consummate with another man just because he was the same race as you. Well, now I have all the power in the universe, my queen. And although I want to wipe the universe clean of its filth with a blank slate of equality, I'm more interested in seeing you regret your decision. Seeing you regret leaving my side. Seeing you regret ever having faith in your goddess." It grew silent once more. Zion could sense Vitaliya's heartbeat begin to slow drastically. Her eyes were starting to roll to the back of her head.

The man stood up now. He grabbed Vitaliya by her shoulders and sat her up onto her knees. The woman's upper body ragdolled; she was nearly a corpse now. Zion bent forward and grabbed Vitaliya's head. He gripped her by shoving his palm into her forehead and clutching her hair with his fingers. Zion ruthlessly tilted Vitaliya's head backwards, forcing her to gaze up at the dying sky of her once-glorious Jannah. He placed his left hand over Vitaliya's heart, where all the bleeding was occurring. Zion took a deep breath. He exhaled. Suddenly, the man's eyes glowed with a powerful, white color. The roof of the castle started shaking. Vitaliya's body broke out in a seizure, shaking violently from the intense force of Zion's energy. A whirring sound of celestial matter emitted from the two of them. And with one final burst, Zion delivered a large portion of his life force into Vitaliya.

Will all the murders he had committed. With all the destruction he had caused. With all the genocide on his hands, Zion had amassed enough power to do the impossible. Vitaliya's upper body fell back to the ground. Zion's eyes returned to their dark color. And amidst the silence, Vitaliya gasped for air.

By the god-like power of her worst enemy, the Queen of Syris had been resurrected from the dead. Vitaliya quickly sat up. She was panting heavily. She touched her chest and found the wound was no longer there. Her heartbeat was present again, as strong as it was before. But she felt something worse. The Crystal of Nihaya. Its power… was back.

As soon as she realized this, Vitaliya quickly sprung into action again. She created a sword this time and attempted to execute herself again with another strike straight to the heart. Zion quickly dashed forward and caught her wrist. He snatched the sword from her hand and threw it off the roof. The emperor stared directly into the queen's eyes.

"Don't you dare attempt suicide again. It's pointless," he said. Vitaliya couldn't help but agree with the man. She was entirely out of options now. Zion had become significantly more powerful than her. Or maybe, with the intelligence he had, he was always more powerful than she was. The Queen of Jannah just stepped back from Zion with her head down, defeated. She started crying. Zion moved closer to her and wiped the tears from her face. He lifted Vitaliya's head by gently gripping her chin with his two fingers. The emperor locked eyes with the woman he once loved more than anything in the world.

"Do you remember when we were younger, how we first met?" Zion asked.

"It was at one of the most prestigious institutions on Jannah. The one my parents forced me to go to so that I wouldn't be looked down upon by the other members of the royal estate," Vitaliya replied.

Zion laughed. "Yeah well, while *you* were upset about being forced to go to the elite school, I had to work my ass off just to go there. My father despised Seraphs, thought every single one of you was pompous and spoon-fed. And although I ignorantly agreed with his prejudice, I still wanted to go to that school on Jannah because I wanted to make something of myself. I didn't want to just be another Vectin who slaved away for the rest of his life."

"How did you ever manage to get yourself into that school? It was mainly for royalty."

"I was royalty under my father. But that wasn't enough. I wasn't a Seraph. So I spent a large part of my childhood working hard and making a difference for my people so that I could send myself there. Despite all the money my dad stole, he wasn't going to give me a single gold septim for me to go there. I ran away from home with nothing and spent everything I had on the institution."

"That's probably why you spoke up so much in class. You wanted to make it worth your while," Vitaliya said.

"Speaking up to maximize my education wasn't the only benefit. I also met you," Zion said.

"I remember that day. I came up to you and asked if you could help me prepare for the tests cause I had no idea what I was doing. goddess, I used to hate you so much back then."

Zion laughed again. "Why?"

Vitaliya looked into the man's eyes. "Because you were better than me at everything."

Zion was taken aback, but he kept it together. "Lies. There was so much I admired about you too, Vitaliya. The way you'd command a room and had hundreds of people who trusted you as a leader. But even though you hated me, that didn't stop you from falling in love with me."

"How could I not? You were good at everything. School, sports, volunteering, social gatherings. You were the biggest role model there. You proved to the entire institution that it didn't matter what race you were. Everyone was capable of great things. And when I fell for you, your father didn't approve of our relationship. And neither did my parents nor the *Hakim Nisa'*."

"I remember. It was hard for us. We used to have to sneak and take a ship across planets just to see each other. We used to meet on Mirage, where they didn't care about the fact that we were an interracial couple," Zion said.

"Then we got caught by your father's guards patrolling the planet. And to punish you for disobeying his orders, your father forced you to fight him for the throne."

"That was something I never dreamed of doing. I hated the traditions of my people. But when I was faced against him in front of thousands of people at the arena, all the resentment I had towards my dad boiled up."

"And you killed him," Vitaliya said. "I was there, watching in the audience. You didn't want to, but it was either his life or yours. And you had a difficult choice to make. You broke down and cried. You held your father in your arms after killing him."

"Then you jumped down from the seats. Ran across the field and hugged me. No one had ever shown me so much love before, Vitaliya. That was why I wish we could've stayed together forever."

"But when my time to become queen was approaching… when my parents got sick, they begged me to do what was best for my people. To find a Seraph man and be with him. I told them that the decision was mine to make and I wanted to change the tradition of Jannah by making you my king. But the *Hakim Nisa'* forced their hands and I was locked in my castle until I yielded to their will. They controlled my life and my love. I came to believe that maybe it was best for my people that I didn't go against that grain. That I married a man and found a king that they could trust. I'm sorry I disappeared, Zion. I'm sorry I didn't fight harder for us. I'm sorry I took your heart for granted."

Zion cried. "All is forgiven, my love. I'm sorry things didn't turn out differently for us. But I promise you, I will make the universe whole again.

There won't have to be any more discrimination or pain. When I equalize everything, there will finally be a universe where our love could have thrived. That, Vitaliya, is my final ode to you."

Vitaliya cried with the emperor. "Thank you, Zion."

Zion pointed forward, towards the front of the castle gates. Vitaliya turned around to see what he was requesting she look at. The emperor and queen looked down to the ground level of the castle. "Look down, Vitaliya. Look at your two beautiful sons fighting for what remains of Jannah. It will unfortunately be the last thing you see. So rejoice in the children you raised. They're one of the last things you've done right," Zion said.

Tears poured from Vitaliya's eyes. She clenched her teeth in overwhelming sorrow. "I'm sorry," she said under her breath. Suddenly, everything felt cold. Zion's left arm had pierced through her heart, past his elbow. It was now clutching the tainted fragment of the Crystal of Nihaya. Vitaliya couldn't see anything anymore. She couldn't hear anything anymore. All she could feel was her heartbeat one last time. Zion yanked his arm back out of the queen, finally in possession of what he fought so hard for. "I'm sorry," he said under his breath.

The emperor released Vitaliya, allowing the queen's recently resurrected corpse to fall towards the battle below.

Although amid combat, the brothers could sense an alarming drop of energy in their vicinity. Locked in battle with an army of foes, Carmine looked back. The sight was the most frightening thing he had seen this entire war. The beautiful, platinum hair denoted that the worst had come. "Jonah!!" Carmine shouted over the sounds of clashing weapons. Jonah had just slain two more enemies with a lance. He turned around to face his brother. "It's mom!" Carmine yelled.

Jonah faced forward once more and looked up, attempting to see what his twin had seen. He could see his mother's corpse descending from the roof of the high castle. Jonah quickly dashed forward and leaped into the air, catching his mother. He barrel-rolled onto the ground, cradling her body as daintily as possible. Carmine screamed violently. His energy surged around him as he emitted a powerful shockwave that sent all surrounding enemies flying. This move bought them enough time. Carmine quickly ran over to help tend to his mother. He knelt beside Jonah. Jonah already had tears in his eyes. The princes had immediately become overwhelmed by what had transpired. The blood, the gaping hole in her chest, her soulless eyes. They wanted to vomit from the emotional turmoil. Jonah could only sum up a few words. "Her heart… it's gone."

Atop the roof of the most powerful structure in the universe, a more powerful being was born. Zion gazed at the 2nd Sun setting behind the gray clouds covering Jannah. He observed the glowing fragment of the Crystal of Nihaya in his hand. Its power was quickly fading, so he had to act immediately. Zion raised his right hand and shoved the crystal into his heart, planting it within the center. The pain was excruciating and the blood poured. But the results, exhilarating.

With a powerful burst of astronomical force, light emitted directly from Zion. A pillar of purple and black energy shot from his body and into the sky, parting the clouds above him. It shook the entire royal estate. Soldiers, as well as the princes, screamed in shock. Jonah and Carmine looked up at the roof of the castle. This was the beginning of the end. Zion roared powerfully, his voice echoing like the chant of a god. Lightning was drawn from the sky, striking around his position. Emperor Zion's hair changed into a pure white, exemplifying his infinite wisdom. Then, the man began sprouting a pair of wings. They grew from the shoulder blades in his back, beginning with a scale-like flesh and soon growing black feathers thereafter. Once the transformation was complete, Zion began to rise into the sky. His arms were horizontally outstretched as if he was being crucified. The man laughed. His goal had finally been achieved.

Zion, Emperor of Kremlin, Newborn god of Eon V

The Newborn God

About one-hundred feet into the air, Zion stopped rising. Amassing such an extraordinary amount of power from the beings of Syris had given him the ability to fly flawlessly. It was unreal. His massive wings flapped slowly, keeping him afloat. Finally, a halo emerged over Zion's head. It was composed of piercing black energy that glowed brightly. A trail of purple lighting flowed across the halo, like electricity on water. The Vectin now had the appearance of an angel, a perfect being. Zion looked down at the Chosen Ones and his army behind them. Then, he turned his attention to the burning mountains in the far distance. Zion put his two hands together and created a javelin, coated with his pure purple celestial energy. It was frightening for Jonah and Carmine to see. He had now attained the almighty ability to create from the mind, just like the Seraphs. Possibly better than their species. Zion raised the javelin behind his head and hurled it towards the distant mountains. A sharp, high-pitched wail trailed behind the weapon traveling at an indescribable speed. The javelin struck one of the mountains and exploded, destroying the entire natural structure. The army and princes screamed. Jonah and Carmine covered their mother's body from the oncoming rubble and dust created by the massive explosion. When they opened their eyes, the mountainous landscape had been completely demolished. One single attack and Zion

was capable of destroying dozens of miles on the planet.

Zion had yet to say a single word. Perhaps the intelligence he had amassed rendered him incapable of explaining his logic to mere mortals. The emperor turned back around, still flying. Now he was facing the 2nd Sun of Jannah in the infinite skies of space. Zion raised one hand and clenched his fist. The gray clouds started dispersing, revealing the purple glow of the setting sun. It was as if Zion was stripping Jannah of its life force and making it vulnerable. He gazed directly at the 2nd Sun, unfazed by its radiance, for his own radiance far exceeded the miracle of the greatest planet in the universe.

The emperor couldn't think of anything but the past at the moment. He reminisced on his adolescence, remembering what it was like to dream about a future of equality. Now he could feel the entire vision be realized by his bare hands. It was time to begin the end of the current universe and the dawn of a new one. Zion roared, releasing a powerful chant as he began his next attack. The man clasped his hands together, interlocking his fingers. Suddenly, in the skies of space, the 2nd Sun began shaking. At a deeper glance, asteroids could be seen striking the 2nd Sun. Zion had become powerful enough to pull interstellar structures together through the force of gravity. These masses of iron and other elements were pelting the Sun with incredible force. After every impact, they stuck to the star, slowly covering its bright light with their rocky exterior. Within seconds, all of Jannah's 2nd Sun had been completely covered in asteroids, to the point where it looked like nothing more than a large rock.

Zion finally unclasped his hands. He began his next attack. All the mortals could do behind him was watch in awe and fear. The emperor raised his right hand and pointed his four fingers towards the suffocated Sun. A beam of purple energy fired directly from his hand and into the massive star. It had managed to cross several million miles into space in a matter of seconds. Suddenly, the cracks within the asteroids covering the Sun had begun to glow with his purple energy, almost as if they were supercharged and ready to explode like a ticking time bomb. Zion released his grip on the Sun momentarily. With this final move, he was planning to end it. Zion crossed his wrists and grunted. Then, he raised both his arms into the air, screaming violently. The emperor's eyes rolled to the back of his head. The 2nd Sun of Jannah was shaking so much, it could be heard down upon the surface of the planet. Finally, it

exploded. It was so loud that all mortal ears shrieked with a deafening sound. The shockwave of the destroyed Sun released solar winds upon the surface of Jannah, setting more fire across the entire planet. It knocked the army and princes to the ground. The airships of Zion's forces in the sky came plummeting to the terrain in a nosedive, the solar winds disrupting electromagnetic signals and cutting off all power. Explosions occurred all across the royal estate, and a massive purple fire covered the sky. Chaos ensued, meteors hurtling towards Jannah like rain from the Underworld. It was immediately followed by ash that glistened from interstellar elements. The ash glowed with a beautiful, luminescent purple.

The newborn god, Zion, looked down upon the princes. It was obvious that his next goal was to tie up the final loose ends. A menacing look appeared on the man's face.

The brothers' jaws dropped in overwhelming fear. This seemed hopeless. Zion raised his right hand with an open palm and fired a blast towards them. "Look out!" Carmine shouted. He dodged along with his brother who cradled their mother's body. They narrowly avoided the oncoming blast that exploded, killing many of Zion's own soldiers. It had become clear that this man had finally lost the little shred of regard he once had for mortal life. With Raakel and Vitaliya gone, the only thing that mattered to him was achieving his goals. Jonah and Carmine barely collected themselves into a crouched position. Zion had fired again. Another piercing wail trailed behind his blast, followed by an explosion. Panels of the pavement struck the back of the princes.

"Get into the castle!" Jonah shouted desperately. His brother helped him carry Vitaliya's body as they quickly burst through the front doors.

The emperor watched silently. It was blissful to be so far above Jannah's royal castle, to be a god amongst gods. Dealing with the rest of the immediate Sultan family could wait. For now, he had to prevent any escape from the royal estate. Zion simply snapped his fingers. Suddenly, several of the oncoming meteors had fallen under the control of his gravitational force. They stopped mid-descent and floated close behind him. There were about fifteen meteors. Zion started clenching his fists tightly as he turned his head to observe the catastrophic weapons he had behind him. As he clenched his fists, he began reshaping the meteors. They transformed into perfect spheres, Zion abusing the powers of a god to do as he pleased with the natural structures of space. The emperor quickly waved both of his hands horizontally, dictating the motion of the meteors. They scattered, each landing into the ground around the castle to form a perfect perimeter. Zion stretched his arms forward and clenched his fists again. The ground of Jannah bent at his will, filling in the gaps of the barrier formed from the meteors. Finally, as he wished, he artificially created a barrier around Jannah's castle. It curved to form a dome. Zion knew it would take extraordinary power to get in or out of the royal estate now. Without the 2nd Sun, darkness ensued. All that remained were the glistening purple fragments of ash falling from the sky, dimly lighting the planet. The moon was still coming over the horizon to witness the most destructive battle in the universe.

From the windows inside the castle, Jonah and Carmine could see the rock barrier Zion had formed around the perimeter. Trying to stay calm, they both carried their mother forward, down the once glorious red carpet of the throne room. They were approached by eleven of the twelve *Hakim Nisa'*. A frightened look appeared across all of their frail faces when they saw Vitaliya in her children's arms. "The queen... no," one of them mumbled miserably. Everyone in the throne room began to cry. This was quite possibly the grimmest moment in Seraph history.

"Her heart's gone. Zion took it with his bare hand, along with the Crystal of Nihaya fragment," Jonah said. Carmine watched as his tears fell onto his mother's beautiful face. Her skin was already turning pale. "He's won. Zion's achieved his goal. And he will kill everyone remaining in this castle until there isn't a single Seraph left in this universe," Carmine said. The *Hakim Nisa'* all looked at each other; there was only one option left. One of them approached the princes.

"Boys. Take your mother up to your father in their room. He's still unconscious, but her spirit will want to be beside her husband. Kanya is upstairs monitoring him," one of the Wise Women said.

"But Zion's going to come in here any second. What will we do to stop him?" Jonah asked.

One of the women touched the boy on his shoulder. "It's okay. Take your mother upstairs and we will repel Zion for the time being. Kanya will explain everything else. You didn't realize this yet, but your Automa friend managed to get the teleporter activated. It's your only hope of escape. So you must use it," she said.

"Repel *Zion*? How? He's become the most powerful being in the universe! And the *Hakim Nisa'* are not meant to wage in the wars between us mortals," Carmine said.

"This is about more than just political conflict, Carmine. This is about defending the entire universe as a whole. Now go!"

In the end, the Chosen Ones respected the *Hakim Nisa'* and trusted their wisdom. They pushed onward and took their mother's body upstairs to let her rest. They debated whether fleeing was their only option or not. There had to have been a way to save everyone.

The *Hakim Nisa'* all stood in a straight line, shoulder to shoulder, ready to defend what remained of Jannah's great castle. They all raised their hands and used telekinesis to grab furniture, cobblestone, and leftover sandbags to barricade the doors to the throne room. They created a supernatural forcefield to increase the defense. With their heightened senses, they could feel Zion nearing their location. The power he possessed was strange. Not only was it immense, but it was tamed. His newfound energy had a presence not like that of a weapon, but like that of a gift. It was refined, intelligent, and all-around superior to anything the women had ever encountered.

"He's close!" One of the *Hakim Nisa'* shouted. They all knew they were not born to fight. But they knew there was a chance their powers could be capable of subduing Zion.

The newborn god approached the door of the throne room. He simply closed his eyes and walked forward. The Wise Women had prepared for a full onslaught from the man, but as a god, he had now exceeded the need to constantly engage in violence. The unthinkable had happened. Zion phased through the door and barricade objects, turning his cells into some type of transparent, permeable form. The emperor now stood before the Wise Women, his physical form returning to him. They were all in shock and awe at his abilities.

"How is that possible?" one of them shouted.

Zion smiled. He took a deep breath. "Allow me to explain, dear *Hakim Nisa'*. You see, attaining the fragment of the Crystal of Nihaya was more pertinent than meets the eye. It wasn't just for blind power. After spending the past several years learning the techniques of the species of Syris, I still didn't have the raw strength needed to fully harness it all. No. This mortal body was limited. With the crystal fragment embedded in my chest, the powers of Syris are not simply added together. The Crystal of Nihaya unified them, significantly magnifying all the strengths of our glorious brethren into me. The problem was that you Seraphs neglected intelligence. You spent so much time focused on the physical prowess of your species and the spiritual connection to your goddess, that you underestimated the value of pure knowledge. My new era will have no such thing. And that means… you must die."

His words were enough. The *Hakim Nisa'* knew that this was the final stand. It was now kill or be killed. In perfect sync, the women released a mass of their energy. Its color was faint, almost completely transparent. The force surrounded Zion, attempting to trap him in a cocoon-like structure. Zion roared powerfully, dispersing all the energy around him. It wasn't anywhere near enough to stop him. Four of the Wise Women charged and fired a blast at him. Zion blocked with both his hands and quickly fired it back. All four of them were knocked to the floor. The remaining *Hakim Nisa'* faced him directly. They used more of their cosmic energy to launch wisps of purely concentrated power at Zion. Their attack pierced the man's body multiple times but they saw that Zion almost couldn't bleed. It was as if his skin was impenetrable now. The women attempted to strike him with more power, but Zion quickly froze time in the vicinity in front of him. They couldn't move, completely paralyzed in place. Zion raised his two index fingers and fired small beams of energy at the *Hakim Nisa'* at a rapid pace. Two, four, eight, sixteen, blasts had pierced through the women's bodies. They all dropped to the floor, suffering from tremendous pain. For the first time in what felt like forever, the Wise Women had watched their blood spill.

Two of them arose to continue the grueling battle. They swung their arms upward, lifting Zion into the air with forceful telekinesis. Another *Hakim Nisa'* joined in the attack, noticing what her sisters were doing. She yanked the massive chandelier from the ceiling with telekinesis and threw it at Zion. The newborn god was smashed into the ground with the object. Cracks emerged across the throne room floor. But it still wasn't enough. Zion emitted an inordinate amount of power, his giant aura exploding the chandelier on top of him. The *Hakim Nisa'* were all blown away towards the walls. The newborn god was growing angry.

Another two *Hakim Nisa'* persisted in the attack to buy the children some time. They leaped into the air and each did a frontflip. In their landing, they each swung a foot down to kick Zion in his head with their heels. He hunched over from the impact of the hit. Three more *Hakim Nisa'* joined in the attack and surrounded Zion. With a wave of their fists, they manipulated the golden floors of the room and used them to bind the emperor. The floors wrapped around Zion, all the way up to his neck, encasing him with the supernatural force of the Wise Women. They attempted the finishing blow. One of their sisters jumped high into the air, harnessing a mass of energy into her two palms. As she descended, she prepared to fire it directly at Zion in hopes of stopping him. But the man had become more powerful than they could've ever imagined. Zion suddenly opened his mouth. A surge of energy was forming in between his jaws. The man roared and fired a cosmic blast at the Wise Woman attempting to strike him with the final blow. She fell out of the air and plummeted to the floor, her body scorched by purple flames.

Zion amassed more of the surrounding energy and emitted a powerful shockwave across the room. He set himself free and knocked the *Hakim Nisa'* down once more. It was time to end this. Using telekinesis, he pulled two of the women towards him and quickly struck them both with powerful elbows to the face. Zion raised both his hands and swung them downward. Suddenly, a bolt of purple lightning came through the castle roof and struck the center of the floor, hitting three of the Wise Women. Smoke emerged. Finally, Zion waved his right hand horizontally, from left to right. A powerful explosion trailed behind his motion, suddenly sparking from the ground. It violently hit the remaining *Hakim Nisa'*. Purple flames started consuming the throne room now. Zion was victorious once more as the most powerful beings in the universe lay before him, defeated. Now the newborn god had proved that he was second to none in this realm.

"Feeble women. You may have all the power in the universe, but your mortal bodies can't help your spiritual prowess reach its full potential. The power to create. The power to proliferate evolution across the galaxies should be *mine* to control. Only then, will the universe witness the rise of a greater species," Zion said. A maleficent look emerged in his eyes; his limitless intelligence had given him a genius idea.

Suddenly the *Hakim Nisa'* arose to attack him once more. All eleven of them moved in sync and faced their palms towards the newborn god. Zion was lifted into the air once more, ensnared by a force seemingly more powerful than telekinesis. "Sisters! Now! If we cannot defeat him by brute force, then we must use what our goddess granted us. Zion can't harm us in this realm if he is unmade!" a Wise Woman shouted. They all concentrated their power and began manipulating the atoms within Zion. The emperor screamed in agony, but he felt no real pain. All he could sense was the anatomy of his energy beginning to shrink. When he looked at his body, he could see his left arm start to change state. It was reduced from a solid to a liquid, to a gas, to nothing. Zion watched as his left arm faded. There was no dust, no residue. It was simply going from existing to disappearing completely. It became evident to him that the *Hakim Nisa'* were fully intent on unmaking him. Taking all of the cells in his body and eliminating all traces of them from the universe. He had heard about the Wise Women using such an extreme technique on one of the most dangerous Seraph criminals Syris had ever known. But to see it happen to himself, before his very eyes. It was… inspiring.

It had partially worked. A purple and black aura appeared around Zion. The wings on his back flapped vigorously and his halo glowed brighter. Zion screamed. In one burst of energy, he managed to set himself free from the *Hakim Nisa's* final attack. He was constantly capable of using his raw force to counter any tactic the

Hakim Nisa' tried to eliminate him.

Zion began plummeting from the air but caught himself mid-fall using his wings. The newborn god landed safely upon his feet. He stepped back from the opposing Wise Women. Zion looked at his left arm and saw that nothing was there anymore. There was no blood, no flesh, no bone. It was just the absence of his left arm, denoted by what remained of his shoulder.

"It's over Zion. If you don't stop this war, my sisters and I will not hesitate to erase the rest of you from existence," one of the Wise Women said.

The emperor was panting heavily. It seemed impossible to combat against a force so capable of manipulating the laws of nature and physics. But he had become smarter than this. He had become more powerful than them. The newborn god had briefly turned around to look out a window of Jannah's castle. The catastrophe was beyond what he could have ever imagined growing up. The man was now a god. What would possibly stop him from fully realizing his goal of rewriting the entire universe? He had gotten so close. This was his destiny. Put the universe's greatest species through genocide, cleanse the worlds of imbalance, and kill anyone who gets in his way.

Zion laughed. After a brief mo-ment of intense concentration, his arm appeared again, almost out of thin air. The *Hakim Nisa'* all gasped in absolute shock. They had never seen a mortal powerful. What he thought, he could simply do.

"Regeneration?" one of them questioned.

Zion shook his head. "No... reanimation. If only you were strong enough to unmake me in one instance. But my power continues to exceed what you could've imagined. I continue to learn by simply watching your every move. Every cell you attempted to erase, I recreated. I'm capable of more creation than the Seraphs. And it took the knowledge of this entire solar system to achieve such legendary attributes. You won't get another chance at that little trick! It's over!" he shouted.

Zion pounced forward at lightning speed. The *Hakim Nisa'* couldn't even catch a glimpse of his movement. After they blinked, they saw that Zion had created a sword and stabbed one of their sisters straight through her chest. She died immediately. The newborn god kept attacking, continuing to move faster than the speed of sound. He brutally attacked the *Hakim Nisa'* with melee combat. An elbow to the jaw, kick to the sternum, punch to the throat, knee to the nose, stab in the side, slash across the back, a bullet to the chest, gunshot to the shin. In a matter of seconds, all of the relatively elderly women were sprawled out across the floor, badly beaten.

Now, the newborn god truly stood victorious. He had slain one of their sisters as a warning but saw no harm in executing more of them. "Pathetic," he said. Zion looked down at all of the women. One woman before him was managing to crawl back up to her feet. She faced the emperor with blood across her face, panting angrily.

"Zion. You may be a god. You may have the halo and wings of an angel. But… you're nothing more than a devil. A demon sent upon the universe. Your actions are nothing more than sin. And… with goddess as my witness… you will pay someday," she said. Her breath became more labored. Zion approached her slowly, never ceasing his eye contact with the woman. He stood before her, three times her size. Not another word was said.

Zion grabbed the Wise Woman by her face and raised her into the air with one hand. All her sisters could do was sit by and watch, nearly crippled from his attack. Zion concentrated the forces of Syris into his physical body and closed his eyes. He gripped the *Hakim Nisa's* face tighter and inhaled. The ground started shaking. A black aura surged around his and the woman's body. Then, blood began

emerging upon his arm. The *Hakim Nisa's* blood. Zion had done the same thing he did to his wife. He sucked the Wise Woman's remaining life essence into his own. All of her power, her spirit, was now within him too. The Wise Woman's body deflated. All blood, then organs, then bones, were simply evaporating. Zion stopped. He threw the hollowed-out sack of the *Hakim Nisa's* skin onto the floor. He was restored. Now, everything could end.

The remaining *Hakim Nisa'* wailed miserably. They bawled loudly. This couldn't have been possible. Two of their sisters had just been brutally murdered right before their very eyes. And now that Zion had absorbed small fragments of their power, he was surely more unstoppable than before. The newborn god simply stood there, basking in his legendary presence. Victory was near.

Suddenly, the Chosen Ones had appeared before him. Jonah and Carmine stood beside the shattered thrones that their parents once sat on. They clenched their fists and clutched their elbows to their sides. Their forearms stuck outward. The princes released a powerful chant. Their power ignited once more. Jonah's golden aura and Carmine's platinum aura emerged again. This was it. The most powerful beings in the universe had failed to stop Zion's tyranny. Working with Aunt Kanya upstairs, Jonah and Carmine were prepared to execute one final plan. The last resort.

"We won't let you win so easily Zion. We Seraphs fight until there is nothing left!" Jonah shouted.

Zion smiled peacefully. It would be a worthy death for these two boys.

"Now… face us demon!" Carmine shouted.

Jonah and Carmine, Princes of Jannah, Chosen Ones of Eon V

For Paradise

Before The Chosen Ones could move an inch, they felt a sudden energy shift. Zion dashed towards them at the speed of sound, his physical form completely dispersing from the godly momentum he had used. Someway, somehow, they managed to dodge on instinct. Jonah pivoted his feet and tilted his upper body to the right. Carmine mirrored his motion to the left. They narrowly evaded Zion's charge. The emperor dashed between them, accidentally driving his fist into the wall behind the thrones. Nearly the whole wall shattered from his single punch, creating a gaping hole in the throne room, which revealed the nearby corridors of the castle.

Jonah and Carmine's mouths gaped. They stared at each other, no more than ten feet apart. The frightened look on their faces revealed their true feelings, their true understanding of the magnitude of the situation at hand. If they lost, Zion would win, meaning that the Seraphs would become extinct at the hands of his genocide. Once the Seraphs would become extinct, the laws of nature in the entire universe would change forever. Newly terraformed planets would be made in his image, one that he claimed to be of an equal philosophy. But at this moment, it had become obvious that Zion obtained even more power after absorbing one of the *Hakim Nisa'*. He did this using the same powers of the Nanomorphs. The Nanomorphs were typically incapable of absorbing a being that far exceeded their powers. But with the fragment of the Crystal of Nihaya in his chest, Zion amplified all of the Syris species' abilities to god-like levels.

The princes both tilted their heads towards Zion, whose fist was still raised after striking through the wall. They had to act fast. Jonah and Carmine each raised a hand and fired a massive cosmic blast at Zion. This managed to knock the man down momentarily, smoke trailing behind the collided explosion. "Run!" Jonah shouted. Carmine followed his brother, both of them setting their plan into motion. It was something they had thought of with Aunt Kanya and it was their last hope of stopping the newborn god.

Zion arose from the floor, angrier than before. He watched as the two princes sprinted towards a hallway, leaving the throne room and running towards the back of the castle. Zion dashed forward with a fist again in an attempt to hit them, but the brothers quickly dove out of the way. The emperor struck a wall again. He turned to his left, watching them continue their escape.

"Fleeing? Is that your brilliant plan?" Zion raised both his hands and fired beams from his fingers, traveling over several hundred miles per hour. As the princes ran down the hall, they were suddenly hit by dozens of small blasts in their backs, legs, and arms. Zion pursued them, still shooting. Unable to handle much more of this onslaught, Carmine quickly turned around and created a shield made from pure cosmic energy. It glowed with his platinum aura. Carmine blocked the remaining shots from Zion and Jonah quickly leaped above his brother. He fired a massive blast directly at Zion. It didn't hurt the newborn god but surely bought them some more time. Zion took the brunt of the blast, only sliding back several feet on his heels.

The Chosen Ones continued running down the halls, wanting Zion to chase them. He dashed forward again, getting his targets back into his sights. Zion raised both his hands and began manipulating the narrow hallway. He clenched his fists and crossed his arms over each other. Suddenly, the hallway started twisting counter-clockwise, the walls jutting into the ceiling and floor. The hallway was completely shrinking around the princes. Zion was trying to crush them. Jonah and Carmine sprinted as fast as they could. They jumped forward, narrowly avoiding being crushed by the collapsing hallway. They both took a right turn. Zion restored the crumbling walls to their original position and moved forward. Carmine quickly summoned explosives and planted them on the wall as they ran. They exploded, the rubble and ceiling blocking the corridor. It bought them a few seconds.

The newborn god quickly destroyed the rocks, shifting their anatomical makeup from a solid to a gas in a matter of seconds. Zion resumed chasing the princes. He saw them turn to the left. Watching them run down yet another corridor, he attempted to manipulate the room again. Zion slid his left foot forward across the ground, then punched the air towards the brothers. Suddenly, the floorboards of the corridor moved like a tidal wave. Although the Chosen Ones attempted to outrun it, they were knocked right off their feet, falling forward. They rolled across the floor of a nearby room. Lucky for them, this was exactly where they wanted Zion to follow them. They quickly made their move for their final attack.

Zion made his way into this room. It was dark and full of unknown paraphernalia used for scientific research and experiments. The emperor didn't move much. He looked around, attempting to heighten his senses to see where Jonah and Carmine had gone. "You cannot hide forever boys," Zion said. But something was strange. He couldn't sense any of the princes' power in the vicinity. But… there was someone else in the room with him.

A sound was made in the corner. A metal door was slammed and sealed shut. Zion grunted angrily as he immediately directed his attention towards the presence behind him. It wasn't Jonah or Carmine. It was a girl. An Automa. It was Leola.

"Time to die you son of a bitch!" she shouted. Leola quickly jumped from the door and pounced towards a nearby control panel. She pulled a switch that activated the transporter she had worked on hours ago. A piercing blue light emerged between the nodes of the device, signaling that it had already been connected to a destination.

"What?" Zion shouted, confused by the plan unfolding before him.

Suddenly, Jonah emerged from the transporter. The reason why Zion could no longer sense the princes' power was because they were light years away from Jannah in a matter of seconds. "Get down Leola!" Jonah shouted. She quickly dropped into cover. Jonah released a flashing light from his palm, blinding Zion. The emperor screamed violently as he shielded his face. Jonah jumped behind the man, getting to his flank. He charged up his power and started pushing Zion towards the transporter.

"What? What the hell are you doing?" Zion shouted, struggling to overpower the boy. He was inching closer to the device. But the emperor was too strong; Jonah needed help.

"Carmine! Now!" Jonah shouted. Suddenly, the twin prince's arms emerged from the blue light between the transporter's nodes. He grabbed Zion by the chest plate of his armor, yanking him in. The newborn god was completely overwhelmed.

"Let go of me! Now you imbeciles! Before I kill you!" It was still difficult to finish the job. Jonah quickly took several steps back and charged an even greater amount of his power. He screamed powerfully and sprinted towards Zion's back. The prince threw his whole body at Zion, knocking both himself and the emperor into the transporter. As planned, Leola quickly shut off the sending transporter and destroyed the device with explosives. With no way to return to the planet, Zion was finally nowhere near Jannah to harm it.

The Chosen Ones had succeeded with half of their plan. Chaotically rolling out of the receiving teleporter, they fell upon the ground of their new location. Carmine fell backwards, Zion landed on his face, and Jonah trailed behind him, catching himself in a barrel roll. The princes quickly stood up and fired a cosmic blast at the teleporter nodes here, destroying them completely. Zion felt the heat of the explosion and was slightly alarmed. What were they planning?

As the emperor rose to his feet, he observed the twins standing side by side. He looked around at the environment. They were on the warm molten rock with red cracks between them, likely from lava buried underneath. The clouds up above were gray and filled with lightning storms. It rained lightly and volcanic eruptions occurred every ten seconds or so. Zion could also feel the ground shake beneath his feet. The distant, mountainous terrain of this place seemed unfinished. And the capital oceans were spouting hot water from their deep geysers located on their sandy floors. "Your newly terraformed planet..."

Having been on young planets before, Zion immediately recognized the princes' creation. He knew this would be the only planet the brothers would set transporter nodes onto so they could visit it consistently. It showed great promise according to the Seraphs who now lay dead upon Jannah. Jonah and Carmine just stared intensely at the enemy before them. He had taken so much from them in so little time. Zion had destroyed their planet, nearly wiped out their species, ruined their chances of becoming rulers of Syris, murdered their mother, and turned them into violent animals, hellbent on killing any enemy before them. Perhaps it was what Zion always wanted. To destroy the faith of the Seraphs, of the universe, and to leave people to their primal instincts. Only then would they be left to obey the laws of nature. Reduced to nothing more than the assertion of power through force was perhaps a form of equality. For without any faith in their goddess, or any of the planets' gods for that matter, mortals would never see one being as greater than the other. Any praise would be created from someone's actions, not from an ideology that existed centuries ago. According to Zion, a world without religion was a world with peace. A world without blind faith was a world with action. A world without a god to blame was a world with responsibility. A world where faith was only established by science was a world where equality can truly exist.

But according to Jonah and Carmine, he was wrong. "It's over Zion," they said simultaneously. The brothers quickly stepped apart from each other, revealing someone standing behind them. It was Kanya, the only *Hakim Nisa'* who had yet to confront the newborn god head-on. "Now Kanya!" the Chosen Ones shouted.

Kanya performed an ancient hand sign sequence, interlocking her fingers and using her hands to form various shapes. Then, she opened her right palm and slammed it into the molten ground beneath their feet. Strange hieroglyphs started appearing across the entire planet. They glowed with a powerful golden and white light. Zion observed what was transpiring in shock. The cracks in the planet's continents grew larger and lava began bursting into the air. The ground shook violently and the storms intensified. And with one final movement of supernatural force, Kanya, one of the most powerful beings in the universe, caused the interstellar structure to self-destruct. A massive explosion emerged from the core of the unnamed planet. The sound barrier shattered in the wake of such a cataclysmic event. As a bright flame consumed the entire planet in a powerful yellow color, fragments of the celestial body scattered into Space. The fires could be seen from light-years away. As the dust settled in the center, the explosion ceased.

This was the final resort. The final plan. For paradise. Lure Zion to the newly terraformed planet and destroy it. At the very least, if it wasn't powerful enough to kill the god, it would have left him lost in the depths of Space. It would be physically impossible for him to get anywhere near Syris now that he was trapped light-years away. The Chosen Ones, Princes Jonah and Carmine of Jannah, were willing to lay their lives on the line for the greater good of the universe. It was what their mother had done, facing a newborn god on her own. And yet another *Hakim Nisa'* was lost amidst the war. The only rationale behind the sacrifice for the three of them was to defend a faith that could now continue to persist in the universe. The faith of their goddess. The end of the war, the end of Zion's tyranny, was an outcome equal to their actions. It was finally over. Or... so they thought.

Suddenly, the stray fragments of the planet were given life. They shook violently and began moving towards each other with a phenomenal intention. It almost looked as if the entire explosion was rewinding. More so, the unnamed planet was reassembling. Piece by piece, continent by continent, ocean by ocean, the unnamed planet was forcefully being dragged back together. The flames that had scattered about the solar system had retreated into the core of the planet once more. A bright light briefly flashed through the cracks of the reassembling structure. As they sealed shut through molten rock, its surface breath emerged once more. The planet was alive again. Its atmosphere spawned, the storms brewed, and volcanoes resumed eruption.

To hear all the sounds. To smell all the scents. To see all the sights. It was terrifying. The Chosen Ones, alongside the *Hakim Nisa'* Kanya, were profoundly appalled by what had just transpired. A horrifying look appeared upon their faces. The erupting volcanoes were heard bursting in the distance. Once again, rainfall occurred. Zion, the newborn god, had one hand planted on the ground, the same way Kanya did moments ago. The hieroglyphs that were scattered about the planet's surface were now receding. Zion finally stood up, facing the Seraphs once more.

"In the same way that you are capable of destroying planets at will, I can recreate them. It took a moment to understand, but I have almost entirely made half of the *Hakim Nisa's* power my own," Zion said. The emperor quickly dashed past the princes and appeared behind Kanya. It was too fast to comprehend. He had his forearms wrapped around the frail woman's throat, his claws digging into the back of her head. Zion gazed into her mortified eyes. "You won't get another chance at that trick." Kanya panted violently. Zion tightly grabbed her by the chin and cranium. With a swift pull of his arms in opposite directions, he snapped Kanya's neck in two. Her body jarred and collapsed onto the molten floors of the unnamed planet. She died instantly.

Jonah and Carmine screamed violently. "Kanya!!" Although they wanted to unleash an onslaught upon this wretched excuse of a god, they were deeply terrified of what type of damage he could do to them. Fists clenched, they simply stood by, crying angrily over their aunt's murder. Zion did nothing more than stare at them. It was his actions that had now nearly wiped out the entire Seraph species. For once, the princes weren't sure if the man would ever see his judgment day. Perhaps their goddess wasn't an advocate of fairness, as they had originally thought.

"What's your plan now, Zion? So what? You killed Kanya! You wiped out the Seraph race! But you're still stuck here on this godforsaken, terraformed mess!" Jonah shouted.

Carmine joined in his brother's verbal attack. "Perhaps if you weren't so vindictive you would have acted more intelligently! But I guess now, the three of us can stay here until we rot!"

Zion briefly closed his eyes and smiled softly; there was hardly any limit to his power. "I suppose that's where you underestimate me again, boys. The same way you thought destroying an entire planet would be enough to stop me. I'll let you know that I have just enough power to travel through the 4th dimension and teleport myself back to Jannah. So... I'll spare you. You can spend the rest of your waking days watching your planet evolve and regretting the day you didn't join in my regime. Farewell."

Terrified, Jonah and Carmine charged forward. "No!" they shouted. They attempted to tackle Zion, throwing their bodies forward. But before they could touch the god, he vanished into thin air, leaving nothing behind but a trail of cosmic particles. He changed his physical makeup into one that could travel through the 4th dimension. This technique had never been done since the Nephilims Eons ago, but it had become clear that Zion had become capable of groundbreaking feats now. It was fitting for a god.

The princes fell flat on their faces and rolled across the molten ground. They panted heavily as they gazed up at the sky overwhelmed by storms. The Chosen Ones slowly arose from the ground. The distant sounds of erupting volcanoes and thunder dominated once more. Jonah and Carmine looked back at Kanya's dead body. Then they looked forward, up at the sky towards Jannah, light-years away. Not another word was said. They lost. Zion won. His regime was at hand. Now stranded, the brothers just collapsed to their knees as their jaws dropped. This was the end. The Era of Progeny was over.

The Era of Egalitarianism was ready to begin. Zion had made it back to the planet he destroyed. Jannah. Heaven. The newborn god entered the throne room to find some of his most elite guards taking complete control of the area. Flags were planted, homes were burned, and citizens were arrested. The legendary army stood by, awaiting the return of their new ruler. Amidst Zion's military were the remaining people who fought for the Seraphs. Adelrik, Evelyn, Leola, what remained of the *Hakim Nisa'*, and other civilians. They were terrified to see Zion return to the planet without Jonah, Carmine, or Kanya reigning victorious. It had become obvious that the princes' plan had failed. Whether they were alive or dead was something their loved ones didn't want to think about now. It was impossible to tell what would happen to them next. For the very fabric of the entire universe was about to change forever.

Zion walked across the gilded floors of the throne room, centered upon the red carpet. He marched silently towards his throne. His entire army bowed their heads as he walked by. The newborn god's aura was magnificently intense. It shook the castle and rattled the royal estate. It was as if his destiny had finally been fulfilled. After decades of suffering, he had finally achieved what he had deserved for so long. Zion walked up the few steps to the royal chairs. His guards quickly removed the shattered thrones of the king and queen of Jannah and brought in the emperor of Kremlin's throne from his palace. Zion's guards removed his cape and he claimed his place upon the royal chair. Before him was the first link towards starting the new era. The scraps of mortality that he must amend to create a universe founded upon equality. His guards placed both Adelrik and Vitaliya's crowns on his head. Vitaliya's was thin enough and small enough to fit within Adelrik's more extravagant crown. It was the best way Zion felt he could honor the sacrifice of his beloved wife, Raakel. She had put her life on the line to achieve his dream. And Zion truly believed she was here with him, right at this very moment.

There the newborn god sat upon his throne. Zion inhaled deeply. He had become greater than what he was destined to be. A king with two crowns. Zion clutched the arms of his new throne tightly. The man began shedding tears of overwhelming happiness and achievement. The war he had faced to make such a hallmark victory across the stars was one he would never wish upon even his worst enemy. All the suffering he had endured was something no one should have to go through ever again. This was for the world, for the universe, for the All. This was what the galaxies were meant to witness. Him. Victorious. Zion inhaled once more.

"Kneel before me," he said proudly.

And it happened. Beings from across the entire Syris Solar System dropped to their knees and bent forward, placing their head and hands upon the gilded floor of the throne room. More tears fell as Zion clenched his teeth. He accidentally let out a breath of sorrow, a slight wail of inundating emotion. Then… he bawled. Not only had he seen his dream through, but the universe would finally be free from its suffering. The universe would finally be free to imagine. The Era of Egalitarianism was now.

The Era of Egalitarianism

While awaiting the development of their newest planet, Jonah and Carmine created one of the most significant points in the entire universe. Although the Syris Solar System had been celebrating the 25th anniversary of peace and the twins' 18th birthday, all joyous excursions had been brought to a halt. What came to light after the war was a reminder of the corrupted nature Seraphs had created during their time. Zion, Kremlin's emperor, became an almighty god by pure force. The first of his kind. A mortal made nearly immortal. Because the Seraphs abused their god-like power, Zion was able to assemble an army full of other rulers who were quite keen on the thought of betraying Adelrik and Vitaliya. Zion's year-long war tore apart the fabric of the legendary solar system and possibly the entire ancient universe. Taking the powers of gods to become one himself was the first step towards Zion's self-made era. After he obtained his two crowns as the high king of the universe, Zion began to exploit the *Hakim Nisa's* tremendous abilities. Threatening their lives and the lives of the remaining Seraphs, Zion forced the Wise Women to abide by his goals for the evolution of the universe. Every new planet that he created was intentionally made without the ability to use the cosmic energy surrounding them. Instead of powers, Zion granted all his species intelligence. A commodity he deemed much more important than the chaotic forces of war. Stripping most of the universe of their powers, Zion made all mortals equal. Instead of fighting, they learned. They achieved evolutionary advancements through science, mathematics, and language. Thus, the foundation of the Era of Egalitarianism lived on stronger than ever. Soon, not many beings in the universe had the powers that the species of Syris once had. As the ancient species became extinct, the newer ones were left with nothing more than their intellectual prowess. To Zion, that was the true determinant of power. The new era of species relied on natural selection, common sense, and the development of their imagination. They were all equal.

Earth, the Last Resort

The stories of what occurred with Jonah and Carmine after Zion's victory are still scattered about the universe. It's rumored that they somehow managed to continue the battle. That the princes had worked with forces to attack Zion from afar, coordinating guerilla tactics across the galaxies. But without Jannah emitting its holy life force, the princes knew the afterlife no longer existed. All Seraphs who died had no hopes for reincarnation. And this was surely true for the entire universe. But their new planetary structure was the last chance for the afterlife to return. While much of the universe was either dead or enslaved in concentration camps to impose equality, this unnamed planet was the last hope of creating a new uncorrupted species. Jonah and Carmine found a purpose for their incomplete terraformed structure. That purpose was

to provide life for the lost Seraph souls. Towards the end of the princes' days, it's believed that the divine bacterium they placed shortly before the war continued evolution at a very slow rate. Without the assistance of the *Hakim Nisa's* powers, the planet was left to faith. This final relic of the Era of Progeny was eventually called Earth. Named for its start of new hope from the bottom. The ground. Without the assistance of the Wise Women, our planet, Earth, took 4.5 billion years to develop on its own. The recklessness of such a species led to a rather disastrous evolutionary timeline. Aquatic creatures reigning before dinosaurs, who were eventually destroyed by meteors because there were not any Seraphs to defend the growing planet from the natural disasters of space. Then, sea-level changes and ice ages emerged before the complete rise of *Homo Sapiens*. The process of evolution couldn't be nurtured and Earth faced countless years of chaos during its early development. But today, it stands as the final remnants of Jannah's godly power of creation and the last hope to restore the afterlife. Earth, within the current era foretold in this prophecy, is the prototype for a new Jannah.

The Era of Humanity
and Our Existence

Amidst all the extinction and mass genocide initiated by Zion, many planets were unable to house any species. Today, many hollow structures surround the universe visible to Earth. They remain as distant relics left behind by Zion as worlds with untold stories. Whatever species that once existed in the surrounding Andromeda, Pinwheel, Tadpole, or other galaxies, were likely wiped out or forcefully enslaved to proliferate Zion's universe. Now, Jannah continues to be consumed in darkness. With heaven's destruction being absolute, there's no longer any guidance for the lost souls of our existence. Everyone who dies in this reality has no place to go except for Purgatory. Without the ability to access the higher realms of heaven, mortals' souls will forever be lost. And the souls of the ancient Seraphs have no true being to reincarnate as. Some suggest many of the Seraphs' lost souls currently embody humans to simply exist once more and escape the wretched depths of Purgatory. Many of them are believed to still retain remnants of their ancient memories. For the first time, reincarnated into humans, Seraphs fear death. They fear Purgatory, as should we. As should all species in the universe. Heaven is dead.

The Chosen Ones
of the Present

Much like their lost kin, Princes Jonah and Carmine also have no body to turn to for reincarnation. With faith rapidly dissipating in the universe and Earth, the struggle to revive the afterlife continues to become even more challenging. Nonetheless, the twin brothers refuse to give up hope. In a realm unknown to mortals, they are trying to find a way to guide the lost souls of Jannah to undertake the biggest task of the millennia. If they succeed, Jonah and Carmine hope to reincarnate these souls into Earthling bodies to protect the Chosen Ones of the present. The Chosen Ones are prophesied to be two orphan brothers born with the task of restoring the afterlife and reopening the gates of heaven. The princes intend to assign many of Jannah's greatest Seraphs' souls to significant humans with the intent of having them assist The Chosen Ones on their quest. Before this new timeline was formed, it's believed that the princes decided to break all rules of reincarnation and inexplicably bestowed a godly power upon The Chosen Ones in the name of the universe. This power is believed to prevent the orphans from true death and confinement in Purgatory. Lost words from the princes that traveled into this realm suggest that the ability for the orphans to reincarnate into their own bodies is extremely crucial to help them restore the afterlife. War is approaching. And Jonah and Carmine believe these two children are capable of deciding the fate of the afterlife and the universe as we know it. But first, they'll need all humans to band together as one unified species for the common goal of restoring heaven for the entire universe.

Eon VI
Imagination

Imagination represents the current Eon that mortals exist in today. The status of the universe as we know it is doomed for a life without heaven. All passed souls are left to wander in Purgatory without a home to go to. The details of this section of the Scripture provide the teachings of how many gods in the past had taken steps to ascend to a higher spiritual level. Imagination may be perceived as a curse left behind by Zion in his new era, but it's the universe's truest remaining power to reach life after death. Harnessing the power of Imagination is only the first step towards becoming a spiritual Paragon. Regardless, it was paramount towards making strides for the betterment of the societies around them. This current Eon is presented with only fragments of the massive amount of teachings that the ancient gods once practiced. It is through these practices that one can find themselves closer to peace within their heart. According to the gods, finding inner peace was the most necessary step towards creating peace throughout the universe. Although the Newborn god, Zion, had diminished these practices millennia ago, the princes are believed to have put their faith in the newest generations. This is where the preceding stories of the few gods before our time harmonize. Imagination is important because it's the ability that pervades our existence. It influences everything we do, think about, and create. Imagination leads to elaborate theories, dreams, and inventions in any profession, from the realms of academia to engineering, or the arts. Meaning is only found through the eyes of the reader. And when that meaning is put to good use, an individual can use the power of their imagination to become a hero and make the world a better place.

The Present

And so it took astronomical occurrences for the beings of this universe to become what they are today. Although this ancient scripture only tells a few of the stories of some of the universe's most influential figures, there are many more out in the depths of space, meant to be discovered. These are the stories of the past. More remains for the stories of the future.

With a tremendous loss of faith in our societies, beings from across the galaxies have started to rely on a new phenomenon established during the Era of Egalitarianism. During this era, mortals no longer possessed supernatural abilities. They no longer possessed the powers that allowed them to live as if they were the very gods that created them. This equality has continued into today, to which many beings have chosen to live at the mercy of gods and do as is told from the religious principles they have either chosen or been forced to believe in. This new establishment of religion by mortals is what has allowed them to maintain faith for so many centuries. These remnants of faith were crucial for survival. Religion became the last vestige of the universe that had been established during Eon V.

But that faith has long since begun to disappear. As faith continues to fade, the new phenomenon emerges in the present of Eon VI. Imagination. On many planets and for many species throughout the universe, faith fades as the years go on. Less and less of the upcoming generations choose to live beyond themselves and make the sacrifice for others the most important part of their existence. With the Newborn god, Zion, eliminating supernatural abilities and emphasizing intellect for every species, evolution changed. Mortal brains grew larger over centuries and they became more capable of creating. Not with cosmic force, but with the power of their minds. Imagination surged across the stars and mortals strived to become smarter than the previous generation. And through the implementation of intellectual status, faith continuously became abandoned. As Zion wished, the new generation of mortals started to neglect to see the purpose of religion. Whereas the be-

ginning of their existence stressed a life guided by religion, their children soon sought different things in life. Money, power, and status over the principles of self-sacrifice. As heaven continues to be consumed by darkness and as the afterlife continues to fade from existence, mortals will soon lose all meaning of their faith. All passed souls will never return to this universe reincarnated. Instead, their ethereal forms will forever be left to wander between the planes of reality and heaven forever. These souls would be left in a Purgatory that has been tainted by the current generation's loss of faith.

However, imagination hasn't come to exist in the present as a crutch to the mortal races. Imagination is in fact one of the greatest powers that mortals have left. The final remnant of what the gods, Gia, Mustafa, He, She, and Alkulu were capable of. Imagination has become the great bridge between what exists in the spirits of mortals into a fully realized, tangible product of life.

But over the Eons of the universe's existence, there has been a trade-off between imagination and omnipotence. The more the mortals became capable of free thought and creativity, the less they became capable of god-like creation. The gods of Time, Space, and Gravity waged war over the universe like elements naturally forming a compound under the laws of physics. The paramount gods collided over dominating the universe with various nebulae without any comprehensible thought to their action. Alkulu became the product of such violence and knew nothing more than to harbor the universe with structures made directly by its cosmic powers. And so forth, the twin gods soon developed attachments to the immortal Nephilims they created. The Nephilims also created. They formed societies and practiced a life determined by hyper beings. Yet they, including Mustafa, always remained beneath the gods. And with the rise of the first child in existence, the next generation had gained free will, at the cost of all cosmic powers. They chose to pursue a life of service that benefitted mortals everywhere. With the sacrifice of Gia as Mother Nature to this united dimension, the powers became restored with a need for all beings to fight for their religion. Although this faith initially created harmony in Syris and the rest of the solar systems for centuries, it soon led to war. Absolute destruction over the ideologies that came from species of different dimensions. And so Zion sought to destroy these ideologies by relinquishing mortals of their need for blind faith and providing them with

confidence in their new power, imagination. The pure creativity of the mortal soul became a new reason for existence. Species everywhere arose with faith but soon evolved into imagination. With full belief in their own capabilities, the meaning of the afterlife continued to fade. Mortals no longer sought to help others in their lifetime for the sake of entering the gates of heaven. No, they sought intellectual prowess for the sake of materialistic gain. They abused imagination. Which begs the question of whether imagination is truly a gift or a curse.

Mortals were once derived from the existence of beings greater than gods. Creation itself. The All. But mortality ensued upon the universe and the power of the gods faded as time persisted. Omnipotence deteriorated. Much of what beings had was lost through the same thing that separated Time, Space, and Gravity; war. Today, all that's left within the mortals is a feeling. A gut sense of what it was like to have the power of pure creation, expressed through their imagination. This is their only connection to heaven. A belief that there is something beyond our understanding of the universe. For at one point in time, all beings didn't simply understand heaven, they lived it. Now, with the afterlife gone, the final fragment of our past existence is doomed to fade. Faith will die and imagination will fully corrupt us. Without a balance between the two, the materialistic gain will only remain. And today, upon many planets, species continue to lose their faith and let their imaginations dictate their thirst for power.

However, one species has yet to truly fall into the trap of corruption. A race left behind to evolve on its own, through the flames of the natural world. On this planet, Earth, humans are relatively young. They haven't entirely abandoned faith and they haven't entirely abused the rewards of their imagination. Hope remains for them. For they have the new Chosen Ones in their population, meant to restore the afterlife and rescue the lost souls in Purgatory. What their intentions are remains unclear, but the balance of the universe is indeed in their collective hands as a united species.

Becoming a Paragon

The entire universe is full of various cultures, traditions, religions, and species. One planet may comprehend its place in the universe in a completely different way compared to another planet. Despite the many differences apparent between the species across the stars, many of them have a strong similarity. The desire for spiritual enlightenment. The drive to ascend to a higher plane of spiritual understanding. Regardless of one's choice in faith, spirituality is a trait inherent to everyone in the universe. Understanding such a key component of existence is the key to discovering the freedom to live your life to its fullest experience.

Throughout ancient history and the few stories of the scripture, it's clear that many have yearned for some form of spiritual awakening. The desire to comprehend life at a higher level is the ultimate goal for many beings when pursuing spiritual enlightenment. The same way Alkulu sought to use its power to achieve new heights or how Mustafa wished to communicate on the level of gods. Many mortals and gods not mentioned in the stories of this scripture have found peace of mind, heart, and soul through their path towards enlightenment. It's this level of spiritual affinity that granted so many beings with powers beyond cosmic forces and instead, ones that forever changed the shape of the universe. Ones that even performed miracles.

Some of the greatest beings to achieve spiritual enlightenment were the Seraphs, the Paragons, who became the epitome of transcending from this physical realm into the celestial Cosmos at will. And with what was learned in the planes of another existence, many prophets came to fully comprehend themselves and the universe around them. Although this enlightenment is impossible to determine from one specific moment, it's still rumored to be achieved through certain tactics. Each journey is different for everyone. Luckily, this means that any mortal in this dimension can achieve such enlightenment by creating their own path. A person doesn't have to indulge in institutional religion to experience such a blessing. Spirituality is within us all. It's the same force that once took mortals from reality through Purgatory, into heaven once they passed.

Many of the spiritual leaders of the past have experienced some commonalities in their steps towards awakening. And many have determined it to be one of the most significant processes to serve the world to your fullest capacity. Some form of self-awareness, understanding of the connectivity of the universe, and willingness to sacrifice are required to sufficiently help those around you.

Surely the collective information of these ancient spiritual leaders can, at the very least, help raise a mortal's consciousness. Serenity and tranquility are key components for enlightenment. It provides someone with the tongue to speak the language of the beings that exist in a higher plane.

Many gods hope that all species learn to live in harmony by speaking this same language. Achieve peace by finally being able to listen to each other not with their auditory appendages, but with their hearts.

Understand that the three major forces of the universe are connected to three major forces of your being. They are listed with their connection below. This is helpful to keep in mind as you go through the first phase of becoming a spiritual Paragon.

Space

الفراغ (*Alfaragh*) = Body

Time

زمن (*Zaman*) = Mind

Gravity

الجاذبية (*Aljadhibia*) = Spirit

The first aspect of becoming a Paragon is the foundation of every being, which is their very existence. The existence of an individual is synonymous with their feet, the appendages that are most often connected to the surface of their planet. The concept of connecting with our existence is strengthened by the feet and lies within the naval. The navel is where many beings received nourishment before birth and it continues to be at the core of your foundation. With the feet and navel united, an individual is capable of coming one step closer towards relatively understanding their existence better. This applies to every aspect of becoming a Paragon. For future aspects, understand that the attachment is the part of the body through which the location of the energy is strengthened.

The color that applies to each aspect is a visual representation of the energy that most closely resembles it. For existence, that color is black. Black is associated with the color of Space. At the beginning of everyone's life, the possibilities are so deep, full of so much depth, that black is the strongest association of existence. Existence itself is full of so many complexities or so many simplicities. It all depends on how the person views their existence. Life itself can be a deep reservoir of infinite information and possibilities, or it can simply be viewed as an empty space meant to be filled. Black is the symbol of existence.

The following are practices and steps commonly necessary towards purifying one's attunement of each aspect. Purifying doesn't imply that corruption is absent. Purifying any one of the aspects of becoming a Paragon involves finding a balance between the positive and negative energies associated with the sense. There are times and purposes for every emotion that a person feels and the goal of becoming a Paragon is to understand them all and find peace with them. With that said, listed below are a set of practices that can help a person discover their inner peace and find balance. Not all of the practices are required to purify one's sense. These are examples of how someone aspiring to become a Paragon can connect with their spiritual selves more. Each individual has their own unique experience when going through their journey towards becoming a Paragon.

Existence

- **Location**: Navel
- **Attachment:** Feet
- **Color:** Black
- **Purified by:** Connectivity, Foundation, Acceptance, Detachment, Unity
- **Corrupted by:** Separation, Excessive Attachment, Feeling Lost, Unappreciation for the Universe

Step 1: Walk Barefoot

Walking barefoot connects you with the surface of your planet. It harks back to the existence of the ancient ancestors who roamed the universe with nothing in their possession. Doing so for a week, for a majority of the day when possible, can reignite the understanding of existence. Especially walking outside barefoot; this strips you of the confines of your dwelling and brings you more closely connected with your home planet.

Step 2: Exercise the Legs

The legs are the appendage of the body that fully unites the surface of the planet to the core, where the naval resides. It's important to strengthen this part of the body through exercise. Squatting and running are some of the easiest ways to build muscle in your legs. Do this every day for a week, then remain consistent with it once a week thereafter. Staying healthy is an important part of lengthening your existence, from this dimension into the next one.

Step 3: Garden

Gardening is more than just growing the plants of your planet. It's building a direct connection with the products that your planet provides. Building this relationship is synonymous with you graciously bringing life into existence for the universe. You don't have to go to the extreme and plant an entire garden if it's not normally possible. But even choosing to own and nurture a few live plants can profoundly impact your relationship with nature. Pansies, Basil, Sunflowers, Succulents, and Mint are good places to start without experience. Committing to growing a few plants until they mature is crucial to understanding that everything in the universe is alive. And we all have a part in creating or destroying life.

Step 4: Go on a Hike or Walk through Nature

Bringing a plant you've grown, trek out to nature. Whether it be a hike or a walk through a wilderness trail, it's important to travel to a place that is rather disconnected from much of inner cities. Take the plant along the trail and bring it to the end of the hike or as far as your body is willing to take you. When the area feels right, leave the plant and its pot out in nature. If possible, you can take it a step further and transfer the plant into the new soil. Allow it to endure what nature has to offer it. Releasing the plant in a foreign habitat exemplifies your control over life and death with the world around you.

Step 5: Learn About the Universe

Many beings throughout the universe take their existence for granted. They lack the appropriate understanding needed to appreciate the minute chance that they were even born. Gaining this perspective is important to make sense of how you came to exist amongst the chaotic cosmos. Reading excerpts of text about the general universe and viewing content to learn more about it is helpful. The Big Bang Theory is one of the most important concepts to learn more about. Let the mind wander through whatever subjects it's curious about within the universe.

Step 6: Stargaze

After learning more about the universe, the next step is to connect with it on a more spiritual level. Simply going outside in a place where stars are visible and spending time viewing them will ground you in their existence more. Connecting the information learned to what you see before you should open the eyes to a greater truth about how they came to be.

Step 7: Meditate on your Place in the World

Outside, grounded with nature, meditate on your place in the world. Take time to meditate in solitude and indulge in the surrounding sounds of your planet. Understand that everything is energy. Much like what occurred throughout the universe ages ago, one form of energy was transferred to another. It's never created nor destroyed. Analyze your own existence and how you may have come to be in the universe. Ponder about

the beings of the universe that preceded you and one day led to your existence. The loss of one life may be the gift of life to another. It becomes even more important to appreciate the gift of your own life and the rare chances of it occurring in the way it has.

Materialism

- **Location:** Tongue
- **Attachment:** Hands
- **Color:** Red
- **Purified By:** Healthy Foods, Positive Habits, Charity, Volunteerism, Intangibility, Internal Happiness, Sacrifice of Ownership
- **Corrupted By:** Unhealthy Foods, Guilty Pleasures, Greed, Tangibility, Needless Possessions, External Happiness

Step 1: Exercise the Arms

The arms and hands are appendages directly linked with the act of holding materialistic possessions. They are the part of the body that feeds the personal mouth and soul. However, they are also the part of the body that can help others. It's important to strengthen these appendages. Spiritual strength and physical strength can become connected if trained properly. The means of push-ups or using weights are sufficient when exercising the arms. Do this every day for a week, then remain consistent with it once a week thereafter. Weaker arms are more inclined to unhealthy habits and frail resilience. Stronger arms show strength for others who may lack it. To help the fellow being. To lend a caring hand and help lift others with strong arms.

Step 2: Give Up your Guilty Foods

The arms can force you to yield to temptation or help you resist it. The food touched upon the tongue not only nourishes the body, but also the soul. For two entire weeks, resist your cravings for foods that damage your body. The corruption of materialism comes from more than just possessions. It exists within food too. Eating healthy foods for two weeks and giving up unhealthy cravings will cleanse the tongue. Maintaining this habit in moderation thereafter will keep poison from spilling from the tongue and intoxicating those around you.

Step 3: Give Up your Guilty Pleasures

The habits that you impose upon yourself are often ones that give you instant gratification. Things like sex, drugs, excessive entertainment, and technology are forms of materialism that taint the mind. Instead, spend two weeks giving up your guilty pleasures and replacing your poor habits with healthier ones. Consistent exercise, reading, learning, and meditating are just a few things that can cleanse your hands. Using your hands more constructively is crucial towards enriching the soul. Giving up your time for others is an especially powerful way to use your hands for good. Properly managed productivity can lead to more overall time and moderately maintaining positive habits thereafter is important to lose the need for instant gratification and pleasure.

Step 4: Donate to Charity

To learn the value of your possessions, you must understand that most of what you own is needed by someone less fortunate. Kindly giving to them will teach the lesson that materialism is more about what one has in their heart, not in their hands. Learn more about the charities in your locale and be willing to donate as much as you can reasonably provide. Currencies are a big factor in materialistic possession. However, money can always be earned again. Live life in abundance and donate to a worthy charity of your choosing at least once every month.

Step 5: Volunteer

However, giving away money to worthy causes isn't enough to truly help others. The greatest commodity of life, greater than money, is time. It's important to contribute that time for the benefit of those less fortunate than you. Find ways to volunteer in your locale and commit yourself to serve a cause of your choosing at least once every month, if possible. The best way to overcome materialistic desire is to realize that greater happiness comes from the happiness that you give others. Your hands will be put to better use and your tongue will speak of kinder things. Just so long as you sacrifice your time to make someone else's life better, even for a day.

Step 6: Meditate on the Objects you Desire

Within your home, meditate on the objects that you desire. Understand why you desire them and question if they would really equate to happiness. Reinforce the popular lesson that materialistic objects don't make you happy. Practices like vision boards focus on materialistic wants and therefore fail in many cases. Instead, strive towards a feeling you want for yourself and that you want to create for others, instead of an object in your possession. Objects are meaningless in death. Yet objects are

also what create many wars. Choosing to hinge your goals upon feelings of emotional fulfillment and true happiness will hopefully stop the needless desire for competition amongst the population. When corrupted materialism is overcome, you and your united people can see that the objects you create and earn are better off in the hands of those less fortunate for you. That's how you can achieve long-term happiness; helping others find happiness.

Consciousness

- **Location:** Crown of the Head
- **Attachment:** Nose
- **Color:** Light Blue
- **Purified By:** Self-Awareness, Knowledge, Sleep, Ability to Look Within, Understanding, Improvement, Memories, Forgiveness, Redemption
- **Corrupted By:** Absent-Mindedness, Mundanity, Betrayal, Complacency, Exhaustion, Unnoticed Flaws

Step 1: Aromatherapy

One of the best tools to use as a catalyst for the senses is aromatherapy. The essential oils and other compounds will be able to enrich your physiological and psychological well-being. Engaging in this practice within a calm and relaxing environment will soften the possibly overreacted nature of your senses. This will cleanse the nose and prepare you to look within without the disruption of your external nerves.

Step 2: Sleep

Begin sleeping early for at least two weeks to observe the improvement of your habits and awareness. Moderately continue this habit to the best of your ability thereafter. Sooner than two hours before midnight should help tremendously if you normally sleep later than that. In many instances, constantly fluctuating sleep patterns or late nights without productivity disrupt your ability to observe throughout the day. Fixing this poor habit and avoiding staying up late on technology will help you avoid absent-mindedness and help you become more aware while you are awake. It will cleanse the crown of the head and improve rational thought. Sleep is the cousin of death. Poor sleep habits leave you walking throughout life without being truly alive.

**Step 3: Learn More
About Your Heritage**

Through whatever means most necessary, whether it be a relative or public information, learn more about your cultural heritage. It's almost essential for people to learn more about the hardships their ancestors have endured and the achievements they have strived towards. This will hopefully spark a conscious understanding and appreciation for the sacrifices of your history. Moving forward, you will know that you, yourself, are the history of your future generation. This thought alone can improve self-awareness about a person's true place in life.

**Step 4: Admit to Your
Greatest Flaws and Strengths**

This will require solitude. Look within and admit to your greatest flaws, but also your redeeming qualities as well. Becoming a Paragon is much less about perfection and more about finding balance within yourself. Write a list of your flaws and strengths. Then, think about a scenario in which each of them has played a part in who you are. Accept that you have made mistakes but that you have also made great strides in your personal development. The key to growth is to avoid letting these flaws overtake you and instead find ways to use these unique natures to your advantage. Consciously utilize them in a way that may be considered positive.

Step 5: Observe Memories in Solitude

If possible, be alone in a time and place where you feel emotionally ready to look back on your past. Whether digitally or through photographs, observe pictures of your memories. Simply indulge in your past and the actions that you have taken in your life thus far. Beyond simple gratitude, be consciously aware of what it took for you to get to your current place in life, good or bad. Accept your current path and be prepared to do what you can to make more beautiful memories. Never forget those you have loved and lost. Loss happens in life, but love is what makes us feel as though the people who are gone never really left us.

Step 6: Apologize

To indulge in full consciousness of your interaction with the world and others, you must learn to eliminate any toxicity that's in your relationships. If possible, meet or contact those you have betrayed in the past. It can be someone that you harmed emotionally, neglected, or never truly appreciated. Apologize for your wrongful actions in the past or simply tell them how much you appreciate them. Societies today hardly engage in love to its fullest potential and many people are unaware of how much they take their relationships for granted, new or old ones.

Step 7: Forgive

Next, forgive the people who have betrayed you. Unconscious toxicity in life is two-fold. It requires the person to apologize, but also requires them to accept that they, themselves, have been hurt in relationships as well. If possible, meet or contact those who have betrayed you in the past. In any capacity that the pain they caused still lingers within your soul, simply explain the harm they caused you. Then, wholeheartedly forgive them for what they have done. Whether they agree they betrayed you or not, understand that your pain is valid but should never be imposed upon other people. Grudges are the bane of fully conscious relationships and damage their ability to thrive. Get rid of the grudges you've had up to this point. Move on and grow from the experiences you've faced.

Step 8: Meditate on Your Past

Learn more about yourself through isolation. Smell, being an innate sense, also deals with unconscious memories. Before beginning, clear the sense of smell with vapor incense to facilitate pure breathing. Meditate on a behavioral habit that you dislike and make a promise to yourself to change it for the better over time. Then, meditate on the memories of your past that you're not proud of. Acknowledge what you did wrong and accept those mistakes. However, it's important to be conscious and redeem yourself. Vow to perform the opposite of those actions in your life today. Don't let things like anger, hatred, and misery continue to plague the way you interact with the world. Consciousness is about accepting your flaws and improving your strengths. They must always live in harmony within yourself. But you must never let one feature take over the other. You're not just your flaws and you're not just your strengths. Your past is composed of both and they make who you are as a conscious person.

Determinism

- **Location:** Spine
- **Attachment:** Ears
- **Color:** Green
- **Purified By:** Destiny, Guidance, Resilience, Posture, Clairvoyance, Leadership, Silence, Listening, Commitment
- **Corrupted By:** Excessive Hindsight, Following Others, Voices, Media, Trendy Behavior, Envy

Step 1: Listen to Brown Noise

The sounds of the outside world can be full of toxicity that damages your ability to walk your path. To cleanse the ears, listen to brown noise, a much softer tone of white noise. This static sound should be listened to for 30 minutes a day for at least a week. Continue to do this whenever the ears must be cleansed again. This will hopefully prepare you to listen to your inner voice and determine your own path.

Step 2: Block Out Sound

Life can be dictated by the environment around us and the sounds it makes. To further cleanse the ears, block out almost all distracting sounds for a day, if possible. This can be accomplished by using some form of earplugs. Take this time to listen to yourself. Write down some of your significant thoughts throughout the day. How you feel when you're alone with yourself. Being able to pursue a day on your own merits and voice is essential towards finding your destiny and becoming your own leader.

Step 3: Exercise the Back

The back is the foundation of a person's structure, posture, and form. Having a strong back shows that you are capable of carrying your burdens and walking along your path with poise. Strengthen the back through the means of a pull-up bar or weights. Do this every day for a week for about 30 minutes, then remain consistent with it once a week thereafter. Not only does exercising the back help with your ability to stand on your own with power, but it enriches the spirit. Leaders who have strong backs can carry others if needed, are willing to demonstrate their independence, and can guide others to walk their own path with a similar posture as them.

Step 4: Avoid Social Media

Overconsumption of media is perhaps the greatest corruption upon determinism. The ability to abide by your destiny is constantly tainted by what others suggest is right for you. The universe, at many times, is shaped by the actions of others through the means of technology. This idolization of someone else's life is extremely unhealthy. The soundbites that resonate through glimpses of their happiness plague the mind. It can fool you into believing that what another person has, is what you need. To continue cleansing the ears, don't consume masses of social media or the lives of others for at least two weeks. Be sure to moderately continue this habit as you see necessary. Being able to trust in your destiny and listen to your in-ner voice gives you structure in your own life. Drown out the voices of others to build your spiritual contentment with where you will go in the future. Being at peace with your choices in life is how you become a leader. Everyone walks their own path and has their own fate, making the act of following others for the same result a useless endeavor.

Step 5: Explore a New Path

In many instances, our daily actions are dictated by others in ways beyond technology. It's important to find a balance between the guidance of others and that of your own destiny. Absolute determinism created by others' voices will lead to a life of misery and unfulfillment. Start exploring a new path that you want to commit to for some time, on your own merit. For instance, explore new career opportunities if possible, new hobbies, or even new areas to have fun without the absolute recommendation of others. Walk new grounds and try to dedicate some time to doing something new. Volunteer in new places or learn a completely new skill. Set your own goals for yourself during the process. Attempt to commit to this new path for several weeks. If it's not for you, be willing to start over with something new. True growth and leadership are found when you're willing to begin anew for the sake of yourself and your development.

Step 6: Meditate on your Destiny

Truly listen to yourself. While performing this meditation, it's important to listen to classical music. This will enrich the ears and stimulate free-form thoughts that connect to the foundation of the spine. During the meditation, think of something you do or have done for so long that you have lost all conscious thought with it. A habit that you consistently do, not because you want to, but because you were told to. Big or small, this could be a goal you're pursuing that you don't necessarily believe is yours. Choose to forsake this destiny for some time and see if you're happier walking along a new path. Attempt to do an activity and further pursue the new path you explored in the last step, whichever one you loved the most. Creating a new path and abandoning an old one is crucial for full growth. As you meditate on the possibilities of starting something new and finding your destiny, think about the happiness you can find along the process. After your meditation, physically write out a plan to fulfill this new destiny that you hope to try. Pave your path and become the leader that you were destined to be.

Free Will

- **Location:** Stomach
- **Attachment:** Mouth/Throat
- **Color:** Orange
- **Purified By:** Communication, Healthy Foods, Positive Words, Choices, Diversity, Risk
- **Corrupted By:** Toxic Words, Unhealthy Foods, Conformity, Being Controlled, Emotional Enslavement

Step 1: Do Not Speak

Whenever possible, spend a single day without communication from the throat. When society is plagued by too many people who speak their minds without listening in proportion to others, we become corrupted by our own words. To cleanse the mouth and throat, set aside a day where you won't speak to anyone at all. Indulging in this silence can help you appreciate the value of every word that comes from your mouth. You will hopefully be able to choose your words more wisely every time you conduct this exercise.

Step 2: Consume Healthy Foods

The actions of the gut tend to be facilitated through what we put in our bodies. Consuming healthy foods for at least a week and in moderation thereafter will cleanse the stomach.

When the body is full of more enriching nourishments, the mind will thrive and choices will be made with better alignment with the soul. Your will becomes sufficiently energized to make more positive decisions throughout the day. A healthy body is more suitable for taking risks and chances.

Step 3: Journal Your Thoughts

In many instances, hastily vocalized thoughts don't represent what a person is thinking. Hence the lesson: think before you speak. It's important to take time to write down your recent thoughts about the world around you. Whether you're upset, happy, or sad, your emotions can be rationalized better when they are properly thought out on paper. After journaling your thoughts for as many or as few pages as you feel necessary, the next step is to vocalize your thoughts to yourself. Taking a moment to vocalize your more rational thoughts will help you understand the differences between your two voices. The hasty one that plagues your throat isn't the same as the one that really represents what you feel. Learn to distinguish between the words that emerge without thought and the ones that emerge with careful consideration.

Step 4: Spread Positivity Through Words

Words have more of a profound impact on others than most people realize. Take time to spread positive words to those you love and those you don't. Whether it be family, friends, or strangers, spend a week going out of your comfort zone to brighten others' days. It can be in the form of genuinely complimenting a stranger or reaching out to your loved ones to tell them what you admire most about them. Interact with multiple people each day with this type of energy. Words of kindness likely spread and people who receive the language of positivity from someone are more inclined to give it to another. Realize the impact that words have and attempt to use them for good instead of evil as often as possible.

Step 5: Do Something Different Every Day

If possible, spend a week exercising your free will. Many people take their ability to choose for granted and give in to the restrictions of society's expectations every day. This type of life leads to mundanity and a lack of control. To exercise your free will, spend every day of a week trying something new, something out of your routine. It can be as simple as running in the morning, trying new foods, or reading something new. Or it can be as drastic as visiting an attraction on impulse or picking up an entirely new skill. In many cases, people find themselves doing the same thing every morning. Spend this week doing things completely out of your routine. We all have the will and the ability to dictate a large portion of how we interact with our day, regardless of what society expects from us. We cannot take this power for granted. After a week of trying something different each day, attempt to continue this behavior moderately to avoid falling into complacency and mundanity.

Step 6: Take a Risk

When you're prepared, take a bigger risk. The greatest test of what type of choices you are capable of lies in your gut decision to take a risk. Free will exists in the stomach and in many instances, is exercised on impulse. The health of the gut depends on your ability to make decisions that involve risk almost based on your first reaction. To better train your psyche for such a future occurrence, choose to take a risk on your own. Whatever activity or interaction with someone you have been afraid to take for so long, prepare yourself to do so. This can be a small investment of your currency, the sacrifice of your time, ap-plying for a new career, or just a conversation with someone. Give yourself no more than a week to prepare for the confrontation of the risk. Regardless of the result, be proud that you were willing to do something that you had feared for so long. Accept the outcome and be prepared to take more risks in the future.

Step 7: Meditate on your Will

Meditate on the things you've missed out on but have always wanted to do. Throughout many people's lives, their free will is stifled by their mental limits. It's important to train the mind to understand that the power of choice can grant opportunities. Rather than running from the obstacles that require a choice of will, it's better to take advantage of them. While meditating and thinking of the opportunities you may have missed out on in life, decide that you'll redeem yourself. To do so, see if you can reclaim this opportunity or commit to something similar to it. Once you make your commitment, do your best to stick with it for as long as you see fit. You will have exercised your free will to its fullest by acting upon an opportunity that you once missed. Looking forward to the future, start to eliminate your fear of opportunity. With free will, you should avoid missing out on activities you have always wanted to attempt. The choice is always in your hands.

Faith

- **Location:** Mind
- **Attachment:** Sternum
- **Color:** Yellow
- **Purified By:** Religion, Meditation, Words of gods, Peace, Conquering Challenges, Learning, Service in Others, Kindness, Tolerance, Good Deeds, Sacrifice, Trust
- **Corrupted By:** Anger, Hopelessness, Selfishness, Sin, Chaos, Ignorance, Intolerance

Step 1: Deep Breathing

Begin by cleansing the sternum, lungs, and mind simultaneously. To do this, spend every morning breathing deeply in solitude for a week while sitting with the legs crossed. Do this for approximately 15 - 30 minutes quietly to maximize the benefits. This will start your day with a peaceful mindset and the airways clear of toxicity. After performing this every morning for a week, continue this practice in moderation thereafter. A few times each week, if possible. Especially when the mind feels clogged with anger or hopelessness.

Step 2: Learn a New Skill

Strengthening the mind is key to opening it to faith. The mind is easily strengthened through the process of learning. In many instances, there are some skills that people have been too afraid to learn or have entirely forgotten. Attempt to learn a new skill that you have considered in the past or relearn one you used to know. It can be an athletic talent, musically related, or technically inclined, for example. Simply becoming a novice at a new skill or learning new aspects of it are enough to power your mental fortitude and reduce ignorance.

Step 3: Challenge and Conquer

To add upon learning a new skill, the mind needs to flourish. When the mind thrives, it can find peace with whatever circumstances it exists in at the moment. To fully expand the mind and soul, find something that has challenged you in the past or something that you know can challenge you in the future. This can be losing a certain amount of weight, passing a certain test, or confronting a situation, for example. Whatever it may be, accept the challenge. There will be fear and chaos in the process. It's all necessary to succeed. Once you succeed in conquering this challenge, you'll learn to have faith in your capabilities in a brand new way.

Step 4: Indulge in Religion

Although religion may not be something everyone wishes to wholeheartedly partake in, the concept of religion is a very powerful insight into the moral compass of any being. To open your mind to another form of faith, indulging in religion for a brief time is essential. The stories told through various forms of faith have been the foundation for existence across the galaxies. The gods who have been described in such stories are recognized as epitomes of a certain type of behavior and what people should strive for in their lifetime. If possible, attempt to attend any place of religion during a sermon or gathering and spend time understanding the reasoning behind such faith. If this is not viable, seek out someone you know or don't know who is religious. See if they're willing to provide detailed insight into their faith and practices. This will build tolerance and open the eyes to what others have chosen to believe in life. Many lessons from every religion can be a helpful guide for morals in everyone's life.

Step 5: Volunteer

Once again, volunteering is a great way to sacrifice your time for the betterment of others. But beyond this, volunteering is an important part of providing faith to your kind. Knowing that there are people out there who wish to help others out of the kindness of their hearts is a big part of what many religions preach. Being able to provide faith to another person helps you understand your own and what morals you choose to live by during your time in these planes of existence. Find more ways to volunteer in your locale or return to a place you have volunteered for in the past. If you have stayed consistent with volunteering every month from Materialism, then you're on the right track towards engaging in this similar step. But now, this isn't just to give your time as a commodity but to show that you have faith in the goodness of others. Especially through continuously helping people in need.

Step 6: Perform Good Acts

Fortunately for the worlds in the universe, more good acts exist beyond volunteering and service for the community. The type of good act required for this step is more than only a day spent assisting others. Find someone you know or don't know who needs assistance. Many people are likely conducting their own projects or dealing with their own problems. A strong lesson of faith is being kind to your fellow being. As long as the task doesn't derail you from your path, be sure to see through assisting someone with what they need. This can involve taking part in their project or helping them during their dark times. Another method of performing an extensively good act could be going to great lengths to show someone how much you love them. This could be a combination of gifts, attention, and time spent reassuring them about how meaningful your relationship with them is. Good acts such as these are just a few examples of greatly restoring a single person's faith. Attempting to do this multiple times nourishes both souls in the process.

Step 7: Meditate on your god

Whether you believe in a god or not, as stressed in this aspect of becoming a Paragon, faith is a powerful part of realizing your true potential for others. Take the time to meditate upon the being you pray to or that you would prefer to pray to for this practice. If you don't believe in any god, meditate on whatever higher power you answer to. For example, many people in various galaxies have chosen to believe the universe is a higher power in and of itself, which is true in many ways. Before meditating, be sure to learn more about the god or higher power and the possible religion behind it. Understanding the basics of the god's teachings is crucial to appropriately communicate with it in its realm. It shows respect for the faith that it has provided the universe with its sacrifice. While spiritually connected to a higher realm of gods or a higher power, spend time speaking with it. Confess to the god; learn and rationalize the meaning behind faith. This will fully open your mind to what faith is and can bring you one step closer to finding your inner peace. The worlds themselves can be full of pain and suffering and there's a great reason why people put their faith in something higher than themselves. The words of the god or higher power will hopefully aid in your search for your purpose in life.

Imagination

- **Location:** Heart
- **Attachment:** Eyes
- **Color:** White
- **Purified By:** Purpose, Love, Appreciation, Honesty, Openness, Clarity, Art, Passion, Talent, Expression, Gift Giving
- **Corrupted By:** Loss, Blindness, Hatred, Reservation, Regret, Inability, Lack of Gratitude

Step 1: Observe Nature

Nature is a fundamental law of the universe that many people take for granted. On many planets, nature has been taken advantage of and exploited by the very people it serves. To enrich the eyes, observe nature in solitude for an afternoon. If time permits, several hours should suffice. Meditate in a peaceful setting and appreciate the nature before you. This will calm the heart and soul. Starting fresh will prepare the heart to exercise its imagination.

Step 2: Be Blindfolded

To cleanse the eyes, spend the majority of a day blindfolded. Be sure to prepare any necessary food ahead of time and make sure you're capable of navigating your own home without any hazards to harm you. Once this is done, use a blindfold or makeshift one to eliminate your sight for a day. This will teach you to spend time without a sense that many people don't use to its fullest potential. The eyes may simply take in an image, but they aren't the sole part of the body used to make judgments. The heart and eyes fall hand in hand. What the eyes witness, the heart expresses emotion to. We feel certain ways when we see someone we love, something that makes us sad, etc. Therefore, take the time to be blind and understand what your heart truly feels inside. Explore your mind and imagine without having to see what you may believe in. See it within yourself first.

Step 3: Observe Art

Now to do the opposite. Once the eyes have been cleansed, they should hopefully be more capable of appreciating the arts more profoundly. Observe various arts of your interest in person if possible. Viewing arts in person is very crucial to truly appreciate the magnificence of what imagination can create. If it's entirely impossible to view art in its physical form, it may be done so digitally. Either way, it must be done in a quiet setting and observed with a true appreciation for an extended time. Until you truly feel satisfied with the message the art pieces convey to you.

Step 4: Draw

After observing art in its true form, take the time to create your own. Exercising the imagination is crucial for opening the heart. Simply draw consistently for a week. Attempt to create full works of art and a full image. Don't finish until you're satisfied with the work, but it must be done within a day. Spend every day for a week drawing, whether it's good or not. Express yourself through this form of art and learn more about what your imagination is capable of.

Step 5: Write

Very similar to the previous practice, write consistently for a week. Writing is one of the most profound ways that people transmit their imagination, creativity, message, and history to last for centuries. Writing is a powerful way to find your voice. You may write about anything you want, whether it be creative or autobiographical, for example. Simply write a sufficient amount every day. You may contribute your heart towards a single piece of work for the week or a new piece every day. Be sure to review your writings to learn more about yourself. The words you choose to write within a finite amount of time may reveal a lot about what your heart truly desires.

Step 6: Make Music

Another powerful form of expressive art that has impacted many corners of the universe is music. The creative process of making music seldom involves the use of your eyes, aside from technical application. Overall, music is primarily felt with and comes from the heart. If possible, invest in an instrument of your choosing at a modest price. Whatever instrument you choose, be sure to do what you can to learn how to play it. The massive web of information will likely have instructional content to help

with learning the instrument. Play the instrument every day, for a week. Watch yourself grow and learn more about how music is a unique form of expression, even if learning can frustrate you at times. Music serves as a unique language for the heart. This will further exercise the imagination and help your heart grow as it hopefully develops a tie to musical art.

Step 7: Create Gifts

Illustration, writing, and music are core components of imagination. They all serve as languages for the heart and creativity. You may use some of the new skills you learned for this next exercise if you wish. Create gifts for those you love and those closest to you. Give the gifts to them without reason. Giving and finding ways to share love is not only expressed through talents but through the creativity of presents too. Be sure to put sufficient thought into the gifts. They can be sentimental or provide a certain function that the person needs. Using a physical item to show love is very common, but not always necessary. Creating gifts for your loved ones will remind you just how near and dear they are to your heart. And showing them such affection without a specific reason will help their hearts grow as well. It's a significant step towards appreciating your loved ones while you exist in this realm. Life for everyone is short, so it's extremely important to show them gratitude while you have the chance.

Step 8: Meditate on your Loved Ones

Take one of the final steps towards the first phase of becoming a Paragon. Before engaging in this practice, gather photographs of the people that you hold near and dear to your heart. Within your home, meditate upon those you love and those you have lost. Accept that people come in and out of your life. Everyone's time and place in the world vary greatly, which makes it even more important to try to open the heart and express love as often as possible. Think about how you feel when you see the ones you love and how it feels to wish you could see the ones you have lost. Indulge in the feelings they elicit. Tend to every loved one that you want to meditate upon. Despite the loss of life, understand that the best you can do is love them to your fullest capacity while they're in this realm. Appreciate them. After you've finished the meditative practice, the final step follows. Openly and honestly tell your family members and friends how much you love them and how much they mean to you. Tell them how much they matter. Tell them of the feelings they brought out from you when you took the time to meditate upon them. Imagination is primarily strengthened when your heart is open and full of happiness. Rejoice with your family, and if you haven't done so in some time, spend a day with them. Be happy. Remember that in life, the only thing that never truly dies is the love in the hearts of the universe's people.

Conclusion

The previous series of steps only comprise the first phase of the full journey of becoming a Paragon. The Paragons, as you may have read, were an elite warrior of people in the ancient universe's history. Being a Paragon of Imagination means you set the example for others. You have used your imagination and continue to use it to make great impacts on your community. Most importantly, as a Paragon of imagination, you use your creativity to inspire the world and make it a better place. In the past, the Paragons were capable of supernatural cosmic feats. But greater than their powers was the way most of them devoted their lives towards bettering the worlds around them through sacrifice. Although some became corrupted by greed, fame, and power, others were true practitioners of the spiritual enlightenment that made the Seraphs models of good throughout the universe. The following phase of becoming a Paragon is more intense and requires more than spiritual alignment with the ways of the Seraphs and the gods that preceded them. To further walk down the path of becoming a Paragon requires intense devotion to the world around you. It requires rigorous action and true sacrifice for your fellow beings. It is told that The Chosen Ones, who are believed to arise by the rite of the princes, will help guide the universe further down the path. They will receive direct messages from the spirits of Jannah and pass their inherited wisdom to the masses of the population. Knowledge is the truest way towards peace.

The Chosen Ones request that you open your eyes and watch the universe around you, for this is only the beginning. The knowledge of the Ancient Scripture is only the first step of a lifelong journey towards a new way of life. Witness the world around you change as the new truth is finally revealed.

Thank You

The Ancient Scripture was not written by the Chosen Ones. However, it is a text discovered by the two brothers at the beginning of their mission to restore the afterlife and save the universe. As their powers emerged, the location of the sacred text became revealed to them by the spirits of the ancient universe. After reading the entire scripture, the brothers knew it was best to pass the text across the galaxies. This is only a small fragment of an entire list of texts created by beings that have long since passed all across space. The Chosen Ones will continue to do their best to unveil any additional knowledge and grant it to the universe. But with what knowledge you now have, they ask that you use it as a catalyst to help the world around you. Use your imagination, become a hero, and make your planet a better place.